DREAMHEARTH

DREAMHEARTH
BOOK 3 OF THE DREAMHEALERS SAGA

M. C. A. HOGARTH

mcahogarth.org

Dreamhearth
Book 3 of The Dreamhealers Saga
First edition, copyright 2018 by M.C.A. Hogarth

M. Hogarth
PMB 109
4522 West Village Dr.
Tampa, FL 33624

ISBN-13: 978-1986741361
ISBN-10: 1986741362

Cover art by MCA Hogarth

Designed & typeset by Catspaw DTP Services
http://www.catspawdtp.com/

A-UTHOR'S NOTE

THIS BOOK CONTAINS EXCERPTS of a Peltedverse story for which I feel an enduring affection. It was written when I was fifteen, and has all the virtues of its enthusiastic and naïve vices. Any criticism directed at Young Me's efforts should not be taken as critique of the romance genre as a whole. It shouldn't be taken as critique of Young Me, even, whose only sin was inexperience.

Some part of me will forever be Rexina Regina, and that's as it should be.

Enjoy the story, ariisen.

TABLE OF CONTENTS

———∞———

Chapter 1

*T*HE TODFOX HAD NEVER SEEN *anyone like her. Like a fairy: delicate, fragile, with the bloom of roses on her lips. Her furless skin seemed to shine like polished marble, and yet, she breathed! He couldn't see her and not love her: love her as one loved a fair maiden goddess, pure and not of this world.*

Would she? She did! She turned that perfect face and met his eyes across the crowded lobby. Such a gaze! So limpid, a pellucid blue, to be so wise! His heart raced in his breast. If only he could be brave enough to talk to her. Would she answer? What would her voice be like?

Would he ever recover?

Vasiht'h put the data tablet down on his forepaws and touched his fingers to his brow. He couldn't decide whether to laugh or hack the taste of the lurid prose from his mouth; what he was sure of was that his mouth was twitching. When his sisters had assured him they'd taken care of his entertainment for the trip back to the starbase, he'd assumed they'd bought him a book or two. But this? He brought up the cover and stared ruefully at the Tam-illee foxine holding a swooning Eldritch woman in his arms. HEALED BY HER IMMORTAL HEART. What in the worlds had they been thinking?

Paging away from the novel, he sent a group message to his sisters.

This book is terrible!

He was close enough to the world to be certain of an answer soon, but while he waited he returned, reluctantly, to the story of Thaddeus WeavesDNA and the Eldritch woman who was either a statue or a sprite, depending on the paragraph. It was hard to concentrate, though (and not just because the story was ridiculous). He couldn't believe that he was finally a graduate, with a degree and a license to practice xenotherapy with a partner of his choosing. That he had that partner, a real and rare Eldritch, who had chosen him as the other half of a mindline out of legend. And who was, Vasiht'h glanced at the novel and managed a grin, not at all as pure and innocent as a maiden goddess. Though he could grant the polished marble as the sort of metaphor that would occur to someone who'd only read about Eldritch and never seen one. Jahir was pale, yes, but not like stone. Like a pearl, with veils of color and shadow and the blood flush of a living man beneath it.

And now he was beginning to sound like a romance novel. But he loved Jahir. And he was—apparently—no more eloquent than this particular author. With a sigh, Vasiht'h applied himself again to the narrative. The woman had the voice of an angel, apparently. Of course.

Having left notifications on, he was interrupted at length by his sisters. Not just one, but several of them, leaving him messages. Ranging from his eldest sister Kavila's "HA HA HA" to Sehvi's more coy, "We thought it would help you with your relationship."

He scowled at the glowing letters and tapped back: *I'm completely sure this author has never been within a sector of an actual Eldritch.*

Sehvi, responding: *She's writing about a woman! Maybe their women are different.*

Vasiht'h lifted his fingers, paused, then wrote: *I am not walking into that trap, ariishir.*

He could imagine her delighted giggles. *What page are you on?*

Goddess, what page *was* he on? Vasiht'h made himself look. *Twenty-six.*

Keep going! It gets better!

Better good? Or better worse??

No response to that, naturally, but he hadn't expected one. He looked toward the window alongside his seat and his reflection was grinning. Well, maybe the book was serving its purpose— would continue to serve its purpose, since he would soon be at the edge of the solar system and the Well drives would take him beyond his family's reach. He'd have to imagine their merriment as he dutifully slogged through their offering, comparing it continually and unfavorably to the reality he was on his way to meet.

Jahir Seni Galare. His very own Eldritch. His best friend in all the worlds, with whom he had survived grief and terror and trial. In whom he had found a joy he somehow doubted the well-meaning author of his romance novel would understand, owing nothing as it did to sexual attraction. What had drawn him to Jahir was better than that—to him, anyway. He had found a soulmate, and he was going home to him.

And home, for now, was a starbase neither of them knew at all. Vasiht'h had stopped there on his way to join Jahir on the capital world Selnor for the Eldritch's residency period . . . and that layover had been long enough for him to decide it would be the perfect place for the Alliance's newest xenotherapists to set up their practice. Jahir had left a week ago to start scouting a likely place for them to live. Had he found it by now?

Silly question. A more likely question was had he found a place that was within their means, and what exactly was *their* means? Because the two of them were still feeling their way through questions like 'who should pay for things, even though you're possibly rich enough to buy anything you want.' Exactly the sort of questions, Vasiht'h thought ruefully, that he most needed advice on . . . and that he probably wouldn't find any answers to in HEALED BY HER IMMORTAL HEART, Sehvi's hopes notwithstanding.

Still, it was something to do while he was en route. Vasiht'h resumed his reading, and in his breast, his heart stretched out toward the man awaiting him a sector away.

⎯⎯⎯⎯⎯⎯⎯⎯⎯

For his part, Jahir was in an office he would have called gracious on any other day and might perhaps call so again, when he was feeling more charitable. He was not, at the moment, feeling very charitable. "Perhaps you might explain these distinctions to me again?" he said with iron courtesy to the Karaka'an felid on the other side of the desk. Behind the woman's head, the trees seen through the open veranda doors were rustling.

"Certainly," she replied. "We have four types of residency on the starbase—on any starbase, you understand, Lord Seni Galare." She held up a finger. "Permanent residents are just what they sound: they stay here for as long as they like, and their families and children are welcome as well. Then there are semi-permanent residents: those are people whose work is based here, but who are rarely present. Merchants who maintain dwellings on the starbase but spend most of their lives on their ships, for instance. Then we have transients, people who are passing through. Usually passengers, or people whose business might take them here for several months, but who aren't staying. And then we have provisional residents. Those are people who'd like to live on the starbase, but who haven't been approved for permanent residence."

"And you are telling me," Jahir said, "that there are no problems with my application, but that my partner is on this . . . provisional status list."

"That's correct."

"My partner," Jahir said. "Without whom I cannot run my business. For some reason I am approved and he isn't?"

"If I may be frank, Lord Seni Galare?" She paused, tilting her ears toward him and waiting for some sign. He inclined his head and she continued. "You're a member of an allied alien species, sir. Because of this, you have a freedom few other Pelted have.

You've taken on a Pelted business partner, which is commendable, and on most worlds what you're requesting wouldn't be a problem. But a starbase is a closed environment. We can't bring in more people than we can sustain. Where the professions are in demand—engineers, farmers, that sort of thing—residency status is granted faster. But we don't need more psychiatrists right now."

"You mean to tell me," Jahir said, "that this enormous habitat cannot support one more person? I have seen the maps, alet. The city sphere is vast, and it is only the first. There are empty modules throughout the skin of this starbase for expansion."

"And no doubt we will expand, as our population does," the Karaka'An said. She sighed and leaned forward, threading her hands together on the table. "I know it seems like a straightforward process, alet. You see the fields that stretch over what you perceive as the horizon, and tour the aquaculture and agriculture spheres, and you reason that there's space for everyone. But there are already permanent residents here who have families, whose families are growing. Nor can we reasonably turn away any relatives they might want to invite to join them. We have to plan for their additions to the population. And every person we grant permanent residency to is adding to that future population. We can open new habitat spheres, Lord Seni Galare. But it's not cheap, and we have to balance what we're producing versus what we're consuming." She shook her head. "It's not simple. And I don't like making decisions like this. But you are—An forgive me—a reasonable risk, because while you'll be around a very long time, it's unlikely you're going to end up with two hundred great-grandchildren."

"No," he said. "But my partner isn't even married."

"Glaseah," she said, "don't reproduce quickly. But when they start, they have big families."

He slowly sat back in his chair, having failed to realize he'd been leaning toward her. A subconscious effort, he thought wryly, to induce a compromise by mimicking her body language. Much good that had done. "So in essence, you have a place for me, but not yet a place for him."

"Basically."

"And how soon will we know if you will let him stay?"

She shook her head. "I don't know. We try to be fair. Six months is typical while we wait and see how things fall out."

How things fell out. What things? What imponderables were they weighing, and how could he influence them in their favor? And what good was it to be what he was—rare allied species to the Alliance and rich by their standards beyond measure—if he couldn't so much as procure a place to lie down for a few years for their heads? "And there is nothing we might do."

She hesitated, hitched a shoulder uncomfortably. "We don't like to tell people anything, sir. But we tend to keep people who are useful to the community."

"Useful to the community," he murmured, then rose. "Thank you for your time, Administrator."

"My pleasure," she said. "I'm sorry that we had to have this discussion, but I'm confident that things will work out the way they should for the good of all parties."

Was she? He wished he had her confidence. "Good afternoon, alet."

Outside the housing office, Jahir lifted his head and stared, squinting, into the pellucid blue sky, straggled with clouds. Past those wisps he could just espy the thin white tracery of the starbase's spindle as seen through the artificial atmosphere of the city's bubble. Somewhere, up past those clouds and a layer of flexglass so thick he probably couldn't span it with his arms, was the vacuum of space, and the interior of the gargantuan starbase where Fleet's vessels lay tucked into their slips, awaiting repairs or refits. He would never have known it by the breeze, which to every sense was authentic. It smelled of spring, of the pollen of unfamiliar flowers, and slightly, of a wet humidity that would have suggested rain somewhere without climate control.

That the ecosystem of this starbase—this vast and unlikely and astonishing piece of engineering—might be so fragile that the addition of even a single permanent resident to it might be enough to offset its balance felt frankly unbelievable . . . and yet, he could not imagine the science that had gone into Veta's making, and knew better than to think himself up to the task of second-guessing the housing authorities. It was their work to understand how many people could live on Starbase Veta's civilian grounds.

It was his, apparently, to prove to them that they were too valuable to send away. His, and Vasiht'h's. Thinking of what the Glaseah would say in response to this setback, Jahir sighed. It would be a week before he saw Vasiht'h again, and in that time he had to formulate a plan. Not because he expected Vasiht'h would not be capable of one, but because it would be a distraction from his friend's initial response to the housing authority's decision. But what to do? He could go this very instant and buy a house in his own name. But what good would that be if Veta decided to deport Vasiht'h in half a year? He'd have to sell it, and the bother of extricating himself from a permanent residence would be far greater than to leave a hotel.

Jahir joined the throng heading down the thoroughfare, careful of their edges and his. The thoroughfare was for walking traffic only, and broad, but it was midday and busy. The outdoor cafes were doing good business; Jahir suspected they never did poor business, given that there were no inclement days on the starbase. He selected one purely on the basis of how it smelled and had a seat, ordering a cup of coffee. From this vantage, he watched the people of Veta stream past. Unlike Seersana, where he and Vasiht'h had gone to school, Veta's populace was far more varied: there were no preponderances of Seersa, as he'd come to expect, but a broad mix of Pelted species, along with some of the aliens rarely seen at the university. Overwhelmingly the language spoken was Universal, but he heard the occasional chatter in unknown tongues, and the impression he derived from this sun-drenched bustle was of exuberant health, prosperity, and purpose. This was the Alliance at its absolute best, he thought. Vasiht'h had been right. If ever they belonged anywhere, it was here.

He would just have to figure out how this was to be accomplished. Taking out his data tablet, he settled in to make plans and had gotten no further than bringing up his income when he was interrupted.

"You have the look of a man with a question."

Glancing up he found a woman standing near his table, one hand resting lightly on the back of the chair opposite his. She was one of the wolfine Hinichi, and an elder from her voice, and the whitening of her pelt around her mouth and nose. There was nothing old about her eyes, though, which were merry and kind, and the polite but distancing comment he'd been about to speak evanesced. Instead, he said, "I hope not."

She laughed. "Now I know you have questions, and vexsome ones, and a man of your good looks shouldn't be troubled by anything that would wrinkle that brow. Can I help?"

"I don't know," he admitted. "I admit I am . . . puzzled."

"Puzzled," she repeated, her eyes dancing now.

"By a conundrum."

"By a conundrum." She nodded sagely, then added, "One that defies easy solution."

"That would suppose it to be a problem," Jahir said. "And I have decided it will not be."

"Ah!" She laughed then. "A man of decision! I appreciate such men. One gets to be my age and the action of youth is often all the diversion one needs to maintain one's zest for living."

"And you so old, mistress," Jahir said, mouth quirking.

"Perhaps not older than you," she said, considering him. "Though what would I know of Eldritch, eh? Shall I sit and help you with the conundrum you've decided will not be a problem?"

"That depends," he said. "Are you a resident, alet?"

"Ahhhh," she said. "So that's it, is it." She pulled the chair back and disposed herself in it, one leg folded over the other and her hands resting easily on her knee. "You want to stay. And there's some problem? I can't imagine the housing authorities saying no to one of you!"

How much to tell her? If he was home . . . nothing. But he

was not home. He was here, on Starbase Veta, in the Alliance . . . and the Pelted had a different culture of privacy, and a far more useful culture of community. "But not to my friend, without whom I will not travel."

"Ah!" Her ears pricked. "A friend!"

"A very good friend." Jahir thought of Vasiht'h and smiled. "The very best."

"Another Eldritch?"

Drawn from his reverie, Jahir said, "No. No, a Glaseah."

"A Glaseah!" She appraised him with interest. "Well, there is nothing for it but to make sure you are both accepted, then. Veta needs an Eldritch and Glaseah who are bosom friends."

Jahir found this bemusing. "Does it?"

"Most certainly." She leaned forward, grinned. "The unexpected is challenging, and challenge grows us up, young man. Just the sight of you is unexpected enough to challenge a dozen people. You with a centauroid Pelted friend!" She chortled. "Yes. My starbase needs you."

"Your starbase," he said.

"My starbase," she agreed. "My name is Helga. I was born here, have lived here all my life, and my daughter and her family live here too. I am allowed to call myself a fixture of the community. So then. Your friend must not have a useful career, or the authorities would have written him a ticket immediately. What is it that he does?"

"We," Jahir said, "are xenotherapists."

Her brows shot up. "You're what?"

"Xenotherapists," he repeated firmly. "With a specialization in dream therapy."

"A what?"

He found her incredulity amusing, partially because she did—her eyes were alight with that merriment he'd found so attractive when she'd first stopped at the table. "We are espers, alet. We've found that when we affect the dreaming minds of our clients, we can help them with their subconscious conflicts."

"That sounds potentially dangerous," she murmured. "Does

no one trouble you with questions of ethics?"

"We trouble ourselves with the questions all the time," Jahir said, and paused as a waiter stopped to see if the woman would have anything. She ordered tea and scones, enough, he noticed, for two. Once the man had departed with her request, he continued, "We received some guidance during our studies, but our professors told us that in the main we would have to write our own manual, if you will. There is apparently no one doing what we're doing in all the Alliance."

"I'd be surprised if there were," she said, considering him with an expression he was hard pressed to define. "So. Do people actually use this dream therapy of yours, or does it scare them out of your office?"

"Vasiht'h had the clinical trial of it, originally," he said. "And those who undertook the regimen returned, and brought referrals. The clients we saw during our practicals also seemed pleased with our results."

"So it had measurable results?"

Jahir inclined his head, just a touch. "It sounds absurd when described. But . . . it does, yes. And we have nothing but the health of our clients in mind when we work. Is that not how all healers should conduct themselves?"

"It's how they should, yes." She pursed her lips. "Well. You are a novel thing in the world, alet, and a novel thing in mine, which is even more astonishing. I would love to see what the xenotherapists already on Veta think of your new-fangled ways!"

He paused in the act of reaching for his coffee, just an infinitesimal hesitation. Of course Veta already had therapists. It was a city, and a busy one; even if no one had a private practice, the hospital would have several attached to its staff. But he had not gone so far as to wonder what they would think of the arrival of two new members of their profession. Did he ask Vasiht'h, the Glaseah would no doubt tell him that their colleagues would welcome them, because that was how the Pelted did things. Jahir thought of the closed ecosystem and could not help predicting a less positive outcome.

"Hadn't thought of that, had you."

"We have a license to practice in the Alliance," Jahir said. "I hope there is no other requirement? No . . . guild, or extra fee, or test?"

"Nothing like that, no. If you have the license, you can set up shop." She chuckled softly. "Just . . . expect to be outsiders, for a while."

"Alas," Jahir said. "We may never be anything but, if we cannot convince the housing authority of our utility."

"Well, go find yourself somewhere to live," she said. "And I will send you a client!"

He looked up at her, startled. "You would?"

"Oh yes." She grinned. "I have a friend with a very stubborn resistance to any form of therapy, though she says she needs help. I happen to agree. She just doesn't like any of the therapists available." The woman leaned forward, sunlight shining on her eyes and the enamel of her teeth, so slightly pointed. "Maybe God sent you, alet. I've been praying for many months now for *something* to help Ametia. And here you are."

"I cannot promise that we'll succeed," Jahir replied, because even knowing the devotion of Hinichi he couldn't allow her to believe them her miracle. "But I will promise we will do everything in our power to help her."

"Excellent!" The old woman laughed, leaned back. "This is going to be tremendous! I can just feel it. And here are the scones." A plate was deposited between them, and the things on the plate had as much relation to scones as Jahir thought his guest had to a real wolf. They shared bones, maybe. But these blonde confections, crisped to golden crowns and draped with a lemon-scented glaze, accompanied by great mounds of pale clotted cream, looked more like pastries than any scone he'd ever seen.

"This café makes the best scones on Veta." Helga used a knife to transfer one onto a small plate and set it in front of him, dolloping half the cream over for encore. "Every day a different flavor, and every single one of them delicious. You must have one."

Since she'd already put the plate before him, he could hardly protest without seeming impolite. "You are too kind—"

"You are too thin." She eyed him, amused. "Or is this a species feature? You are all elongated?"

Would agreeing be a breach of the Veil? Jahir said, "I have always been this way. I assure you, it is not a sign of ill health."

"Maybe not, but I won't take wagers on the shadows under your cheekbones." She waved a spoon vaguely in that direction. "I will bet, though, that you forget to eat when you're worried."

He couldn't help staring at her now, and was grateful she was occupied serving herself. Or he thought she had been, because she was chuckling when she lifted her head and met his eyes, and the look in them was so mischievous and so knowing that he couldn't help a laugh himself.

"You get to be my age and you notice a great deal that younger people overlook. One day maybe you'll be the same."

"I will hope," he said, because saying he was already older than her and had yet to develop her facility would be either embarrassing or rude, and he had no desire to be either. She had recommended their first client! And where on the starbase would they hold that session, when they had no place to live!

"There, see?" Helga tapped the top of his cup with her spoon. "You're off doing it again. Worrying instead of eating. Don't waste these while they're warm!"

So he didn't. And while they were far more confectionary than any scone he'd ever had, they were delicious, so he ate his serving in its entirety and even recovered enough of his aplomb to ask after his guest's family and her life on Veta. Nor did she press him about his family or life, which was a diplomacy she hadn't expected; she did want to know about Vasiht'h and he told her willingly how they'd met on Seersana, and a little of their schooling—he kept the details of his residency to himself—and this seemed to intrigue her.

Tapping her mouth with her napkin, Helga said, "Yes. A most excellent beginning to what I hope to be a profitable enterprise for us both. You have your data tablet with you, so let me give you my comm-tag and you can tell me when you're ready for Ametia." She lifted a finger. "I warn you. She will be a challenge!"

"We will do our best by her," Jahir promised.

She grinned. "I know you will. And now I'll be off and leave you to your hunting. Look . . ." She turned in place and then waved a hand vaguely. "In that direction, I'd say."

"Yes, alet."

Helga laughed. "And you will, I'm sure. Good afternoon to you, young man. Don't forget to eat until your friend shows up to remind you."

He started, but she was gone before she could note his reaction . . . probably, he thought ruefully, because she hadn't needed it to confirm her suspicions. He'd said nothing about his relationship with Vasiht'h that should have allowed Helga to guess how frequently the Glaseah was his reminder to take care of himself, but he was somehow not surprised that she'd derived it anyway.

A most formidable woman, the Hinichi. Jahir found himself smiling as he paid the tab, picked up his tablet, and headed in the vague direction of "that way" to see what might be on offer.

CHAPTER 2

HALFWAY TO THE STARBASE, Vasiht'h started annotating HEALED BY HER IMMORTAL HEART with the intention of sending his sisters a dissertation on just how wrong everything about it was—well, that was unfair. There were things about it that weren't wrong, mostly about the Tam-illee hero. Vasiht'h suspected the author was Tam-illee herself, but a woman, maybe even a young woman, because her descriptions of the todfox's emotions were on the right track but felt more like projections or extrapolations than authentic experiences. When he flicked to the author's biography, he found a cartoon portrait, so stylized it was hard to pin it to any one species, and a ridiculous description: Rexina Regina was the author of over thirty novels of "stirring romance," and lived at home with her "loving family and two pets," having returned there after a life of "adventure" that had prepared her for her new role as a domestic goddess with a data tablet ready at hand for dictation of her heart-warming stories. Obviously a pen name, and when Vasiht'h flipped through Regina's catalog it was almost entirely stories about fainting Eldritch in the arms of Pelted swains, or swooning Pelted in the arms of Eldritch knights. Eldritch knights! Were there even such things? And yet here they were, painted with actual steel armor! Vasiht'h tried to imagine Jahir carrying sixty pounds of chain mail and metal plate on his body and stifled a guffaw. No, not likely.

He wrote Sehvi a quick comment: *You picked this author for extra ridiculousness, didn't you.* Then he returned to the narrative. Thaddeus, the reproductive engineer, had finally seen the woman come into his clinic because, apparently, she wanted a baby and couldn't conceive—though how this was going to turn into a romance given the impossibility of Thaddeus helping her directly with this problem, Vasiht'h couldn't fathom—and they had spent several sessions staring at one another longingly. As the shuttle chimed the two-hour-to-dock warning, he began to read another one of these scenes of unrequited desire when it culminated, abruptly.

And then she offered a trembling palm to him.

Was this what he thought it was? Was she asking him to touch her? Without words, the only way she could, because of course she couldn't tell him she wanted him—him, an alien, a Pelted, a doctor! He stared at her skin, softer than a peach and so light he could see the delicate sapphire traceries of veins in them, like precious stone in marble. And then he reached for her, and rested his fingertips on hers, and shuddered!

Vasiht'h set the tablet down, and not even the absurdity of the author describing the woman's skin as both a fruit and a rock could distract him from his own memories of how it had felt to touch Jahir for the first time. How would Vasiht'h have described the texture of an Eldritch palm, if pressed, and would he have been any more lucid than Rexina Regina? Hadn't he shuddered? Goddess, poor Thaddeus. At least Vasiht'h and Jahir had had some hope of a future. There was nothing like that awaiting a todfox who was sexually drawn to an Eldritch woman, both of them barren and both of them wanting children. That he could feel pity for this doomed couple despite the prose was more a function of his own personal experience, he thought . . . but it was real anyway.

And then Regina ruined it by waxing poetic on the cherry color of the Eldritch's lips and the teeth like pearls behind them. Pearls! And cherries! To his data tablet, Vasiht'h said, "It's either precious stones or food! Pick!"

"On behalf of the crew of Flight UR-Veta-12, we'd like to welcome you to Starbase Veta. Please wait until our pilot snugs us into our berth before rising and collecting any carry-on baggage you have stowed in overhead or underseat compartments—"

Muttering about Sehvi's taste in books—and jokes—Vasiht'h tucked the data tablet into his shoulder bag and waited for the shudder that preceded the stillness of the engines winding down. He'd packed lightly, and everything he needed was either in his messenger bag or the saddle bags he retrieved from under his seat and buckled onto his barrel.

Barring catastrophe, he was home. And Jahir would be waiting. Vasiht'h's heart swelled with the anticipation of both.

The familiar sight of the Eldritch was nothing to the re-raveling of the mindline; as Vasiht'h jogged toward Jahir across the terminal, the bond between them woke, bringing with it the Eldritch's delight: soft and cool and bright, like the sun off a stream. Definitely not his memory: when had he ever seen a stream? Grinning at the gift, Vasiht'h came to a halt in front of Jahir and looked up at his friend.

"Welcome back," Jahir said, with that brook-burble pleasure.

"It's good to see you." Vasiht'h knew better than to hold out his hand, and Jahir didn't offer his, but that was all right. The evidence of his friend's happiness at the sight of him was good enough for him. "So how've you spent the past week?"

"I hesitate to say productively. . . ."

The jumble that clotted the mindline then made Vasiht'h's brows lift. Shadows and amusement and the taste of lemon and tea and the smell of flowers and a faint itch like irritation. "I can't tell *what* that is, but it feels complicated."

"Perhaps I should say 'there is good news and bad news,'"

Jahir answered, rueful. "Maybe we can repair to a café to discuss it."

"I could eat."

"Then I know a good place."

———⚬⚬⚬———

The good place was outside beneath a perfect sky, with the smell of flaky fresh bread emitting from the door that opened for the waiters seeing to the people at the patio tables. How Vasiht'h could tell the bread was flaky and not dense just from the smell he had no idea, but his mouth watered anyway. Jahir found them a table beneath a delicate flowering tree, and Vasiht'h gladly unloaded his bags onto the chair he couldn't use and sat beside it, curling his tail over his feet.

"You've at least found a few good places to go, I see." Vasiht'h glanced over his shoulder at the sunlit thoroughfare. It was late afternoon, and he found himself suddenly wondering if the starbase simulated sunset or if there was some other transition from day to night.

"A few," Jahir allowed. "Was your trip back uneventful?"

Vasiht'h thought about expounding on the many flaws of his sister's gift, but looking at Jahir he found . . . he just couldn't. Rexina Regina had never had her own Eldritch, but who could blame her for wishing? And wouldn't it sound ridiculous to discuss some Pelted writer's tired clichés about Eldritch with Jahir, who would probably find them more painful than funny? "I spent it reading," he said. "So tell me the good news and bad news. Any order."

Jahir folded his hands on the table. "Then I will say the good news is that we might have our first client."

"We do?" Vasiht'h straightened, eyes widening.

"And the bad news," Jahir finished, "is that we might not be able to stay."

No wonder the mindline had been such a confusion of impressions. Before Vasiht'h could speak, Jahir said, "But I have engaged us a temporary housing situation." And then, significantly, he paused, and the mindline felt like a held breath. Vasiht'h waited for the exhalation, and when it didn't come, he peered at Jahir.

"You're . . . waiting?"

"I thought you might be . . . distressed."

Vasiht'h sorted through the mindline's hesitances, found the memory of his reaction to their off-campus apartment, among other, less defined things. "Because . . . we might not be able to stay, and because you did something about it in the meantime? But I'm not surprised, arii."

"You're not?"

Before he could answer, the waitress interrupted them. The list of specials was long enough that Vasiht'h lost track of them before she was done, but she finished with, "And our evening scones are the cardamom spice, with rosewater-infused cream—"

"Those sound deadly," Vasiht'h said.

"We'll have an order," Jahir said. "And coffee. And—?" He glanced at Vasiht'h.

"Better make that two cups of coffee," Vasiht'h said. "I'm not sure about rosewater cream with kerinne."

The waitress, a ginger-coated Asanii, wrinkled her nose. "No. I wouldn't be either."

After she'd left, Jahir said, "The scones here are well regarded."

"They sound it. Anyway, as I was saying . . . I didn't expect them to handwave us in. Citizenship is complicated. I don't know much about it, but a lot of it is political. I did a little reading on it when I went to Seersana." Vasiht'h shook his head. "No, I'm not surprised. I hope we'll be able to stay, though. I'm guessing they need to approve us for permanent status?"

That delicate hesitation was more sensed through the mindline than observed. Jahir touched his water glass and said, "Something like that, yes."

Vasiht'h watched him not fidget and chuckled. "Let me guess. They can't wait to let you in, but they aren't as excited about yet another Pelted." That earned him a look that was almost—almost—mournful. Grinning, Vasiht'h said, "Goddess, arii, who could blame them?"

Surprising him, Jahir said, "I could."

Vasiht'h blushed, flattered. "Well. Tell me about this client. How did we end up with a client before we even managed residency? And where are we living? Transient housing, I'm guessing?"

"Not . . . quite, no. I toured the transient housing," Jahir said. "I didn't think it would suit us."

"By which you mean. . . ."

"It was. . . ." Jahir hesitated. "Colorless. And not very comfortable."

"Not very comfortable."

Jahir did smile then, one of those whimsical smiles Vasiht'h loved so much. "I am rather taller than the average Pelted, and you are rather longer. An apartment engineered to suit the common averages, and meant for short occupancy, is not ideal for such disparate roommates."

Vasiht'h squinted at him.

"They also had no full kitchens," Jahir said.

"Oh." Vasiht'h grimaced. "Then, no. You're right. What did you find instead?"

"There is an area to the northeast here known as the Garden District, and I found a woman there letting her cottage to tenants. I engaged that cottage. It was not overmuch money and I was concerned someone might take it while we were discussing it."

"Not overmuch money," Vasiht'h repeated, torn between skepticism and resignation.

"It is not a permanent solution. We have only half a year to prove ourselves to the housing authority or we'll have to find someplace else." Jahir hesitated. "I know it doesn't seem long—"

"It doesn't, no, but that's all right. We can do it. And if we can't, then that's the Goddess telling us this wasn't the right place, or the right time." Vasiht'h grinned at him. "Besides, we've done more in less time."

A breeze blew through the mindline, like a sigh, like spring evening: Jahir's relief made manifest. It lifted the fur up Vasiht'h's spine. "I suppose we have, at that."

"So, this client?"

Jahir told him about Helga as they ate, and Vasiht'h found the whole story completely unsurprising. Of course his friend attracted the attention of a person who could help him, and wanted to—because who didn't want to help Jahir? Even Thaddeus Does-Something-With-DNA had that much right—and of course it had resulted in their first patient, plus a place to live which he had no doubt would be just right for them. The Goddess was probably smiling somewhere.

Also, the scones were tremendous, and as usual, Vasiht'h had to encourage Jahir to eat his fair share.

"They are good," Jahir said. "Just . . . rather overwhelming at speed."

"Then eat slowly," Vasiht'h replied, amused. "And we'll find you an ice cream place as soon as we're settled." He set his spoon down and added, "Would you look at that!"

Over the tops of the buildings the sky was streaked in deepening gold. As they watched, the blue over them began to creep away from the sunset, slowly, slowly, as if they really were on a world. When the waitress came by she followed their gazes and grinned, ears perked. "New to the station?"

"I am," Vasiht'h said. "I didn't think there would be a sunset."

"And I never thought to question it," Jahir admitted. "The verisimilitude of the environment is convincing."

"We do get sunsets and sunrises," the waitress said as she cleared their plates. "And they're different every day, just like on a planet. They happen earlier and later in the year, depending on the time of year. The only thing we don't get is violent weather."

"Does it rain, then?" Vasiht'h asked.

"It dews!" She laughed. "But it's not rain like you're thinking, big soaking things. That would be a real mess to clean up."

"I imagine," Jahir murmured, and his bemusement suffused the mindline like the clouds that probably never touched the starbase's sky.

"Feel free to stay if you want," she finished. "It's worth seeing.

And watch out for our local stars! That's the spindle, and all the Fleet shuttles moving around. We love our night skies."

They did in fact stay, in perfect peace with one another, sipping their coffee and watching the sky change color. The night sky drew the spindle into relief; no longer a distant white lattice barely visible against the light blue, it glowed with rich and visible colors, pinpricks of blue and green and red and white, with streaks here and there that suggested the frame. There were lights in motion, as promised, and Vasiht'h wondered how many Fleet vessels were moving there, nuzzling into their docks for service, or being towed by tugs or swarmed over by whatever machines were needed to fix up starships.

"I hope we can stay," he said.

"As do I, arii."

CHAPTER 3

THE GARDEN DISTRICT WASN'T far from the commons. Walking the thoroughfares with their lanterns, Vasiht'h wondered if Fleet could see them as well as they could see Fleet—wouldn't that be something! But maybe the atmosphere distorted the lights? Then again, one could see cities from space. Was the spindle closer to the city-sphere than a ship in orbit was to a planet?

"Strange thoughts," Jahir said aloud.

"Interesting ones." Vasiht'h hooked a hand around the strap of his messenger bag. "When I left home my plan was to get away, really expand, experience things I couldn't while living on Anseahla. Seersana was good—the culture there's not much like the culture we've got at home—but it's still full of Pelted. And Selnor. . . ." He trailed off, then shifted his wings, refolded them. "I didn't really experience much of Selnor."

"Neither did I." Rueful, with a sour and apologetic taste. Vasiht'h wrinkled his nose and tried not to smack his lips.

"Anyway. This place . . . I think this place qualifies." Glancing around, he added, "Though if you didn't know we were on a star-base, you'd probably never realize from the architecture."

"No," Jahir agreed. "But it has a pleasant look, I thought. And the gardens are rife."

"I guess that makes sense, given the name. Who's our landlady?"

"Her name is Ilea EveryLivingThing."

Vasiht'h hmmmed. "A Tam-illee, from the name? What's she like?"

"I'm not certain. We made the arrangements over the data tablet. She said she'd be waiting to show us the establishment."

So blandly said that Vasiht'h almost missed the implication. He shot a glance at the Eldritch. "You haven't looked inside the place?"

"I saw a viseo of the interior," said Jahir, and this apology was less sour and more meek, and smelled like a delicate lady's perfume.

Vasiht'h burst out laughing. "So if I ask you why I'm smelling flowers, you probably won't tell me."

"It would require chasing the association down, and I'm not certain I can." Jahir cleared his throat. "If it doesn't suit, we will find something else."

"Of course we will," Vasiht'h said, amused. "Lead on."

⟨∞⟩

Such a relief to find that Vasiht'h was not distressed! Neither over their precarious circumstance, nor over his precipitous housing arrangements. Jahir had worried. But now that the Glaseah was back, he found those worries receding beneath the pleasure of having him by again. When he'd left Vasiht'h to the remainder of his family vacation, the mindline had slowly attenuated until at some point it had become a vague film, a sense of presence without weight or detail, and while he'd been grateful that it hadn't snapped he'd become aware that he was now . . . accustomed . . . to having company in his thoughts.

A tremendous thing, this. For one of his kind, particularly. What would his people say did they know how closely he'd yoked himself to anyone, much less an alien? Even Eldritch lovers didn't cling to one another, mind to mind—it was considered too great an intimacy, the sort of thing parents cautioned their adult children against embracing lest it poison the union. 'Best not to know everything about someone,' they said. 'Hold your privacy dear.'

So much they were missing, Jahir thought, and let some of that pleasure through, like an evening breeze, and received in return the sound of wind chimes. Perfect accord, he thought, and brought the Glaseah around the corner and down the street where their accommodations were waiting. This part he knew; he'd walked this way and seen the 'For Rent' sign himself before looking up the listing. He'd liked the cultivated loveliness, the neat little houses with their gardens overgrowing their delicate wooden fences, the mingled scents of their blooms, the constant shifting sunlight on the leaves that nodded in the clean-scented wind. Pedestrians had been using the thoroughfare in the afternoon, but strolling rather than striding; the businesses here were few, little corner stores with victuals and boutiques and plant nurseries. He'd found it charming.

The Garden District in evening was no less so, lit by sleek lamps with warm light and from beneath by cool-hued string-lights glowing along the edges of the walkways. And if anything, the perfume in the air had grown denser. There were still people strolling, talking together, and others on their patios, rocking in chairs or swinging on them, enjoying the weather or visiting with neighbors.

"This is beautiful," Vasiht'h murmured.

There was an undertone there that felt like a cold shadow on Jahir's back. He glanced down at his friend. "Arii?"

"I mean it," Vasiht'h said. "But this is . . . ah . . . probably a very expensive neighborhood."

Jahir had yet to understand the Alliance economic system. It was probably an impossibility, given the size of the polity—what was true on one world, or even in one world's city, would not hold true for some other—but he still felt he should at least grasp the basics. In this case, "And . . . we would not normally be capable of affording it?"

"I certainly wouldn't, not on a xenotherapist's salary. Unless we became . . . I don't know. Rock star xenotherapists famous throughout the known worlds, with scores of articles in juried medical journals and rounds of talks scheduled in all the prestigious universities in the Core." Perhaps some of his puzzlement leaked, because Vasiht'h squinted up at him. "You really have no idea, do you. How money works. Does money just appear in your account, tagged to you?"

Saying 'yes' would probably dismay the Glaseah. Jahir settled for, "I grew up with a different system."

"I'm betting," Vasiht'h muttered. Then, louder, "Is that your Tam-illee?"

Since the woman was standing alongside the property, Jahir said, "It is, yes." And calling to her, "Alet. Good evening. We are your new tenants."

"I figured from the look of you." The foxine grinned at them. He'd seen her portrait when making arrangements; had, in fact, made those arrangements based on his instinctive reaction to the settled lineaments of her face, the perk of her ears, the vitality in her eyes. Stills could lie, of course, and were carefully chosen by their user to project a certain personality, but that she'd chosen such a forthcoming and energetic one had surely said something about her.

Meeting her now, those hopes were borne out: Ilea EveryLivingThing was a middle-aged Tam-illee, her coat some dark lustrous hue made non-specific by the gloaming, and she bounced on her heels, hands folded behind her back until their arrival prompted her to offer Vasiht'h her palm to cover.

"I'm Ilea," she said. "And welcome. Let me show you around."

There was a door at the gate that led to the main house, but Ilea took them to a second door, and this one took a shorter route through the garden directly to a small cottage. "As I mentioned," the Tam-illee was saying, "It's really not intended for multiple tenants, but if you're sure you're fine with small spaces—"

She opened the door. "Then this is home."

The room she revealed was as cozy a thing as he could have

imagined: a single room with a couch, a small kitchen, and a table beside the window where the flowers were doing their best to enter. The sleeping chamber, such as it was, was a nook in the back, where a single bed with a thick quilt was tucked beneath the lowered ceiling. A single window hung alongside it, open to the sweetly scented evening air.

"I know it's a little strangely shaped," Ilea was saying as she turned on the lights. "But there's a ramp outside that leads to a roof garden. If you're not sure—"

The surge of desire that flooded the mindline surprised Jahir, and delighted him. Vasiht'h said, firmly, "It's perfect."

"Then let me make you a cup of tea to celebrate." The foxine beamed at them. "I'll tell you a little about the neighborhood to get you started, since you'll be relying on your neighbors and their shops for most things."

"You're not here much?" Vasiht'h asked as he investigated the table, straightened the tablecloth.

"Oh, no." She took down a tin from a cupboard and started a kettle. Another of those magical Alliance contrivances that worked without visual evidence of heat, Jahir noted, despite the rustic furnishings. The lace curtains could have come out of an Eldritch gentlewoman's sitting room . . . but no Eldritch lady would ever have had hot water within seconds of deciding she wanted it. "I'm a ranger—do you know what we do?"

"Not at all?" Jahir offered, taking one of the seats at the table. Vasiht'h sat alongside him, the mindline between them humming with the Glaseah's excitement.

"What you're looking at out there," Ilea said, waving her measuring spoon, "is essentially an enormous terrarium, aletsen. The grass, the flowers, the trees, the soil, all of it . . . it has to be maintained by the judicious application of supportive fauna. It's not just the farming spheres that need bees and treerunners and birds and bugs. Without those things we'd be living in a giant metal ball, full of girders and glass and steel. It would be pretty, I guess, but it would pall quickly. To thrive, we need a real ecosystem to support us. Not just mentally—" She tapped her temple, "but physically as well. I am technically a kind of environmental engineer, but here on the stations, we call ourselves rangers. We monitor the health of the station's ecosystem."

/*Fascinating,*/ Jahir murmured.

/*I'll say,*/ the Glaseah replied privately before continuing aloud. "So there's more than one of you?"

"Oh, it's a job for several teams, certainly. That's not even counting the Fleet folks who do the weather. They're the ones in charge of aerating all the spheres, the gas ratios, the water." She poured for them, brought a tray to the table and sat on the remaining chair. In the light, her fur was revealed as a glossy brown—a very handsome woman, in her prime and very settled in her work, Jahir thought. "Since the base is technically Fleet property, they feel strongly about things that are either security or infrastructure-affecting. We let them handle that. Honestly there's enough work without worrying about oxygen leaks." She grinned at them. "The short of it is that I'm often sleeping off in some field somewhere, trying to set traps for wildlife, or spending a few weeks tracking the penetration of new colonies of damselglitters or grubs. I love my work, but it doesn't leave me much time to enjoy the fancy house I bought because of it."

"I'd say you're enjoying yourself fine without it!" Vasiht'h said.

She laughed. "You're probably right, at that. So let me tell you about the neighborhood and I'll let you all go from there. You're paid up for six months so no pressure."

There was a faintly ominous cloud now in the mindline that Jahir chose to ignore. "Thank you, alet. We're listening."

⸻ ◈ ⸻

The rundown on the neighborhood was about what Vasiht'h had expected from the walk and the introduction. They had access to boutiques and farmers' markets, all very neatly designed to be as picturesque and pleasant as possible. Unlike their landlady, their neighbors were frequently home, either running these shops or taking advantage of their wealth to rock in chairs on their porches or pursue what were probably ridiculously expensive hobbies at their leisure. From the Hinichi on the corner who was studying comparative religions when he wasn't conducting services in the discreet chapel at the end of yet another beautiful alley to the Asanii grandmother who made wind chimes to sell to tourists, they were one and all the sorts of people Vasiht'h would have expected in a book—and not like HEALED BY HER IMMORTAL HEART. More like a cozy slice of life thing.

He knew Jahir could sense his rue through the mindline, but didn't broach the topic even after Ilea had left. He washed the tea cups, enjoying them wistfully, and let Jahir turn down the bed and unpack. When at last he finished in the kitchen, he found the Eldritch sitting there with his hands folded in his lap, looking for all the worlds like one of Vasiht'h's younger sibs awaiting a lecture.

He couldn't help his laugh as he gathered the spare pillows. "It's not a permanent solution."

"It is a little small," Jahir said, cautious.

The size of the place wasn't the only problem, but since it was one of them, Vasiht'h said, "It's fine." Because seeing how worried his friend was, he couldn't feel anything else. The Eldritch had tried so hard . . . ! And it was beautiful, really. "Do we have a plan for tomorrow?"

"We should . . . look . . . for someplace to host clients," Jahir said. "An office? But offices do not normally have beds, do they?"

"No," Vasiht'h said, plumping a pillow. There was no space left beside the bed for a pallet, but he didn't mind a makeshift nest on the floor. "But a bed could be brought into one, I guess. Maybe we should split up and see what we find? And then we could find out more about this client we have."

"Yes," Jahir said, exhaling, a sigh Vasiht'h caught only because the mindline magnified the otherwise minimalist sound. "I'm glad you're not . . . distressed."

"No," Vasiht'h said, amused, settling down on the pillows. As the Eldritch went to prepare for bed, he added, "Things will work out as they should, arii."

"I pray so."

"So do I," Vasiht'h murmured.

CHAPTER 4

"HE'S COMPLETELY UNAWARE OF the most fundamental things," Vasiht'h said, "And I love him but it makes me a little crazy too."

His sister Sehvi had her cheek in her palm, staring at him across the parsecs from her student apartment on Tam-ley, where she was studying reproductive medicine. The display in Vasiht'h's new flat was of supremely high fidelity: he could see the darker rims around her brown irises, just before her cheeks crinkled and occluded some of them. "And there's no advice to be found in your reading?"

Vasiht'h growled. "No, and you know it. 'My bonded doesn't understand money' is a little too mundane for the romantic caricatures in that ridiculous piece of fluff."

She laughed. "You *are* exasperated! Why does it bother you so much? So he's paying for everything right now, and he doesn't seem to understand why that's extraordinary. Maybe he's rich. Maybe you should enjoy it."

"What if he's not rich?" Vasiht'h asked. "What if he's going to run himself into debt spending like this?" He rubbed a circle into the fur at his temple. "No, it's almost worse if he is rich and he just doesn't realize most people don't live in fancy places like this, and never worry about bills."

"That seems a little harsh," Sehvi said. "You did rounds with him for your internship, didn't you? Did he seem like he didn't understand those things?"

"It didn't really come up!" Vasiht'h forced himself to sit back and sip some of the mint tea he'd brewed before making the call.

"I find that hard to believe—"

"Well, it came up in that people were worried about money, but when people worry about money there's a root there. Security. Fear. A need for safety or stability. Or the sense that you're pulling your weight, or that other people value you in a context that society understands. . . ." He trailed off.

"So now we know why you might find all this troubling," Sehvi said with a crooked smile.

Vasiht'h sighed. "None of that's a surprise, is it? Of course I want to feel like I've . . . I've arrived."

"After years of Bret telling you that you needed to straighten out and start acting like a responsible adult? I'm sure."

Even hearing his brother's name afflicted Vasiht'h with a vague sense of guilt. Rueful, he said, "I want to be his partner, Sehvi. Not his . . . his kept friend."

"Kept friend!" Sehvi exclaimed with a burbled laugh. "Now there's a mess of a construction."

Vasiht'h wrinkled his nose. "Well, 'kept man' has implications that don't apply." He smiled a little. "But that's the gist of it, yes. On my part, anyway. I don't know what's going on in his head."

"Even with the mindline?"

"Even with. The mindline's a little more mysterious than you'd think from reading about it. I thought it meant we'd just . . . know each other the way we know ourselves? It turns out it's . . ." He trailed off, looking for words.

"Whimsical? Capricious?"

"Complicated," Vasiht'h said, firmly.

"That makes sense," his sister said. "People are. And their minds, definitely." She looked past him. "So this is the place? It is fancy. But small?"

He nodded. "Too small for us to see patients. That's where he is right now . . . looking around for places we could see someone. We already have a client, even, if we can figure out where to receive them."

"Your first client!" Sehvi exclaimed, sitting upright. "Already?"

"Well, you know," Vasiht'h said. "These things just . . . fall into his lap."

"And that bothers you?" she asked, peering at him.

Did it? Vasiht'h sipped his tea, searching for any resentment and finding none no matter what corner he peeked into. "No," he said. "No, I . . . I *like* it, Sehvi. I like watching things happen to him, the way I did. Everything delights him. Everything fascinates him. He's grateful for every new experience he has."

"He reminds you to be, too."

"I admit, I sometimes wonder if the Goddess didn't decide I needed a good swift kick in the rear," Vasiht'h said, chagrined. "If only to keep from disappointing Bret."

Sehvi huffed. "The only person responsible for Bret's disappointment is Bret. If he didn't have such a hidebound idea of what everyone was supposed to do or how they were supposed to act—"

"Then most of us would still be rambunctious kits without the first idea of how to get by," Vasiht'h said. "Be fair, ariishir. Dami and Tapa were too busy to raise us all without help, and for better or worse Bret wanted the job. And he does love us."

"Sort of," Sehvi muttered.

"Sehvi!"

"Fine, fine," she said. "I know he cares. He's just so officious it makes me want to pinch his flank once in a while."

"That's natural," Vasiht'h said. "He is our brother, after all."

Sehvi considered him at length. "You really are all right. I mean, you look it, but it's my job to be sure, right?"

"You're my younger sister, Sehvi, not my older."

"Still," she said. "I'm the one who loves you best, and don't deny it." She grinned. "So?"

"I am all right," Vasiht'h said. "I mean that. We've got things to work out, but what couple doesn't? We'll figure it out. And in the meantime . . . we're here. You know?"

"I know," she said, her smile relaxing into something gentler, and they shared a moment despite the distance that separated them.

"So," Vasiht'h said. "How's *your* relationship going? Ready to marry him yet?"

She mimed throwing something at him.

"Oh, so it's serious! Wait, let me see if I can find a romance novel to educate you on handling your nascent love affair! I'm sure there's got to be one for two Glaseah—"

Sehvi was already laughing. "Yes, I'm sure it's called THEY'LL GET TO IT EVENTUALLY."

"Don't wait too long, Dami will be disappointed," Vasiht'h said with a grin. "And unlike Bret, her disappointment actually matters."

He expected a tart response. But Sehvi said, "I don't think I'll wait long." He wasn't sure what to say until she grinned again. "But don't worry. I'm not there yet."

Vasiht'h exhaled, pressed a hand to his breast in theatrical dismay. "Don't worry me like that, ariishir. If you grow up and become a responsible adult with children, I won't have any choice but to do the same!"

She guffawed. "More like you won't have anyone between you and Bret's critical eye."

"That too, ariishir. That too."

The mindline had remained warm and present throughout his call with Sehvi, and consulting it after they'd parted brought him the distracted, distant feel of his friend about the work. It was tempting to go out after him, but the garden was beautiful. Vasiht'h refreshed his cup of tea and used the ramp outside to reach the low roof. Surveying the surrounding houses, girdled in their lawns and extravagant landscaping, the Glaseah sighed. The chances of their being able to stay here were . . . very low. Even without the price, which he was sure was exorbitant, it was too far from the center of everything. He hadn't come to a starbase to hide in its outskirts. But for now . . . for now it was just right.

Watching the flowers nod in the slight breeze, Vasiht'h sipped his tea and brought up the painful adventures of Thaddeus WeavesDNA. He doubted there would be anything in it about making a home, but it would give him something to blame his sister for when he talked to her next. At least this scene didn't feature the goddess-like presence of the Eldritch love interest, though he wasn't sure three pages of internal monologue expounding on the guilt and yearning of the hapless Thaddeus was an improvement. He was wondering whether he should skim to the next break when he became aware of his partner's gentle amusement. Looking away from his reader, he found the Eldritch standing in the garden below him, like . . . well, like a romantic hero serenading a lady fair.

The book was definitely getting to him.

/This distraction is unlike you,/ Jahir offered.

/My sisters,/ Vasiht'h said by way of explanation. Truthful, if not entirely. He still felt odd about inflicting his complaints about the novelist's caricature on his friend. /They're incorrigible./

/And consuming,/ Jahir said. /Or you would have noticed the market a few streets down. You must have a view of it from there. Or heard the sound?/

/Glaseah don't hear as well as most Pelted races./ Vasiht'h set the reader down and rose, stretching a hind leg as he leaned toward the roof's railing. /And I don't see anything either, except people walking on the streets. And the tops of trees. There's a market?/

A hint of lemon chiffon amusement, edible as pie. /You could buy groceries./

/I could!/ Vasiht'h trotted down the ramp and finished aloud, "You just want me to bake."

"I'd like to cook with you," Jahir said. "And we do have to eat."

Vasiht'h cocked his head, looking up at his taller friend. "How did the office shopping go?"

Jahir held open the garden gate for him. "I can tell you about it afterwards."

"That good, ah."

A faint resignation soughed through the mindline, like the dim childhood memory of a breeze over grass. "Somewhat in that vein, yes."

"Groceries it is."

The market was everything Vasiht'h had hoped from the hints of color and bustle in the mindline. One of the streets had been overtaken entirely by tables and booths with awnings that rippled in the breeze. Several dozen people were browsing the offerings, and it was everything from honey and preserves to freshly baked pocket pies, and all the odd bits that seemed to accrue at the edges, like cross-stitched aphorisms and little metal sculptures of birds to decorate a person's garden.

Looking over the artisanal popsicles—what did a pistachio popsicle taste like anyway?—Vasiht'h did his best to sit on his chagrin.

/You could try one and find out?/ Jahir suggested, having apparently caught some part of that. Looking over the rows of colored ices, he finished, /I am tempted, myself./

/I bet there's a fancy ice cream seller here somewhere,/ Vasiht'h said, making his way to the next booth with its yeasty aroma. Rows of fresh-baked breads were stacked on the three tables. Rosemary and new Attican olive. Chives and handmade cheese from, he noted, a vendor on the other side of the market, who apparently kept goats somewhere? He looked for plain bread and found some narrow loaves at the end of the table, in a bin. For, apparently, the barbarians too uncouth to appreciate the exquisite flavor pairings designed by people with far more time on their hands than Vasiht'h could ever hope for, if he wanted to be able to afford a house without leaning on his partner.

His conversation with Sehvi about his need to feel like he'd arrived loured over him like a cloud. He sighed.

"I would like ice cream," Jahir said.

"You'd always like ice cream."

"I do, yes." Jahir paused and looked down the street. The sun gilded the hair that was shifting in the breeze, just like something out of Vasiht'h's novel. Unlike that perfect maiden, though, his friend was . . . frowning. A normal frown, a little pinch between his brows, not some thunderous, dramatic expression.

/There is something wrong with this,/ Jahir guessed as he finished his survey.

Vasiht'h stood alongside him and looked too. Really looked. So many species represented, far more than they were used to at the university. Wolf ears and Phoenix feathers, curly cat tails and the smooth skin of humans, gleaming in the sunshine. Tamillee bartering for fresh vegetables with long-eared Aera, Harat-Shariin children chasing their Seersan friends. Little old women and men, reminding him of family gatherings on Anseahla, selling quilts that . . . no one here needed, really, because of the perfect climate control. And yet he still wanted one, because someone had made it and it was beautiful.

/There's nothing wrong with it,/ Vasiht'h said. /It's just . . ./

/Not right,/ Jahir said. More firmly, /I saw an ice cream parlor in the commons, walking back. We should go./

"Have you even eaten lunch?" Vasiht'h eyed him.

"There are always scones. . . ."

"That's not lunch," Vasiht'h said.

"It is when you put herbs in them and serve them with salmon mousse," Jahir observed, and that expression was a little pained. Vasiht'h couldn't help but laugh. Smiling too, Jahir said, "Ice cream?"

"Fine. But lunch after." Jogging along after Jahir, Vasiht'h added, "You are incorrigible."

/Only because ice cream is delightful./

The parlor in the commons looked like the one near the art college at Seersana U where they'd had so many desserts. It was not manned by a calico Asanii, though, but by a serious-looking Harat-Shar: one of the rarer clouded pards with a ragged splotchwork pelt and a set of impressive teeth which Vasiht'h had time to admire when the woman smiled at them. More or less. Her mannerisms were stilted and formal, and natural smiles seemed a stretch for her, though she obviously considered the effort worth making. She was also retiring until Jahir's question on the composition of the ginger ice cream unleashed an astonishing disquisition on the topic, one which segued into explanations of every other flavor, their weaknesses and strengths, suggested uses and ideal servings (including mix-ins), and a step-by-step breakdown on how best to take advantage of the current customer rewards structure. Vasiht'h had never been so well-informed about ice cream; the pard made the artisanal ice cream makers at the market sound like dilettantes.

Halfway through this narrative, he started catching silvery glints of humor in the mindline. Jahir did nothing so gauche as glance at him to share his reaction, but by the end of it, Vasiht'h was grinning.

The Harat-Shar paused, ears flicking outward. "Did I discomfit you? I discomfit people sometimes."

"On the contrary," Jahir said. "We find you informative."

"We think you're great," Vasiht'h agreed.

"And the ice cream is sublime," Jahir murmured over his sample of the ginger. "We should come back."

Vasiht'h laughed. "We haven't even left yet!"

"The future does not take care of itself without a sufficiency of planning."

Squinting at Jahir, the pard said, "You mean that."

"He does," Vasiht'h said, still chuckling. Rising up on his toes, he added, "I'll have the dulce de leche. With the espresso drizzle, like you suggested. What's your name?"

"Karina," the pard said. "What size?"

"Medium, please. But he'll have a large."

"I—" Jahir paused. "I . . . will have a medium ginger, with the fresh figs. But I will also have some of the cinnamon biscuits you suggested. Should I have tea or coffee?"

Karina wrinkled her nose, eyes narrowed. "Tea. But black.

We have a Harat-Shariin homeworld blend that's full-bodied with a fruity aftertaste. You should order that. Don't sweeten it."

"As you say," Jahir said. "Thank you, alet."

"You're welcome."

It was, Vasiht'h reflected once they were seated with their selections, nothing like their old ice cream haunt, and everything like it. His contentment saturated the mindline, melding with Jahir's, and that left him prey to the unexpected question.

"Why did it distress you? The market."

Now, he thought, would be an excellent time for handy tips from the heroes of HEALED BY HER IMMORTAL HEART. Naturally, the only advice he could remember absorbing from the book involved buying gifts to hint at affection. Did the ice cream count? Come to think of it, which of them had paid for it? "We should probably open a joint bank account."

"It would behoove us to earn a salary first, perhaps," Jahir murmured.

"Well, we have a client," Vasiht'h said. "Do we have a place to see her?"

Jahir sighed, and drew his data tablet from his messenger bag, sliding it across the table. "I have put them in order of best to worst."

Vasiht'h picked it up and thumbed to the first. "Using what criteria?"

"Whether the environment is professional and safe," Jahir said. "And whether its location inspires confidence."

"And whether we can afford it?" Vasiht'h asked, lipping his spoon.

"I fear our choices are already rather limited," Jahir said. "And it hardly matters how much the location costs if we won't be able to stay."

"Sort of like the cottage." Vasiht'h sighed, looked over the top of the tablet. His friend's eyes were somber, matching the muted fog in the mindline. Jahir knew something was wrong. It was unfair to keep him guessing like this. "You know it's bad to live beyond our means."

"We don't yet have a means," Jahir murmured, eyes dropping to rest on the ice cream.

"That's the problem. Ordinarily we'd be taking out a loan . . ." Vasiht'h trailed off. "But you don't need one. Or you already have one?" When Jahir didn't answer immediately, he said, "Don't tell me that your monetary situation is one of the things you can't talk about."

A sheepish smile, and a faint apologetic brush through the mindline. Vasiht'h groaned and put his head in one hand. "Great."

"I know it bothered you as a student," Jahir said, obviously picking the words with care. "But . . . I had a question about this."

"Go ahead?"

"You . . . do not appear to be poor either." Jahir broke one of the biscuits in half and then into quarters. "You are the son of two working professionals, who had the money to send you to a university on another world. I do not perfectly understand the economic model of the Alliance, but my observation is that you have never seemed to be want for money."

"I . . . no. I'm not poor," Vasiht'h said, then winced. "All right, my *family's* not poor. But all of us kids . . . we're expected to go out into the world and make our own living. We can't be a burden to our parents. That's part of the point, right? We get old enough to help them."

"Is it?" Jahir wondered.

Trust the Eldritch to ask the unexamined questions. "Yes? I think?"

"I doubt your parents had you so that you could support them," Jahir said.

"Fine," Vasiht'h said, on firmer ground now. "*I* want to help them, and not be a burden. And that means I don't ask them for money. I earn my own. I maybe send the rest of my family some money sometimes." He tapped the spoon on the table between them. "And that means . . . I have to know if I have the potential to earn that money, which I can't right now because I have no visibility into our expenses. This is above and beyond what we set up so that I could buy furniture for us once in a while. If I'm going to be your partner, I want to be your partner."

⸎

Jahir had thought the mindline had capped the intimacies he could develop, because surely being bonded to an alien's mind was as close as one could manage in this life. It was probably inappropriate to be delighted to discover otherwise: that his own ignorance of the Alliance could continue to surprise him with the ways he had yet to engage with Vasiht'h, and everyone else.

This was, he thought, a better reaction than alarm. But he acknowledged that there was some of that as well. "You are my partner," he assured the Glaseah. "But you forget that I'm not certain what that means to you. I didn't assume money to be involved."

"I didn't either until it became an issue." Vasiht'h's resignation glittered in the link, hinting at humor. At least this wasn't entirely depressing his mood. "But it turns out it matters to me. So. What do we do?"

"I am not adverse to a joint account," Jahir said, when in fact he meant he was greatly in favor of one. It would allow him to keep the account the Queen had been pouring his stipend into separate, because God and Lady alone only knew what Vasiht'h would make of the balance. He'd known intellectually that the Queen must be wealthy because Ontine had not fallen apart like the remainder of the Eldritch homeworld: there was food in the palace, fresh food; someone was doing maintenance on the grounds; there was a private landing pad for her couriers, out of sight of the xenophobic citizenry. But he had not properly understood just how wealthy until he'd seen what she considered a minor stipend. Living here, he had a sense of how she might have accomplished it. Hundreds of years of interest in carefully selected investments could compound at an astonishing rate, and if Liolesa had inherited some of those portfolios from Maraesa before her, or even Jerisa who might have maintained some of them on Earth. . . .

No, he would never want for money. But watching Vasiht'h

push his ice cream around with a spoon—without eating it—
Jahir thought his friend would very much not appreciate learning just how extreme they differed in estate.

"That's a start," Vasiht'h said. "I don't have almost anything
to put in it, though. When I decided to leave Anseahla for school
my parents budgeted out what I'd need to live offworld and
gave me all of it in a lump sum, and left me to figure out how to
manage it."

"That must have been . . . exhilarating," Jahir offered,
cautious.

Vasiht'h snorted. "It was terrifying at first. I'd never had
that much responsibility before. For the first couple of months I
barely ate without checking my bank balance. But I figured it out
pretty quickly. I don't really have many wants, you know? Above
the basic stuff."

"Cookies," Jahir murmured. "Pillows. Incense."

Vasiht'h chuckled. "More or less. Presents for other people."
He shook his head. "But we're doing things that require . . . well,
a lot of money. Renting a place to see patients. Renting a place
to live. We'll need to buy advertising. Food . . . food here is more
expensive, probably because it's a closed environment. You need
clothes—"

"I have clothes?" Jahir offered.

"They'll wear out," Vasiht'h said. "And while you're probably
going to try to mend them, at some point your time is more valuable than the money you'd spend buying a replacement."

The idea was fascinating, and disarming. He'd never thought
of his time as valuable; he had so much of it, and at home there'd
been so little to fill it with. But the Glaseah's speech had given
him an opportunity to sense the texture of the emotions that
accompanied them, and this allowed him to say, "What is this
really about? If it is not impolite to ask." At Vasiht'h's sharp
glance, Jahir said, "I can hear echoes of something, and it is
linked to pride, and Sehvi's voice."

Vasiht'h looked away, feathered ears sinking against his fur.
The mindline vibrated with some tension: not anger, he thought,

but determination. Frustration, maybe. At last, the Glaseah said, "I want to be an adult, arii. I can't do that until I can take care of myself."

It seemed the wrong time to suggest that they'd spent several years learning that sometimes even adults had to ask for help . . . or could even build their lives around partnerships that involved sharing self-care with another. Vasiht'h had in fact crossed several sectors just to prove that to him. But . . . he had needed to survive the wet epidemic on Selnor before he made peace with his need for help in those areas where he was weak. Perhaps Vasiht'h needed this struggle to understand a similar lesson.

Was that hubris, he wondered? Transference? Did he want his friend to have problems with autonomy and dependence because he'd had them?

Looking at the melting dulce de leche ice cream, now a dulled light brown from the constant mixing that had made short work of the drizzle, Jahir thought not.

"I understand," he said. "Shall we pick our office out? I am partial to the first choice on the list, but there is honestly not much to differentiate the selections. I am not strongly wedded to any of them."

"In that case," Vasiht'h said firmly, picking up the data tablet and thumbing through them, "let's take the one we can afford."

Jahir suppressed his sigh and sipped the tea.

CHAPTER 5

A METIA WAS A HARAT-SHAR. Not just any Harat-Shar, either, but a member of the smallest intrarace, the one based on cheetahs. Like them she was rangy and restless and arresting, from her golden eyes to the enormous thick bars of her pelt, for she was striped like one of Terra's king cheetahs. They called it royal patterning among the Harat-Shar, and it was supposed to indicate a direct link to the young girl who'd befriended the angel Kajentarel, the major figure in the homeworld's primary monotheist religion.

Ametia certainly carried herself like a queen, dropping her bag into the chair in their office and standing, hands on her hips, her direct gaze a challenge. "So. Helga sent me."

/Goddess preserve us,/ Vasiht'h muttered.

/Her aid would not go unappreciated./ Jahir said, "Alet, would you like a seat? A cup of tea?"

Ametia was studying them both. "Weirdest therapists I've ever seen, and I've seen a lot of them. But they're invariably Core race bipeds, and the one exception wasn't much of an improvement. But for reasons I entirely understand." She quirked a brow at Vasiht'h. "A Glaseah. And an Eldritch? Really? What's that story?" But she did sit down, at least, though her tail tip flicked constantly.

"We met in school," Vasiht'h said. "And discovered that we did well together."

She huffed, ears flattening. "Isn't that the way it's supposed to work." At Vasiht'h's questioning look, she finished, "I'm a professor at the university here, in the history department."

"But you have observed that it doesn't always work that way," Vasiht'h guessed.

She folded her arms, leaning back. "I'm not going to trot out my rant for you to psychoanalyze. I've been through that a half dozen times, and I'm tired of it."

"Fortunately," Jahir said, "We have a couch for you to sleep on, and no need for you to elucidate your reasons for needing it."

That perked one of her ears up, though the look she awarded Jahir was skeptical in the extreme. He found himself thinking she must be a very animated lecturer, and that class with her was probably challenging. "Helga did say you had surprising methods. So what are you going to sell me? Do I solve my problems by sleeping through them?"

"Not an inaccurate description of the modality," Jahir said.

"You dream," Vasiht'h said, "And we watch your dreams, and if they seem troubled, we nudge them."

Such a fascinating flurry of emotions through her face then. Vasiht'h said, /We've at least surprised her./

/That may be our best way into her, at that./

"That seems . . ." She trailed off, frowned. "Chancy."

"It requires a trustfall," Vasiht'h said, which made her laugh. Jahir sent a puzzled question and received an image of someone falling backwards into the arms of a friend. "But if you aren't willing to open yourself to a therapist, you shouldn't be here. We can't practice on the unwilling, alet. Before we can help anyone, they have to be willing to let us help."

She rested her elbow on the chair's arm and put her cheek in her hand. "My. That's some straight talking."

"We don't want to waste your time," Vasiht'h said. /Goddess, I hope I'm doing this right. But I'm not even sure she wants to be here!/

/She may not want to be,/ Jahir murmured, studying her. /But she needs something./

/Maybe we'll be the lucky ones to help her find it?/

/God and Lady willing. I would hate for our first appointment to be an abject failure./

Vasiht'h's wince felt like the little shock on skin after a static electricity discharge.

"You talk to each other," Ametia said. She had grown calmer, watching them, as if the intellectual puzzle had distracted her from her agitation. Still radiating that sense of energy and purpose, though. This was perhaps closer to what she was like when contented, this intent focus like a huntress in the savannah. "You're doing it now. Are you?"

/We really need to work on that,/ Vasiht'h said. Aloud, he continued, "We do, yes."

"I thought espers needed to touch one another to hear each other's thoughts?" Her eyes roved from Vasiht'h, sitting on the ground on one side of the small table, to Jahir, seated on the chair. "Angel, that's fascinating. Could you always do it?"

"No," Jahir said. "It was a choice we made."

That gave her pause.

"You're thinking it sounds like a commitment?" Vasiht'h said. "It was."

"Interesting," Ametia said, studying them. And suddenly, "So, I just take a nap on your couch?"

"That's how it works, yes," Jahir said.

"We only listen to your dreams," Vasiht'h added. "Nothing deeper."

She laughed. "Good one, aletsen. Use it on someone more naïve. You want to tell me my dreams aren't as revealing as my thoughts? Maybe more so?" She rose, stretching all the way to the curl of her dark tail. "I hope you have a blanket. I like it warm. That's assuming I can even fall asleep."

"We can make you a calming tea," Jahir said.

"I'd rather you didn't." She eyed the couch, then flicked her eyes at first him, then Vasiht'h. "Presumably you're not going to stare at me while I try."

"No," Vasiht'h said, sitting up. "We'll be . . . over there." He pointed at the door. "In the foyer."

She snorted. "Fine sight the two of you will be loitering out there. How exactly are you going to know when I've dropped off?"

/Good question,/ Vasiht'h said with a sigh.

/We would not have been able to anticipate all the problems with the process without trying it,/ Jahir answered. To Ametia, "We will give you a reasonable amount of time before re-entering."

"And what's a reasonable amount of time?" She sat on the couch and gave them a look straight out of one of their lecture courses: the professor, waiting for the student to work through problems with their methodology.

"If we divulged the number," Jahir said, "you might become anxious about whether you will sleep by the deadline, and fail to fall asleep."

She guffawed. "All right. I suppose that's good enough." She made a little shooing gesture with a hand. "Off you go, then."

The foyer outside the office they'd engaged felt far too formal to Jahir, a sentiment he found surprising in himself. But standing beside Vasiht'h and watching the people passing through on their way to their offices, he found it too quiet, and yet, too busy. Nor did he feel there was enough protection for their patient with only the one door between them and the world they'd left. Some part of him longed to create more of a separation, so they could make a reasonable transition from the vulnerability of both therapy and slumber to the responsibilities and requirements of the waking sphere.

"We know it's imperfect," Vasiht'h said, sensing no doubt his discontent through the mindline. "But it's the best we can manage right now."

"Is it?" Jahir asked.

Vasiht'h glanced at him and said, deliberately, "Yes. Because we don't even know if we can stay. You can't put down roots if they're going to get ripped up in half a year."

"We do not know whether they will be," Jahir said. "And if

we act as if they will, does that not create the fulfillment of our assumption?"

Vasiht'h watched two Karaka'A stride past, talking over a milkshake they were passing to one another along with the conversational baton. "Not everything is under our control, though. We learned that the hard way, didn't we?"

Jahir inhaled carefully, felt the flex of ribs that could move against the gravity here. "Yes. I suppose we did, at that."

When they entered the room fifteen minutes later, Ametia was asleep with her head on her folded arm and her tail slopped over the side of the couch . . . and yet, even sleep had not stilled its twitching tip. They both saw that detail, shared a chagrined look. Vasiht'h offered his hand as he had so many times on Selnor, and Jahir took it, and together they reached for their client.

And leaped back out of her mind again, immediately.

"All right," Vasiht'h said aloud, if softly. "At least we know there is a problem."

"We knew that the moment she entered our office." Jahir sorted through his blood-soaked impressions of battlefields, the screams of jaguars and tigers, the lightning forking through skies taut with storms that never broke. Ametia had been in the center of it, fighting at the side of a winged Harat-Shariin lion twice her height.

/Goddess, what a mess,/ Vasiht'h muttered. /The end of the world, practically./

/No,/ Jahir said slowly. /There was exhilaration there. She is fighting for a noble cause./

/And . . . she's staring at us, arii./

She was, her eyes open and considering them. Noticing their attention, she grinned with teeth. "So?"

"Your cause will win through in the end," Jahir said. "But you may lay your life down in its service, and not live to see the culmination of your aims."

Vasiht'h looked at him. /Arii . . ./

Ametia shoved herself upright abruptly, pushing her hair out of her face. "Say that again."

"You have given yourself to a righteous war," Jahir said. "That you may lose, personally. But you feel you must fight it."

"What in all the hells," she said, wide-eyed. Looking at Vasiht'h, she managed, "What about you, then? Going to agree?"

Jahir's shoulders tensed. He had made an intuitive leap without consultation, and knew that the Alliance's long history of peace did not lend itself to the formation of individuals who understood the immediacy of war. Nor, he thought, had Vasiht'h grown up with the stories of blood and necessary death that he had.

"You wouldn't have drawn Kajentarel into your dreams to fight at your side if you hadn't thought he'd approve," Vasiht'h said slowly. "And honestly . . . I'd be the last one to tell you that the appearance of a god in your dream is just a figment of your subconscious." He smiled a little, rue seeping through the mind-line like a low fog. "I've had my share of dreams about Her, and She usually only shows up when I need to pay attention."

She looked from one of them to the other. "You are the *strangest* therapists I've ever been to. Bar none."

"Because we believe in the Divine?" Vasiht'h asked.

"Because we believe in your fight?" Jahir said.

"You don't even know what my fight is!"

"Why don't you tell us, then," Jahir said.

She stared at them with round eyes. Then . . . she started talking.

⸺⸻∞⸻⸺

"That went well," Vasiht'h said, satisfied, as they walked from their office toward the likely-looking café they'd chosen for lunch. He was definitely ready for food. "I had my doubts there for a minute."

"We did not affect her dreams," Jahir observed.

"I don't know about you but I don't think I could have stayed in them very long," Vasiht'h said with a shiver that lifted the fur along his sides. "She has a vivid imagination."

"She is a historian, and no doubt there is more than enough captured video for her to have internalized its horrors."

Something in the mindline there tasted strange . . . like a bitter tea, something associated with sickness. Vasiht'h wondered but decided the oblique approach was, as usual with his friend, best. He could be patient. They had years to figure one another out. "Do you think she was right? Her dreaming self. About losing the fight personally."

The rant Ametia had declined to share with them when she'd first entered their office had involved the treatment of humans, both as students and in history. She argued that there was prejudice against humans on campus, and that the history texts that spoke only of the Exodus's necessity elided the contribution of the humans in that time period who helped the Pelted flee their progenitors. That history was complex, and that widespread denigration of the species was unreasonable, and a reflection of the Pelted's continuing issues with their creation rather than any factual understanding of humanity as a whole. She felt called to protect her human students, of which she'd accumulated a great number because she was one of the few faculty members who protected them from discrimination, and to fight for the human perspective on the events prior to the Exodus, and after the Rapprochement.

She was, Vasiht'h had thought while listening to her unleashed eloquence, an extremely magnetic personality and a deep thinker. Which probably got her labeled a radical. A human rights activist. Was that even necessary?

Apparently that last thought had been very loud. "She thinks it's necessary," Jahir said. "It is not our task to evaluate whether the prejudices she reports are valid. Only that she feels they are, and is living with the consequences." He glanced at Vasiht'h. "Do you believe she's correct?"

"About human prejudice?" Vasiht'h thought about it, trotting alongside his taller friend. "I don't doubt it exists. I just don't know . . . I guess I wouldn't. If it affects a lot of people, or if it's just this particular university. . . ." He trailed off, then said, "Honestly, what would I know about it? I'm not human."

"No," Jahir said. "But you have gone to classes with them, and lived in a society that includes them."

"The Alliance isn't a monoculture, though," Vasiht'h said. "What I saw in class on the medical school of a university in Seersana doesn't necessarily apply to the rest of the Alliance. It doesn't even apply to the other side of campus . . . !"

"And yet," Jahir said. "Something must give rise to the stereotypes we know." Vasiht'h glanced at him, and his friend said, "You know them. Glaseah are not passionate. Harat-Shar are hedonists."

"Eldritch are mysterious?" Vasiht'h tried, teasing.

"You see? That one abides because there is truth in it. Even Lucrezia fought her own stereotypes among her own people."

"Because they weren't her people, really," Vasiht'h said. "She was colony-bred. Those were her people." He sighed. "Well. No one said it wasn't complicated, living with people who aren't like you." The mindline twinged a little. Humor? Maybe? Except there was a pinched feeling under it. "And you would know."

"A touch," Jahir allowed as they found the café.

"Look!" Vasiht'h said. "No scones."

"I look forward to having something simpler."

"Though the scones were good," Vasiht'h said, surprised to feel a touch of wistfulness.

Jahir only smiled and opened the door for him.

———∞∞∞———

That evening, Vasiht'h went to shop "at a reasonable grocery," leaving Jahir to make notes on their single client and wonder at the fortune that had allowed them entrée to her concerns. Was it luck that had led them to an approach unusual enough to intrigue her? Or the hand of some guiding power? His partner would surely suggest the latter. And possibly, in addition, that the goddess helped those who attempted to solve their own problems.

Of course, a promising beginning portended nothing. They might fail with Ametia, eventually. No course then but to walk the path and see where it took them, as he had been doing for years now. He had not always made the wisest choices, but then, what he'd learned from those mistakes had been knowledge irreplaceable, and he doubted he would have accepted the lessons so wholeheartedly without proof of their relevance.

The chime of the real-time comm request startled him out of these ruminations. Few were the people who had access to that particular tag, but he trusted them all, so he was delighted—if surprised—to find his mentor from Seersana, Lafayette Kindles-Flame, resolving on the screen of his data tablet.

"I had not expected to hear from you," he admitted after their exchange of greetings. "Is all well?"

"Don't worry, there's no tragedy," KindlesFlame said with a grin. "More in the way of good news. I have a professional conference on Tam-Ley at the end of the year and Starbase Veta's on the way; I'll probably layover there. I thought I'd come visit, if you're amenable."

"I'd be glad to host," Jahir said. "If we're still here."

KindlesFlame quirked a brow. "Well. That begs a question."

"It is not that we find Veta unpleasant," Jahir said. "But rather that we might not be allowed to stay. Because they must decide whether there is room for Vasiht'h."

"And if he has to go, you go."

"They said we'd know within six months," Jahir said. "So . . . I will perhaps be here when you come, or perhaps not. Dependent on, apparently, whether we can make ourselves useful to the community."

"There's a nebulous metric," the Tam-illee said wryly. "I don't suppose they gave you any clearer directives?" Something in Jahir's face must have revealed him, because the healer chuckled. "No. I guess not. So what are you doing to meet this goal?"

"We are attempting to build a practice," Jahir said. "And have, in fact, seen our first client."

"Went well?"

"Rather," Jahir said, and glanced at the Tam-illee when he chuckled. "It is early yet. I would not venture to guess at how completely our effort will succeed."

"Of course you wouldn't." KindlesFlame grinned. "So is that what you're working on? I can see something turning in your head."

Jahir paused. Ruefully, he said, "I should ask how you divined this, but you will tell me . . ."

"There are too many very minute pauses between my responses and yours." The Tam-illee was smiling. "But don't worry. You'd have to have hours of observation at various cafes to have picked up on it."

Strangely, it pleased him to know that someone other than a mindbonded friend could read his body language. He would not have wanted to be the closed and foreign individual Professor Sheldan had accused him of being, once upon a classroom. "Then may I ask you something, alet?" When KindlesFlame waved a hand, he continued. "It is something in the way of a strange question."

"This should be good then."

"Is there poverty in the Alliance?"

Both KindlesFlame's brows went up. Few expressions crossed the Tam-illee's expressions that he did not allow, in Jahir's experience, so that was probably as much a planned reply as any words. "I guess that would depend on where in the Alliance."

"That . . . seems to be a common response to my questions."

"That would be because it's a common response to most questions. 'It's more complicated than it looks on the outside.'" The Tam-illee leaned back, folding his arms. "You know some of our history?"

"I have a gloss of it. I would not call my knowledge extensive or deep."

"Mmm." He nodded. "That would be the other thing. Because history is inextricably a part of why groups do anything. Or even why individuals do anything." He lifted a brow. "Yes?"

"Yes," Jahir allowed, smiling. He found himself wishing for a cup of something warm to drink; this was obviously going to be another of his impromptu lessons, so like the many he received from KindlesFlame over a coffee shop table.

"Those early Pelted wanted to be different from who they were, arii. They'd been created as property. To decide otherwise required them to leave that identity behind. On one hand, it's good to know who you are and where you belong; we all need that. On the other, they longed to assert the independence they'd been denied. The early history of the Alliance is hip-deep in that struggle. To create a new identity. To discover that individuals wanted to have different identities, and to find a way to respect that need. To balance that against the competing need to be a part of a community. So you get the Alliance. Not just the scattered worlds, but the scattered races, divided as much on beliefs as on what they looked like. And we allow all those worlds and peoples as much latitude in deciding how to live as possible." KindlesFlame lifted a hand, palm up. "But where you have freedom, you have people making bad choices."

"Yes," Jahir murmured.

"Everywhere you go, then, the people have made their own rulings on how much of that is allowed. So . . . yes. There's poverty in parts of the Alliance. Even places like Selnor where anyone can apply to the local government for the basic necessities will produce people and communities who don't, or won't. Or can't. For reasons as varied as there are communities and individuals."

Thinking of Vasiht'h's parents, Jahir said, "I suppose the cost of schooling is also one of those things that varies depending on where one is."

KindlesFlame nodded. "Most worlds are fairly elastic. Where things become less so is when you cross boundaries. Just like in everything else, the interstitial spaces are difficult to bridge. So someone who might have a good living where they were born might have to make sacrifices to live on some other world."

"It seems strange," Jahir said, tentative, "that such a vast polity, with such resources, could not . . ."

"Solve all problems?"

"Put that way," Jahir murmured, "it does sound absurd, yes."

"Just say . . . complicated instead. Which brings us around to the beginning again, you'll note." KindlesFlame tilted his head. "Are you worried about money, then?"

"No," Jahir replied, honestly. "I am worried about context."

"Ahhh." The Tam-illee chuckled softly. "Good. You should be."

CHAPTER 6

GIVEN THE CHOICE BETWEEN sleeping and talking, Ametia preferred talking. Which ordinarily would have suited Vasiht'h, because he liked listening, but by the third appointment his pelt started itching the moment she arrived. Letting her vent her frustrations with her work situation didn't seem to be hurting her, but it certainly wasn't solving her problems either.

"You are distressed," Jahir said as they tidied up after her fourth visit.

"She has a problem," Vasiht'h said. "But we don't seem to be helping her find a solution."

"Is that what we should be doing?" Jahir asked, interested. That smelled like percolating coffee, fragrant and innervating.

"Fine," Vasiht'h allowed, smiling a little. "We aren't necessarily here to help people solve their problems. But to help them find better ways of coping with them? That's not too much to ask."

"If Ametia was displeased with us, she would have stopped coming after the first visit, I believe."

"Oh, I don't doubt that." Vasiht'h watched Jahir fold the blanket and set it on the couch. "But I'm not sure it's good for her either, to come here and relive all the things that are upsetting her. That re-opens the wound."

"One would think working at the university is what does that." Vasiht'h frowned, and Jahir looked up. "Arii?"

Shaking himself, Vasiht'h said, "Nothing. Still, she can't live on outrage. She'll eat through her own stomach lining eventually. Listening isn't enough. And going into her dreams . . . I don't know if I can handle it. What would we do to fix them subconsciously? Turn her righteous war against prejudice and bigotry into a tea party where she politely explains how things should be and her enemies have an epiphany and change their ways?"

"Somehow I doubt that would work."

Vasiht'h snorted. "Because it wouldn't, no."

Jahir looked the office over, then picked up his bag. "It takes time to develop the therapeutic relationship, arii. She will have to trust us before any of our help will fall on fertile ground. Perhaps we are still in that stage."

"I hope you're right," Vasiht'h said with a sigh, standing to follow him out. "Because I could use a sign that we're on the right track."

— ⊶∞⊷ —

The next week, Ametia did not arrive alone.

"This is Lennea," she said of the retiring Karaka'An felid standing alongside her. "A friend of mine who works in the city's primary school system."

Lennea was a soft gray in color with darker stripes, a soothing coloration that made the contrast of her odd eyes startling: one blue, the other brown. She also had white-furred hands, kept folded in front of her, and a white tail-tip. She was dressed as conservatively as her demeanor, in a long cream-colored tunic over a white blouse and grey pants, and sandals. The latter was the only thing that seemed out of place, because few of the digitigrade races bothered with shoes, and usually only did so for decoration. Lennea's had little sequins on them, and the right one had a blue felt flower.

"She's been talking about therapy but never got around to it, so I told her about the two of you and here she is."

"May I make an appointment?" Lennea asked politely.

"We can see you after Ametia, if you like," Jahir replied in kind. "There is an intake form you can fill out while you're waiting."

"That would be wonderful, thank you."

/What?/ Jahir asked as they saw Lennea out.

/Seeing the two of you talking,/ Vasiht'h said, amused. /You're both so . . . cordial. I want to put out a tea table./

/You always want to put out a tea table . . ./

/Oh, no, be fair. Sometimes I prefer kerinne!/

Jahir hid a smile and said to Ametia, "Thank you for the referral."

"My pleasure," Ametia said, dropping onto the couch. "She's so tightly wound. I worry about her. Anyway, let me tell you about the latest ridiculous thing . . ."

Vasiht'h inhaled. /Here we go./

/Yes. But we have had our first referral./

/That is something./ Vasiht'h forced himself to exhale. /That's a very big something. I'm grateful./

"So, you got your second client?" Sehvi propped her muzzle on her palm and lifted her brows. "Another firebrand like your first?"

"No," Vasiht'h said as he deglazed the pan and stirred it to lift up the tasty bits on the bottom. He added a little more stock. "She was a relief after our first client, honestly. Quiet. A little shy."

"Big problems?" Sehvi asked.

"Are anyone's problems small by their own standards?" Vasiht'h wondered.

Sehvi snorted. "No. But we don't measure by internal standards, do we?"

"Don't we?"

His sister shook her head. "We live in a society that gives us context. I don't see how that can't affect us, and how we view our own problems."

"I don't know," Vasiht'h said. "I think it's possible to be utterly self-absorbed. And easy."

She grinned. "You sure?"

Vasiht'h wrinkled his nose at her.

"What about your problems? Has the book helped with them?"

Vasiht'h rolled his eyes. "Thaddeus What's-His-Name has finally kissed the perfect Eldritch girl."

Sehvi squealed, clapping her hands. "Wasn't that fantastic? I don't think she could have fit more adjectives into that scene!"

"It was disgusting," Vasiht'h said. "I really didn't need all the details about the tongues that felt like heavenly velvet. Seriously, ariishir. Velvet. Tongue. Tongues are *wet*."

His sister giggled. "I know, that's what made it perfect. I love the way she writes."

"You know, I don't even think you're kidding . . ."

"I'm not!" She laughed. "Don't worry, the sex scenes become such a confused muddle of metaphors that you can't really tell what's happening."

Vasiht'h pressed a hand to his forehead. "There's a *sex* scene? Why didn't you warn me?"

"I did! By giving you a romance novel! Her bodice was unlaced on the cover! Didn't you notice?"

"I don't stare at people's clothes!"

"Now that's a lie," Sehvi said mischievously. "You do all the time."

"All right, fine. But only to see if they've missed a button or their shirt hem is showing. . . ." He pointed the spatula at her. "Stop that. It's not like you notice these things either."

"Oh, I don't know. Kovihs's tongue . . ."

"Stop," Vasiht'h groaned, covering his face. "Stop right there. I don't want to know about your paramour's tongue."

She snickered.

"What!" he demanded.

"Paramour," she repeated.

He couldn't help it . . . hearing her say it made it sound ridiculous to him too. He started laughing. "You're terrible. Go away so I can finish cooking dinner."

"Yes, sir!"

He was still smiling when Jahir pushed open the door to the cottage to reveal not just himself, but an elderly Hinichi. "That smells delicious, arii, and I hope there's enough for a visitor."

"There's always enough for visitors," Vasiht'h said, looking at the woman, whose twinkling eyes belied a mischievous nature that even Sehvi would have been hard-pressed to evoke with such style. "This must be . . ."

"Helga," the woman said. "And I'm very pleased to meet this partner of the starbase's only Eldritch." She grinned. "Alet. I hope you like scones, because we brought some."

"No salmon mousse, though," Jahir murmured.

"Thank the goddess," Vasiht'h said. "Salmon mousse would not go at all well with chicken pomodoro."

In retrospect, running into Helga at the scone café was completely expected. She'd sent them Ametia and it had been almost a month since that referral; no doubt she was curious about how things were proceeding, if she hadn't already heard from the cheetahine. And the last place they'd met had been the café, so why wouldn't she linger there, now and then, in hopes of catching sight of him? It wasn't as if he was difficult to pick out of a crowd.

"So, alet," she'd said, joining him at the take-out counter. "Settling in well?"

"As well as can be expected given the circumstances," he'd answered.

"Oh, no, it can't be as bad as that!" she said with a laugh. "Not with Ametia so pleased with you. She's a difficult woman to please, you know."

"Working with her has been a pleasure."

Helga looked up at him, snorted, grinned. "That was nicely done. The soul of discretion, are you."

"She is our client," Jahir said, smiling back. "It is not for me to disclose anything leading."

"What you consider leading makes me wonder just how good you are at sleuthing!" She glanced at the counter. "I see you're on your way home. To this partner of yours, I assume? I'd like to meet him."

His first instinct had been to invite her on some other date. But seeing the merriment in her eyes, and knowing how Vasiht'h liked company, he couldn't resist the implicit request. "He's making dinner now, but I'm certain he'd enjoy meeting you if you came with me. Would you like to do so?"

"For a home-cooked meal I don't have to cook myself I'll walk a lot farther than the Garden District! But let me buy. I'd hate to arrive empty-handed."

"As you will, alet."

The pleasure that flowed through the mindline when he brought Helga home was all the confirmation he needed of those initial instincts. As the Hinichi set out her offerings, he said, tentatively, /I'm glad you're pleased./

/To meet this mysterious stranger who sent us our first client? And I get to feed her! Of course I'm pleased. And this is going to be a good meal, too. I haven't had a chance to make this recipe for a while./

"Bread," Helga said. "For sopping up juices? It smells like there are juices to sop . . ."

"There are," Vasiht'h said. "You can leave that on the table. I'm guessing the scones are dessert?"

"They are double-chocolate scones with chocolate chips, pecans, and powdered with espresso, crystallized sugar, and cocoa," Jahir said.

Vasiht'h stared at him over the counter and started laughing. "Goddess. She talked you into those? Are you made of magic, alet?"

The Hinichi beamed. "Oh, you know how it is when you get old enough. People hate saying no to you."

"I suppose we shall have to have them with coffee." Jahir put the box on the counter.

"Those things? Absolutely not," Vasiht'h said. "Kerinne. All the way. Even for you."

"Good for you," Helga agreed. "Make him eat more."

"I like her," Vasiht'h said.

Jahir sighed, though he let the mindline pulse his affection. "I knew you would."

"So," Helga said over dinner: not just the chicken, but a salad Vasiht'h had hastily thrown together to accompany it. "Ametia's happy with you, and you've netted Lennea as well. Nicely done!"

"You know them both?" Vasiht'h asked. "Do you work in academia too?"

"Oh, no, no," Helga shook her head. "I'm just a friend. And I have a great deal of children, you know. Grown-up ones with children of their own. You inevitably get involved with schooling when you help out with the family." She grinned. "I've been here a while. I know everyone, you'll find."

Vasiht'h tilted his head, looking up at the ceiling. "Karina?"

"Spoons ice cream on the commons," Helga said. "Her birthday is in fall. You'll like fall here, it's pretty."

"Is it?" Jahir asked. "Substantively different from how it looks now?"

"It gets colder, so the trees turn their leaves." The Hinichi wiggled her eyebrows at Vasiht'h. "Got another for me?"

Vasiht'h wrinkled her nose. "Hinichi woman, a little younger than you. In Fleet. Brindled pelt."

"Sounds like Alfreida," Helga said, unconcerned. "But could be her cousin, Henrieta. Henrieta just moved here four years ago." She speared another piece of chicken. "You are an excellent cook."

"'Just' four years ago?" Vasiht'h repeated, bemused.

"I have lived here all my life, alet!" Helga answered. "And I like people. If I don't know everyone, I at least know *of* them. I've made it my business to know."

"And now you know us as well," Jahir observed.

"Not as well as I'd like," she said, smiling. "So maybe you can tell me about yourselves, now that you're both in one place. When I met your partner here, Vasiht'h-alet, he told me a little about how you met. I'd like to hear it from your side, if you'd like to tell the tale."

"Only if you'll trade, and tell me something from your life," Vasiht'h answered.

Helga laughed. "I'll tell you about how I met my husband, God keep his soul. That's a good story. Yes, it's a deal. So tell me how it happened. And pass me the plate, I need another serving of this." She tapped her fork on Jahir's plate. "You stopped eating. Finish eating."

"I like her!" Vasiht'h said again to him.

Jahir hid a smile.

The dinner remained congenial: both Vasiht'h and Helga enjoyed talking about their families, which gave Jahir ample opportunity to listen over the dessert course, which they ate disposed around the sitting room. Vasiht'h relented and allowed him coffee instead of kerinne; given that the scones were dense and crumbly and powdery, he was glad of the contrast. The evening slowly deepened, bringing a gentle breeze through the windows, and the sound of night insects, and the murmurs of conversations engaged by those on their constitutionals.

"You like this," Helga said, startling him out of his reverie. He found her examining him with far too perspicacious eyes; worse, he felt the pressure of Vasiht'h's sudden interest in the mindline, and knew a great deal was riding on that interest.

He chose his words carefully, and said as little with them as possible. "It is pleasant."

"Pastoral," Helga said. "Quiet."

"Quiet can be good."

"But?" She refilled her kerinne.

Jahir glanced at Vasiht'h and said, "I did not come here to rusticate."

From the loosening in the mindline, that had been the right answer, and he hadn't even known it had been a question.

"You can commute, you know," Helga said, and something about her tone struck him as curious. As if the answer mattered. "It's not a long walk. Or you could use the Pad."

"There's a Pad nearby?" Vasiht'h asked, one ear sagging.

Helga snorted. "It's the Garden District. Of course there is. The people here work all over the starbase. Why should they walk? And no one flies, you'll notice."

"We could . . . commute," Jahir said, tasting the word, sensing its consequences. Imagining how it would work. "But it would place us at a remove. I would prefer to see if we need the remove before we commit to it."

"And you would need it if. . . ."

"If our work proves too emotionally taxing." Jahir glanced at Vasiht'h. "I would not want to go through Selnor again."

"No," Vasiht'h said. */You said that out loud? You trust her with that story?/*

/Should I not?/

Vasiht'h glanced at the Hinichi and smiled. */I know what I'd answer. But I'm not you./*

/No. But I believe I made my choice when I accepted her help in the first place./

Helga was sipping her kerinne, the very picture of nonchalance. Addressing her, Jahir said, "Alet, you are fooling no one with this look."

She grinned over the rim of her cup. "I suppose not. But I find it evokes a lot more confidences when I pretend to innocence. People find it humorous in the elderly, when they are mischievous."

"You work that angle pretty hard," Vasiht'h said, amused.

"You work with what you have, alet," Helga said, and her tone was more serious, if gentle. "And people do age, and that affects how they're treated." She set her cup down. "So, you don't think you wish to 'rusticate', do you."

"I think it might be a fine thing to live in the commons, if we stay," Jahir said. "But first we must earn our stay."

"Keep on doing what you're doing," Helga said, patting her

lips with her napkin. "I'm sure it will come. That was a fine dinner, aletsen. My compliments to the chef."

"Thank you," Vasiht'h said, smiling. "You should come by again. I like feeding people."

"I imagine you do," she said, eyes sparkling. "Else you wouldn't have found yourself someone so in need of it, mmm?" Rising, she said, "I will take you up on that another time."

At the door, Jahir said, "You have not asked."

The Hinichi lifted her brows. "Of course not. What would we talk about next time if I had? Good night, aletsen!"

He remained by the door, watching her recede into the dark. Behind him, Vasiht'h began washing the pan and the plates.

"She didn't ask about Selnor," he said at last.

Vasiht'h laughed. "Of course she didn't. We were expecting her to. I don't think she likes to do the expected thing. It would be boring."

Thinking of their first conversation, Jahir smiled. "Yes. I expect you're right. Shall I help with the plates?"

"Just to put them away. Those cabinets are taller than I am." As Jahir picked up the stack, Vasiht'h finished, "You know, I think our luck is going to turn?"

"It has not already?"

Vasiht'h paused, chuckled. "Good point. I'll have to see if there's a siv't nearby. I'm obviously overdue."

CHAPTER 7

THERE WAS A MAN WAITING for them outside their office when they arrived, so it was fortunate indeed they'd decided they should at least spend part of every day there. He was a Seersa, golden fur going silver in threads that sparkled when he turned his face, but striped in dark brown to match his hair. His blue eyes were direct, and his clothing utilitarian but very neat. At their approach, he offered his palm to Vasiht'h.

"Pieter Strong. I'm glad I caught you."

"Alet," Vasiht'h said for them. "What can we do for you?"

"My kids think I need therapy," he said. "Saw your form, filled it out, and here I am."

"Why don't you come inside?" Jahir said. "We can discuss it."

"That would be fine, thanks."

Inside their office, the Seersa settled on the couch with his leg crossed, ankle on knee, and both hands resting on the leg. He watched them as they followed him inside, and did not seem to miss any detail of their disposition. /Observant,/ Jahir said, picking up the data tablet to scan the form.

/Takes good care of himself,/ Vasiht'h added, his perplexity astringent, like tea steeped-too-long. /Another person who doesn't really want therapy for himself, but got pushed into it. Why us?/

"I saw you were new in town," the Seersa said once he'd decided they were ready to listen, and there was no question he'd been waiting. "Since the last guy they sent me to didn't seem to do anything for me, or so my kids tell me."

"They perceive you to have a problem you don't?" Jahir asked.

"So they tell me." He smiled crookedly. "I feel fine. I'm just restless. They're old, they've left the nest. I have time to myself for once. I'd like to do something with it."

"That seems perfectly normal to us," Vasiht'h said. "Why do they object to it?"

"Oh, they think the things I like to do are too dangerous." He shrugged. "They're both risk-averse. I don't blame them. I'm sure one of you would say it's because their mother died young." He cocked a brow. "But I'm no therapist."

"Dangerous," Jahir mused.

"You know. Shooting. Zero-g skiing. Fun things."

/Sounds within the realm of normalcy to me,/ Vasiht'h said uncertainly.

/Except that it frightens his children. Can we talk to them?/

"Do you think they'd tell us why they think it's dangerous?" Vasiht'h said. And offered, "Maybe they're the ones who need therapy, not you!"

The Seersa laughed. "Maybe. Sure, you can talk to them. I don't care. They're worried about me, I respect that. Love 'em for it." He shrugged, looking away. "For all I know, they're right." He rolled his shoulders. "Anyway. Your listing said you do something with dreams. Am I supposed to tell you about them?"

"No, you're supposed to fall asleep and let us examine them," Vasiht'h said. "We read minds."

/Rather an extreme approach to divulging this . . . !/

/I'm riding a guess . . ./

"Huh," Pieter said. "Sounds interesting. I lie down here, then? Got a bigger pillow? Oh, thanks, that works." He lay down on his back, covered his eyes with his arm. "That'll do me."

"We'll turn off the lights and leave you alone for a bit, then," Vasiht'h said.

The Seersa chuckled. "Don't bother. I learned to sleep through anything in Fleet. The one lasting lesson of the Academe: if you have sack time, take it." With that, he re-settled himself and promptly fell asleep as they watched, astonished.

/He didn't mention anything about Fleet in his intake form,/ Jahir said. /Perhaps we should revise it to prompt more specificity? The information that he was once in Fleet seems pertinent./

/A risk-taker who used to be in the military and isn't anymore? Indulging in dangerous behaviors?/ Vasiht'h frowned. /That does seem leading./

/Leading where, though . . ./

/I guess that's what we're here for./ Vasiht'h offered his palm and Jahir took it. /Let's have a look./

But if there was a clue as to Pieter's problems in his dreams, they did not find it. Adventure a-plenty, certainly, for when any imagery resolved it was of their host snowboarding, engaged in maneuvers that seemed implausible, like skidding off exposed rock into flips. The satisfaction of their client when the board smacked onto the ground again, spraying snow in crystalline fans, resonated throughout the dream like a perfectly tuned pedal harp. They tarried for some time, waiting for revelation, and instead withdrew nursing the vague feeling they'd been on vacation.

/This one is going to take time, I guess,/ Vasiht'h said ruefully.

/They all will. It is the nature of our work./ Jahir glanced at him and smiled a little. /Do not be so afraid of failure that you belittle your own powers, arii./

Vasiht'h wrinkled his nose. /I do not need therapy./

"I did not say so," Jahir said aloud, because he didn't trust himself to say it over the mindline without contaminating it with his sense that his partner was, in fact, fretting overmuch. They had money. They had clients. They still had five months. Perhaps Vasiht'h understood because he sighed and smiled.

/I should trust Her./

/You do trust Her,/ Jahir reassured him. /But it would be unreasonable to expect you not to have doubts, now and then. Shall we *wake our client?/*

Vasiht'h mantled his wings, twitched them back into place, smiled. */Yeah. Sorry about all this./*

/It passes,/ Jahir said. */All things do./*

/I'll be better about it, promise./

———⊸∞⊶———

This promise was on Jahir's mind on receiving the latest missive from his mother, which held the expected news associated with the conclusion of the winter court: the political situation remained tetchy, and he did not envy her the need to associate with people so antagonistic to the Queen's aims, particularly with them becoming more open about voicing that dissent. No, it was the final paragraph that filled him with chagrin.

I know not how time keeps in the Alliance, my son, but here the new year has sped and brought with it the prospect of a tender spring. I advance you this token for your natal day, thus. It remains blazoned in my mind as one of the happiest of my life. You and your brother are very certainly the greatest gifts ever granted me by a beneficent Lady. Do you go and celebrate in some fashion, and know that I remain:

Fondly,
—Your Mother, Jeasa

The enclosed "token" had already been deposited in his account, and it was enough to pay their office rent for the remainder of the year.

He was not minding the emotional bleed into the mindline, either, because on the other side of the cottage, Vasiht'h looked up from his data tablet and said, "Something wrong?"

"Not wrong, no." Lying was distasteful, but he didn't want to belabor the point either. "My family has sent me a small gift for my natal day. I am pondering whether it will come at the same time next year; I cannot imagine the days align perfectly."

Vasiht'h made a face. "Ugh, no, and it's confusing as

anything."

"Birth anniversaries," Jahir said. "I realize I do not understand the custom. Or even if there is a custom that applies to everyone."

"It does to a lot of us." Vasiht'h set the data tablet down and stretched his forelegs. A good sign . . . this was a conversation that both interested and relaxed his partner. Perhaps they'd gotten past the small gift entirely. "There are cultures in the Alliance that don't celebrate birthdays, of course, but they're pretty rare. I can think of more that celebrate conception days on top of birthdays than I can think of people who celebrate neither . . . !"

"Conception days," Jahir repeated, bemused.

"Oh yes." Vasiht'h rose, shook out a hindleg: asleep, from the bright prickles in the mindline. "I'm going to make myself lemonade. Want some?"

"I would, yes."

"So, yes, conception days," Vasiht'h said, padding into the kitchen. "Since so many of us died in test tubes before we left Earth, and afterwards so many of us were only questionably fertile, there are pockets of people who celebrate successful conception of a baby. That's usually about the parents, not the child, though. The birthday's for the person being born. The conception day's for the parents to celebrate having gone through that challenge and made it. Though there are groups that make the baby part of it too."

"Fascinating," Jahir murmured. The Eldritch would not take such a celebration amiss, but that they had lost the technology to pinpoint a date. He felt a pang for all they had lost—or thrown away. "So, when do you celebrate your birthday, when you travel? By the date of your homeworld? Or the date of your residence?"

"Most people go by homeworld date," Vasiht'h said. "I do. I was born at the beginning of our second dry season—the year goes dry, wet, dry—and that put me in summer on Seersana."

"That must have been . . . strange."

"Not as much as I thought?" Vasiht'h squeezed the lemon into the first glass, one hand over the other. "It's warm or hot all year round at home, so it's not like I perceived it to be all that different. Drier, maybe." He paused, thoughtful. "Funny how what you cue into is the atmosphere around you. It makes me wonder if all that stuff about the zodiac is right."

"The zodiac," Jahir repeated, uncertainly.

———— ⌘ ————

Vasiht'h looked up from the glass at the wobble in the mindline. He couldn't help a laugh. "Let me guess. Never heard of it. Why would you?" He shook his head, marveling at how many little things his friend still didn't know. Which gave him the pleasure of introducing him to them. "Lots of people believe that the year and the season or day you were born determines your personality."

"Ah." Musing in this context felt like ruffling papers. Vasiht'h wondered at the association. "We have something similar. The seasons, we say, influence one's temperament."

"Right, like that," Vasiht'h said. "Except that everybody's got a different idea of what time of year makes you like what kind of person. Maybe that makes sense if it's the local stars that are doing the influencing, but if it's the seasons, then you'd think they'd be similar across worlds? But what do I know. No one else does either." He grinned. "As a "beginning of the second dry season" baby I'm supposed to be nervous, but also stable, and a seeker/wayfarer, because I miss the rains. How does any of that make sense together?"

"I'm not certain," Jahir said, thoughtful. "I don't know that it fails to describe you."

Vasiht'h snorted. "It could describe anyone. What's your birthday say about you?"

A pause: gathering thoughts, Vasiht'h thought. Jahir said, "I am purportedly emotional and intuitive. And enigmatic."

Vasiht'h laughed. "Great. So basically you're an Eldritch?"

A winsome smile, apologetic. "Just so."

Shaking his head, Vasiht'h finished the first glass and moved to the next. "Come get your lemonade. And tell me what you want to do with your birthday money. I assume it's enough to buy a small starship."

Was that a blush? He'd made his friend's cheeks color. "Not so much as that. But I have been adjured to celebrate in some fashion."

Tempting to ask Jahir what season it was on the Eldritch homeworld. Would that be too much prying? Maybe. If he waited enough years, he'd have a sense of the length of the Eldritch year, though, based on how Jahir's birthday moved across the starbase calendar . . . what a thought! To have to work so hard to learn such a tiny detail. Thaddeus didn't seem inclined to explore the mysteries of his crush's background, and Vasiht'h couldn't fathom why. The not-knowing was part of the pleasure of having Jahir as a partner . . . that sense that he'd be forever uncovering new things.

Come to think of it, that was why Jahir was in the Alliance, wasn't it? The Goddess had definitely known what She was doing.

Which made it obvious what they should do to celebrate. "I know just the thing, if you're willing."

Jahir glanced at him. "Ah?"

"Leave it to me," Vasiht'h said with a grin.

"Oh, but no, arii," Jahir said immediately on entering the train station. "You must allow me to pay for this. It is why I was sent the gift!"

"I promise I'll show you the bill," Vasiht'h said complacently, padding alongside him. Jahir's wonder was bright as new sunlight and so strong he swore he could feel the warmth on his back. Vasiht'h snuck surreptitious glances at the Eldritch as they joined the throng heading onto the platform, and the wide-eyed solemnity was everything he'd hoped for when he'd bought the tickets, because nothing less would have done than to take his friend on the same train tour that had convinced him they belonged here, on this station.

Come to think of it, he could use the reminder himself.

The station was worth seeing all on its own, because it was three stories high. One entire wall of it was a flexglass portal to the interstellar view, overlaid in translucent schedules and tags as ships passed in and out of view. Since the station abutted the civilian docking facilities, there were a lot of ships; one of the starbase guides Vasiht'h had read recommended the train station as the best place to shipwatch, and from the brisk business being done on the cafes on the balconies above them, plenty of people came to do just that.

"I admit I don't know why there should be trains," Jahir said, keeping close to him. "Surely Pads are more economical?"

It should have been an easy question. Instead, it made Vasiht'h realize just how little he understood about the Alliance himself. He took for granted that Pads weren't used for every kind of transport but had no idea why. "I don't know. But I know at least one reason the trains are here."

Jahir glanced down at him.

"Tourism," Vasiht'h said firmly. "Come on, that's ours over there."

They threaded their way through the throng, with Vasiht'h leading a little to open the way for Jahir so he wouldn't have to bump into anyone. It was a lot of fun, species-spotting. The races that were uncommon on Seersana were still rare elsewhere, but the port brought a lot more of them through than planetside did. */Look, that's a Phoenix child!/*

Said child was in front of them, with its parent: mother, Vasiht'h thought, though it was hard to tell with the tail and wings obscuring the line of the torso. The Phoenix were mammals, but they weren't as dimorphic as some of the other races.

The child, though, was as perfect as Vasiht'h could imagine, a little miniature in copper and burnished brass, each feather's edge shimmering as if honed, with a short beaked face and enormous eyes a luminescent aquamarine.

/I have never seen the like,/ Jahir said, wonder suffusing the words.

/We should child-spot on our trip./ Vasiht'h grinned. */Could*

even play the traveling game my sibs and I did when we were younger.
You count up the number of things you spot./

/Ah, so, whoever sees it first . . . ?/

/Right./

/Then you are one point ahead of me, but you shall not remain so
long! As I am taller, and that makes it easier for me to see./

Vasiht'h chortled. */Yeah, but I'm closer to their level. See, look,*
over there: two Asanii kids. Look at that pelt!/

/Looks a great deal like Lennea's,/ Jahir observed. */The gray*
with the stripes./ He shook his head minutely. */Three points. But*
I am on my mettle now. There, an infant in that Tam-illee foxine's
arms./

Vasiht'h glanced that way and saw the little face swaddled in
a blanket, and the tiny pointed ears, and thought the cuteness
would slay him. */Look at the little nosepad./*

Jahir smiled a little. */This game would have pleased our friends./*

That came twined with the smell of the hospital, and the
sound of voices: Meekie, Kayla, Amaranth, Kuriel. Vasiht'h
smiled too. */Yes. I think so./*

Jahir nodded, a dip of his chin. "There, our train, arii."

"The starbase awaits," Vasiht'h said. Grinned. "And it's still
three to one."

∞∞∞

The train was a marvel, and stepping into it Jahir knew at once
it was not intended for mundane transport. Each roomy car was
composed almost entirely of flexglass windows that extended
up into the curved ceiling. Padded benches lined the walls and
there were two circular sofas in some smooth, leather-like fabric
in the center aisle. He claimed one of the benches, and Vasiht'h
settled on the floor beside him. As the other passengers entered,
he looked down the row toward the next car and found its adjoin-
ing door only by the enclosed bathroom facilities.

"There are sleeping cubbies, I'm told," Vasiht'h said. "And a
car for working, with desks."

"I cannot imagine working through a trip even of this

duration," Jahir said.

"No," Vasiht'h agreed, looking out the window at the people jogging past on the platform. "Me neither. You'll see."

And he did ten minutes later, when the train pulled smoothly from the station. The car darkened as it entered a tunnel close enough that he could see the veins of the starbase's ducting along the inside wall, and then streaks of blue and green lights as they accelerated. And then they burst free into a faerieland of lights and ships. Their train was running along the exterior skin of the starbase, one entire side and its ceiling exposed in the transparent tube, and the rate they were traveling was dizzying and yet the starscape barely moved. The ships before it did, though.

Would it ever cease to astonish him, the audacity of the Alliance's engineering? To have flown here on one of the Queen's couriers was one matter, and had seemed astonishing enough. But he'd been enclosed in a cabin for the entirety of that flight, and the portals had been engaging but he'd been aware of experiencing his journey from a remove. This . . . this was naked somehow. He felt close enough to those ships to touch them, and their stars.

"Oh, arii," he whispered.

Vasiht'h just leaned against his bench and smiled.

His birthday train ride was two days long, and took them past the civilian docks and over the skin of the starbase alongside one of the colliders used by Fleet to create fuel for their ships. Those enormous tunnels were not open, of course, but they were lined with emitters that reported their status, and when someone had noticed how striking those lights were from space, they'd been enhanced. Now there were "light sculptures" programmed to entertain passengers, their patterns and colors prompted by the particles that happened to be bouncing in the tube at the time. Some of those sculptures were stationary, helices of light or fireworks displays that the train slowed to observe; others paced the train in showers and ripples, sometimes dancing over the tube entirely so that the passengers stood in the center and pointed up at the ceiling and gasped or laughed. There was, inevitably, a stop at what was surely a distant workplace, a bubble of a market with its useable hemisphere facing the starscape, and there the passengers could descend to shop, nap, or eat at any number of restaurants from the very fine to diners with counters that faced the void.

Vasiht'h chose their lunch, a small restaurant run by enthusiastic Aera who stopped every ten minutes to perform dance routines, long ears waving and long limbs undulating. The music was mostly drums. Jahir found the whole experience invigorating, as was no doubt his partner's intent from the grins he kept receiving over their fried fish. ("Why fried fish?" "Because we're at a port? Sort of? It made sense to them.")

They returned to the train, and ended the external trip by circling the Fleet base at the starbase's pole, where they could see the warships clustering at the slips or gliding in and out of the ingress to the spindle, where the more serious drydock and building facilities were sheltered. The base was a riot of colors and movement, even from the distance permitted a civilian tour, and their viewing was narrated by a retired Fleet officer who came by later to shake hands and answer questions.

Afterwards, the train dove back into the wall and began its tour along the interior skin. That segment took them to the agriculture and aquaculture spheres, where they stopped again for shopping and sightseeing. More food ("Fish again." "Makes more sense, this is the aquaculture dome."), more browsing in stores and people-watching. The train stopped overnight at the agriculture dome, and they slept in a room off the station's platform, which was mounted high enough over the land that they were afforded a spectacular view of the croplands and forests. Jahir left the windows open, and though the smells and sounds were foreign, the superb quiet of it, and the freshness of the growing things on the breeze, almost made him feel that he was home again.

The journey back to the Veta city sphere was considered a

low point for most of the travelers, which was why there were several events scheduled within the train: parties, games, awards ceremonies for the children who'd played the scavenger hunt throughout the trip. Jahir found it as fascinating as the rest of the journey, as it took them through some of the empty cradles. Those would hold spheres as the starbase expanded; seeing them, he had some sense for why the administrator had insisted the inauguration of new ones was not a minor undertaking. The scale of those hollow vaults beggared his imagination even as he stood looking down into them, his mind struggling to make sense of the distances when the clarity of vacuum made details so crisp even so far away.

And yet, the Alliance had created this starbase, and had such a sufficiency of power that it could afford to install follies solely for the delight of tourists. The light sculptures were purely pleasure, as were so many of the other things they'd seen. The entire train trip . . . he wouldn't be surprised to discover that almost the entirety of the train industry on Veta was based on such tourist trips.

He had believed that continued exposure to the Alliance would help unravel some of its puzzles, and yet, sitting on a bench that had no doubt been engineered by some team to be comfortable, durable, and easy to clean, in a train car that had been designed and rigorously tested by another team for safety and maximal exposure and then no doubt re-engineered by a team that had assessed it for its ability to earn back the money spent on staffing, cleaning, and maintaining it, being carried through a starbase that he literally could not imagine the first detail of its construction, Jahir found himself even more mystified than before. The economy that had created this immense marvel was also the economy that could drive his partner to fretting over coins.

He wondered if he would ever understand it, and some part of him was glad. How tiresome it would be, and how disappointing, to know everything!

One of the most memorable sights of the journey was not

provided by the company running the train, however. They were nearly home when a clot of people passing revealed another traveler several benches down, and at his feet. . . .

"Is that a dog?" Jahir asked.

Vasiht'h craned his head past the bench Jahir was on. "It is, yes."

"It is strange to see one," Jahir said, realizing it. The Eldritch did not keep pets, for the good reason that few had survived the transition to their new world. Livestock they had in plenty, for the maintenance of that livestock had been essential to their survival, and so he had handled in the course of learning his duties everything from goats and pigs to sheep and horses. He had not become attached to them, for such behavior was discouraged. His cousin Sediryl had kept bees, but the Seni had never had an apiary. Of the remaining animals available, birds were the only ones cultivated for pleasure, and one could not call them companions. They were never kept indoors or trammeled in cages, but rather fed by indulgent nobles who liked to see their colored feathers in the gardens. But he had read stories of the faithful companions of early Eldritch, and the sight of a dog was strangely affecting. It was a large animal, leaning against the knee of its owner, with dark coat, pointed ears, and gray hairs brindling its long muzzle.

/Human, of course,/ Vasiht'h said of its owner. /Pelted rarely keep pets./

/Ah?/

/Cultural thing,/ Vasiht'h said. /The original Pelted species were bred as pets. It's given most of them a distaste for it. Sentients are meant to be free./

Studying the dog, so patient under the gentle hand of its master, Jahir offered, /There are animals that prefer companionship./

/I'm sure. But it's slippery-slope material for a lot of Pelted, where 'it wants to be kept' starts becoming an excuse to keep things that shouldn't be kept./ Vasiht'h shrugged, a flutter of his lower wings and a lift of shoulders. /I don't really have an opinion on it, and I suspect most people don't either. They just don't do it because no *one else does it, and it's become a habitual reaction./*

/So only humans keep pets./

/Only humans keep pets regularly,/ Vasiht'h said, emphasizing the final word. */There are Pelted with pets. Just . . . not a lot of them./*

/A stigma?/

Vasiht'h flicked his ears back. */I wouldn't call it anything that strong. It's not a taboo./*

/Even though other passengers are looking at the man askance?/

Vasiht'h looked past Jahir's leg. */Are they?/*

/It is not so much a look,/ Jahir conceded. */As a not-look. If you understand. No one is paying them any attention, and it is a lack of attention that requires effort./*

"Huh," Vasiht'h said aloud. "Nice catch."

"I have had practice interpreting such things," Jahir murmured, thinking of the veiled disdain of the courtiers of Ontine.

/Maybe it's one of those signs of human prejudice Ametia keeps talking about,/ Vasiht'h said.

/We should ask her./

Vasiht'h sighed. */Won't she like that./*

Jahir smiled. "We should think about aught else."

"Like?"

"Like where we shall dine at the final stop of our trip." Jahir hesitated, then let his gratitude through the mindline . . . carefully, so as not to overwhelm, because his joy over the experience was complex and expansive. "This birthday gift . . . I have never had one like it."

Vasiht'h's flush of pleasure felt like the first sight of flowers after a long winter. "I'm glad you liked it." And then, satisfied, "I thought you would."

"You know me well," Jahir said. "Though you have set an impossibly high standard for future gifts, I fear."

"Oh, that's not a problem," Vasiht'h said airily. "If we stay, it's concert tickets, all the way. Veta's got an arts complex you're going to have to see to believe."

"Oh," Jahir said, reining in his avarice with difficulty.

"Then . . . you shall have to show me, so that I might try."

Vasiht'h grinned. "Dinner, then."

"Mmm," Jahir said, innocent. "One last chance to catch up with my score in our impromptu game of 'spot the child.'"

"Goddess, send me a field trip!"

CHAPTER 8

"PREJUDICE? AGAINST DOGS?" Ametia snorted as she fluffed up her pillow. "Ridiculous. Dogs are fine. No one can hate a dog. But no, most people think pet-keeping is in poor taste. Yet another ridiculous holdover from our origins. And they say we don't hold grudges." She snorted. "Not a dog's fault, any of it."

"I see," Jahir said, his bafflement a faint peppery taste in the mindline. Vasiht'h wondered at the aggression of the spice . . . usually his partner's confusion was milder. "Are you sleeping, then, alet?"

"I am," Ametia said. "I've had a long few days, aletsen, and if you don't mind I'd like to spend my session unconscious." She pulled her bag over and dragged a brightly colored afghan out of it. "Look, I decided to help you decorate."

"You brought a blanket?" Vasiht'h asked.

"I brought you a blanket, because one blanket isn't enough. What if you have clients with thin skins? Like me?" She poured herself onto the couch. "You're trying to keep it professional, I understand. But there's nothing professional about sleeping. Even when you try to apply scientific rigor to it. Especially then. I don't know why they bother with clinical sleep trials when it's patently obvious that people aren't going to sleep in a

hospital room the same way they sleep in their own bedrooms."
She yawned and pulled both blankets over herself, the motley
afghan on top. "No offense, aletsen. Go away. Come back when
I'm unconscious."

Outside, Vasiht'h said, "She brought us an afghan."

"She makes afghans?" Jahir sounded curious.

The mental picture of their restless client sitting somewhere
long enough to crochet one granny square, much less seventy,
was so funny that Vasiht'h laughed. "Oh, I hope so. That would
be too good."

Ametia's dreams remained pastiches of war scenes, though
lately they'd begun including moments of quiet between battles.
Mending armor, sleeping in a cot, bent over maps in a tent while
outside the muffled rumble of thunder called to mind storms,
or the movement of artillery. */Maybe we're doing some good?/*
Vasiht'h said when they withdrew.

/Hard to say,/ Jahir replied. */One would have to assume that
these pauses represent a cessation of her worries, and yet, they don't./*

*/If it's a war she doesn't think she'll win in her lifetime, maybe
this is her admitting that even she has to rest sometimes./*

/One can hope./

"Thank you for the afghan," Vasiht'h said to the Harat-Shar
when she was leaving. "Did you make it yourself?"

"I did," she said. "I don't crochet often, but I get these wild
impulses and then I'll just up and do one in half a day. Yarn
everywhere . . . it's a total mess." She grinned. "But I get something concrete out of it. There's something about that. Making
a thing, rather than building ideas and thoughts and contexts."

"You are making a context," Jahir offered. "It is merely a
context of pattern and fabric."

"Hah!" She shook her head. "Maybe. Anyway. We can talk
more next time. Not about the dog, though. That's Allen's business. And probably stupid tourists who don't know him gawking.
The people in the city know better."

"I beg your pardon?" Jahir said for him, which saved Vasiht'h
the trouble of asking.

"Allen," she repeated. "Allen Tiber. The only big dog around here is Trusty, and Trusty belongs to Allen." She grinned, showing a tooth. "I'm surprised you haven't met him yet. He's a big name in the therapist community. I saw him for a few sessions. Before you ask—we didn't click. Probably because he's human. How can I complain about human prejudice to a human? There's no way he could keep it from getting personal. Or maybe I'm doing him wrong. Maybe he could have managed . . . but then, would it have mattered if I hadn't been able to believe him capable of it? Anyway. Next week, aletsen."

The floor-dropped-away feeling in the mindline wasn't a perfect approximation of how Vasiht'h felt at having this dropped on them, but it was close. "Why didn't she tell us that in the beginning?"

"Why would she have?" Jahir said. "It was not an important detail, apparently."

"Like the fact that strangers for some reason are snubbing him and his dog?" Vasiht'h frowned. "Is that because he's human and she sees human prejudice everywhere? Or because he's human, and so people are prejudiced against him?"

"Or the third possibility?" Jahir offered. When Vasiht'h glanced at him, the Eldritch paused, then said, carefully, "Perhaps he is not easily liked."

Vasiht'h folded his arms. "A therapist who isn't liked doesn't stay in business long."

———— ∞∞∞ ————

That week, Pieter's children came to visit them: two adult Seersa, both caramel-colored, but the male had a darker cast and lacked his father's stripes, which his sister sported along with striking ventrals of cream. Their mother must have been a handsome woman, Jahir thought as they settled on the couch.

Their differences in coloration did not extend to their eyes, which shared their father's bright hue, and were identically determined.

"We're so glad Tapa decided to come to you," the female,

Brenna, said. "We're worried about him."

"He needs therapy," the male said, Roland. "He's going to get himself killed on some of these crazy trips of his. It's like he's trying to die." His ears flicked back. "He's not . . . do you think he's suicidal?"

/This is more your arena than mine, I fear, arii,/ Jahir said. */My instinct is to reveal nothing, but they are Pelted, and the Pelted feel differently about medical privacy issues./*

"What makes you think he might be?" Vasiht'h asked aloud.

/Nicely done!/

/Let's just say I've been taking notes since we met./

Jahir tried not to let his rue tinge the mindline.

"He's always been a model father," Brenna said, taking up the narrative. "Dami died when we were young, and he left Fleet to take care of us when he could have handed us to our grandparents, or had us in a boarding school. But he felt strongly that he should be there for us. He was always there for us."

Roland nodded. "Responsible. Dutiful. He told us how those were important ideals. It's what drove him to Fleet, I'm sure. Though he never talked much about what he did there. It was always about us. How were we doing in school, what could he help with. What did we need to take whatever next step we'd decided on."

"He was good at listening," Brenna agreed. "He doesn't talk much, but he listens really well, and then he acts on those things."

"That's how we knew he loved us," Roland said. "He showed us. But we grew up and we moved out, and maybe that was hard on him. He's got nothing left, you know? He spent twenty-five years on us and now that's done."

"He's earned a life of his own, but . . . he's acting like it's over!" Brenna wrung her hands. "He goes on these crazy vacations where you shoot animals in the outback, and there's no safety gear, and we're never sure if he's going to come back. Or he'll do stunt sports . . ."

"He likes skiing and snowboarding," Roland agreed.

/So those dreams were real!/ Vasiht'h exclaimed.

/*Astonishing,*/ Jahir murmured.

"We're worried," Brenna said. "That he misses Dami so much that we were the only reason he was . . . you know . . ." She looked away.

"That he was staying alive for us," Roland finished. "And now that we're grown up, he thinks it's safe to move on."

/*Plausible,*/ Jahir murmured.

/*Kind of sad that it's such an easy diagnosis that even a couple of kids could make it.*/ Vasiht'h sounded troubled; Jahir glanced over and found him pressing his forepaws together. /*It almost seems too easy.*/

/*Then perhaps it is. We should make our own evaluation. It is why we have been engaged.*/

/*True.*/ Aloud, Vasiht'h said, "How young were you when your mother died?"

The rest of the interview garnered them a picture of the Strong household, enough to confirm that from Roland and Brenna's point of view, they'd had a very good childhood. Roland as the elder had clearer memories of their mother than Brenna, who'd lost her at five years, but they both recalled their father's devotion to her. It seemed to be in keeping with Pieter's character, for he'd certainly shown the same devotion to his children. A man who'd prioritized his family, Jahir thought.

"Maybe he just really likes risky sports and didn't want to take any chances when the kits were young?" Vasiht'h said after the two had gone.

"Mayhap," Jahir agreed, going into the cabinet for the afghan. "The question becomes what part we play."

"It's beginning to sound like the part we play is 'mediator'," Vasiht'h said, the mindline tacky with the memory of embarrassment, like something spilled and left without cleaning. "Goddess knows I've untangled enough squabbles in my family to know sometimes what you really need is a third party to translate. You can grow up with someone and still find them incredibly alien."

"We could suggest group sessions?" Jahir said.

Vasiht'h glanced up at him. "I feel a 'but' in the mindline."

That made him smile—how well his friend knew him already. He brought down a fresh pillowcase. "But from our own observation, and from the children's, Pieter is not a talkative man. If we put them in the same room it's likely they will do all the talking and he will obligingly listen, and nothing will be accomplished."

"I wonder if group sleep therapy is possible," Vasiht'h muttered.

The idea was not quite appalling, but close. "One dreaming mind is a sufficiency."

"You're probably right," Vasiht'h said. "But wouldn't it be something to be able to . . . !"

That was honest-to-gods enthusiasm in the mindline, and it made Jahir wonder what about the prospect could possibly be so exciting. The extent of their powers was already enough for him. To be capable of more was . . . disquieting, when more was so often associated with villains out of myth. The gifts they'd been given were enough, and he let that conviction tint the mindline, and received in return an acceptance that felt like a hug. He glanced over his shoulder—

"You're right. We should be grateful for what we have," Vasiht'h said.

"I am," Jahir agreed.

⸺·❧·⸺

Lennea was the most retiring of their clients, and the most willing to use the couch for the purpose they'd intended it. Her dreams were anxious things that they soothed according to the scene they found: they quieted raucous children in classrooms, eased tensions in staff rooms, provided gentle breezes and the distant sound of wind chimes to rambles outdoors and diffused tensions in awkward family dinners. From this, and her hesitant talk sessions, they gathered that she was a peacemaker, and that work sometimes forced her into positions of more responsibility than she was comfortable with: usually temporary, but always distressing until she was able to resume her normal duties. There was no darkness lurking in her, and little urgency to their work when she came.

"More like what we signed up for," Vasiht'h said when they were shutting down for the day.

"It is as Healer KindlesFlame told me once," Jahir said. "A practice is mostly catarrhs and broken bones, and only the occasional emergency."

"Did he actually say catarrh?" Vasiht'h wondered.

Jahir paused, then said sheepishly, "Probably not. But 'virus' seems imprecise."

"You could say 'head cold.'"

"But what if it is in the chest?"

Vasiht'h eyed him and Jahir let him sense the peeping mischief in the mindline. It was not on the level of Helga's mischief, certainly, but it was enough humor to light his friend's eyes.

Yes. He could certainly live like this. For a very long time. And enjoy it.

—∞∞∞—

The charge for the train trip just . . . vanished.

Even expecting it, Vasiht'h found it unsettling. They'd gone to open their joint account, as promised, accepting the token fin coin from the bank—explaining that had been a fun conversation, particularly since Vasiht'h didn't know why banks always gave new account holders a single coin. Almost no one used coins except for their symbolic value, so he'd riffed on that, but the moment they'd gotten back to the cottage he'd looked it up to make sure. Thankfully, he'd been on the right track, though as with everything there was a strange and long story behind it.

So they'd had their joint account, and they'd attached all their assorted bills to it, including the vacation. And the day after, that debit was gone, and their account still had the same balance. It was as if he'd left someone with a gaping, bleeding wound only to return the next day and find the patient jumping around outside, playing flying saucer.

It was their day off and Jahir was exploring the recreational complex in search of a pool, so Vasiht'h settled on the roof with his book and hoped to find some insight, no matter how oblique, in his sisters' gift. The sex scene was as appalling as Sehvi had reported, not because it was erotic and he found thrust-by-thrust descriptions of sex uninteresting, but because it was so clogged with metaphors and vague allusions to what the characters were doing that he couldn't figure out what was happening. In a sex scene! He would have thought it would have been fairly easy to at least guess!

He was on the sixteenth paragraph about how they were completing one another spiritually and looking up the word lubricious when the tablet chimed a priority message. Spreading it, he found his sister, leaning so far toward the screen that her nosepad was out of focus. The few seconds it took for the well-connect to finish negotiating meant she was halfway through his name when the sound finally started working. "..siht'h, Vasiht'h, ariihir, he proposed!"

"Kovihs?" Vasiht'h said. "Already??"

"Already!" She laughed. "Ariihir! I've known him three years!"

"Oh!" Vasiht'h said. "Then he's quick, good for him." He grinned at her peal of laughter. "Well, you know. THEY'LL GET AROUND TO IT EVENTUALLY."

In between squeaks, Sehvi said, "Yes . . . I know!" Wiping her eyes. "Tell me you're happy for me."

"The only reason I'm not thrilled is because you're on another planet and I can't come over and hug you, and hug him, and have an impromptu party," Vasiht'h answered, beaming. "Have you told Dami and Tapa yet?"

"No! You first," she said, eyes sparkling. "It's the middle of the night on Anseahla, they're going to have to wait. Well, no, I'm going to have to wait. It's so hard to wait! But it's mid-morning for you, so I figured I'd hit you first."

"And the rest of the family?" Vasiht'h said with a studied air of innocence.

That made her laugh harder. "You really mean 'did you tell Bret', don't you. No, I haven't, but I look forward to it. Knowing him, I'll get a lecture about how to properly set up a marital relationship before embarking on it, and do I really know what I'm doing, and have I considered the practicalities?"

Vasiht'h grinned. "Do you know what you're doing? And have you?"

"Yes. And I don't care." She snickered. "That felt good to say. No, seriously, we have discussed the sorts of things you need to know before you start, like 'do we have congruent plans for our lives' and 'do we both want children', and 'do we both have similar sex drives.' I'm not ten years old anymore. I'm a little more cognizant of basic reality than I used to be."

"I never doubted it," Vasiht'h said. "Well, except maybe briefly while reading this book. Can I send it back to you so you can use it as relationship advice for your forthcoming marriage?"

Sehvi snickered. "I've already read it! Find me a new one!"

"With better sex scenes," Vasiht'h said. "It's pretty bad when you can't tell whether they're done or not from the text."

"You're just not reading it carefully enough."

"If I was reading it more carefully, my eyes would start bleeding," Vasiht'h said dryly. And then sighed and added, "So have you and Kovihs discussed money, and if so, how did you make it work?"

"Have you run out of fin already?" Sehvi leaned toward him again. "I thought you had clients!"

"We have three clients," Vasiht'h said. "I'm pretty sure they're not enough to cover the monthly rent."

"Pretty sure," she repeated, her ears fanning in confusion.

"We just got the joint account," Vasiht'h said. "And one of our bills disappeared, and now I'm wondering if others are going to disappear. And if so, if they're disappearing because they're drawing on our money, or because he's putting extra in."

She shook her head. "Oh, ariihir. For once, I have actual advice for you!"

"Good! I need it!"

She wrinkled her nose. "Don't let your need to think of yourself as an independent adult—to please a brother who's never going to change!—introduce problems into your absolutely amazing relationship with your best friend."

"It's not just Bret," Vasiht'h protested, pressing his paws together. "I want our parents . . ."

"To be proud of you?" Sehvi interrupted. She snorted. "They already *are*, ariihir. And they've always loved you. Look, we're both young. Even by Pelted standards. And you're already out on your own with a partner, running your own practice! On a starbase!"

"Maybe," Vasiht'h said. "If they let us stay."

"If they don't, then you'll go somewhere else where they will let you stay, and you'll set up again. Or you'll come household with me and Kovihs and we'll run a huge joint medical office—wouldn't that be fun?" She sighed. "I wish I could hug you, because you need one. Stop second-guessing yourself, big brother. You're doing great! And if you keep picking at this scab with your Eldritch, you won't be doing great, because you'll disturb him, and you'll upset yourself, and all for what? Because you can afford to pay your bills? Just say 'yay' and go buy a cake!"

"I guess that makes a lot more sense than fretting about it," Vasiht'h admitted. "But I can't seem to do it." He smiled a little. "I guess that teaches me, right? I'm so ready to help people who come to me for therapy be confused and anxious for as long as they need to be, without judging them for not just getting over it. And here I am, not getting over something."

"If you tell yourself you're not getting over it you really won't, and then you'll be in trouble," Sehvi said. "Don't make any prophecies you're going to be compelled to fulfill."

He chuckled at that. "Ugh. Maybe you should be here doing this job . . . !"

"No thank you. I'm far too impatient." She grinned. "You're the understanding one, ariihir. All I'd do is kick people in the pants and then wonder why they were lodging complaints instead of paying me."

That picture made him laugh. "All right, I'll try harder! But enough about me? When are you doing the ceremony? Where?"

"Oh, you know the family will kill me if I don't go back to

Anseahla . . ."

They spent the remainder of the call discussing Sehvi's plans. Not just for the wedding either, but for the life that she and Kovihs wanted together, and Vasiht'h was astonished at how neatly they'd tied everything into one package. It helped that they'd met in school doing similar work, of course. But he still couldn't help saying at the end, "I wish I had as clear a picture of what I'm planning as you do!"

She blew out a breath, exasperated. "You have the worst case of tunnel vision ever, ariihir. You're *already* doing what you were planning to do! Now it's just 'continue doing it', so of course it doesn't sound very deterministic."

"But if we have to leave . . ." He trailed off. "I'm doing it again."

"You're doing it again," she agreed firmly. "So stop doing it. Go do something else. Read more of the novel!"

Vasiht'h sighed. "At least tell me it gets better."

"Oh, goddess," she said, eyes dancing. "You're about to get to the best part."

There was nothing for it, then, but to make lunch and resume reading, this time in the garden outside. The table had been designed for bipeds, but he brought a couple of bolsters out and settled himself at a good height. The chirping of birds was far more interesting than the book, but he resumed reading over his butternut and ginger soup, nibbling on a soft sour bread roll as he turned pages. Thaddeus and the girl, whose name he finally remembered as Alana after half a book of nicknames like 'the sweet maiden' and 'the gentle goddess', had recovered from their episode of sexual completion and were just discovering . . .

"What!" he exclaimed at the tablet. "You have got to be kidding me. She can't possibly be pregnant!"

⸘

The recreational complex was not Jahir's sole destination, though it was enough of a primary one that he felt no twinge at what someone might have otherwise construed as misdirection. And he did, indeed, go there, and was unsurprised—and enchanted—by the landscaped park with its jogging track and playgrounds, and the swimming pools set into them in imitation of natural lakes that connected with the water environment for the aquatic races. There was a separate area for competition training, with the facilities he'd come to expect from the university and the hospital on Selnor, but he found the more natural areas charming.

But much as he wanted to linger, he was drawn on toward the commons, and the list of addresses there.

Two of the five names on his list he dismissed: they were medical therapists attached to Veta's civilian hospital, and did not take personal clients. But there were three other names, and he wanted to see them. He had no plan to engage with them, but the need to face them was irresistible, and he could no more have explained it to his Pelted friend than he could have failed to do it. Some needs did not belong to this civilized society.

The first address took him near the university where Ametia must work. Not on campus, but near its greenways, the office shared a building girdled in trees and little café tables with a coffee shop, a bakery, and a bookstore. Jahir bought a cup of espresso in a thick-walled ceramic cup, hand-glazed in teal and orange and dark brown, and sat outside to watch the clientele drift through the area. This was Minette Dashenby's practice, Karaka'An therapist, and most of her appointments looked like university students.

The coffee was good, if strong. The breeze gentle and the sunlight warm. He spent an hour there and regretted leaving.

The second office took him to the city's most peculiar landmark. Looking up at the city's sky one saw an uninterrupted view from horizon to horizon, with only the distant lattice of the Spindle to suggest the artificial environment. But the city was in fact bisected by the starbase's external wall. The interior of the wall was thick with the warehouses, factories, and industrial works necessary to the maintenance of the civilian port and its vessels, which were on the vacuum-facing side.

But the wall of the starbase was invisible until one crossed some magic line, and then it hove into very abrupt view, rising out of sight in uncompromising lines. He would have thought it to be uniform in color—gray—but like the outside of the base it was patterned with projections that allowed its murals to remain vivid no matter how long they stayed up . . . or to be reconfigured in an instant whenever the person charged with that particular bit of real estate decided. And there were, as with everything the Pelted did, so many windows. It was less grim architecture and more a piece of sculpture, and he found it fascinating that it existed and was hidden.

At the foot of the wall, and along its balconies, were a number of shops and apartments, more technological in style than the rest of the city, more like what he'd imagined a society like the Alliance would create. But the second of his addresses was not along these boulevards, but in the Wall itself. It took him some time to locate, in fact, because there were so many offices in the Wall. But eventually he found it, a luxurious practice on the outward facing skin, with glass doors and a lobby with an enormous window overlooking the city from a breathtaking vantage.

This was Allen Tiber's office, and he took a seat on a bench nearby to watch the stream of people in the hall as they separated into passersby and clients: several Karaka'A. A Tam-illee. A delicate, dark-haired Malarai, her soft gray wings folded behind her. The people entering Tiber's office were wealthier, and more varied in age, and there were a lot more of them. And strangely, while he found the style of the office repelled him, whenever the doors opened he smelled something bright and welcoming and it kept him in place long after he would have left for his final stop.

The third office was in the commons itself: not in the city's center, but close enough to it that he could have walked to any of its cafes and shops. He liked it instantly: the proximity to the bustle while also maintaining a remove, the way it was integrated so nicely with the surrounding shops and homes, the trees nodding over the lane and the pedestrians passing. This was the Healer's Knot, a clinic that should have had several doctors in practice? But no one was entering its door, and when he stopped there he found a sign indicating that it was no longer open for business.

Three general practitioners, he thought, walking home. And one gone. That left a vacancy, and a vacancy was—just perhaps— enough space for him and Vasiht'h to fill.

CHAPTER 9

THERE WAS A GARDEN OUTSIDE. Vasiht'h knew nothing about gardening, but it felt impolite to let it get overrun. And while he preferred baking to pulling what he hoped were weeds, he couldn't spend all his time inside. The cottage, so welcoming at first sight, was beginning to feel a little small. How that was possible when he and Jahir had lived practically stacked on one another in the hospital apartment on Selnor, he had no idea. But it wasn't about living with Jahir, specifically, because he felt the same restlessness when Jahir was off on a walk or an errand. Something about Veta made him want to spread out, breathe more.

So he pulled up common guides to gardening, figured out the climate zone the starbase was maintaining in this part of the city, and set to work learning to identify which plants were ornamental and which needed removal. This was a much better distraction than wading through HEALED BY HER IMMORTAL HEART, which he'd abandoned after the todfox had magically impregnated the entirely alien Eldritch girl.

He still found himself muttering about that sometimes.

"Well, this is a nice surprise!" came the voice of Ilea EveryLivingThing. Looking up he found her leaning on the garden gate, arms folded and a smile on her lived-in face. "I didn't expect you to do any maintenance on the yard, you know."

Vasiht'h sat back on his hindquarters, one scrawny plant dangling from a hand. "Alet! Ah . . . I hope I'm not hurting anything."

"Not by pulling that never-do, you're not," she said, amused. "I came by to see how you two have been getting on, now that it's been a couple of months. Still happy with the place?"

"It's wonderful," Vasiht'h said. "The roof patio in particular. I like to read up there." Or he had, before the mystical impregnation. "Can I get you anything to drink? Lemonade? Tea and biscuits?"

"Lemonade sounds nice, thank you. And here, leave that plant with me, I'll tuck it in your waste bag there."

Bemused, he handed her the plant. By the time he got back with the tray, he expected her to be weeding, and she was, whistling to herself as she plucked up the plants scraggling along the edge of the pavers. "So how is the starbase ecosystem?"

"Getting along," she replied cheerfully. Straightening, she brushed her hands off on her pants and took a seat at the table, and a long sip of the lemonade. "My, that's good. Did you buy that down at the corner market or . . . no, you made it, didn't you." She grinned. "I could tell by the look on your face. The idea of buying something like this that you could make more easily is offensive, isn't it."

"It's not that it's easier, it's that it's easier and mine tastes better," Vasiht'h said.

"I can't argue that. And these?" She picked up the biscuit. "Don't tell me you make these too."

"Yes. But not the cheese." Vasiht'h managed a lopsided smile. "I don't raise goats."

Ilea laughed. "No, only Margery's crazy enough to do that. But we all have to keep occupied somehow. So, you and your partner doing well? How's business?"

How was business. Good question. "We have some clients," Vasiht'h said. "We could always use more."

"Who couldn't!" she said with a chuckle. "Though I expect

you're doing pretty well, to pay the rent. Xenotherapy . . . there are easier ways to make money."

"Are there?" Vasiht'h suddenly wondered if he could find one, maybe make up the shortfall they would have been experiencing had they not been floating on Jahir's largesse.

"Pulling weeds, for one." She sliced herself a wedge of cheese. "But I would think so, since it's what I like to do."

Thinking of Lennea, Vasiht'h said, "Sometimes we do things and they don't end up being what we imagined, though."

She snorted. "Of course not. How else do they stay interesting?"

It was such an unexpected response that he laughed. "Well, some people like routine, you know!"

"Even the people who like routine need some shaking up now and then. Otherwise, how would they know they've got a routine? Sameness dulls your sensitivities." She waved a hand at the garden. "That's what I do, after all. I introduce random variables to a system that would otherwise be too sterile. That's the spark that keeps things moving. Otherwise, entropy would run it down eventually." She ate another biscuit, expression complacent. "Nature knows that. It's why there are trees that only release their seeds after fires. The unexpected needs to come."

Vasiht'h refilled her glass. "How much do I owe you?"

"Beg your pardon?"

He grinned. "For the therapy session."

She barked a laugh. "Oh, alet. That's not therapy. It's just common sense. You know it yourself, or you wouldn't be in the profession, eh?" She rose, stretched. "So, you want me to teach you which of these plants need to stay and which to go?"

"Sure!"

"Come on, then. You were on the right track, but leave those fermilions there, some people think they're a nuisance but in autumn they turn golden against this backdrop of evergreens I've planted and it looks like filigree."

Jahir found him outside several hours later, still tidying.

"I did not know you gardened."

"I don't," Vasiht'h answered, amused. "That's why it's taking me so long. Is that supper?"

"It is at least salad greens." Jahir set them on the table beside the tray. "Did you entertain, then?"

"Our landlady came by to see how we were doing." Vasiht'h gave up the effort for now, squinting at a sky that had turned periwinkle blue. He could just see the lights of the spindle starting to wink. "She gave me an impromptu lesson on how to keep the patio pretty and it was a nice day out."

"The days seem unlikely to become less nice," Jahir observed, drawing one of the chairs out and settling on it. "Even summer must be mild."

Something in the mindline felt vague, like a mist. Or the distant smell of perfume, or flowers. Vasiht'h narrowed his eyes, puzzled. "Do you miss weather?"

"Do you?"

He thought of the flash floods at home, and the torrential downpours, and then the abrupt days of clear skies with a brassy sunlight that seemed to sharpen the edge of every leaf. Then he thought of the mud on his paws, and drenched fur, and the discomfort of damp skin. "No. Weather is a nuisance. I could be very happy in a place with no weather."

"We are certainly in the right place for that," Jahir said.

Vasiht'h eyed him. "You didn't answer the question, though, and this time I want to know the answer."

The amusement this time tasted like cream on strawberries. "I have not been away from weather long enough to miss it."

Which was another evasion, Vasiht'h thought. But an acceptable one, because behind that sweet-scented amusement there was something melancholic that he didn't want to push. Instead, he said, "Ilea EveryLivingThing thinks that we all need some change to shake us up now and then. So maybe we should take vacations to places with weather. You know. See some snow. Get rained on. Dance in a thunderstorm."

"Dance in a thunderstorm!" Jahir said, laughing.

"All right, you can dance in a thunderstorm. I'll huddle under a rain cape and cheer you on." Vasiht'h grinned. "I'm going to go rinse off. You can bring the salad greens in."

"Maybe we can eat on the patio?" Jahir said. "You have put such work into it. It seems a pity not to."

Which they did, while the afternoon deepened into a cool purple twilight, so beautiful that they walked to the commons to the ice cream shop, where Karina declaimed on the latest flavor. Vasiht'h watched indulgently as she pressed several samples on Jahir until at last he settled on a decadent more-almond concoction topped with great curling shavings of dark chocolate and grains of pink salt.

"She says it needs coffee," he began, and stopped when the pard appeared at their elbow with a tiny cup of espresso. "Ah, thank you, alet."

"I'm fine," Vasiht'h said firmly, before she could eye his choice too carefully.

The contrast between their quiet patio table in the Garden District and this table in the brightly lit parlor on the commons main street could not have been more distinct. The river of people passing, holding shopping bags or drinks, talking, laughing, strolling or striding purposefully past the glass storefront, versus the quiet murmurs of the occasional pedestrian back at the cottage . . . there, the lights had been dim and discreet, and the loudest noise the rustle of wind through the plants. Here lights were strung over the byway to accent the lit displays from the stores and restaurants, and conversations were so numerous he could hear their hum even inside the insulated parlor.

"Seersana was not so busy," Jahir observed.

"The university wasn't," Vasiht'h said. "The capital was, the few times we visited. This is just . . . city-living." He glanced at his partner. "It doesn't make you uncomfortable? So many close by?"

"But they are not close by. They are there, and we are here."

Vasiht'h snorted. "Very minor distinction. We have to walk out there to go home."

"But you are with me," Jahir said, eyes still following the passersby outside.

Vasiht'h tried not to let the flush of pleasure overwhelm the mindline, but that was a lost cause from the beginning. He was blushing when the Eldritch glanced at him and cocked his head, one of those little smiles on his face.

"Yes?"

"Always," Vasiht'h said, spooning up the ice cream to keep from meeting that gaze.

"Then, what worry do I have?"

"It's too bad we can't live here," Vasiht'h said. "It would be nice to be in the center of things, wouldn't it? Not just work there, you know, in that office building."

"It would be pleasant," Jahir murmured. "Perhaps, when we know . . ."

"Yeah." Vasiht'h smiled a little. "When we know."

"It will be well," Jahir added, quietly.

"I know. Just . . . it would be nice to know for sure."

"So it would. And yet, so few things are certain. Are they?"

Vasiht'h snorted. "What I'm certain of is that you should finish that ice cream, because you need it more than I do."

"Well," Jahir said with a measure of primness the mindline informed him was staged. "Perhaps some things are eternal."

Vasiht'h grinned. "The best things."

⁂

Preparing for bed later that night, Vasiht'h divulged his concerns about Lennea. "Do you think we're helping her any?"

"She returns," Jahir observed, thoughtful.

"People do that sometimes even when things aren't helping."

"We could ask?" Jahir said at last, and maybe something of Vasiht'h's reluctance seeped through the mindline because he finished, "We may do so without seeming incompetent."

"Are you sure?" Vasiht'h asked, rueful.

"To admit to mistakes must improve trust between healer and patient," Jahir said, straightening the duvet and turning his pillow. "That is what we are aiming for in these preliminary sessions. We cannot pretend to omniscience, arii."

"No," Vasiht'h said. "The Goddess we are not."

———ᘒᘓᑯᘒ———

But it preyed on his mind through another week with the Karaka'An, during which she scheduled an extra session. At the conclusion of that second appointment, Lennea said, hesitant, "I was wondering . . . one of my students' father is a friend of mine, and I thought I could refer him to you?"

Asking if she was sure that was wise was not a good idea, and yet he found himself opening his mouth.

"Do you believe we can assist him with his coping skills, in a manner similar to what we have done with you?" Jahir asked before Vasiht'h could speak.

She flicked her ears outward, thinking. "Not exactly. It's that you don't try to help me cope that helps. If that makes sense? I've been to two other therapists before and they wanted me to work on my skills. I've read up on them myself. I've done guided exercises out of the u-banks. I know what I should be doing. But the only place I succeed in doing any of them . . . is here!"

"Here?" Vasiht'h repeated, mystified.

She nodded firmly. "Here, I actually put my head down and I sleep, and I sleep restfully. And everyone's right! If you do get good sleep, you are better able to handle things. But I could never figure out how to rest on my own. Something you all do . . . do you still go into my mind? No, don't tell me, or it might break whatever you're doing! Anyway. I come here and I lie down on your couch and . . . I rest. And when I wake up, I feel refreshed." She exhaled, eyes closing. "Good sleep is such a blessing. I had no idea."

"It is a vital part of our health," Jahir said.

She opened her eyes and smiled at them, and she had dimples Vasiht'h had never noticed before. "Yes! It is. And that's what I want for Joyner. Do you have time for him? I'll tell him to come straightaway . . . he's never had luck with therapy, but I bet one real nap a week will do more for him than an hour of talking."

"By all means, send him to us."

"Wonderful." She rose, smiling again. "What you all do . . . it's really magical. I have to say. I don't always leave here happier, but I always leave feeling stronger, if that makes sense."

"It does," Jahir answered for him. "And you honor us."

Her ears flushed. "Well. I'll tell him to get in touch. Thank you. See you next week."

The door closed on her and Jahir tilted his head, waiting.

"Real sleep," Vasiht'h repeated.

"There is an element of mystery in what we do," Jahir said. "I suspect our role now is to be open to it, rather than attempt to corral it into a modality we understand."

Vasiht'h sighed, chuckled. "All right. I just wish . . ."

Jahir did not push him to finish the sentence, but did he have to? They were both aware of their deadline.

CHAPTER 10

JAHIR KNEW OF HIS PARTNER'S agitation, but he could not help but find their situation promising. One client had become four, one of whom had begun seeing them twice a week, and of those four two had been referred by existing clients. Such a pattern boded well, even if, like Vasiht'h, he was often mystified by what benefit their clients were deriving from their naps. The rounds they'd done as students in the university clinic had not prepared them adequately for solo work—perhaps because these were working adults, and not young people? He didn't know why it seemed different, but it was. But that too fascinated.

They had time. Even if they had to leave, they would have time to explore the many permutations of the humanoid psyche. Including, he thought, his own.

The time on Selnor had marked him, as surely as the long-ago duel that had left the scar on his shoulder. He knew it for the tendency to glance at the hospital's job vacancies, and the vague itch that drove him to buy chemistry textbooks, and medical ones.

He did not want to be a healer—yet—but he missed the camaraderie of the hospital. There had been a pleasure in being part of a team.

"So you miss working in a group?" KindlesFlame said to him

during their next call. "Or is it the type of work?"

"Yes?" Jahir answered, and smiled as the Tam-illee guffawed. "I am not being obscure intentionally. I don't know the answer."

"I suspect not," KindlesFlame said. "Do you regret going into private practice?"

"No," Jahir said, and that answer he was sure of. "Even given the youth of our business, I still find it rewarding."

"And you still enjoy working with your partner."

Jahir cocked his head. "That sounds like fishing, alet."

KindlesFlame grinned over his coffee. "Believe it or not, it's not. It's just that working with someone outside the university's sheltered environment . . . it brings out problems and personality conflicts you might have missed while you were still operating with a safety net. Running your own practice is complicated, and establishing yourselves . . . well, it's a lot like the first stages of a marriage. You're figuring out how to work together, live together, pay bills, resolve problems. Sometimes you discover you can't make it work."

Did he worry about that? Not on his own behalf. But Vasiht'h was fretting. "I have some concerns. But without the challenge, there's no opportunity for growth."

"You say that like you're hoping I'll agree with you," Kindles-Flame observed, sipping from his cup.

"Do you?"

The Tam-illee chuckled. "Yes. But sometimes growth takes you away from people, as well as toward. I hope you have a fall-back plan, in case this doesn't work out for you."

The idea distressed him. To plan to leave Vasiht'h? "No," he said, so reflexively that his mentor pricked both ears toward him quizzically. "I don't doubt my relationship with Vasiht'h," he said. "The mindline does not permit it. We are too close."

"Dissolving the business relationship doesn't have to dissolve the emotional partnership," KindlesFlame pointed out. "Your Glaseah could do something else with himself. You could go work in a hospital. You might be happier that way, instead of trying to make something work that's creating stress in one or both of you."

That sounded eminently reasonable, but Jahir still hated the idea. Working with Vasiht'h was a source of peace he couldn't imagine surrendering. And yet, if Vasiht'h never settled, would it poison their ability to work together? Jahir liked to think he could ignore his friend's surface agitations, but if they dragged on for years . . . would it become easier to deal with, or harder?

KindlesFlame was watching him with far too much canniness. Jahir exhaled slowly. "I admit I find this discussion uncomfortable."

"I know," the Tam-illee said, not unkindly. "But I'm interested in your welfare, not in helping you preserve a status quo that might not be serving you."

"Still my advisor, despite my graduation?"

The foxine chuckled quietly. "You can take the student out of the university, but you can't take the student out of the advisor's schedule. Besides, I can see too clearly that you're not done yet. You might not come back to school for your continuing education—though I'm willing to bet that you're going to end up back here again—but you're not done learning, Jahir."

"I hope I am never done learning," Jahir said.

"I hope not either. I'm a strong proponent of the value of education." He grinned, let the smile fade. "More seriously, you could consider a compromise."

"A . . . compromise."

The Tam-illee nodded. "Most hospitals do have a number of part-time contractors. You might see if you can be put on their contractor list. You'd get some work that way, but it wouldn't be the commitment that becoming full-time staff would be."

"I hadn't thought of that," Jahir murmured.

"Now might not be a bad time to establish yourself with them, before your practice gets busier."

That too made sense, though he found himself wondering how much friction it would create in his relationship with Vasiht'h if he developed a second income stream when his friend wanted so badly to be financial equals.

"Still not good?" KindlesFlame guessed.

"The heart is rarely reasonable," Jahir said.

"That it isn't," KindlesFlame said. "And you should be grateful. It keeps you in business."

———❦———

Vasiht'h might never have finished HEALED BY HER IMMORTAL HEART had he not checked the annotations. He wasn't even sure why he did. He was thinking of Sehvi, maybe, but his tablet checked him when he selected her name from his list of contacts to build a call. 'Local time on Tam-ley, Timezone 2, is three hours after midnight. Do you wish to continue?' And of course, he said no, because just wanting to chat was no reason to wake her up.

He was agitated. He knew it because he was catching himself rubbing at his own feet again, and if he didn't stop soon he'd wear away another patch and that, no doubt, would inspire his partner to ask him what was bothering him. 'I'm just worried,' wasn't enough of an answer when everything looked like it was going so well. They had clients. The clients kept coming back. Two of them had even sent friends. They were developing friends and acquaintances of their own: Helga, who now had the habit of stopping by for dinner every week, the waitstaff at their two favorite cafes, Karina at the ice cream shop. Ilea wandered past too, though her visits were erratic. They had a place to live, and money to spare, and it was all going so well that the fact that it might be amputated by the housing authority was painful. Worse, the nagging feeling that he was somehow failing at learning how to be an independent adult kept waking him up at night. That he wasn't an independent adult, technically, both did and didn't help; he was profoundly grateful—proud, pleased!—to have Jahir as a partner, but he wasn't sure he was pulling his weight, either.

He missed Sehvi, and in lieu of talking with her he pulled up the book. Since he still didn't want to read it, he checked the sidebar and found the annotations function active. That was how he stumbled onto a conversation between his sisters about what the mystical Eldritch/Tam-illee hybrid was going to look like.

> **KAVILA:** I'm voting for an Eldritch with fox ears.
> **SEHVI:** Humanoid with skin and fox ears isn't materially different from how some Tam-illee already look.
> **TAVYI:** Well I want a snow-white Tam-illee with tragic eyes. And floor-length white hair.
> **MANDARA:** She would have a voice sweet as jingle bells!
> **KAVILA:** They put those bells on harnesses, you know.
> **MANDARA:** Maybe she'll be into that?
> **SARDA:** Ugh, don't even go there, yucccck
> **NINEH:** I'm voting for bilateral asymmetry. The right half of the baby can be Eldritch, the left Tam-illee.
> **KOVRAH:** Maybe it'll be bisected at the waist instead? Top half Eldritch, bottom half Tam-illee? So it'll have the cute tail.
> **SEHVI:** I've got it! Twins! One Eldritch, one Tam-illee!
> **TAVYI:** Boooooring.
> **MANDARA:** Yeah, who wants a reasonable answer? Stop reproductive-sciencing at us, Sehvi.
> **SEHVI:** Fine. How about the baby can turn from one species to the other at will?
> **SARDA:** Yes! Totally good with that!
> **TAVYI:** PLOT TWIST—Dad is actually a Chatcaava!!
> **MANDARA:** Great, horror instead of romance! I'd read that!

Their annotations littered the text: underlined passages they'd found funny, wailing over ridiculous plot twists, extended commentary on what they would have done as one of the protagonists ("why'd he bring her flowers? She's pregnant! I bet she wants sardine sorbet or something"). He paged back to the beginning of the book and found they'd started early. Had all of them read it?? He checked the list and found all seven of them contributing. Grinning, he started re-reading, and in his mind he heard their voices as clearly as if they were scattered around him, throwing pillows or brushing out one another's coats. It reminded him that he had a family that loved him, that wanted to include him in their jokes and their lives. He sent Sehvi a message for when she woke, asking her who'd decided to buy the book in the first place, and how long it had taken all of them to read it, and then set it aside to look out the window. The morning sun was bright on the street, and Jahir was taking a walk. Maybe he should too.

And, he decided, he would walk through the Garden District, and confront his discomfort with living there directly.

The morning was glorious; if he hadn't known he was on a starbase, he would never have guessed. There was even dew jeweling the edges of the plants, and he could hear birdsong. And people were out, jogging or strolling. They had the tranquility of people with a great deal of leisure time, and Vasiht'h let their calm infuse him. They didn't have to live here forever, after all— and what a startling thought that was, when he was spending so much time fearing that he wouldn't be able to! He stopped in the middle of the street, bemused. How ridiculous that he was both convinced they should leave the place they were living— the Garden District—while also upset that they might be forced to leave the place they were living—the Starbase. How could he hold both those things in his head without it exploding? Vasiht'h chuckled and resumed trotting down the street.

Maybe it was his chuckle that attracted the attention of the human on the porch. As he approached, the man called, "Good morning!"

It was such a merry greeting that Vasiht'h halted alongside the steps leading up to the deck. The human was old, his hair nearly entirely white and laugh lines sketched around his mouth. His hands, resting on a gaily-patterned quilt, had the thin delicacy of age, though they looked strong yet. But he had clear eyes and there was laughter in them, and Vasiht'h couldn't help grinning back. "I recognize you," he says. "You're the man who sells quilts at the weekly street market."

"That's right," the man said. "And you're half of the new

couple that moved into Ilea's rental, aren't you."

"We're not a couple—"

He lifted a hand. "Pair. Sorry! I don't mean to imply anything."

"I'm sorry to jump on you about it," Vasiht'h said. "A lot of humans don't know how we work. We Glaseah, I mean."

The man chuckled. "That's fair. A lot of Pelted don't understand how we humans work either."

Vasiht'h thought of Ametia's rants and winced. "Probably not, no."

"Not a very good beginning," the man said, smiling down at him. "Maybe I can fix you a cup of tea and we can start over? Without assumptions? It's a nice day to sit outside and get to know your neighbors."

"I'd like that," Vasiht'h found himself saying before he could censor himself, and the old man beamed and rose from his rocking chair.

"I'll be right back."

So Vasiht'h walked up onto the porch and sat on the opposite side. He inhaled the freshness of the morning air, smelling the water in it, and watched the faint breeze ruffle the broad-leaved plants that edged the wooden deck. The plants in this man's garden grew closer than the ones in Ilea's, and had darker foliage. It reminded him a little of home.

The fragrance of tea preceded the man as he returned with a tray, one with folding legs. Setting it up, he said, "My name is Hector Avila. I'm an old hand here in the neighborhood . . . been living here since I was twenty-two when I moved here with my wife."

Vasiht'h looked toward the front door.

"You won't find her there," Hector said. "She's dead these past fifteen years." His smile was gentle. "I do miss her, but I feel her nearer every year. Here, do you take sugar?"

"No thank you," Vasiht'h answered, accepting the mug. "I'm sorry for your loss."

"I am too," Hector answered, chuckling. "But she wouldn't thank me to mope. It's why I took up quilting. She loved quilts but never had the patience to make them. When the one she loved best started coming apart, I tried my hand at putting it back together."

Vasiht'h grinned. "The beginning of the end!"

"Of my life of sloth!" he agreed. He sat back in his rocking chair with his mug and pushed it into motion with his toe. Without, Vasiht'h noted with bemusement, sloshing the tea. "But then, retirement was getting boring. I like working. It gets me out, talking to people. Gives some structure to my days. What about you, then? What do you do? And what's your name? I'm gone and rambled on and didn't even ask."

"I'm Vasiht'h. As you noticed, my partner Jahir and I are renting the cottage while the Starbase decides if it wants us. We're xenotherapists."

"Therapists!" Hector nodded. "That's a useful thing. I can't imagine them turning you away."

"I'm glad someone can't," Vasiht'h said ruefully. And added, "Is that one of your quilts?"

The man beamed. "Why, yes." He set his mug on the tray-table and spread the quilt out on the porch rail. The pattern reminded Vasiht'h of stars, and they'd been sewn in bold blues and whites that reminded him somehow of Jahir. "This is a Mariner's Compass design. I think it quite smart . . . it's one of my favorites."

Vasiht'h reached out and petted it. "It really is beautiful. I was looking at your quilts at the market."

"But?" Hector asked.

"I don't get cold very much!" Vasiht'h fingered the edge, admiring the stitching, and the cloudlike softness of it. "I could hang it, I guess, as art."

"Oh no," the human said, shaking his head. "Quilts are meant to be used. They're like a hug you can carry with you. Maybe you know someone who needs a hug?"

Vasiht'h thought of Jahir wrapped up in a nautical blanket and smiled. Somehow he couldn't quite make it work. But Lennea popped up in his head and he stopped, struck.

"Ah, you do know someone," Hector guessed, grinning.

"I think they'd work very well for my couch at the office," Vasiht'h said. "We've been looking for ways to personalize it a little. Maybe you could show me your inventory? If you have inventory?"

"Do I have inventory!" The man guffawed, slapped his knee. "Don't I. I'd be delighted to show it to you. But!" He lifted a finger. "After tea. Business after pleasure. Or what's the point of retiring?"

Vasiht'h said, baffled, "I don't know. I haven't thought that far ahead." And then laughed. "Oh, my, that probably sounds ridiculous to you."

"I'm not saying a word. . . ."

"But you're thinking it, and you should." Vasiht'h laughed. "So tell me how you ended up here at twenty-one, and what you were doing to make the starbase decide you were a good bet."

About an hour later, Vasiht'h left his neighbor's company with a bag and a great deal on his mind. He'd enjoyed the morning, and the fact that this surprised him was . . . strange. He liked people; talking with them was one of the pleasures of his job. Had he become so insular that he no longer thought of striking up conversations with strangers? He was letting worry drive him from the habits that gave him strength, and how could he conquer his anxieties if he relinquished those coping mechanisms?

What a field day a therapist would have with him! He chuckled ruefully. No doubt this was all just new adult problems, and he would figure them out the way he did the problems that beset him when he decamped for Seersana University. But it certainly felt like the sky was falling. Shaking his head, he trotted back to the cottage and found Jahir returned from his walk.

"You bought something that smells good," he said as he came in the door.

"Scones," Jahir said. "Inevitably." He set out a box.

"And what flavor are the inevitable scones this time?" Vasiht'h asked, amused.

"Blackberry, with cream whipped with honey. The honey

is . . . some sort of special flavor also, but I have forgotten what."

Vasiht'h peeked in the box, swiped a finger through it. "Delicious, whatever it is. I bet Ilea could tell us what kind of flowers it came from. Unless it's imported?"

"I don't know," Jahir admitted. And added, "You have been shopping also?"

"Yes!" Vasiht'h brought the quilt from the bag and spread it out to show off the pattern, soothing blues and greens and happy yellows. "I bought it from one of our neighbors. This one is a 'flying geese' quilt. I thought we could use it for the office, for the people who find the afghan too heavy. Or too holey."

The mindline grew flowers in the same yellow color, and the blues and greens in the quilt seemed to flow through it. "It is lovely. And a good thought."

"I thought so." Vasiht'h sat back, added, "Do you ever think of what we'll do when we retire?"

The flowers in the mindline faded. While Vasiht'h wouldn't have called the breeze that blew past them arctic, it still had a touch of autumn in it, one that reminded him strongly of the nightmares his friend used to have. Paling, he said, "Ah, you don't have to answer that."

Jahir smiled at him, a tiny crooked smile that didn't break Vasiht'h's heart, quite . . . but did bruise it a little. "Shall we eat?"

"I'll make coffee."

Their next session was with Pieter, who arrived and gave them the same nod and exchange of courtesies he always offered on the way to the couch. Jahir didn't perceive him to be withdrawn or taciturn . . . it was more that he preferred action to words, a point his dreams re-emphasized repeatedly. They'd come to regard their sessions with him as invitations to 3deo entertainments they would ordinarily never have consumed.

/What do you guess it'll be this time?/ Vasiht'h asked him, resigned. /Whitewater rafting? Big game hunting with a low-tech bow and arrow? Parachuting off an airplane?/

But it was none of those things. When they took hands and slipped into the Seersa's dreams, they fell into an adrenaline rush and the sound of their own breathing in an enclosed space. A helmet? Flashes of light strobed against part of their vision. They were spinning—they'd been flung from the hull of a ship. The tightness of their chest was an effort not to vomit against the unexpected rotation. Toggling the suit thrusters too quickly wrenched something in their back, but it stopped the spin and the disorientation.

This allowed them to see how far they'd been thrown from the ship.

Never had they been so isolated. Hanging alone amid the stars in all the preternatural clarity of airless space, they felt nothing but awe: awe, and excitement that they were here, that they were able to share, in some small part, in the glories of an endless creation. That it was their daring that made it possible. And that it was now their responsibility to make their way back to the ship, without surrendering to panic.

When they withdrew from that dream, Vasiht'h whispered, voice separating into a multi-part whisper like a choir softening out of song, /Wow./

Jahir squeezed his fingers and let them go.

When Pieter woke, he accepted a glass of water and rolled his shoulders. "That was interesting."

"Did it happen?" Jahir asked, quiet.

The Seersa nodded, ears flipping forward. "Remember it clearly. Kind of a pivotal moment."

"I believe it," Vasiht'h said. "You weren't scared at all?"

"Scared?" He frowned, a little wrinkle of furred brow. "No. Startled, certainly. But what was there to be scared of? I'd had extensive training on EVA emergencies. I had plenty of power to get back to the ship. I knew exactly where she was, too. Pretty straightforward problem to solve."

"You miss it," Jahir said, voice still quiet.

Pieter looked at him without flinching, his eyes steady. "Yeah. I guess I do." He rose, brushed off his pants. "Same time, next week?"

"Of course," Jahir said.

/You're working on something./

Was he? Jahir stood to escort their client out, feeling a vast emptiness in his head, one that trembled with tension . . . much like Pieter's reaction to the void when he'd found himself faced with it, alone and unbowed. /Yes, I think so./

/What do you think?/

"Have a good week," Pieter said with a nod, and turned from them only to pause.

There, standing across from the door into their office, was the human man with the dog from the train.

"Doctor Tiber," Pieter said.

"Pieter-alet." The human studied him, then looked past him at Jahir and Vasiht'h. His eyes narrowed before he finished, "It's good to see you. How've you been?"

"Well enough, thanks," Pieter replied. "Kids wanted me to try these new therapists, so I've been seeing them. Been going fine."

"I'm glad to hear that."

There was a pause then. It was evident that the human— Allen Tiber, one of the base's established therapists—wanted to talk with Jahir and Vasiht'h, and that he had nothing more to say to Pieter. But the Seersa remained where he was between them. He folded his arms, his stance already wide, and though he remained relaxed he gave the strong impression of a man preparing for a fight.

/What is he doing?/ Vasiht'h asked, baffled.

/Defending us, I think,/ Jahir answered, and stepped up beside Pieter. "Next week, then, alet."

Pieter cocked his head, looking up at the Eldritch—no, searching his eyes. Jahir let his calm seep through, hoping the Seersa could read it, and apparently it worked. Pieter nodded, satisfied. "Fine. Next week, aletsen. Thanks for the session. They've been helping."

"Our pleasure," Vasiht'h said, the Glaseah's confusion still tainting the mindline.

"We aim to serve," Jahir agreed, and that made the Seersa smile before he turned and headed off. That left them with the human, and it was easy to see why Pieter had reacted to him. His entire body spoke of his agitation, and the fist at his side was actively aggressive. The only thing that mitigated the portrait was the soft hand on his dog's head.

/Is he angry at us?/ Vasiht'h said. */What in Her name for?/*

/I suspect we're about to find out./

"So you're the people siphoning off everyone else's clients," the man said.

"I was not aware there was any prohibition against seeing clients who made appointments for therapy," Jahir answered as Vasiht'h came to stand alongside him.

"It is when you're using a dangerously untried modality." The man lifted his chin. "Of course, I've only heard rumors. Hearsay can be wrong. You might not actually be forcing yourselves into their minds?"

/Great,/ Vasiht'h muttered. */Not only is he angry, but he's ignorant./*

/He is concerned for the welfare of his former patients,/ Jahir murmured.

/You sure that's what it is and not hurt pride that we stole them from him?/

/No,/ Jahir admitted, smiling faintly. */But let us assume the best before we assume the worst./*

/If he really cared about his patients he'd be preserving their confidentiality by having this spat with us in private, not out here in the open. And he'd be willing to hear our side of the story . . ./

/Would you, if you heard someone was doing something you considered potentially dangerous to your client?/

Vasiht'h growled in the mindline, but the noise was colored with his exasperation. Tiber did not know him well enough to perceive the affront in his extremely punctilious reply, but Jahir heard it as if someone had rung a gong by his ear. "We don't force ourselves on anyone, alet. That's a prosecutable crime. By the way, I don't think we've been introduced. You are . . . ?"

The dog at the man's side was beginning to show signs of agitation, ears flicking back and head lowering. "Doctor Allen Tiber." A pause. "Licensed xenotherapist. I've worked here for six years."

"It's nice to meet a colleague," Vasiht'h said. */Usually./* "My name's Vasiht'h. This is my partner Jahir. We just moved here."

"Someone licensed you to practice by invading people's thoughts," Tiber said.

"As I said, we don't *invade* thoughts." Vasiht'h's ears had flattened, and Jahir could feel the fur on his lower back bristling like a tingling ache over his own spine. "That would be actionable. We use our abilities to help people address subconscious impulses that might be hobbling them. And we have a license. And a degree from Seersana University, which is renown for its medical school."

"You can't help people solve their problems by tweaking their thoughts for them," Tiber said. "If you do the work for them, you rob them of the chance to develop the skills they need to cope with their challenges without you."

"Are you accusing us of fostering codependency in our clients?" Vasiht'h asked, his incredulity a weight so heavy it bowed the mindline. "First, you want to tell us we abuse our esper abilities, and now you suggest we're manipulating people to keep them?"

"I call them like I see them," Tiber said.

"You're calling them wrong," Vasiht'h answered. "And I think that's a pretty good end to this discussion."

Tiber scowled at him, then looked at Jahir. "And you? Nothing to say for yourself?"

"We have begun what might have been a collegial relationship rather poorly," Jahir answered, choosing his words. "I would not be averse to beginning anew."

/I would!/

Jahir hid his smile in the mindline, and his resignation as well, where he felt it chasten his partner. He finished aloud, "I know I, for one, am curious how Terra educates its therapists."

Tiber frowned. "How did you know. . . ."

"You said you were a doctor," Jahir answered. "That is a human title, indicating training in Terran educational facilities."

This hesitation in the conversation felt like an opportunity. Perhaps he had succeeded in pushing Tiber off-balance, enough to consider re-evaluating his opinion? But the mask fell back over the human's face. "I'm not interested in pursuing a relationship with people I consider to be practicing an ill-conceived modality—if I can even call it that!—on vulnerable patients. I don't know what you think you're doing here, but it's not therapy. And I plan to tell all my clients so."

/Calmly,/ Jahir said. "As you will, alet."

Tiber hesitated, waiting for something else. When Jahir didn't give it to him—or let Vasiht'h do so—he backed away and left, spine stiff. The dog trotted at his side, occasionally glancing up at him as if worried.

/The nerve! Coming here and . . . and accosting us in front of our own office. To accuse us of . . . of raping our clients!/

Jahir winced. /Arii—/

/You're going to tell me to calm down but . . . but what he just accused us of, it's a crime. It gets you stripped of your abilities on Anseahla. It's not the kind of thing you just casually say about a person. About anyone!/

Jahir stopped at the door, startled. /You can do that? Take telepathy away?/

Vasiht'h stalked past him into their office and sat in front of the couch, mantling his wings. /Yes. It's not pretty. Sometimes you get other parts of people with it./

The shiver that ran his spine . . . Jahir sat, arms folded and head bowed.

"You're not sick, are you?" Vasiht'h asked, fretful. "Did he upset you?"

"No," Jahir said. "Surprised me, certainly. Puzzled me. But upset me . . . not the way you are thinking." At Vasiht'h's frown, he offered, "Why did he do it?"

"Do what? Come assault us?"

Jahir clicked his tongue. "Hyperbole."

"Fine," Vasiht'h said. "Confronted us. Aggressively. And without evidence."

"Why?"

"Because he's an angry and controlling personality who can't stand that we took something from him?" Vasiht'h answered, tail flicking.

"Possibly," Jahir allowed. "But rather the worst reading we could take on the situation."

Vasiht'h sighed gustily. "Fine. Maybe he lost some clients, tried to figure out where they went because he was worried when they didn't show up again, and discovered them in the office of the newest therapists in the base, who were also doing things to them he doesn't understand and can't find any ethical or procedural frameworks for. And that upset and worried him, so he came down to . . . yell at us? That's the part where it breaks down. What did he hope to accomplish?"

"Maybe he wanted to judge our reactions to his accusations." Jahir leaned back. "Or perhaps he hoped he could shame us into giving up our work?"

Vasiht'h snorted. "Given the people we've dealt with already . . . he's going to have to work a lot harder than that to get us to give an inch."

Jahir smiled a little.

"Maybe he didn't have a plan," Vasiht'h said finally, reluctant. "Maybe he was just so upset he couldn't stop himself from taking it out on us."

"Or perhaps a little bit of all these things."

Vasiht'h threw up his hands. "Great. He's not even a client and we're psychoanalyzing him."

"Perhaps we should send him a bill," Jahir answered, demure. And that won him the laugh he'd hoped for. "There is no use refining too much on it, arii. Unless he interferes further."

"And how much you want to bet he won't?"

There was no taking that wager, because Jahir knew as well as Vasiht'h that he would lose. He suppressed his sigh.

"Exactly." Vasiht'h tugged on the mindline, let an apologetic breeze blow through it, smelling like the aftermath of a storm: wet and heavy. "I'm sorry. I shouldn't have overreacted. It's just . . . that really is a serious accusation back home."

"Something he no doubt failed to realize when he made it. You were correct about his ignorance."

"Yeah," Vasiht'h answered. "But it's not like he'd have many opportunities to learn about it, would he? Humans don't produce espers, or at least, they don't as far as I know."

And the reasons for that, Jahir thought he could keep to himself. "More interesting to me, however, was Pieter's reaction."

"Pieter's . . . you mean to Tiber?" Vasiht'h frowned, crossing his paws and stretching the topmost absently. "He seemed civil enough. I would guess there was no hard feeling between them? Or maybe he didn't even say he was leaving?"

"Perhaps," Jahir said. "I was more interested in that he felt compelled to protect us."

"He did what—" Vasiht'h stopped abruptly, the mindline blossoming with fireworks. "Goddess. He did, didn't he? You said it yourself . . . he was defending us. I didn't even notice."

"That surprises me, given how often you have interposed yourself between me and anyone you believe to be attacking me," Jahir said, smiling.

Vasiht'h's blush did not show on his face but it colored the mindline like a drop of dye spreading in water. "I imagine you've had a lot of practice observing it, then."

"Which makes it easier to identify in someone else." Jahir folded his arms. "I wonder, a little, if we are taking the wrong approach with Pieter."

"In what way?"

"We have been working on the assumption that his need for adventure is a condition to be coped with," Jahir answered, slowly, testing the words as he spoke them. "What if the real issue is that he's not in the right place?"

"You mean . . . here?" Vasiht'h leaned back, eyes narrowed. "Physically. Like his life."

Jahir sorted the puzzle pieces, thought they locked together too well for anything but truth. "He needs to go back to Fleet."

Both Vasiht'h's brows rose.

"He left it to raise his children, and his children are grown," Jahir said. "There's no reason for him not to go back to the work he obviously loved."

"If there's no reason, why hasn't he yet?" Vasiht'h asked, thoughtful. "Habit?"

"Perhaps he's waiting for permission from his children."

"Or maybe it's something out of his control." The Glaseah tapped the couch cushion, thinking. "Can he just go back to Fleet after years out of it? How does that work?"

"I don't know," Jahir said. "But even if there was some pro-hibition from him rejoining—is that the correct term?—there's no reason he can't take up some other similar work. Passenger liners and cargo ships need crew. Or he could become an instruc-tor for the sports he enjoyed so, or a ranger on some remote ski slope . . ."

Vasiht'h eyed him, his bemusement blurring the mindline's edges. "You want us to suggest to our client that he should cope with his feelings of confinement and disappointment by . . . switching careers."

"Not all problems arise from within," Jahir said. "Sometimes they are a result of a mismatch between the interior mind and the environment. If the environment can be addressed. . . ."

Vasiht'h made a face. "But how do we go about doing that? We don't even know why he's still here instead of hightailing it for the nearest Fleet recruitment center."

"I don't know," Jahir admitted. "But we have time to consider it."

"Time," Vasiht'h said, scowling at the door, "in which we hopefully won't have to deal with people camping outside our door, waiting to ambush us with baseless accusations."

"Allen Tiber is no doubt a busy man." Jahir picked up the data tablet to pull up the information on their next appointment. "He will have limited time to hound us."

"From your mouth to Her ear," Vasiht'h muttered.

CHAPTER 11

$\mathcal{J}$OYNER MAKESDO STARTED their session by explaining his Foundname. "It was a joke when I was younger," he said, sitting on their couch with his fingers threaded in his lap. "I was clumsy and not great at math, and I'd improvise a lot, or try to figure out workarounds for things I couldn't do the way they taught me. That usually worked out for me, so I kept at it. When I started my first job and we didn't have the resources we needed, I'd make a go at it anyway with whatever I could find . . ." He paused, ears sagging and a chagrined smile on his face. "Sometimes that went well and sometimes it exploded in my face. But my mother used to say that I was a wizard at making do with what I had, and it just sort of stuck." He paused and added, almost defensively, "It's not . . . you know. Some kind of statement that I'm not happy, or that I'm getting along because I don't think I deserve any better."

"Of course not," Jahir answered for them both.

"Anyway, Lennea said I could come here and take naps, and that they're the best naps in the world." He glanced at the folded blankets on the couch, and the pillow. "I admit it does look kind of nice in here. Though you could probably diffuse some essential oils or something. Or have flowers, flowers smell good."

"That is a nice idea," Vasiht'h said. "I thought about incense, but the dust makes some people sneeze."

"Incense is too specific anyway." At Vasiht'h's curious look, the Tam-illee finally released a hand to wave in a vague way. "You know. They're used for a lot of spiritual and religious ceremonies, and everyone's got a different incense, so you smell it and you think 'oh, that's not right.'"

/Perhaps we should hire him to decorate our permanent office,/ Jahir said, amused.

/I'm not making the mistake we made with Pieter this time,/ Vasiht'h answered sternly. /Let's make sure he didn't leave anything important off the form./ To Joyner, he said, "So what is it you do?"

"I'm a carpenter."

/Not an interior decorator, but right track, at least,/ Vasiht'h said, and Jahir's silent amusement tickled like the bubbles in carbonated lemonade. Which . . . sounded good. He might have to try that later. "That sounds interesting."

"Oh, it's great!" Joyner's other hand loosened in his lap. "For a while I worked for a big shop designing things meant to be machine-assembled, or genie-created. But I started out doing it by hand, and I'm back in a shop doing that now. I love it. And I love my family, too. And living here. It's all good."

"So . . . what can we help you with?" Vasiht'h asked.

"That's the thing." Joyner's ears sagged. "I feel like I'm so lucky, and yet I can't stop being anxious that it's all going to vanish. Like, the next time I breathe in, when I exhale, something awful will happen to make up for the years I spent happy."

Vasiht'h could sense Jahir's mind working through the link, grouping possible causes: organic ones, like diet and exercise and sleep problems, or historical ones, like a childhood example of someone losing something important. It bemused him, the speed at which his partner assembled the permutations. Pieter's dreams of leaping over obstacles on ski slopes came to mind, the ease and the exhilaration of competence.

"That's not unusual," Vasiht'h said. "Anxiety plagues a lot of people. Particularly people with good imaginations."

"I never thought of myself as having a good imagination," the

Tam-illee said with a frown.

"You design furniture," Jahir offered. "That requires the ability to imagine it, turn it in your mind, see it from multiple angles, and conceive of how people might use it."

"Or misuse it," Joyner said, chuckling. "The times I've thought 'no, if I do that someone will smack their shin into it when they turn away' or 'that corner's got some baby's bruised forehead written all over it' . . . !"

"Exactly," Vasiht'h said.

"And you will note," Jahir added, "that your ability to foresee negative outcomes is not always undesirable. That quality allows you to plan for the safe use of your designs."

Joyner's eyes were wide. "I never thought of it that way."

"The goal, then, is to keep it useful and learn to put it away when it's not," Vasiht'h said. "But I'm guessing you've been to other therapists before?"

"A few," Joyner admitted. "They taught me a lot of things. Some of them work, but I forget to do them and then they stop working."

"Like what?" Vasiht'h asked.

"Well, like not eating any trigger foods," the Tam-illee said, starting to tick them off on his fingers. "And not listening to music that depresses me, or has bad lyrics. Talking to friends. Getting enough physical contact with people I trust. Exercising regularly. Getting enough sleep, and sleeping at the same time every day." His smile was embarrassed. "When I do all those things, I'm almost not anxious at all. But that's a lot of work, you know. It's like I have to be an entirely different person to manage my anxiety."

"It can certainly feel that way," Vasiht'h agreed, sampling the rue in the mindline. /That certainly takes care of all the things we might have suggested./

/So it has./

"Which of these strategies worked best for you?" Jahir asked.

The foxine wrinkled his nose. "Honestly, the one I liked least. Exercise. I know it's good for me, but I've tried like six different things and they all bore me. I always find something I'd rather be doing. Or I get busy and it's the first thing I sacrifice to make up time. You know how that goes."

"And the second best?" Vasiht'h asked.

"Well . . ." Joyner drew out the word. "When I was exercising, I slept better. And that seemed to help a lot." His smile was lopsided. "That's why I said yes when Lennea told me about you all. Another therapist . . . I've seen enough therapists. I'm tired of talking about what I'm supposed to be doing. Being able to put my head down and get an hour of quality sleep sounds divine."

"By all means, then, lay your head down." Jahir rose. "We will leave you to compose yourself."

"Thanks. This means a lot to me!"

Vasiht'h chuckled. "You're paying for our help, alet. It's what we're here for."

Pulling the blanket over himself, Joyner said, "Sure, but it's never a bad thing to say thank you."

Outside in the foyer, Vasiht'h sat with his tail curled over his paws and chuckled.

"What amuses you?" Jahir asked.

"How often we know what's good for us, but we don't do it anyway," Vasiht'h said. "Why do you think that is?"

His partner looked up at the atrium ceiling. "I suppose there are as many answers as there are people."

"Do you really believe that?"

That inspired a longer pause. Through the mindline, Vasiht'h sensed his partner's mind at work, and it felt like . . . weaving? Something complex with a pattern, and a lot of touching, separating threads. "I believe there are as many permutations as there are individuals. But perhaps the roots of those reasons are narrower than that."

"What do you think Joyner's reason is?"

"I don't know that we know enough about him to guess," Jahir said. "But if we can find that out, perhaps we'll be able to advise him in a way that makes it easier for him to change."

"Maybe," Vasiht'h said, still finding the situation funny. "Or maybe he'll just keep coming to us for naps."

Jahir glanced down at him. "Would that satisfy you? To never serve any greater purpose than to offer a moment's respite in a busy week."

Because Jahir had asked, Vasiht'h sat on his glib reply and really thought about it. "It would be a lot more satisfying to wave a magic wand and help people resolve their problems obviously and immediately. But maybe that's a selfish desire? Because that's what I need out of this, maybe. Maybe what some of the people coming to us need isn't a fix. Or maybe the fix they need is some gradual thing we won't be able to see from the outside." He considered that possibility and nodded. "And that does make me uncomfortable. I want to be able to tell we're helping."

"It is not often given to us, to know these things."

Vasiht'h cocked his head, smiled up at him. "No, you don't get out of this with cryptic comments. We're therapists now, arii. If we don't help our clients, we shouldn't be in business."

"And yet, the uncertainty remains. There is no avoiding it. We serve at the pleasure of life—your Goddess—and that is all we might do."

Vasiht'h inhaled, let the breath out slowly, counting. "And yet, we're called to be responsible for ourselves and our decisions."

Something in the mindline then tasted bittersweet. Like salt on lips. And then Jahir smiled. "No one said the answers would be easy, nor that they would be given to us."

Vasiht'h snorted. "That must be why the manual I sent away for never came." He shook his head. "Let's see what Joyner MakesDo's dreams are like."

The Tam-illee was snoring contentedly on their couch when they entered the room. His dreams, when they looked, were a montage of normal concerns; nothing in them suggested some dire trauma, the resolution of which would inspire a miraculous remission of Joyner's anxiety. Naturally. Vasiht'h found himself smiling as he and Jahir soothed the most unsettled of the images from their client's dreams. He wondered if doing therapy constituted therapeutic intervention for himself as well as his clients and wasn't surprised to find Jahir studiously not noticing the idea.

On waking, Joyner yawned and peeped over the edge of the quilt at them, eyes bright. "That was the best sleep I've *ever had.*" He paused. "Well, maybe I slept better as a baby but I don't remember that." He grinned and sat up to stretch. "Fantastic!"

"We're glad you enjoyed it," Vasiht'h said, grinning. "And next time, we'll have some essential oils."

"Even better. You should try lavender. Or citrus. Or . . . hmm. You could have different ones at the start of the session, and have a new smell to wake people up? Like peppermint." He rubbed his nose. "I know someone who sells them. She sets up shop at the commons market every weekend—have you been to one of those?"

"No?" Vasiht'h said. "There's a market in the Garden District . . ."

Joyner waved a hand. "Tiny. Come to the one in the commons. It's on the university side of town. I'll send you the name of my friend, she'll set you up." Standing, he added, "I'm guessing my session is over? I could have stayed another hour! Can I do that? Schedule a two-hour session?"

"Yes?" Jahir said. "You may even wish to talk through part of it."

Joyner laughed. "Maybe! I'll be back next week. Thanks, aletsen."

After the Tam-illee left, Vasiht'h stripped the pillowcase from the pillow as Jahir took a fresh one from the cabinet. "So, what are you thinking?"

The Eldritch cocked his head. "Am I?"

"Very busily," Vasiht'h said. "But not a lot of thinking. A few thoughts, moving briskly? It feels like a little trickle of water."

Jahir chuckled softly. "That would be apt." He handed down the pillowcase and unfolded the new sheet set. "I am thinking there is at least one material suggestion we can make Joyner that no one has yet. Perhaps."

Vasiht'h paused. "Oh?"

"He should probably see someone about the snoring," Jahir said. "He cannot be sleeping well thus."

That struck Vasiht'h as hilarious, and sensing his partner's puzzlement he couldn't begin to articulate why. The practicality of it, maybe, coming from his dreamier Eldritch friend, when Vasiht'h thought of himself as the down-to-earth one. "I'm sure that affects his sleep quality, definitely. Every little bit?"

"Helps," Jahir replied, serene but still bemused.

"Do you think we become like our partners?" Vasiht'h asked Sehvi.

"In what context?" Sehvi asked.

Vasiht'h was preparing a marinade for the night's dinner, whisking citrus and thinking unavoidably of Joyner's essential oil suggestions. He took a deep whiff of his mixture and tried to imagine it in their office. "Well, do you think we inevitably start sharing traits. Like if someone's good with money, their partner starts picking it up from them?"

Sehvi rolled her eyes. "Do you ever think of anything besides money, ariihir?"

"It was the example that came to mind!"

"Find a better one."

He grimaced. "Fine. He's the mystical one, and I'm the practical one. I wonder if he'll start becoming more practical and I'll start going mystical?"

"Start," she repeated, droll. "The one brother among us who never, ever forgot to go to temple."

"That's different." Vasiht'h whisked harder. "The goddess is real."

"And your impractical friend," Sehvi continued, face leaning on her palm. "The one who found and arranged for your housing."

"He was the one who was here!"

"And found your first client. And scouted all the offices for rent." She lifted her brows. "That impractical friend?"

"He doesn't know how money works here," Vasiht'h said.

"I think you're mistaking 'enigmatic and inexperienced' for 'impractical,'" Sehvi said. "For all you know, he's some kind of Eldritch business magnate and that's why he's so rich."

The idea was so absurd Vasiht'h stopped working on the marinade and pressed his hand to his nose to keep from snickering out loud. "I am completely sure he's not a tycoon."

"What I'm sure of is that you have just as idealized a picture of an Eldritch in your head as Rexina Regina," Sehvi said. "And that's why I sent you that book."

Vasiht'h's ears flicked back. "You did *not* send me that book to make a point about my preconceptions about Eldritch. You sent that book to torment me."

"I sent that book to make you laugh! And also to make you think about your preconceptions about Eldritch." She shook her head. "It's not just you, ariihir. We all have romantic concepts of love that get bruised up when we finally stumble into a relationship we want to keep."

"And you know so much about this from the position of your venerable years and experience," Vasiht'h said dryly.

"No," Sehvi agreed. "I know this from the position of 'nearly youngest sister in a long chain of sisters, all of whom talk incessantly about what's irritating them.' You did read the comments we left in the margins, didn't you?"

"Only up to the pregnancy part," Vasiht'h admitted. "I quit there. Because it was *ridiculous*."

Sehvi giggled. "I know. Wasn't it great?"

Vasiht'h shook his head. "Your idea of great is freakish, ariishir."

"What can I say. Bizarre genetic sports interest me." She tapped her finger on her desk. "But I'm serious about the preconceptions. You have ideas about how partnership should work from seeing how our family does it. But you've gone and harnessed yourself to someone whose family is completely different. And you don't even know how! So you can't stumble along assuming it's going to work out. You're going to have to talk about it."

"This is the part where I know a little more about the situation than you do." At her skeptical look, he pointed the whisk at her. "Eldritch? Don't talk? Ever?"

"All the more reason to approach this with an open mind! An opener one anyway."

"Opener isn't even a real word."

"But you knew what I meant." She watched him, sighed. "I don't mean to poke you—"

"Much," Vasiht'h muttered.

"It's just that I can tell you're worried and I want to help!" She grinned. "I guess when you find the perfect someone for yourself you suddenly want everyone else to find their perfect someone."

"I've done the finding," Vasiht'h said. "Now I just have to worry about . . ."

"What?" she asked when he didn't finish.

To say 'the keeping' felt histrionic. He didn't believe he would lose Jahir. Not with a mindline to connect them.

Could he?

Shaking himself, Vasiht'h said, "About making it work for us both. That's all."

"That's a lot," Sehvi pointed out.

He sighed. "I noticed."

After they'd signed off, Vasiht'h wondered at his own fears. He and Jahir had gone through so much to get to where they were, and it had felt . . . it had felt like he'd finally made it. Why was he finding all these reasons to fret all of a sudden? Was that just part of moving through life? That you thought you had things figured out, only to discover another challenge waiting for you on the other side? Pieter and Ametia would probably find that exhilarating, he thought. Routine bored them—maybe that's why Ametia couldn't give up her crusades, or find some better way to handle them.

Or possibly that was unfair. If she truly did care about discrimination against humans, how could she rest while it still existed? Even if she didn't accomplish as much as she hoped?

Whatever the case, Vasiht'h was not a thrill-seeker. He found himself far more in sympathy with Lennea. A calm life, filled with productive work, a large family, and the small pleasures of the world, like good food and soft pillows, was all he wanted.

With the meat in the marinade, Vasiht'h considered the rest of the afternoon. Walk? Read more of the novel? Garden? Weed-pulling sounded soothing, but he felt he owed it to Sehvi to finish the book, particularly after getting whacked in the face with the reason she'd sent it. His preconceptions about Eldritch. He huffed to himself. He took his data tablet back to the roof garden with a glass of mint lemonade and settled in to read. The newest chapter began with an extended celebration of the miraculous conception of the child (on which Vasiht'h's sisters had much to say in the marginalia, all of it far more engaging than the text).

> **KOVRAH:** This is the most unbelievable part yet. They're not arguing how to decorate the nursery.
> **SARDA:** They just had a cross-species baby and *this* is the most unbelievable part?
> **KOVRAH:** You weren't around when Tek and his wife were expecting their first. You wouldn't believe the drama.
> **TAVYI:** I'm still waiting for the big reveal about one of them being a shapeshifter.
> **SEHVI:** You're going to be waiting a lonnnnng time.
> **TAVYI:** There's not much left in the book?
> **SEHVI:** There are sequels.
> **SEHVI:** So many sequels.
> **NINEH:** What
> **MANDARA:** what
> **KAVILA:** What??
> **TAVYI:** YAY
> **KOVRAH:** Wait, seriously? YAY?
> **TAVYI:** Aww, you have to admit they're kind of a cute couple. Plus, Eldritch babies with fox ears?
> **NINEH:** If it's not Eldritch on the right side and Tam-illee on the left, I am quitting this book.
> **MANDARA:** You can never quit this book. This book will

haunt you for the rest of your days.

Vasiht'h hit his forehead with the data tablet. Gently.

CHAPTER 12

SEVERAL DAYS LATER, THEY ARRIVED to their office to find a woman with a basket. Jahir had never seen a Pelted as fluffy as this Karaka'An, whose tawny fur had been shaved into decorative patterns on her arms like a rug with multiple height piles. The hair on her head, a lighter, buttery yellow, fell in a curtain of braids, all different thicknesses, tied off with bangles and beads in brass and steel and silver. She wore rings in similar hues on all her fingers, and on the toes she left unshod as was customary with the digitigrade Pelted.

Her brown eyes, studying them, were incisive and curious. But Jahir saw no malice in them.

"I hope you don't have an appointment this early," the woman said.

/Another client?/ Vasiht'h wondered, puzzled.

"You find us free, alet," Jahir said. "What can we do for you?"

She grinned and shifted the basket onto her free arm so she could thrust out a palm. "You can tell me all about yourselves, because I am obviously so behind on the gossip. I'm Minette Dashenby. I practice over by the university. And you all are the new therapists!"

"You're not here to tell us to get out of town, are you?"

Vasiht'h asked.

She rolled her eyes. "No. That's more Allen's bailiwick."

"Good." Vasiht'h covered her palm. "I think one threat was enough."

/Coming it a bit too strong, perhaps,/ Jahir murmured.

/It was a threat and I'm not going to soft-pedal it. You shouldn't either./

The musical metaphor startled him, coming from a partner who'd never shown much interest in it.

"He can be a little overbearing. I wouldn't let it bother you. Oh, here . . ." She offered the basket. "A little welcome gift. Did I ask your names yet? What are your names?"

The mindline was growing lighter now, like sun breaking through dissolving clouds. "Thank you. I'm Vasiht'h, this is my partner Jahir. Come on in, I don't think we have anyone for another hour . . . ?" Vasiht'h looked toward Jahir quizzically.

"An hour and a half," he agreed, and opened the door for them both.

The woman stepped inside and clapped her hands. "Look at this! It's so cozy! I didn't think you'd be able to redeem the cold 'tower of glass' motif outside, but this is fantastic." She fingered the quilt. "Very homey. Do you mind if I . . ."

"Please," Jahir said.

She plopped onto the couch and looked around, grinning. "No wonder Allen was so incensed. Did he accuse you of running a massage parlor? Those have bad reputations on Terra."

/I'm . . . getting the feeling we've fallen into the middle of something./

Jahir suppressed the urge to look at his friend and settled for sharing the feeling that would have inspired his wry smile.

/Right./ "So, alet," Vasiht'h said. "You're one of Veta's xenotherapists?"

"That's right. You've met the other two, so I figured I'd complete the set."

"The other . . . two?" Vasiht'h asked.

"Sure. Allen, of course. And Helga? Who's been sending you

her clients? She wants to retire, you know." Dashenby fluffed the pillow beside her arm and leaned on it. Seeing their expressions, her mouth creased into a grin and she pressed her hand to it. Her eyes were merry. "No, don't even say it. She hasn't told you."

"No," Vasiht'h said.

"But we are not surprised," Jahir said.

/We're not?/

/Are you? Truly?/

The mindline grew empty with the anticipation of the answer as Vasiht'h thought about it. Then he said, /No . . . no, I guess I'm not either./

"She's old," Dashenby said, unconcerned. "A grandmother several times over . . . actually, a great-grandmother by now, I think. I'm not surprised she kept it to herself. She's fond of teaching moments." She grinned. "And when she finds out I've spoiled this one you can tell her it's my fault."

"We shall do so," Jahir promised. "Was she then the owner of the property that stands vacant now?"

"The Healer's Knot? You found it, did you?" She nodded. "She used to work there with her eldest daughter and son-in-law. A doctor and a physical therapist, respectively. It was great for patients, a real family business, and you felt like you were home, you know? But her daughter moved away, back to Hinichitii. After that, she rented out the extra space to a couple of other people, but it was never the same and eventually she let it go vacant. She's been talking about retirement for a while now, but she hasn't committed to it." Her grin returned. "Looks like she's changed her mind."

"Should we even ask," Vasiht'h said.

"It was always a question of where her clients should end up. There's not that many of us, you know? And here you are. I bet if I looked at your client list, I'd find all her patients on it."

"I thought they were Tiber's," Vasiht'h said.

"Oh, sure, they're his for now, because where were they going to go on her reduced schedule?" Dashenby propped her cheek up in her palm, smiling at them both. "It was him or me, and I don't like working long hours. I have a family; getting home in time to read my kits bedtime stories isn't my idea of spending enough time with them. Allen's divorced and has three times the energy of mortal men. If he wants to work until midnight, that's his business, and I thank him for it. Keeps me from having to."

/*Great. So he really is crazy.*/

Jahir didn't answer, tasting the reluctant compassion threaded through the acerbic observation. Tiber's behavioral pattern was all too obvious to them both—and to Dashenby too, if he read her expression right. She spoke of Tiber with the complacency of long acquaintance, and without derision.

/*You see it too,*/ Vasiht'h thought with a sigh.

/*Yes. Which begs the question . . . if Tiber can sustain a collegial relationship with other therapists, jealousy may not be the driver of his animosity toward us.*/

/*I still say he was threatening.*/

/*But discovering why is important.*/

Dashenby, unlike some of the other people they'd met, did not seem to notice them conversing in silence. She was too busy examining the particulars of their office, admiring the afghan, twisting to look at the walls. "You should put something on those. If you stay here."

"We will hope to be able to do so," Jahir said. "If our residency applications are approved."

"Are you worried about that? With Helga retiring and starting to send you her clients?" Dashenby laughed. "I wouldn't. Unless you mess things up. Which brings me to my next question . . . why *is* Allen so convinced you two are hacks? He told us both that you were dangerous and said something about . . ." She waved a hand. "Mind powers and vulnerable clients and not respecting the client/therapist boundaries."

Vasiht'h strangled a noise.

When Dashenby looked toward him, startled, Jahir said, "Please pardon my partner. The accusations Tiber made against us are considered serious crimes on his homeworld, and slanderous."

"Goodness." The Karaka'An sat up straighter. "I'm sure he didn't realize it. He's usually very letter-of-the-lawish. What . . . can I ask?"

"We are bonded espers," Jahir said. "And we work primarily through observation of and action on dreams."

Her eyes widened. "Goddess dancing. Well. Yes. I can see why that might have gotten him upset." She cocked her head. "That's . . . a real thing? Going into people's minds? They train that somewhere?"

"We don't do it without consent," Vasiht'h said. "And where I come from, it's real. If not formalized."

/Is it?/ Jahir asked, startled.

/It must be,/ Vasiht'h answered. /Because no one thinks anything of it, and there are Glaseah therapists on Anseahla. We do half our communicating mind-to-mind! It's not something we think of as . . . as special. Worthy of notice./

/If you can find evidence of it, that would help us with our naysayers./

/Then I will./

"We graduated from Seersana University's medical program," Jahir said. "And we are properly licensed."

"And we only do this with consent," Vasiht'h continued, the fur on his back starting to bristle. "To do otherwise would be wrong."

"Huh." The Karaka'An frowned a little. "I don't know anything about esper law, or etiquette or . . . well, I don't know anything. Ordinarily, I'd be leaning more toward Allen's side of the debate. Not because I think you all are evil people, but . . . what we do with people, it requires trust. And I can't imagine trusting anyone to go directly into my head that way."

Before Vasiht'h could explode, Jahir said, "And yet . . . ?"

"But Helga trusts you. And from what I've heard, you not only have repeat clients, you have referrals." The Karaka'An played with one of the rings at the end of her braids. "That could mean something sinister, I guess. But Helga's a lot harder to fool than I am." She grinned again. "And after ten years in practice,

I've gotten pretty hard to fool. I've seen charmers swan into my office and make promises and confess to their sins and not mean a word of it." Her scrutiny then was not at all frivolous, and Jahir wondered at the experience in her eyes—how many of those glib liars had come through her hands and scarred her. "You two don't have the polish of the sociopaths I've known."

"Thanks?" Vasiht'h folded his arms.

She burst out laughing. "Sorry, that sounded awful. But you have to look at it from our point of view! What do non-espers know about what it's like to be you? All I think of is 'mind control' and 'brainwashing'. I'm sure you think something different. You must."

/It is not her intention to insult,/ Jahir said to the seething he sensed through the mindline.

/I know. That's what makes it harder to listen to./

/Perhaps this is the form that the discrimination against humans takes, in Ametia's experience./

/Self-justified ignorance?/

"Rest assured," Jahir said, "we have nothing but our clients' well-being in mind when we engage with them. And if you or Doctor Tiber, at any time, would like to experience our techniques yourselves, you are welcome to try them."

/Really??/

/There is only one path out of ignorance, arii./

"Oh!" Dashenby sat up again. "That's quite an offer."

"Unless you think we're brainwashers," Vasiht'h said. "Then it's a threat. Until we're done with you, and you agree that we're the best thing since red velvet cake."

She'd been looking steadily more flustered until the end of the sentence, at which point she laughed. "Red velvet cake! Oh my, have you had the red velvet scones yet? You've found the scone place, right?"

"We have," Jahir said.

She grinned. "Wait until they have the red velvet scones. You will die for joy." She patted her hands together, then let them drop to her knees. "I really am sorry. I can tell I've offended you, and it wasn't my intention at all."

"We understand. What we do is . . . unusual."

"I'll say." She stood, straightening her tunic and tossing her braids over her shoulders. "I've taken up a lot of your time, though. I won't keep you any longer."

"You'll consider our offer?" Jahir asked. "And tell Doctor Tiber?"

"I will." She grinned. "I wouldn't miss the chance, just to see the look on his face." She paused, ears sagging. "Ah . . . that's probably not very flattering, is it. When you've known Allen as long as I have, you'll understand."

"We hope to have the opportunity."

Jahir shut the door behind her and turned to face his partner. And waited.

"For a therapist," Vasiht'h said finally, "she's not very good with people."

"That assumes she came here to befriend us," Jahir said. That caused the Glaseah to lift his head and meet his eyes, and the mindline felt thick with tension, like the air before rain. Purposefully casual, he walked to the basket and set it on the desk, starting on the ribbon. "That felt more like a reconnaissance. Would you not say so?"

The storm pressure eased. Sitting up to watch, Vasiht'h said, "You think she's more Tiber's friend than Helga's?"

"I think she thinks of them both as peers, and that her relationship with Tiber is not antagonistic. If she did not value his professional opinion, she would not have come here to . . ."

"Feel us out." Vasiht'h blew out a breath gustily. "That does make sense. She already had misgivings, but she wanted to see for herself."

"And give us a chance," Jahir said, pushing the tissue paper down. "She did not seem evil to me, arii."

"People aren't evil," Vasiht'h said. "Their personalities just interact badly with other people's."

Jahir glanced at him. It did not seem the time to profess to belief in true evil. If the time came that they needs must confront it . . . perhaps then. But he doubted Vasiht'h, raised in the cradle of civilization, could truly believe what he had never seen. Not really. He studied the contents of the basket. "She is at least generous."

"Shavings for hot chocolate," Vasiht'h said, going through it now with him. "Brandied peaches? That sounds deadly. Oh, look, it's a loaf of that bread from that baker at our market."

"The one you thought too precious to eat?"

Vasiht'h chuffed a laugh. "Yes." And then he was laughing in earnest, and Jahir grinned back at him.

"Do you feel better now?"

Wiping his eyes, Vasiht'h said, "A little." Looking up at Jahir, he added, "You knew about Helga."

"No," Jahir said, but the pattern was beautiful and it had been coalescing for some time. *You are a novel thing in the world, alet, and a novel thing in mine, which is even more astonishing.* He smiled at the memory. "But I suspected."

"I'm guessing you know where this office of hers is, then."

"I do, yes." Jahir glanced at him. "Shall I take you to it?"

"Yes," Vasiht'h said. "But after our clients. Ametia's about due."

Following their work day, thus, Jahir led his partner through the commons to the location of Helga's former practice.

For a long time, Vasiht'h stood beside him, fur ruffling in the breeze and sun glossing his coat. The mindline felt strange between them: taut, but empty. Calm. Jahir couldn't read it, wondered if he would learn to interpret his friend's moods better in the years before them.

"It's a good location," Vasiht'h said at last. "I wonder if she'll rent it to us?"

"Somehow I doubt we will be allowed before our trial is complete."

That inspired the Glaseah to look up at him sharply.

"There is no better explanation for her behavior," Jahir said.

"She is testing us, and this will be our prize if we please her."

Vasiht'h blew out a breath. "Great. Another Ravanelle."

"Ravanelle did not know how to judge us," Jahir said. "I am certain Helga already knows the standards she will use to assess our suitability to take up her mantle."

The Glaseah folded his arms, considering the property. "I guess that's her right."

"She has to believe she is leaving her clients in good hands." Jahir began walking up the street. "No doubt discovering that we are being tested is part of the test."

Vasiht'h chuckled, trotted after him until he was walking abreast of the Eldritch. "I guess that means next time we see her, we'll have to tell her we know. Or . . . would that be too Pelted an assumption?" Cocking his head, he peered up at Jahir. "Would you ordinarily leave her in the dark?"

Would he? Did he need to ask? Where he'd come from, knowledge was power. One did not casually divulge the extent of it. "I would perhaps ask myself what there was to be gained by either course. Silence or confession."

"Logical." Vasiht'h shook his head. "I can't decide whether I'm amused or exasperated. I thought we'd given up tests when we graduated."

Jahir smiled a little. "You should know better."

"Should I?" A surge of curiosity, stinging the mindline like nettles.

The secrecy of his people was based in their belief that knowledge was power. And yet, how much was there to be gained by sharing? With this one particular person? And in the end, this was less about his upbringing and more a personal belief. So he said, "Life is a neverending series of tests, arii. By our successes and failures, we know ourselves."

"That sounds exhausting," Vasiht'h said. "Don't you already know who you are without having to prove it over and over?"

"Are you the same person today you were a year ago?"

"I . . . yes. Mostly." Vasiht'h grimaced. "I mean, I hope I've matured a little. But who I am at heart . . . that doesn't change.

I'll always be . . . me."

"And you know yourself entirely?"

They walked all the way back to the center of the commons before Vasiht'h answered that one. "I know the important parts. I hope. Do you want ice cream?"

"I always want ice cream," Jahir said gravely. "But perhaps I should have a real meal first."

Vasiht'h grinned. "Good point. Dinner, then ice cream."

Jahir let his friend steer the conversation away from the unease in his own mind. They had time enough to wear at each other's anxieties and pains. Little by little.

CHAPTER 13

SLEEP WAS THE FURTHEST THING from Lennea's mind when she arrived for her next appointment. She took to pacing instead, like Ametia, but utterly unlike her. The Harat-Shar swept to and fro in their office, striding as if over the battle-fields of her dreams; Lennea darted and paused and drifted, then halted abruptly. They reflected her disordered thoughts, for she had been talking for several minutes and still Jahir was uncertain what had distressed her.

/She's talking about everything but the problem,/ Vasiht'h guessed.

/A natural reaction./

/But not helpful!/ Aloud, Vasiht'h said, "Lennea? Would you like a cup of tea?"

"A . . . a cup of . . ." She stopped walking, tail twitching behind her. And sighed. "Do you have anything stronger?"

"Hot chocolate?" Jahir offered.

She blinked at him, then burbled a laugh, touching her mouth. "I was thinking of alcohol! But come to think of it, choco-late is the top of the top when it comes to medicating anxiety, isn't it."

"I would not go so far," Jahir said. "But you may find a denser, fattier drink more engaging. You have a great deal of energy."

"I do." She exhaled gustily, shoulders drooping. Covering her eyes, she moaned, "It's been such an awful week, and it's never going to get less awful again."

"Definitely chocolate," Vasiht'h said.

She parted her fingers around her eyes to peer at the Glaseah, let them slide off her face and laughed. "All right. Chocolate."

Tea they could make. Hot chocolate had to be ordered, or fetched. As Jahir went forth to that task, he murmured, /*Having a kitchen adjacent to our office would be useful.*/

A wistful reply, accompanied by the image of Helga's abandoned office. /*I bet she has a kitchen in there.*/

/*One step at a time.*/

/*As usual.*/

They reconvened over little cups of rich cocoa augmented by melted chocolate and thick froths of cream whipped with flavors—mint for Lennea, cinnamon for Vasiht'h and honey for Jahir. "So this thing . . . I . . . my news." Lennea's ears drooped. "I got promoted."

"That does not please you." Jahir said it not because he was surprised, but to prompt the dialogue.

"No! I didn't ask to be principal. I don't *want* to be principal. I don't care that I'm good at the paperwork. The paperwork is the easy part. The hard part is all the . . . the people parts. The soothing angry parents, and talking donors into donations, and keeping all the teachers talking to one another when half of them don't like each other . . ." She sighed. "But no one else could do it. We did a job search, but we didn't have any takers." She stared glumly at her cup before meeting their eyes. "You may not know this, but starbases are actually pretty small communities. We don't normally have loose people wandering around, waiting to fill jobs. Or if we do, they're young people who were born here and are training up into starter positions. They don't have the experience or seniority for positions of this kind of responsibility."

"We know a little bit about it," Vasiht'h muttered.

"Surely if there is a vacancy, someone will be permitted to

immigrate to fill it?" Jahir asked.

"We just started a broader job search, yes," Lennea replied. "But our former principal hasn't left the base, so we have to justify her replacement rigorously to get them in. And everyone wants me for the position! I told them I'd be acting principal until they found someone official, but it's very comfortable for everyone to just leave me there."

"Except you," Vasiht'h pointed out.

"Except me." She sighed. "But I'm not so good at sticking up for myself. The job has to be done, and the kids need someone to do it. I don't *want* it to be me, but if there's no one else, what will happen then?"

"What would happen if you quit?" Vasiht'h asked.

"I couldn't do that!"

"Hypothetically," Jahir said.

"I guess they'd have to have someone else fill in, who wasn't as good at it," Lennea said slowly. "But . . . I wouldn't be able to be a teacher anymore, not there. If I left, I'd be letting them down, and they wouldn't forget that."

"That seems unfair," Vasiht'h said. "Punishing you for not being capable of a job you didn't even sign up for."

"That's the problem! I am capable. And for anyone else, it would have been a great thing, to be promoted. The money. The prestige. All of that." She shook her head. "And they wouldn't punish me on purpose. It would just be . . . this thing in the backs of their heads. They'd remember me as the one who couldn't handle it. They wouldn't trust me anymore." She sighed. "The only way I can get out of this without losing my job as a teacher is to find a replacement who *wants* to be principal. Then I can go back to doing what I love, and I'll be the hero who got them what they needed and then gracefully stepped down to let this new person have their chance."

/She's not wrong,/ Jahir murmured, chagrined.

/No. And she's really smart for noticing all those undercurrents./

/We have always noted her sensitivity. This should be no surprise to us./

/No,/ Vasiht'h agreed morosely. /*I just wish we could help her fix it.*/

"When you entered," Jahir said, "you said your weeks were never going to get less awful. But it appears that there is an exit for you from this situation, yes? If the school succeeds in finding a new principal. They are advertising?"

"For now," Lennea muttered.

"Are they likely to stop?" Vasiht'h asked, ears sagging.

"No! No, I guess that's unfair. At least, I hope they won't." She sighed and rubbed her eyes. "I'm just . . . I'm really upset. This was my first week at my 'new' job and I hated every minute of it except the paperwork and even that was less engaging than my teaching work. And I don't know the first thing about trying to find some person to replace me if the original job search didn't turn anything up." She looked at them, pained. "What do I do? How do I cope with this? Sleeping it off doesn't seem enough . . . !" Tilting her cup to look at the dregs, she added, "A problem that sleep or chocolate can't solve . . . I didn't know those existed."

"You can still make jokes," Vasiht'h said. "That's a good sign."

She smiled weakly. "I guess you're right."

"Let us take apart your issues with this temporary position one by one," Jahir said. "And see if we cannot find coping mechanisms that will help you."

"All right." She looked into her cup again and added, "This was really good. I don't suppose we can have another?"

/*Your turn this time?*/ Jahir asked.

/*I'm on it.*/

Vasiht'h brought back scones, fruit, cheese, and the hot chocolate, and over this repast they separated all of Lennea's challenges and discussed options for minimizing their effect on her. It was a poor bandage over the true wound, though, which was that she was unsuited for the work no matter her competence at its most basic aspects. Watching her depart, Jahir said, "A regrettable situation."

"Very," Vasiht'h said, cleaning up the table. "Poor woman. They're taking advantage of her inability to say no."

"Perhaps this incident will teach her to do so?"

Vasiht'h lifted his head, frowned. "I doubt it. Lennea wants to be helpful and make everyone happy. That's not a bad thing. We can teach her to say 'no' more often, but if she values harmony and peace more than she values her own discomfort, she's still going to default to saying 'yes.' And in a situation like this, where everyone's depending on her?" He shook his head.

"A strange viewpoint for therapists," Jahir murmured.

"Is it? We're not here to turn people into something they won't recognize or like. We're just here to help them deal with their problems and challenges better. In the specific way that works best for them. Ametia's never going to deal with problems the way Lennea does."

That comment set a reaction chaining up his spine, like a moving series of static shocks. The strength of it seized his thoughts so completely his partner looked up abruptly. "Arii?"

"Nothing," Jahir murmured.

"That wasn't nothing!"

"Nothing . . . yet."

That was all Vasiht'h got out of him, too. Pieter came after Lennea, and dropped to sleep for another of his adventures; watching them, Vasiht'h wondered when they were going to tell him maybe he should go back to Fleet. He wondered when they were going to tell Helga they knew about her machinations. He wondered when they were going to tell Tiber to stick his nose in someone else's business.

He wondered why they were waiting. They wandered to the commons market and bought essential oils, as suggested by Joyner; they saw Ametia and their other clients. They ate dinner and lunch and ice cream and breakfast, took long walks, left one another alone when they needed time apart. Vasiht'h worked in the garden, talked with his neighbors, chatted with Sehvi about her wedding, visited the siv't; Jahir slipped in and out of the warp of his days like a weft thread, steady and dependable without ever becoming less mysterious. They lived a life that would have contented Vasiht'h at any other time, except that everything looked settled but nothing was.

"... and it's driving me crazy!" he finished.

Hector mmmed over their lemonades. Vasiht'h had brought the drinks; his neighbor supplied the food at what had become a weekly chat on Hector's porch. The elderly man seemed to enjoy listening; he reminded Vasiht'h a little of his grandfather, who'd also had the habit of bright-eyed interest and pithy commentary. "It's just what my father always used to tell me."

"What's that?" Vasiht'h asked.

"It isn't the mountain ahead that wears you down, it's the stone in your shoe."

Vasiht'h blinked, then chuckled, rueful. "I guess it does sound small, doesn't it."

"The small things grind you down, if you're not careful." Hector resumed setting stitches in his latest creation.

"You don't seem very ground down by anything." Vasiht'h folded his arms on the table, watching. "What's your secret, alet?"

Hector grinned. "My secret? To find the funny part of everything."

"Oh?"

"Like, say, this woman who's secretly a xenotherapist and pretending not to be while sending you all her clients? As if you're one of her grandkids who thinks he's making breakfast in bed for her while all along all the ingredients have been lined up on the counter and all the tools put on shelves in easy reach?" Hector chortled. "Can you imagine how much fun she's having?"

"Watching us be confused?" Vasiht'h said, ears splaying.

"Watching you succeed!" Hector glanced up at him, tufted brows rising. "What else? That's what we want out of people we're helping. We want them to do well. It's a pleasure when they exceed our expectations."

Vasiht'h frowned. "You think we're doing that? Exceeding her expectations?"

"Good question. I don't know." He laughed. "If I ever meet

her, I'll ask her."

Canting his head, Vasiht'h said, "Promise?"

Hector eyed him, tugging the needle through the fabric.

"Just asking . . ."

The man guffawed. "I doubt that." And shook his head, amused. "All right, then, I promise."

"Great," Vasiht'h said, surprised to discover he meant it. He grinned. "I hope you like home cooking."

Two days later, Vasiht'h set out four place settings instead of two and sent Jahir a message to bring back extra groceries. When the Eldritch returned with his shopping bags, the query preceded him in the mindline, a bemused fog. "I invited our neighbor," he told Jahir. "He's a widower."

"Ah, the quilt-maker."

"I thought he and Helga might enjoy each other's company," Vasiht'h said innocently, taking one of the bags. He ignored the stern look, feeling it just fine through their link. Setting the bag on the counter, he added, "Trust me."

"I do," Jahir said simply.

The ease of it flustered Vasiht'h, as it always did . . . that he might have earned the trust of a member of this rare and reclusive race, and this particular member. Who was so much everything. Not an angel, like what's-her-name from his novel, and not a hero chiseled into stone, but something finer and realer. More real? His friend. His *best* friend. Setting the bread in the warmer, he said, "It'll be great."

And it was. Helga arrived first, settling in with her preprandial tea and teasing them both about this or that. Hector came by ten minutes later, and to Vasiht'h's delight he was wearing a carnation in his buttonhole. The two of them sized one another up, and as Vasiht'h expected, grinned at each other with similar expressions of mischief. After that, dinner rolled along, with both Hinichi and human trading amusing stories and bantering.

/Matchmaking?/ Jahir asked when they were clearing away

the plates for the dessert course.

/I think so,/ Vasiht'h said, surprised to discover it was true. Some part of him had known they'd like one another. /Why be alone after your spouse's passed away if you can find company again?/

/Wise,/ Jahir murmured, with a hint of that autumn-wind softness Vasiht'h associated with his acceptance of what life would be like for him in the Alliance. It dissipated when Vasiht'h sent him a twinkle of stars to decorate the sky for that wind. His friend smiled at him over the coffee pot.

"So," Hector said as Vasiht'h set out the flan. "Helga-alet. You've known these youngsters a bit longer than me, I think."

"Since they got here," Helga said agreeably, leaning back with her hands on her now distended belly.

"And have they done well by your lights?" Hector asked. Too innocently, maybe, because Helga rotated one ear slowly toward him.

"I think they're doing fine," she said.

"Oh, come on. They just fed you a meal fit for a queen."

"And flan," Vasiht'h said.

"And flan!"

"Flan is special," Helga admitted, staring up at the ceiling. "But do they grind their own coffee beans?"

"It would be easier to do so in an apartment with a better kitchen," Jahir said.

Vasiht'h sat on his sudden laugh. /You did not say that out loud!/

/She wishes to play with us, in a kind way. It is only polite to join the game./

Helga thought so too, apparently, because she was watching them with a smirk. "A better kitchen, is that it?"

"We do like to cook," Vasiht'h said.

She guffawed. "Let's have this flan, then."

After dessert, Hector took his leave—"Quilts to be finished before the weekend, I'm afraid,"—leaving them with their . . . mentor? Proctor? Self-appointed foster grandmother? Hector had been right. There was an element of humor to all of this, and resting his cheek on his fist and watching the Hinichi drink the last of her coffee, Vasiht'h could finally see it.

/I'm glad it no longer irritates you./

/Me too./

"So, you figured me out, mmm?" Helga asked.

"We have, yes," Jahir said.

Vasiht'h nodded wisely. "We think he's your type."

She'd been about to speak but this comment made the words stop on her tongue. Incredulous she stared at him. "My . . . type?"

"Oh yes," Vasiht'h said. "And we were right! You two liked each other." He grinned. "Don't worry, we'll invite him back so you can keep seeing if he suits you. We know you like to test people out for a while."

Helga's eyes widened, and then she let out a peal of laughter. She laughed until her shoulders shook and her eyes ran and she started squeaking for breath.

/Should we . . ./

Jahir sipped his coffee, eyes lowered. /Let her finish. Laughter is good for the spirit./

Wiping her eyes, Helga pointed at Vasiht'h. "You . . . you are . . . I . . . I deserved that. Possibly." She snorted, exhaled. Snickered. "Oh, that was good. I haven't had a belly laugh like that in ages."

"I take it we can invite him back?" Vasiht'h asked.

She grinned, pushing back from the table and standing. "You do that, young man. I'll see if he suits me. But if things go as well as they did today, I don't think it'll take long." She waggled her brows. "If you know what I mean."

"I think we do," Jahir said.

After she'd gone, they commenced with clean-up. Vasiht'h couldn't help the smug satisfaction that leaked through the mindline. "That went well."

"Do you feel better?" Jahir asked, putting away the plates.

Did he? Vasiht'h chuckled. Did he have to ask? "I do."

CHAPTER 14

PIETER'S DREAM OF THE EVA emergency returned three months into their therapy, and after weeks of hunting with him through jungles and deserts, jumping out of airplanes or off canyon cliffs, and playing innumerable team sports that often resulted in bloody injuries, Jahir was grateful to see it. But also curious. Hanging with Vasiht'h off to one side while their client drifted, staring into the infinite abyss, he said, /Why now?/

/Maybe he's done with us?/

/This is the most genuine expression of his longing,/ Jahir said. /His incompleteness./

Vasiht'h shivered. /That's . . . an extreme way of putting it./

/Do you disagree?/

The Glaseah was silent for a long time, bearing witness with him. /No./

When Pieter woke, Jahir handed him a cup of coffee. The man nodded his thanks and drank.

"There is a question I wish to ask, alet. If you are willing," Jahir said.

"Sure."

"When you left Fleet . . . was it that you retired?"

"Retired? No. I could have, I guess." Pieter frowned over the cup, eyes losing their focus. "But no, I didn't. I applied for a hardship discharge, since I was my children's only surviving parent. The Pelted grant those a lot easier than humans do, so it wasn't difficult."

"Discharge," Vasiht'h said. "That means . . . you're done?"

"I'm not, no," Pieter answered. "Since I wasn't discharged dishonorably. I could re-enlist."

/He's not done, is he,/ Jahir murmured.

/You were right about this,/ Vasiht'h said. Aloud, he said, "So, why don't you?"

"Re-enlist?"

"Yes?" Vasiht'h asked. "Since you could?"

"Because . . ." He stopped. He stopped, and didn't speak again for a while, frowning into his coffee.

Not angry, Jahir thought. Confused, perhaps. "Because?"

"I . . . don't know. I never thought of it as an option. But . . . it is. Isn't it." Pieter looked up at him.

"You're not too old to go back?" Vasiht'h asked.

"No." Pieter put the mug down. "No, I'm not."

"So nothing prevents you from this course of action?" Jahir asked.

"My kids," he muttered. "They're already worried about me."

"They might worry *less* about you if you're not off doing extreme sports," Vasiht'h said. "Fleet's a job, after all. They're going to think of it as something structured and expected."

"You will have companions to watch your back," Jahir added, quiet. "That is certainly safer than to be alone."

Pieter looked at him suddenly.

"They want you to be happy," Vasiht'h said. "You miss your job, alet. If you went back to it, you wouldn't miss it anymore."

"And you would no longer strive to fill that void with other, less meaningful exercises," Jahir finished.

Their client didn't answer immediately. They let that silence sit. At last, Pieter said, "I want to say something. Like. 'I never thought of going back because my wife died, and she was sad that I was often away so much.' Or 'I feel like being happy again after she died by going back would be a betrayal of her memory.' Like I owe it to her to feel grief. But . . . I don't. Feel any of those things. I just don't know why I never woke up and thought of it."

"You got into a routine," Vasiht'h suggested. "This was your new life. Your new life was raising your kits."

"But that phase of your life has ended," Jahir said. "Perhaps the transition was so gradual you did not note it, and so did not think of its implications for your own life."

"I didn't," he murmured. "I didn't at all. This was . . . just the thing I did. I kept doing it until it was done."

"And now that it is," Jahir said, "you may choose a new focus for your life."

"You maybe better," Vasiht'h added. "Because now that they're adults, your kits aren't going to want you trying to push them back into that pattern."

His eyes narrowed. Jahir added, testing, "Or they might need you to change so that they can let go of you, and the last of their childhood."

That softened his expression. /Good guess,/ Vasiht'h said, surprise coloring the mindline with a blooming yellow, like a field of new spring flowers.

/They kept recommending him for therapy,/ Jahir said. /They continue to be very involved with him. Admirably, but perhaps too closely./

Standing, Pieter said, "I'll think seriously about this." He paused after walking to the door, one hand on the handle. Turning to face them, he added, "Thanks. This was important."

"You're welcome," Vasiht'h said.

The man nodded and let himself out.

Vasiht'h blew out a breath. "Well. I hope that worked. And that it was the right thing to do."

"We can only work so far as we trust ourselves," Jahir said.

"I guess we'll see where he takes it."

"Do you think Dami and Tapa had to kick us out of the house to make sure we grew up?" Vasiht'h asked Sehvi later that day.

"What?"

"It was just something I was thinking. About how your relationships have a pattern and unless something disrupts them, you keep repeating that pattern. So, as long as a child is home with the parent, even if they've grown up, they still act like a child . . ."

Sehvi snorted. "You need to find something new to be anxious about, ariihir. This topic's getting old. You're going to chafe it down to the skin, just like your paws." She leaned toward the screen, trying to get a good angle downward. "Should I make you show them to me? I bet there are bald patches . . ."

"Sehvi!"

"Well? Are there?"

"No!" he said. "I wasn't thinking about me. I was thinking about a client!"

"Yeaaaah, tell me another one." She sighed noisily. "When are you going to accept that you're as grown up as you're going to get? And that if you don't feel grown up enough now, nothing's going to convince you?"

Vasiht'h grimaced. "That sounds dire."

"Listening to you complain about it every time we talk? It is."

"I meant me never feeling good enough!"

"Ah hah!" She pointed. "That's it. That's all. You said it. Now you're done, right?"

"What?" he asked, bewildered.

"The core of all your problems!" She held her arms open. "You don't feel good enough. Now that you've figured that out, the rest is easy, right?"

Vasiht'h snorted. "I wish." More meekly, "Do I really talk about it *every* time you call?"

"Maybe that was a littttle bit hyperbolic. But only a little bit. Can we go back to talking about my problems?"

"If you had any," Vasiht'h answered, amused. "I'm sure you'd bring them up."

She snickered. "There, that's better. The brother I know."

After they said goodbye, Vasiht'h sat on the patio with his data tablet, thumbing through HEALED BY HER IMMORTAL HEART in the vain hope that it would have something useful to tell him. "About anything," he muttered to the text. "Life. Feeling good enough. Not feeling good enough. Feeling so lucky something might go wrong. Feeling like you can't move on from a pattern that doesn't work for you. Anything. Go." He let it scroll until it came to a halt and read the top line, hoping for divine insight.

All he got was the end of a sentence. ". . . went there the next day."

"Great," he told the novel. "Not only are you unbelievable as a narrative, you're lousy as a mechanism for revelation."

Setting it aside, he looked at the nodding ferns and the trees rustling in the breeze. It was an odd day, moist and gray; on a planet he would have predicted rain, but it didn't rain on Veta. It just felt comfortable, the right kind of day to stay inside and drink kerinne and read a better book than this one. He didn't think he wanted to read anything about fictitious Eldritch. Maybe next time he could get his sisters to recommend a book without them, though if their tastes ran to ridiculous romances he doubted their next selection would be any less painful.

Kerinne and a chance to do meal planning for the remainder of the week, though . . . that sounded perfect. As he ducked back into the cottage, he wondered where his partner's walk was taking him, and if he spent any part of them wondering if he was grown up enough yet. Or was that something that centuries of living took care of?

Vasiht'h tried to imagine Jahir young and tentative and found the image charming. Maybe one day he'd see a picture. Wouldn't that be something? Rexina Regina would probably faint. He grinned and started a pot of cream before putting his tablet to more practical use.

—⊗⊗⊗—

Jahir was, at that moment, climbing from one of Veta's pools.

The bank farthest from him had been sculpted under an embank-
ment on which a tree-lined path wound, and a waterfall fell from
its lip over the shadowed nook. He'd explored underneath it and
discovered doors into the water environment's private areas,
which he'd elected not to investigate; he didn't know how often
Naysha needed to breathe but he guessed it was far less often
than he did. The opposite end of the pool, where he made his exit,
gradually rose from the water like a mock beach, but without the
sand. It was a charming conceit, though he preferred the rectangular pools for the exercise; it made counting laps easier. But
once he'd finished them, he liked wandering the connected pools,
seeing what the landscapers had made of them and observing
the people using them.

Swimming remained a great comfort, though it was no longer
as urgent a relief as it had been on Selnor, where the gravity had
been more intense. He liked the idea that he was slowly strength-
ening himself against a repetition of that episode. Perhaps one
day he might even become capable of visiting Anseahla for longer
than an hour or so. He would like to know his partner's family
better.

Veta, he thought, was coming along well. The revelation
that an existing member of the community had taken them to
apprentice could not help but make their case for them when
their six months' probation elapsed. So long as they pleased
Helga, chances were good they would be able to take over her
practice and she would retire. In their dinners, the Hinichi had
mentioned wanting to travel . . . she had family on Selnor and
in several locations in the Hinichitii system, but had never had
the time to visit them. That they would make it possible for the
woman to do so was also pleasing. Everyone would benefit from
the situation, and surely that was exactly what the starbase
housing committee would like most to see.

Pulling down a towel from the stack set out for visitors, Jahir
dried himself enough to walk back to the lockers and halted at
the sight of Allen Tiber on one of the nearby footpaths, standing
beneath a tree. At his side, his dog paused, then sat, ears lifted

and head cocked.

"Doctor Tiber," Jahir said. "I didn't expect you. It's a pleasure."

Ignoring the greeting, Tiber said, "You have a lot of gall, you know."

"I beg your pardon?"

"Asking me to come by and sleep on your couch." The man's lip curled. "So you could do who knows what to me."

"You need not take advantage of the offer if you wish otherwise."

"You know I would never. But you offered, so now you can say you did. And I get to be the villain of that piece, because I didn't try it—"

"Doctor Tiber," Jahir said, wishing he was dry and dressed in more than a swim-stocking. "If you are correct and our methods are coercive and abusive, then your refusal makes you the hero, does it not?"

The human paused.

In that quiet, the dog rose from his haunches and padded to Jahir. Sitting, he offered a paw.

"Trusty?" Tiber said, startled.

The dog's expectant look seemed to want a response, but his life had not equipped him to guess at the behavior of companion animals. Livestock, perhaps. Horses, certainly. But dogs? "What is he asking of me?"

"You don't know?"

Jahir glanced up at the human. "I am afraid I have never had a dog."

"Poor you," Tiber murmured. More clearly, "He wants to shake hands." When Jahir hesitated, Tiber said, "Just take his paw and give it a shake. Like you would a person."

That handshaking was not common among the Pelted, who preferred palm-touching, and unheard of among Eldritch who did not touch, Jahir chose not to point out. Instead he went to a knee before the dog. A handsome creature, large without bulk, with variegated fur in grays and dark browns and a black saddle over the back. His eyes were golden and their regard felt almost sapient.

Jahir had never had a dog, but if the histories were correct, he might have had such a companion on the hunt had he been born generations ago. He took the animal's paw in his, finding its narrowness and different textures fascinating: leather pads, furred skin, hard black nails. Warm, it was, but it carried with it no thoughts to unsettle him, only a sense of interest and benevolence. Cautiously, he tried shaking, and the dog sat for it, opened his mouth with lolling tongue, and appeared to grin.

"Is he really smiling?" Jahir asked, surprised.

"Yes," Tiber said. "They have expressions of their own. That's a good one . . . he likes you."

"You can tell so quickly?"

"Sure." The reluctance in Tiber's voice was fading as he spoke, and the enthusiasm that replaced it, and the natural confidence . . . Jahir caught a glimpse of what his clients must find so compelling. "He's relaxed, you see? His body's not tense at all. The ears are up, and he's smiling. He offered you his paw—that means he sees you as someone he can use his trick on. He wants to entertain you." The man crouched alongside his dog and wrapped an arm around his neck, tugging him over to rub his head with his knuckles. "Crazy pup. What are you doing, making up to strangers, hmm?"

Trusty yipped at this treatment, a noise that sounded happy somehow. He and his owner wrestled playfully until Tiber offered both his hands and the dog shifted upright so he could set both his paws in them. Tiber wiggled them. "Good dog. Great dog. Best dog."

Trusty yipped again, ears up.

"You've really never had a dog?"

"No," Jahir admitted, fascinated by the relationship.

"Cat? Bird? Pet goldfish? Anything?"

"No," Jahir said.

Tiber glanced up at him. "I can't imagine not having a dog. Petting them lowers your blood pressure, did you know? And you live longer, with pets."

"You would have a dog even if there were no health benefits to be derived from one," Jahir observed.

"Yeah." Tiber chuckled, rubbing Trusty's ears as the dog leaned into him. "I would." He glanced up at the Eldritch. "Don't think my dog liking you means anything. I still think what you're doing is wrong."

"You seem a man of science," Jahir said. "Does it not offend your sensibilities to dismiss something without first understanding it?"

Tiber snorted. "And how am I ever going to understand it, when I have no esper powers of my own?"

Jahir said, "Do we need to have suffered all the ills of our clients to be capable of helping them? Experience is not the only lens by which we see the world."

"It's the most important, though." Tiber sighed and gave Trusty one more pat on the head before rising. "Look, you might be the nicest people in the world and still be doing the wrong thing. If you've had any experience in practice yourself, you'll know that happens all the time. And you're siphoning off a lot of existing clients, people Minette and Helga and I feel responsible for."

"Helga seems content with our progress."

"Helga . . ." Tiber grimaced. "Helga's her own person, with her own opinions. But I've got mine, and they're no less valid."

"Come try our methods," Jahir said. "We can allay your misgivings, if you allow us the opportunity."

"No." Tiber shook his head. "I'm sorry. Maybe your methodology would serve an esper population, people who might understand it well enough to identify abusive behaviors. But on a population primarily composed of people who have no defense against what you're doing? It's not ethical."

"Doctor Tiber," Jahir said. "Our clients are vulnerable to us no matter our methodology. Our training gives all of us the ability to manipulate and abuse clients without their having any protection against it, whether we do it with our minds or with speech. It is why we have a code of ethics. Can you not trust that we too hold to that code? We swore it in school, and again before the licensing board, and before our deities as well. To do no harm. To hold the health of our clients foremost in our minds. This is our calling."

Tiber eyed him. "Before your deities."

"To them we swear first," Jahir said. "And that oath is the most binding of all. They know our secret hearts in a way no mortal might."

Tiber shook his head. "I regret this, but I can't recommend what you're doing. And in fact, I plan to warn people that in my opinion, it's unsafe." Glancing at the towel, he added, "I'll let you dress now."

As the human departed, the dog at his side glanced back and grinned again at Jahir.

⸺ ❦ ⸺

"So that was a disaster," Vasiht'h said once Jahir had returned home and described the encounter.

"Disaster is a strong word," Jahir said. "But it was . . . discouraging."

Vasiht'h set out cups for them both: kerinne for himself and black tea for Jahir. "I'd call 'respected and established therapist starts telling the community at large to avoid us' a disaster."

"If he was the sole therapist, perhaps. But Helga is no doubt informing the community at large that we come highly recommended."

"And you think they'll cancel each other out?" Vasiht'h snorted, the steam from his cup bending away. "I wonder if Dashenby will come down on our side."

"Dashenby," Jahir said, "will watch from the sidelines until she's certain of the outcome."

"That's a harsh assessment."

Was it? And yet he knew it to be true. "Not necessarily. She is friends with both Tiber and Helga. Alienating one or the other before time would put her in an uncomfortable position."

"Or it might have made Tiber rethink his prejudice. That's

what you do when friends tell you you're wrong, isn't it?"

"One would hope," Jahir said. "But it does not always work out that way."

Vasiht'h was silent, his ruminations weighing the mindline as he sipped from his cup. Finally, he said, "Dogs shake hands?"

"At least one does."

"That sounds . . . kind of cute," Vasiht'h said. "I'm sorry I missed it."

"Perhaps if we win Tiber to our side, you might witness it yet."

Vasiht'h shook his head. "I wouldn't hold our breath."

CHAPTER 15

AMETIA REMAINED THE highest-energy of their clients. Sometimes she napped through their sessions; often she paced, tail lashing, her hands jerking through a series of gestures so abrupt they would have looked more at home in a dueling circle than in a therapist's office. Jahir noted the fire in her eyes when she described her crusades on behalf of her human protégés. He was not the only one who saw it, either.

/Do you think she hasn't figured out how to fix this problem in her life because she doesn't want to?/ Vasiht'h asked.

/Because she enjoys the fight? I had wondered, yes./

/But?/

/But,/ Jahir replied, and could not articulate the reasons he was unwilling to commit to that diagnosis.

Those reasons became clearer to him the next time the Harat-Shar consented to sleep. Ghosting through her dreams, they saw her again at the battle at the side of the Harat-Shariin demigod. Jahir glanced up at a sky bloodied by sunset and storms, out at the battlefield at the moaning and broken. In her dreams, Ametia's zeal was tempered by a sense of grueling determination, and while she went again and again into the fray in her angel's wake, she did not do so singing or crying for victory. She took wounds that bled until they became gore, crusted on her fur. She lifted her mace with power but a great grimace on her face. The entirety of the dream was permeated with the effort of battle.

/*It's not always like this.*/ As always, Vasiht'h withheld himself from Ametia's dreams until he became the faintest of presences, only enough to see events but not to inhabit them. He left that to Jahir. /*Sometimes there's joy here.*/

Jahir could taste his partner's incredulity. He could appreciate it—he found no joy in the fight himself—but unlike the Glaseah his culture gave him a context for understanding the appeal of battle. /*Sometimes,*/ he agreed. /*But not always. That is an important distinction.*/

/*Because . . . ?*/

/*Because if she truly loved the fight, she would never feel the senselessness of it. And this . . .*/ He surveyed the wounded, the weeping. Felt Ametia's frustration and grief as she was forced to leave them behind. /*This is more complex than that. This is regret, arii.*/

They withdrew from her dreams to await her waking, and were not kept long. Her eyes slitted open, considering them; she did not move beneath her blankets. "You found something."

"We're not sure we'd go that far," Vasiht'h said. "More like . . . we have some things to talk about?"

She pushed herself upright, shaking her hair over her shoulders. "This should be good."

"We hope, or what have you been paying us for." Vasiht'h managed a smile. "Do you feel like there's any hope for what you're doing?"

"Excuse me?"

"This fight you're fighting," Vasiht'h said as Jahir watched them both. "Do you think there's any winning it?"

"Of course not," Ametia said. "We're all tribalists at heart. There's no doing away with prejudice. You might quash it somewhere, but that just makes it pop up somewhere else in a different form." She shoved the blankets away and rolled her shoulders. "We always need a 'them'. The brainpower we'd need to hold everyone in our heads as one of us would make our skulls so big we wouldn't make it out of our mothers without surgical intervention. In the end we're all just animals."

"That seems awfully cynical," Vasiht'h said cautiously.

"I'd call it realistic," the Harat-Shar answered, unruffled by the critique. "But anyway. To answer your original question: no. I don't think I'm going to solve the interstellar problem of human prejudice."

"But the local one?" Jahir said.

"Not even that," Ametia answered. "A university's a large populace, and by the time students get to it they're already set in their ideas. They think they're not because they're young and not very introspective, so they don't see that they've already absorbed too much of the world to be really open to change. The ideas they embrace will either be logical extensions of their upbringing, or they'll be antithetical to that upbringing, as a form of rebellion and a way to assert their identity as adults separate from their families. That's not real change . . . that's just reaction." She smiled, showing teeth in a crooked grin. "All the real changing they're going to do once they get to us is going to have to come the way it does to all adults: in the school of life, which doesn't take prisoners. It's a lot harsher than college."

"Yes," Jahir murmured. "We have some notion."

"I'm sure you do. An Eldritch and a Glaseah, practicing on sleeping minds?" She guffawed. "You're in for your share of askance looks. When people aren't jealous of you, they're betting you're doing something wrong just because they don't understand it, and they're probably too self-involved to educate themselves." She shook her head. "I'm glad I'm not you. Being one of the cheetah intrarace is enough trouble for me."

/That is an uncomfortably trenchant observation./

/She never struck me as dumb,/ Vasiht'h said, rueful. "Is that what made you interested in human prejudice?"

"Probably. Or at least, it primed me for it. But I hate injustice anywhere I find it. Don't you?"

"I admit I never thought about it," Vasiht'h said, stumbling over the words.

She snorted. "Because you're lucky enough not to have to." Eyeing Jahir. "I bet you care, though."

"I doubt my partner cares less about injustice," Jahir said. "Lack of exposure to such things does not beget callousness. Ignorance is reparable."

"If you care to repair it." She looked from one of them to the other. "But I bet being stuck with him will make you notice it more. Sometimes that's all we need . . . a close relationship with someone who exposes us to different perspectives." She grinned suddenly. "I like you two. You know how much trouble it is, finding people to keep up with me?"

"I think the only way we're managing is because you spend most of your time with us asleep," Vasiht'h said ruefully.

Ametia laughed. "But you admit it, and I like that." Rising and brushing the lines of her slacks into place, she said, "I'm glad I came. No matter what rumors are circulating."

"Rumors?" Vasiht'h asked sharply.

She grinned at them. "Like I said. The ignorant will always make trouble. Just ignore them, aletsen, and do what's needful. That gets the job done."

As she reached the door, Jahir said, "Ametia-alet? May I ask you one thing before you leave?"

"This should be good. Go ahead."

"Granted the possibility of success . . . do you love the fight more than you want to win the war?"

The Harat-Shar's eyes narrowed. "Rewording the question to see if it provokes a different answer?"

"It is a time-honored rhetorical technique."

She guffawed. "Yes, it is. A pleasure to talk with educated people. Then I'd say . . . if the war could be won, it wouldn't matter if I enjoyed the fight, would it? My duty would be clear."

"And you would find joy in duty," Jahir said.

One of her fine brows arched. "It wouldn't be exciting, certainly. But . . . there would be a certain satisfaction in it. I'd imagine. I don't guess I'll ever find out." She flipped a hand in a casual salute. "Enjoy your morning, aletsen."

Jahir knew better to expect so, given the tumult in the mind-line. When the door closed, he waited for the inevitable explosion, and was surprised to find Vasiht'h frowning in contemplation.

"You are not angry at Tiber?" he asked, careful.

"What? Yes. Of course I am. But I was thinking about Ametia's comment. About injustice, and whether I care about it or not. Because what he's doing is unjust." The Glaseah looked up at him. "Am I overreacting, because I see injustice so infrequently that even the smallest things feel cataclysmic?"

"You did say his accusations were serious crimes on your world."

"Sure," Vasiht'h said. "But he doesn't know that. And how's he going to find out if he doesn't bother to look it up? And why would he look it up if he's convinced he's right?"

Jahir considered those questions and said finally, "Life is complicated."

"Don't mistake me," Vasiht'h said, getting up. "I'm still angry at him. It's unfair that he's balking us this way, and spreading rumors! That's even worse! But maybe if I stop reacting to this like it's a personal thing, and start treating it more like a . . . a . . ."

"Psychological problem to be solved?" Jahir offered.

Vasiht'h wrinkled his nose in a grimace. "Yes. If I can ever get enough distance from it to manage."

"Give it time," Jahir suggested.

"Time is the one thing we don't have."

Joyner missed his next appointment. Vasiht'h tried not to assume the worst—maybe the Tam-illee had gotten sick?—but it was hard not to leap to the obvious conclusion. He definitely didn't want Jahir reading his agitation through the mindline and knew it would bleed over unless he kept himself busy . . . so he pulled out his data tablet and resumed reading.

She was never more beautiful than she was like this. Thaddeus

*watched her strolling the garden, caressing her tumescent belly and
singing to it in a beautiful, alien tongue in her golden voice. They were
going to be a family. Finally, he would have one, and with the love of
his life. He thanked the Laughing God for her, and for this chance. I
won't waste it, he promised. I'll make her and the baby the center of
my world. She deserves it. And with a melting sigh, We're going to be
so happy. He let the curtain fall and reluctantly returned to the data
for his next meeting.*

"What are you reading?" Jahir asked.

Startled, Vasiht'h looked up and flushed. "A book."

"A good one?" Jahir wondered. "I would not object to reading
something less arduous than some of these journals."

"Oh, no, Goddess," Vasiht'h blurted. "This is an awful book! I
wouldn't recommend it to anyone!"

The look Jahir gave him then was justifiably puzzled. "Then
why do you continue . . . ?"

"It was a gift," Vasiht'h said. "From my sisters. If they hadn't
insisted I finish it I wouldn't have gotten past the first chapter,
honest."

"Ah," Jahir murmured. "I see. Duty."

Vasiht'h squinted. "Less duty and more obligation, really."

"What is the difference?"

Trust the Eldritch to ask the impossible questions, and the
interesting ones. There was nothing but curiosity in the mindline . . . curiosity, and an odd shadow beneath it that didn't seem
to belong. Vasiht'h said, thinking out his reply, "An obligation . . .
that's small and personal. But duty is bigger."

"And yet," Jahir said, soft, "Duty can be so very personal."

The shadow had grown under the curiosity, until it crept
over a battlefield that looked a lot like the ones from Ametia's
dreams. Vasiht'h tried not to shudder. He enjoyed learning about
his partner; unraveling the Eldritch mystery was one of the
pleasures of their relationship, in part because he anticipated it
taking so long. But this glimpse made him wonder if there were
parts of Jahir's life that he didn't want to know about.

"Not a book you would recommend," Jahir said at last.

"No," Vasiht'h said firmly. "Not at all." He let the tablet droop as he looked at the door. "He's not coming."

"No."

"I bet it's because of Tiber."

"I cannot think that likely. Joyner was already our client, and had experienced our therapy already, and found it agreeable."

But Vasiht'h heard the hint of doubt in the words, in the way his friend's tone rose slightly at the end as if posing a question. "Some people will believe an authority over their own experiences."

"He may be ill."

Then why didn't he call? Vasiht'h wanted to ask, and knew it was unfair. If you were sick enough to miss appointments, you might be too sick to cancel them, too. Instead he said, "What are you up to? You seem engrossed in it. Maybe it's better than my book."

"I am researching pets."

Vasiht'h's ears sagged. "You're serious? You want a pet?"

The mindline brought him . . . what? A sense of whimsy. Curiosity. It tasted like sea salt and summer. "Not at all. I was merely curious how one acquires a pet, given their dearth on the base."

Curious now himself, Vasiht'h asked, "And . . . ?"

"On Terra there are apparently pet shops and pet breeders from which one might acquire a companion like Doctor Tiber's," Jahir said. "But here there are neither, though there is a veterinarian hospital."

"A . . . hospital. For pets?"

"For animals," Jahir said. "Ilea may know more, since it seems to exist more to support her efforts to maintain the starbase ecosystem than to service animals like Trusty."

"Or the goats down the street," Vasiht'h said, thoughtful. "I wonder why no one thinks of them as pets?"

"They are livestock," Jahir said. "Intended to serve a purpose. The only purpose Doctor Tiber's dog serves is the same all of us do."

Vasiht'h wrinkled his nose. "I'm not sure whether to find that disturbing or . . ."

Jahir glanced at him with interest. "Or?"

"Or kind of charming?" Vasiht'h hated admitting it, especially sitting in an office waiting for a client he was completely certain Tiber had scared away. "The goats . . . they're just there to do what their owners need. If they didn't do something useful, I bet she wouldn't be keeping them. But the dog doesn't have to do anything to be worth Tiber's time and care."

"It was an intriguing animal," Jahir said. "And Doctor Tiber's relationship with it very affectionate."

"I'm not going to forgive him for hating us because he's nice to his dog. I bet there are mass murderers and insane despots who are nice to their dogs." But saying it, Vasiht'h wondered, and grumbled at having to wonder. He didn't want to like anything about Tiber. That might distract him from the important job of being upset at him. "So are you done with your research about dogs?"

"Mostly," Jahir said.

That 'mostly' had an odd flavor, but Vasiht'h decided not to ask. "Well, if he's not coming, we might as well go get coffee."

Jahir eyed him. "And scones?"

"I wasn't going to say that part in case it put you off the idea." Vasiht'h grinned. "But scones do sound nice. And who knows, maybe today they'll be lighter?"

"I doubt it highly." But Jahir put down his tablet and stood. Satisfied, Vasiht'h followed him out. Maybe Joyner really had been sick. And while he would have preferred to make money, he wouldn't say no to a second breakfast.

⸺ ◦∞◦ ⸺

Their appointment with Lennea the following day was revelatory. In a bad way. She stomped in, surprising them both—Vasiht'h had never seen her *angry*—and exclaimed, "I am so upset with Joyner!"

"I . . . beg your pardon?" Jahir said.

"Sit, please," Vasiht'h added. "Do you want something to drink? While you tell us about it? Or you can pace if you want. Lots of people do."

Lennea looked down as if expecting a worn path in the carpet. Today her sandals were the bright blue of damselflies, and one of them had an enamel pin of a sun peeping from behind a gray cloud. The other sported a jeweled flower in pink and yellow.

/Perhaps we should ensure our next office has a rug over the high traffic areas./

Vasiht'h hid a smile. */Her sandals are very fancy today. I mean, both of them. Usually it's just one./*

A pause as he sensed his partner assessing them. */Interesting./*

"I guess tea would be good," Lennea said. "And it can cool down while I pace." She said that firmly, folding her arms over her chest and flattening her ears. "Because I want to pace!"

"By all means?" Jahir said, taking down the tea selection.

Vasiht'h got the kettle. Hot water, at least, they could do in their modest office. Lennea liked a mild tea, made from Hinichi mountain lilacs and Terran chamomile. He showed it to her and she paused, pursing her lips. Then pointed. "That today."

"Cinnamon it is," Vasiht'h said. "Now, pace your heart out."

She smothered a giggle and put her hands on her hips. "I can't stay angry when you make jokes."

"Anger is unlike you," Jahir said. "What has caused this particular disturbance?"

"Oh, I don't know." She sighed. "No, I do know. It's the stress of the new job—no, they haven't found a replacement yet—and it's making all the little things in my life feel like ridiculously huge things. It's horrible. I snap at people for the stupidest things, but it just . . . I'm out of control!" She walked to the door and stopped there, shoulders slumping. "I don't think I even pace very well, do I."

"Everyone paces in their own way," Vasiht'h said. "You should see me try it. And I bet Jahir would make it to the end of the office in two strides and have to turn around."

She managed another tired giggle before returning to the

table and sitting, elbows on the surface and shoulders sunk
inward. She stared at the tea morosely and then straightened,
fierce. "I am legitimately irritated at Joyner, though. He said
he had such good results with you but he won't come anymore
because he heard that your methods are untried and might result
in unintentional harm."

"That sounds like a direct quote," Vasiht'h said, ignoring his
own spurt of indignation.

"It was." She sniffed. "He got it from some message in the
local newsstream. Some other therapist on the base said you all
were doing things in a way they'd never been done and that it
might be appropriate for espers but not for non-espers, and that
there was no testing? It all sounded ridiculous to me. If you'd
been manipulating me, why would I feel better?"

"Maybe we want you to feel better so you'll think well of us?"
Jahir said, and Vasiht'h glanced at him sharply at the tickle of
merriment in the mindline.

Lennea laughed at that. "What, like everyone? If that's
manipulation, we need the whole galaxy to take it on." She shook
her head. "But he's nervous about not doing the right thing. It's
a good thing about him, because it means he cares about doing
the right thing. But it's a horrible thing about him because he
can never decide if he is doing the right thing, or if there's some
better way to do the right thing that he should be choosing and
he's not because he's already chosen some other way to do the
right thing, which will now probably end in disaster. . . ."

Vasiht'h said, wide-eyed, "You know him well, don't you."

"We've been friends for a while." She sipped the tea. "This is
good, but it needs cookies."

"If I had a kitchen," Vasiht'h muttered.

/Would it be bread or some confection?/

/Definitely bread,/ Vasiht'h answered, sourly. /Bread needs to
be pounded, and I could use an excuse./

"I'm going to tell him he's being ridiculous," Lennea was
saying. "Sometimes if I say it often enough, he believes me."

"It's fine if he does not," Jahir said. "We would prefer our clients come to us of their own volition. Therapy requires the consent of its participants."

"It's not fine, because you were helping him!" Her face fell and she finished, glum, "I want to help *someone* if I can't help myself."

"A nap maybe?" Vasiht'h suggested. "You look tired. After you tell us about it, if you want to."

"I do," she said. "But I want the nap too, so I'm going to keep it quick."

Lennea's complaints were repetitions of the previous week's and she was noticeably more agitated . . . but she slept for them easily enough, and the relief on her face when unconsciousness claimed her struck Vasiht'h painfully. */I really hope they find someone who wants this job soon./*

/As do I. Shall we look?/

They did and found nothing expected. Vasiht'h soothed the spastic energy twitching through her subconscious landscape, bringing an evening breeze moist with summer rain and sprinkling it with stars and the smell of tropical flowers. They watched her limbs cease their twitching; her restlessness eased. Backing out of her dreams, Vasiht'h said, */I guess that's all we can do for now./*

/For now,/ Jahir agreed, with that busy weighty feeling Vasiht'h associated with him working through a puzzle. */Arii . . . /*

/If you're going to tell me not to be angry about Joyner, don't,/ Vasiht'h said, sitting on his dull anger. */It's still unfair./* He glanced at Jahir. */Have you seen this announcement in the newsstream?/*

/I may have looked. It was as fairly worded as it could have been, given what he believes about us. No personal attacks, only a warning about our methods./

Vasiht'h flattened his ears.

/If he truly believes what he says, arii, he would have no choice but to act on it in just the way he is doing now./

/I can still blame him for willful ignorance./

Jahir sighed softly and picked up the kettle. */No scones today./*

/What?/ Vasiht'h asked, distracted by the non sequitur.

/We will find you ingredients for bread. You may take out your pique on it./

/But why should I have to just accept this?/ Vasiht'h watched his friend begin brewing a fresh pot of water. */He's wrong. It's not fair!/*

/How do you propose we stop it?/

That question arrested him. If he charged Tiber with slander . . . but would that work? He'd never done anything with the legal system before . . . he didn't even know what bringing an action against someone entailed. Other than it would probably be expensive and newsworthy. Getting in a fight with an established member of the community might make them look like troublemakers when they were trying to present themselves in the best possible light. Worse, he'd be the one getting all the negative attention as the person making the accusation, and he was the one who needed the permit to live here. Jahir wouldn't be a party to it, he was sure. Or he would, but passively, because he obviously didn't approve.

/You know he's wrong./

Jahir dropped teabags into their mugs. */Yes./*

/And you know it's unfair./

/Yes./

/Then why don't you want to do something about it?/

/Because I see no way to bring about the outcome we desire. Forcing Tiber to recant will not help us, arii. It will only prejudice him against us. We would win his silence, but lose forever any chance at a true rapprochement./

/Like that's even possible!/

/But if it is, we will end that potential if we attack him. Arii . . . you are thinking with your heart instead of your head./

/I . . ./ Vasiht'h sputtered mentally. He wasn't used to thinking of himself as the irrational one, but he found his partner watching him over their mugs the way they did with clients who were working through something and he colored. */We don't have time to let him come around the normal way. It's only a couple of months until our deadline. What if he convinces the authorities we*

shouldn't stay?/

/We will ask Helga's opinion./ Jahir pushed a mug over to him. */Perhaps she will have useful advice./*

/I hope,/ Vasiht'h said with a sigh.

When Lennea woke half an hour later, she sat up and yawned.

"Good sleep?" Vasiht'h asked, hesitant. What if his agitation about Tiber had poisoned his work in her dreams?

"Wonderful!" Lennea rubbed her eyes and reached down to start putting her sandals back on. "I felt like . . . I was being cradled in this hammock, drowsing on a warm summer night, and I could just hear the world? People unhappy or upset and talking. But it was so far away, and it was like it couldn't touch me! I was cocooned in my little shelter." She paused to beam at them. "That was so good. I wish the world actually worked that way. Maybe I could pretend through the day that all the things that are upsetting me are far away from me, and I'm safe in my little warm bubble no one can touch."

"That sounds like a useful strategy," Jahir said, no doubt covering for Vasiht'h's momentary speechlessness. "Will you tell us how it serves you next week?"

"Oh, absolutely." She scowled. "And I'm going to wring Joyner's giant ear one more time. I can't believe he'd give this up just because of someone else's fears!" She paused. "No, wait. I really can believe that." She blew a breath up, ruffling her hair over her brow. "Such a great guy and so *frustrating* sometimes."

"We know how that goes," Vasiht'h said, rueful.

After she'd left, the Glaseah said, "I'm . . . glad . . . I didn't accidentally mess that up."

"There is an essential benevolence in our relationship that carries through the disagreements," Jahir said.

You hope, Vasiht'h thought to himself. Now was definitely not the time to bring up his concerns about money, and independence. They were all wrapped up in whether they'd be able to stay, anyway. Because it was his test, wasn't it? Not Jahir's—Jahir had already been accepted, could stay if he wanted. It was Vasiht'h who had to prove he could add value to a community, as an adult, in his chosen profession. *No wonder I'm so worked up.* Aloud, he said, "I think pounding bread is a good idea."

"By all means, then. Let us find groceries."

CHAPTER 16

"ALLEN?" HELGA DIPPED HER churro in the chocolate-bourbon sauce. "Oh yes. Nice young man. Why?"

Jahir ignored the incredulity that surged through the mindline. "Ought we to be concerned over his attempts to discredit us?"

"Is that what he's doing?" She chewed on the confection, her brows lifting.

"Isn't it?" Vasiht'h asked.

Helga chuckled, dipping again. "Such a good sauce. You are an amazing cook, alet."

"I try," Vasiht'h said. "About Tiber?"

/Gently,/ Jahir sent.

/I want to know!/

/As do I, but one does not push a woman given to mischief./

/Or a woman who's holding our fate in her hands?/

Jahir suppressed the urge to eye his partner, instead refilling his coffee. /We are in possession of our fates, arii. The moment we surrender that responsibility, we lose any hope of affecting it for ourselves./

Vasiht'h sighed.

"You're troubled by it, I see," Helga said. "You shouldn't be.

If Allen was really trying to discredit you, you wouldn't still be in business. My broad influence notwithstanding." She grinned at them. "He's concerned. But his conscience will keep him from outright driving you out of town until he knows for certain that you're a danger to the community."

"You think highly of him," Jahir guessed.

"Oh, I like him quite a bit," the woman said. She licked one of her fingers clean of the chocolate sauce and resumed eating. Between bites, she said, "They're both good people, really. Minette and him both. They have their quirks, but who doesn't?"

"You wouldn't know anything about quirky people, would you," Vasiht'h said, grinning finally.

"I'm old, I'm allowed to be eccentric." She leaned back. "If you had another serving of those, I would eat them . . ."

"But fortunately I don't?"

"Fortunately," she said, glancing at the ceiling. "Or unfortunately. I can't decide." Lifting her mug, she said, "Don't let him bother you. Once you've established yourselves, he'll come around."

"Will he?" Jahir asked.

"Oh, I think so. He's not a bad man. Or a stupid one. The opposite, really. A good man, and devoted to his oath. If he didn't take it so seriously, he wouldn't be on your case so much."

"So it's not concern that we might be poaching," Vasiht'h said.

Helga laughed. "God Almighty. No. He doesn't want for clients. In fact, he's got a third again the clients I do, or Minette, as a byproduct of his decision to overwork himself after his divorce. He's only just now starting to think about shedding some of those people, maybe taking on a saner schedule. And before you ask, because I see you want to," she eyed Vasiht'h, "it was a necessary divorce, and it wasn't his fault. He and his wife had decided before marrying that they wanted a family, but she changed her mind."

"Not a matter upon which there can be compromise," Jahir said, quiet.

"None," Helga agreed, stirring cream into her coffee. "He was in a bad way for a while. I'm glad he had that dog of his, because I swear Trusty helped him get through it more than any of the rest of us. I sometimes think we might be missing something as a culture, no longer having pets."

"Would you?" Jahir asked, curious. "Have a pet?"

She laughed. "Oh, I'm old and set in my ways—"

Vasiht'h snorted.

"Not buying that one, are you." The Hinichi snickered. "Maybe it was a little on the unbelievable side. I suppose I'd try it, maybe. Hector's said he used to keep dogs before he married his wife; she was frightened of them, so he gave them away."

"Hector said?" Vasiht'h asked, innocent.

"He did." Her eyes sparkled. "And don't give me that look, young man. I know what you're hoping to hear."

"So am I going to hear it?"

/You are enjoying this,/ Jahir observed.

/There's a little bit of a matchmaker in most Glaseah. We like big families, and settled people./

"We've gone out for coffee," Helga said. "Very stimulating conversation."

"So, a dog?" Jahir said. "Not . . . a different animal."

"Definitely a dog," Helga agreed, setting her now empty mug down and patting her mouth dry with her napkin. "On the assumption that a dog will smell me and defer to me as the enormous, bipedal pack matron. I might not be too old for new experiences, but I am too old to put up with cheek. At least, from an animal." She sighed. "As always, a wonderful meal."

"You'll tell us how it goes with Hector?" Vasiht'h asked mischievously.

"Wouldn't you like to know!" She grinned, tail swishing. "On the whole I think it's better for you not to have all the answers, wouldn't you say?"

"No," Vasiht'h said. "But I'm totally unsurprised that you would."

"Hah! You two are keepers. I'm going to miss you when I go

on my retirement gallivants. Keep yourselves well, ariisen."

They returned from seeing her off and began the familiar chore of cleaning. Jahir brought the plates and cups to the counter and Vasiht'h handled their washing. As they worked, Jahir said, "I have a sense that the pack matron may decide to gallivant in company."

"Her and Hector?" Vasiht'h stacked the plates, the mindline brisk with interest. "That would be good for him. He's stayed too long alone. Not that sewing quilts and selling them isn't bad . . . he's not suffering. But why be content with 'not suffering' when you could also be having adventures with a witty and elegant companion your age?"

"They certainly seem agreeable to the arrangement," Jahir said, amused. "You are satisfied with your part in it?"

"I like making people's lives better. And we're better in company. Most of us anyway."

"Yes," Jahir agreed, thinking of Tiber and his barren marriage.

Vasiht'h looked up sharply. "That's an awfully cold wind."

"Hector does not seem to have grandchildren? Or near ones. Perhaps he might enjoy Helga's." Jahir folded the tablecloth and set it aside for cleaning. "Children are important."

"You're thinking about Tiber."

"From one potential marriage, to one of blighted potentials . . . not a stretch?"

"No," Vasiht'h said slowly. He put away the mugs, handling them one by one. "I wonder if Tiber let it leak. So that he would seem . . . more approachable. You know, 'I've suffered too, so I know what you're going through.'"

"I highly doubt it."

Vasiht'h's surprise felt like the prickle of a limb waking from nervelessness. "Really?"

Jahir considered his impressions of Tiber by the pool. "It does not seem in keeping with his personality. I would guess instead that he was mortified at his lapse in both judgment and strength. If he considers himself a bulwark for his clients, faltering in a way that made him unavailable . . . more likely he thought of it as a failure."

Vasiht'h winced. "All right. Now that you put it that way . . . that's more believable than him manipulating the situation to get something good out of it."

"That seems . . ." Jahir tried to find a word that would not disturb his friend.

"You're trying to say it sounds bad? But I don't think it is." Vasiht'h took up the tablecloth and dropped it in the hamper. "If bad things happen to you, why shouldn't you find something good in it? Make it a way you can strengthen your ties to the community? Ask for help and get it? People don't connect with people who never ask for help."

"Why do you suppose that is?" Jahir asked, hesitant.

"You're worried this is about you, but it's not." Vasiht'h came around the counter and sat, facing him. "You did ask for help. From me. From other people too. KindlesFlame. Helga, even. That's good, because it made you seem less like an impregnable fortress. You can't get into someone unless they let you in, and if you never get in, then . . ." He shrugged. "Then you're not really in. I mean, obviously. You see, though, don't you?"

"Does that require weakness?" Jahir wondered. "Do we only ever trust one another, seeing one another weak?"

"It's not weakness," Vasiht'h said firmly. "It's *vulnerability*." A hesitation. The mindline softened with the smell of rain on warm earth and lilacs, and the sound of that rain drumming, and a gentleness. "My great-grandmother . . . I saw her die. She was old of course, so we weren't surprised, but she was in a lot of pain. We don't get a lot of weird diseases, but." He paused, ears flicking back. "That part's not important. The relevant part is she was dying and yet she wasn't *weak*. She had a dignity of spirit, leaving the world, that made her strong despite her circumstances."

Jahir pulled a chair back and sat in it, leaning forward and clasping his hands. He watched his friend react to his focused attention: a straightening of the shoulders, and a relaxation of the spine, the mantled wings. The tenderness in the mindline was directed at him now, and it made his cheeks tint, to be the target of such affection. But he kept his eyes level on Vasiht'h's.

"So it's not the same thing," Vasiht'h said. "Weakness and being open to other people. You can be open to them and let them in—to help you and love you—without being weak. But you have to show them you're not perfect, too, because otherwise, it's just too hard. Loving a perfect person . . . most people aren't strong enough to do that."

Something about that statement made the Glaseah think of words on a page. Jahir wondered at it, but didn't ask. "Fortunately," he said, "none of us are perfect."

"No," Vasiht'h said.

"Even Doctor Tiber."

Vasiht'h's ears flattened. He folded his arms. "Back to that."

"The lesson seemed relevant?"

Vasiht'h snorted. "You would say that." He rested his arms on the table. "More importantly, how do you feel about kits?"

"Children?" Jahir said, surprised. "Are we not too newly established to be so concerned?"

"Not if we're in this for the long, long run," Vasiht'h said. "Eventually we're going to want families. Right?"

Jahir thought of the housing authority's comment: *Glaseah don't reproduce quickly. But when they start, they have big families.* The idea made him smile; easier to imagine his partner being climbed by Glaseahn children than to imagine his own prospects, and the unlikeliness of his joy in the duty given the choice his heart had made, so precipitously, so young. "I should think so, yes."

"You're all right with that?" Vasiht'h asked, hesitant.

"More than well with it. I should like to see it."

The Glaseah blew out a breath. "Good. Not that I'm leaning that way anytime soon, but . . . I wouldn't want to get to that point and suddenly discover it was a problem."

"We have a slight advantage over the Tibers in that regard," Jahir said. "As we need not rely on one another to obtain our progeny."

Vasiht'h snorted, and again that sense of words on a page,

this time overlaid with . . . pepper? Spearmint? Something that suggested humor. "No. That we definitely don't."

Later, after his partner had retired to read the obligatory book, Jahir went up to the rooftop. The sky remained convincing, and breathtaking, a black sward that lightened to a luminous purple in a halo around the starbase's spindle of glittering lights. It also brightened at the apparent horizon, over the commons; the city did not sleep as early as the Garden District did. Here it was softly glowing lanterns in gold and rose, and the dim silver lights lining the walkways, and a velvety purple dark with the silhouettes of decorative plants bordering the welcoming glow of the houses. It smelled of foreign flowers, like a world, and again it struck him, the enormity of the Alliance's capabilities. This marvel, inconceivable to his people, was a way of life for the Pelted. . . . and he was privileged to be among them to experience it. When his time here was done, would he come home grateful for having had the journey? Or would he cavil at the restrictions?

He was here now, at least. And thinking that far forward did him no kindnesses. He thought instead of the surmountable problems facing them here and smiled. They could wait. First he had an unexpected letter from his brother to read—that would prove interesting, for Amber was usually a indifferent correspondent. Then . . . there were no pet shops on Veta, but perhaps an ad in the local stream would net him a dog he might give to Helga as a gift for her help. It might take him the remaining two months to find one . . . !

Sensing the nearness of his friend, Jahir spread his brother's message and began reading, feeling again the juxtaposition of his cherished but prior life and the joys and astonishments of the new.

What's-his-name and What's-her-name had finished decorating the nursery in the book and were back to gooey love scenes dripping with enough adjectives to fill a dictionary, so it wasn't surprising that Vasiht'h's mind wandered as he read. Inevitably, he thought of Tiber, and his empty nursery. Maybe his divorce had been amicable, or maybe it had been acrimonious, no matter how he and his wife conducted themselves in public. But it was hard not to feel sorry for him when that divorce had not only deprived him of a partner, but of a possible future as a father. Vasiht'h hadn't given much thought to children, except to assume he would have them, but making himself imagine it now—really imagine it, holding a squirming baby, teaching a kit how to lick a spatula clean of cookie dough, dancing for a grown daughter at her wedding—he couldn't imagine taking the amputation of that future well. Tiber looked to be about middle-aged for a human, so there was no reason he couldn't marry again . . . but he'd thought he'd had things worked out, and then it had all been taken away. Vasiht'h had seen plenty of traumas caused by similar scenarios while working in the student clinic.

Had Tiber gone to a therapist himself? Or had he just soldiered on, and held onto that dog as the only thing that hadn't abandoned him? And the Pelted all around him, with their subconscious prejudices against animals . . . no wonder he was prickly.

Vasiht'h sighed and set aside the tablet to fluff up his pillows. He didn't want to like Tiber, but Sehvi would be the first to tell him that he should accept his inability to hold grudges. Tiber was apparently successful enough, so his clients must like him. He couldn't be all bad. Or even mostly bad. Even Helga said so, and Helga . . . well. If you couldn't trust a mischievous Hinichi great-grandmother, who could you trust?

Something, Vasiht'h thought, had to be done.

CHAPTER 17

VASIHT'H WAS STILL CONTEMPLATING this the following morning when a stranger showed up on their doorstep. He was a male Asanii felid with orange tabby markings and golden eyes, wearing the sort of stylish and comfortable clothes associated with service jobs: a white shirt tucked into dark teal pants, and over it a breezy sarong in shades of blue and gold. He offered Vasiht'h his palm. "Hey. I hear you're taking clients? Can I sign up?"

"Sure? Want to sit and fill out the intake form? Then we can make an appointment."

"All right." The male padded in and dropped onto the couch, wriggling until he made himself comfortable. He studied their office as he accepted the data tablet and stylus. "This place is nice. Doesn't look like a den of iniquity or anything."

"I beg your pardon?" Jahir said, entering with the coffee he'd gone to fetch for them both.

"You know. A place where therapists prey upon the subconscious minds of their innocent victims." The Asanii grinned easily, arm resting on a cushion as he went to work on the form. He had long fingers and broad wrists, corded with muscle; it made Vasiht'h wonder what he did for a living.

"Doctor Tiber did not say anything that prejudicial, if I recall correctly," Jahir said.

"And we're definitely *not* into . . . preying on victims while they're sleeping," Vasiht'h added, ears sagging.

"I know." His smile became more natural, faltered. "When I read that bit, I went looking to see if anyone else had talked about you, and the people who've actually had you as clients liked you a lot. So I figured I'd try you, if you're still looking for new clients."

/As if we have so many we don't have time for new ones!/ Vasiht'h said.

/I would not mind being somewhat closer to that situation than the one we are in now./

Vasiht'h refrained from glancing askance at the Eldritch. */Don't tell me you're worried about money now./*

/No, arii. But you are, and what concerns you concerns me./

Vasiht'h tried not to wince. So much for keeping his worries from bleeding into the mindline. "We'd be glad to take you on. What days and times work for you?"

"And perhaps you could tell us a little of what brings you to our office?" Jahir said.

"Sure."

The Asanii's name was Rook Talben, and he described his issue with a casual air that fooled no one in the room: the loss of his older brother had disturbed him 'more than I feel is normal.' By trade, he was a physical therapist, with specialties in massage and kinetic movement, "So you see, I'm used to people waxing hyperbolic about the dangers of a profession they think salacious. You see people while they sleep; I touch people while they're naked. It can scare people."

After he'd departed with an appointment to return later that week, Vasiht'h said to Jahir, "So Tiber lost us one client and got us another one. I'm not sure now whether to be glad or angry at him for his public accusation."

"It was not accusation, so much as strongly-worded warning." Vasiht'h snorted.

"He is doing what he believes necessary, as are we," Jahir said.

"Perhaps you should consider it more in light of a favor. We want only those who are certain of their choice to be our client, yes?"

Saying he didn't want to forgive Tiber for being obnoxious was getting old. Especially since Vasiht'h wasn't sure if it was true or not. Instead he asked, hesitant, "Are you really worried about money because I am?"

Jahir looked at him over the rim of his tablet, his mug in hand. "You have tried not being worried about money because I am not," he said finally, "And that has not worked for you. I thought I might try your way instead?"

"My way is neurotic!" Vasiht'h exclaimed.

Jahir set the cup and tablet down and folded his hands in his lap.

Blushing, Vasiht'h said, "Well, it is. I know it is, it's just . . ." He scrubbed at his face and sighed, irritated with himself. "I should be over this by now."

"You did just tell Rook Talben that the amount of time an issue takes is the amount of time it takes."

"I'm great at *giving* advice," Vasiht'h said, rueful. "That's why I'm doing it, instead of sitting on the couch and listening to it."

Something about that . . .

Shaking himself, he said, "But if you think we're fine for money?"

"Arii," Jahir said gently, "In less than two months, either it will matter a great deal, or matter not at all. To spend these weeks in fretting is . . ."

"Stupid?" Vasiht'h said, rueful.

"Profitless," Jahir said firmly. More kindly, "Veta is beautiful, our neighbors congenial, our work pleasing, and our cottage comfortable. If we are to have only six months here, let us enjoy them."

Vasiht'h sighed. "You're right." He smiled a little. "The food's amazing, too."

———— ∞ ————

That night, though, he couldn't resist looking at their joint account and wondering at the stubborn stability of the numbers. He knew how much should be coming in. He knew what should be going out . . . at least, for groceries. Leaning back, he struggled not to rub his paws together. There was no universe in which he should be upset about this. Sehvi was right: he should enjoy it. Even Jahir had said so, and his partner wasn't known for his ability to *relax*. The very idea made him smile.

He didn't go to bed until after his partner had. Sitting amid the pillows, Vasiht'h looked up at the Eldritch and watched him breathe. This part felt perfect, still. The comfort of being near him. The satisfaction of *knowing* him, of knowing that he braided his hair back for sleep, that he wore long sleeves because he got cold despite the heaps of covers he preferred. That he was Vasiht'h's, in some small ways, to protect and to slowly understand. To . . . to *savor*. The mindline was like an extra blanket cuddled around him, a heart's warmth that never left.

This was precious. The idea that his worries might be jeopardizing it was unbearable.

If Sehvi had been more available, she might have talked him out of it; but his sister was busy with her wedding plans and her finals. As it was, he could hear her objections in his head: that after filling her ears for days about Tiber, he was going to do this? Was he crazy?

Yes, he thought, trotting toward the commons. Yes, he was. That was the reason he was doing this.

Fine, his invisible sister insisted. *Then try that other girl. Or your crazy adopted grandmother.*

But this was the person he needed. And who needed him, Vasiht'h thought.

You know this is going to end in tears. Just like the story of Thaddeus and Name of Girl You Can Never Remember. I totally would remember, though. You should have had this conversation with the real me instead of the fake me in your head.

Yes, he thought with a rueful smile. He certainly should have.

Even so, Vasiht'h would have never tried it had Tiber not had an open office hour every week for walk-ins. Had he had to make an appointment in his own name, he wouldn't have found the courage. Even sitting in Tiber's waiting room was hard, and he thought about leaving. The receptionist—Tiber had a receptionist!—was a soft-spoken young Seersa female, nothing like what Vasiht'h would have expected him to choose. And the room itself was the opposite of the conglomeration of odd pillows and blankets and trappings he and Jahir had begun to acquire. At some point they'd ceased to be clean and professional and had become . . . homey and quirky, he guessed. Tiber's waiting room looked more like the one he'd imagined himself having, with elegant plants, a small trickling fountain, and sleek sofas arranged around a rectangular rug.

He was still staring at the patterns in the rug when he heard boots on carpet. Looking up, he found a Malarai walking down the hall toward the reception desk. Her mask-like face would have been more beautiful had it been wearing more expression; as it was, between her solemn countenance and the black dye job on her wings, Vasiht'h didn't have any trouble guessing what she'd come to Tiber about.

The little top hat jauntily perched on her dark curls, though . . . that was a nice touch. Maybe she wasn't completely sunk in her depression.

The Malarai exchanged quiet words with the receptionist, confirming next week's appointment, and then she left. Not long now. Vasiht'h pressed his paws onto the carpet to keep them still. What would he say? How would he explain himself? Would the receptionist politely look away while they had their fight? Or would Tiber wait until they'd gotten back into his office? Vasiht'h's shoulders tensed; he could hear Sehvi now: *This is a dumb, dumb idea.*

But Tiber did not come down the hall. Trusty did. To his astonishment, the Seersa reached down and ruffled his ears. "Hi, Trusty. Is Allen ready, then?"

Trusty wagged his tail and grinned.

"Great, here's his walk-in, then. Alet, if you'll follow the dog, please?"

"I . . . sure. All right?" Bemused, Vasiht'h rose to his feet and came to a halt before the animal.

"Trusty. Take him back to Allen. Take him to Allen, Trusty."

The dog wagged his tail and turned that grin up at Vasiht'h, then set off back down the hall.

No help for it now. Besides, he was curious. He hadn't realized Tiber brought his dog to work. Vasiht'h followed.

Trusty padded into the office at the end of the hall, which shared aesthetics with the waiting room, except instead of soothing blues and greens, this one was more warm soft golds and sage greens. Instead of a fountain, there was a rock garden the length of Vasiht'h's arm with a little rake set into a table. There was no desk, which he'd expected somehow . . . only a sofa and a few chairs arranged around the table, with enough space on the floor for larger aliens to settle if they preferred that to furniture.

Tiber was leaning down to caress Trusty's head. When he looked up, though, he froze.

"This is not a joke," Vasiht'h said, holding up his hands.

"It had better not be," Tiber said. "Because it would be a damned poor one. What are you doing here?"

"Believe it or not," Vasiht'h said, "I'm here for therapy."

Tiber's eyes narrowed.

"Also not a joke?" Vasiht'h offered weakly. "I could really use someone to talk to who hasn't heard all this before, and who isn't involved."

"Why didn't you go to Minette then? Or Helga, since you're in her pocket?"

See? Invisible Sehvi said. You should have had a good answer ready for that question before you walked in.

"Because Helga's involved. Or at least, I think she is. And Minette's your friend, and I don't want to put her in the weird position of seeing me as a client when you've made your opinion of us clear."

"And yet it made sense to you to come to me. Despite knowing that opinion."

"I'm not asking for you to evaluate me as a therapist," Vasiht'h said. "But as a client." The longer he talked, the more settled he felt. As unlikely as it seemed, this *felt* like the right course of action. "If you don't think you can, then I'll go. But . . . I think you're a fair man, alet. And your clients speak highly of you. If you can help me, I think you will."

Tiber scowled at him. "This is not some backhanded way to make me trust you."

"If it makes you trust me, I won't be sorry," Vasiht'h said. "But mostly I'm hoping you'll help me with something that needs fixing, before it breaks the best thing in my life."

Tiber paused, his hands stilling on Trusty's neck. "All right," he said finally, and everything about him shifted. His body language, his voice, his expression . . . all of it felt receptive, suddenly, and competent. "That sounds serious. Get comfortable, then, and tell me what's on your mind."

Here was the man Vasiht'h could imagine clients returning to continually for help. Satisfied—and hopeful—he sat sphinx-like alongside the table and started to talk.

Of course, talking made him face that he hadn't come here solely to try to fix the rift between Tiber and himself and Jahir. He started with his nebulous feelings of inadequacy, branched out into specifics about his family, explained Sehvi's opinion of the matter, tried not to bellyache about the money situation and his sense that he wasn't contributing enough. It just kept going and going, like he was emptying out a bucket without realizing it had been attached to a lake.

"Am I crazy?" he said, when he was done. By then Trusty had inched over to him and had set his muzzle on Vasiht'h's paw.

Tiber frowned, but not in anger. He looked pensive, instead, as if he was giving serious thought to the gestalt. "You have a lot going on. But no, of course you're not crazy." He eyed Vasiht'h and smiled a little. "As you should know. Mister 'also a therapist.'"

"I know what I *should* know," Vasiht'h said. "That doesn't mean I always listen to myself."

"Yes," Tiber said. "That describes us all, more often than we wish. Would it be accurate for me to say that your issues began prior to meeting your partner?"

"Yes," Vasiht'h said slowly, because it was hard to remember his life before Jahir. He skipped back to those first years in the university, floundering his way through learning how to budget, being embarrassed at all his mistakes, slowly getting it right and wondering when he was going to get it wrong again. "Yes."

"Then this situation with your partner only exacerbated a pre-existing condition."

Vasiht'h nodded. "I'd agree with that." He hesitated. "You want me to pay attention to that. So that I don't go blaming the relationship, I guess."

"I think one of your significant concerns is whether this relationship is good for you," Tiber said. "But relationships that encourage us to confront some of the issues we should be working on aren't always bad. They can be growth opportunities, especially if your partner is committed to your well-being."

"I don't question that."

Tiber cocked his head in a way eerily reminiscent of his dog. "That sounded definitive."

Vasiht'h rested his hand over his heart. "I feel it here. Literally. That would be the mindline."

"A bond, you said earlier," Tiber said, with more interest than Vasiht'h expected given the human's problems with their methodology. It was a clinical interest, but Tiber could have chosen not to ask. "A rare one."

"Right. No one knows how it works, but sometimes people are just compatible with you, heart and mind," Vasiht'h answered. "Sort of the way people are sometimes sexually attracted to one another, I guess. You just are, the chemistry's there."

"How does it manifest?"

"The bond?" Vasiht'h tried petting the dog, whose tail thumped softly on the floor. Dogs were furry. It was a little freeing, to be able to touch something that felt like another Pelted without having to worry about them misinterpreting it. "I hear his thoughts in my head, and often his feelings."

"You don't confuse them for your own?" Tiber asked.

"Goddess, no!" Vasiht'h laughed. "His thoughts are utterly unlike mine. He's like sunshine and tea and music with lots of string instruments. I'm nothing like that. I'm practical and not at all romantic." He made a face. "I can't even get into the one romance novel my sisters sent me."

"Sunshine," Tiber repeated, bemused.

"I know it doesn't make much sense, given how mysterious he is," Vasiht'h said. "But he's not really a dark of the moon kind of person, no matter how many secrets he feels he has to keep, or how many memories he's forgotten because they happened to him decades before I was born. He still feels new to me. And wide, like a summer sky. He makes my life better."

"Even when he's discomfiting you?" Tiber asked, and the tone in his voice . . . was he teasing? It felt very gentle. Vasiht'h hadn't thought him capable of gentleness.

"Even when he's making me face my issues," Vasiht'h agreed with a smile. "I guess I forgot that."

"I doubt that," Tiber said. "It sounds more like you know you can rely on it, so it just doesn't occur to you to question it."

"I guess there's that too." Should he keep talking about this, knowing Tiber's wife had left him? It seemed cruel to prattle on about his own idyllic relationship. Vasiht'h tried for a different tack. "But I do hear his thoughts in my head in his voice, with his intonations, so that's another way I know they're different from mine. And it's different from when I imagine the voices of people I know well in my head." He thought of his conversation with imaginary Sehvi. "It's like his voice casts a shadow in my head, because it's real and has volume and weight. But people whose voices I'm imagining, they're insubstantial. Like ghosts. Even if I know them well enough to be able to guess what they'd say and how they'd say it, it's still not real in my head."

"It sounds fascinating," Tiber said.

"I never really thought about how it works," Vasiht'h admitted. "It's just . . . something I've grown up with. Not the mindline part, but the 'being able to tell the difference between the inside of my head and someone else visiting it.' Some things you just know. I don't think you have to be an esper, either. I think you always know when something doesn't belong inside your head."

"Whose voice is in your head when you think about not having a handle on your life?" Tiber asked.

"Mine," Vasiht'h answered, reflexive. He winced. "I guess I've internalized all the messages I kept hearing from people who might not be right."

"I think the people who were encouraging you to grow up had your best interests at heart, from how you've described them," Tiber said. "And they have a point: we all have to grow up and start shouldering our responsibilities. The only question is why you think you haven't yet."

"Maybe we can talk about that another time?" Vasiht'h asked. "The hour's up . . . I don't want to keep you. But . . . I'd like to come back."

"Absolutely," Tiber said. "Though don't use the walk-in slot next time."

Rising, Vasiht'h smiled crookedly. "I guess I'm an official client?"

"Does that seem strange to you?"

"Yes," Vasiht'h said, finding it funny.

Tiber surprised him by grinning. "Good. Because it does to me too. But if you feel like you want to come back because I helped, then I'm glad you stopped by."

"Me too," Vasiht'h replied.

On the way home, Vasiht'h reflected on the encounter, finding it poignant and funny, the way life was sometimes. He really had felt relieved, unburdening himself to someone who wasn't going to be hurt by the hearing. Tiber had been a good listener, and a sympathetic therapist despite their history. And petting the dog had been oddly soothing. Best of all, talking it out made him realize how lucky he was in his partner, and how much he loved the Eldritch. Sehvi hadn't been wrong to tell him to stop letting his issues poison his relationship. And Tiber's observation about relationships that helped you grow was also trenchant.

How ridiculous it was to be reflecting that therapy could be helpful! He grinned, shook his head, and ducked into the bakery. Tonight seemed a good night for soup. If Jahir brought him sunlight and romance—more real romance than anything poor Thaddeus had access to—then he was definitely the one who brought the good and homey things to keep Jahir grounded.

CHAPTER 18

$\mathcal{J}$OYNER DID NOT RETURN, despite Lennea's urging, but Rook became a regular client following his first appointment: "I get what you're doing here. It's a lot like what I try to do, except I can't have that experience by going to another massage therapist . . . I'm too busy picking apart what they're doing, trying to learn something or critique it. And I want that experience, of someone taking care of me while I relax. So this works for me."

Tiber's warning, then, did not materially harm them, unless it prevented new clients from seeking them out. Jahir supposed it might have been doing so, but as he'd told Vasiht'h, dwelling on the possibility was profitless. His prediction of their future was far more dependent on Helga's goodwill than Tiber's, for he guessed that if they pleased her, she would send all her clients to them, not just the ones she'd chosen as test cases.

That she was testing them was incontrovertible. Vasiht'h attempted to corner her into admitting it over dinner, but she sidestepped direct questions with the skill of an Eldritch courtier; recognizing the techniques, Jahir could only smile over his cup and let her be. She knew, too, because now and then she would spar with him.

/It's like a game of 'how much can you imply but not communicate *clearly,'/* Vasiht'h said one night, listening with sagging ears. His exasperation sizzled, but more like something being seared in a pan rather than something burning under a too-hot sun, so Jahir thought the annoyance minor. */The point of talking is to communicate!/*

/Yes,/ Jahir said. */But sometimes what one wishes to communicate is more complex than an idea./*

/You lost me./

/In this case, how the idea is conveyed tells us something. Yes? She does not wish to commit to definitive responses. That is useful data. And she would like us to know it, because she's making her evasions patently clear./

/Why would she want us to know that she doesn't want us to know something, though??/

/Ah,/ Jahir said, hiding his smile. */That would be the more interesting question, wouldn't it./*

/It still seems unnecessarily convoluted to me./

/Sometimes it does to me as well./ And as for the times it didn't, Jahir let those go unspoken. But he wondered what Vasiht'h felt through the mindline; if the whisper of dresses on cold marble floors echoed into his friend's mind, and the hush of conversations undertaken in shadowed alcoves . . . or if he merely sensed them as an unease, without form or metaphor.

Such a fascinating thing, the mindline. Who would ever have conceived of it?

The days slipped past. They cooked together, and sat in the garden. They walked the charming streets of the Garden District, and the bustling ones of the commons. They explored the city in their time off, ranging through parks and wandering boutiques. And they entertained: Helga and often Hector, Ilea when she chose to come by. There were people who remembered their names; there were several times more people who recognized them and nodded or waved on their way past.

It was not an idyllic existence, to work without knowing what would come of it. But Jahir found it strangely peaceful. And the work itself was wonderful. To join minds with someone like and unlike and serve life by encouraging the health of their clients was balm for the soul. And that he would never have known had he not left the homeworld.

∞∞

Pieter missed three appointments.

"Do you think we did something wrong?" Vasiht'h asked one day, frowning. "By suggesting he go back."

"No," Jahir said. "At least, I don't believe so."

"Maybe his kits didn't take it well."

"Mayhap."

Vasiht'h wrinkled his nose. "I guess we'll never know."

But they did learn, because Pieter returned on the fourth week. He nodded to them with his customary lack of dramatics and peeled off his boots to stretch out on the couch. Within moments, he was asleep, without any word of explanation for his absence or what it might imply about his current needs. Because he was there, and because they had no other ideas, they joined hands and went into his dreams, and found that they had changed. No more riotous adventures; no more sports bordering on dangerous extremes. Instead, they found him hanging again in space, and after staring contentedly into that void for a while, he reeled himself back in and started work on something neither of them understood. It involved welding? Pieter's mind tagged some of it as dangerous—mostly the large pieces of hardware floating alongside in space, being guided into place with technology Jahir did not understand—but none of it alarmed Pieter. He was a man in his proper context, and all of it felt new, the details crisp and interesting.

They all woke together. The Seersa was smiling.

"Your new job?" Vasiht'h guessed.

"On base, yeah. Don't really want anything that takes me too far from the kits. Especially with Brenna expecting. But it's good work."

"Repair?" Jahir guessed.

"And building," Pieter said. "Starships don't come from

genies. Someone's got to put them together."

"And that's you," Vasiht'h said.

"And that's me." He sat up. "So . . . I hate to repay you this way, but . . ."

"You don't need us anymore?" Vasiht'h said, grinning.

"I think I'm good. But if something comes up, I know where to go. And I know where to send any friends." He smiled at them, a sunny, confident smile, with just a hint of mischief, and in it Jahir saw the young man who'd given himself to Fleet in the beginning. "I'll tell them they'll be in good hands."

"We appreciate that," Vasiht'h said.

At the door, Pieter covered Vasiht'h's palm and nodded to Jahir. "You all keep yourselves well."

"We will. Good luck," Vasiht'h said.

"And good hunting, alet," Jahir said.

Another of those unexpected grins. Then Pieter left.

"I can't say I'm glad to lose the money," Vasiht'h said, his satisfaction thick as cream, "but Goddess, that was fantastic."

"It was, was it not?" Jahir said.

"Mmm-hmm." Vasiht'h eyed him. "And why do I feel like you're about to say something funny?"

"I don't think that I am," Jahir answered, modestly. "But I do feel this requires celebration."

"Which means ice cream?"

"Your pleasure tastes like it."

Vasiht'h laughed. "No! Your brain *interprets* my pleasure as tasting like ice cream. That's all you, arii."

"Are you certain?" Jahir asked, innocent.

"I . . . am almost entirely sure." Vasiht'h paused. "Ice cream really is good, though. And pleasurable. Satisfying. I can see the association working."

"You often associate emotions with food."

"Do I?" Vasiht'h chuckled. "I bet I do." He reached for his saddlebags. "Well, let's put up the 'we're out, come back later' sign and see what Karina has today."

On the way, Vasiht'h said, "I'm glad we suggested Fleet to

him."

"So am I," Jahir replied.

"At what point does lifestyle become a necessary part of health?" Jahir asked. "To the point that healthcare practitioners must be obliged to address it?"

Across the parsecs, KindlesFlame snorted. "At the point we're born? You can't separate health from lifestyle, arii. The choices we make intimately affect our bodies and minds." He raised a finger. "Not to say that it's all under our control, of course. But we are the stewards of our bodies, and every decision we make involves them, if it involves us."

"Rather a great deal of responsibility," Jahir murmured.

"But a satisfying one," his mentor said. "Responsibility is the mother of satisfaction. From the moment we leave our childhood behind and grasp that we really are the author of our own destinies, we have access to a kind of satisfaction that we can never achieve without shouldering the duties and responsibilities of adulthood." Jahir eyed him, and the Tam-illee grinned. "Should I be worried that I've just told someone four times my age that growing up is a good idea?"

"No," Jahir said. "One can be very old, chronologically, and not yet mature. Because, as you say, those burdens have not been accepted."

"True. More your bailiwick right now than mine."

Jahir noted the 'right now' and did not comment on it. KindlesFlame had accepted as obvious that one day Jahir would return to the medical track, a path he himself remained uncertain of. But that he had time to decide—that he trusted. "So it is not inappropriate to advise our clients to make changes to their lifestyles. Perhaps enormous ones."

"If you think it will help them, it's your duty to do so. They might disagree with you of course, but that's their prerogative. And in fact, their duty, as well. Because they are their own people, and only they can make the final decisions about their own lives." KindlesFlame canted his head. "I take it you ran into this situation?"

Could he talk about it now that Pieter was no longer his client? "We suggested taking up a job to a client, who did so."

"And did it go well?"

"They no longer require our services."

KindlesFlame chuckles. "If only all of them were that easy."

"I do not know that I would call it easy," Jahir said, remembering. "But it was decisive. Many of the factors that drive people to therapy are chronic conditions, and respond only to management, not direct intervention."

"Like the difference between your hospital stint and a normal clinical practice?" KindlesFlame smiled. "Surgery was deeply satisfying."

"But broken legs and minor viruses are far more livable," Jahir said, smiling back.

The Tam-illee chuckled. "Would that all my students listened so closely to me. It sounds like the work part of your life is going well. How about the rest of it? Has your partner settled down?"

"He seems to have," Jahir said. "Our situation is inherently discomfiting. It is . . . difficult . . . not to be able to plan for your future. We are accustomed to the illusion of control."

"You don't seem too discomfited to me."

Jahir thought of the terrors of Selnor, the fatigue, the grinding sorrow of it, the acceleration of his heartbeat, the contraction of his life. "I no longer fear myself unequal to the challenges typical of the Alliance."

"My, that's quite a statement." At Jahir's quizzical look, the Tam-illee said, "I commend your confidence, my student. Just make sure it doesn't become hubris. Not everything here is about whether you can book enough clients to afford the fancy restaurant or the corner diner."

"I hope I never make that mistake," Jahir agreed. "I have a great deal left to learn."

"Just keep that in mind and you'll do all right." KindlesFlame tapped his fingers on his coffee mug, paused on the way to his lips. "Humility. Humility is key."

"Yes."

"For most of us," he finished, eyeing Jahir. "You might have too much of that already."

"Then what is key for me?" Jahir asked, fighting amusement.

KindlesFlame considered him over the rim of his mug. He said, finally, "Courage."

Surprised, Jahir said, "Truly?"

"It's a long game, arii," the Tam-illee answered. "And in the long game, courage gets us home."

Brenna Strong came to them later that week, during one of their walk-in hours. ("We might as well have some," Vasiht'h had said. "Since it's not like we don't have the time for them.") She thanked them effusively for helping her father, having a seat on their couch and folding her hands on her lap. "He's so much more . . . I don't know. More settled now. I never would have thought that being in Fleet again would make him *less* reckless, but it really has! I guess you can't afford to be reckless when you're welding together starships."

"I would imagine not," Jahir said.

"Anyway, I'm so grateful, and so is Roland. You did an amazing job with him, after no one else was able to help."

"We appreciate you telling us so," Vasiht'h said, smiling. "We don't always hear back."

She beamed at him. "Well, consider yourself told. In fact, you worked such a miracle for him I was hoping you could manage another one for me?"

"For you?" Jahir asked.

"I know. I didn't think I'd ever need therapy," Brenna said. "But then this situation happened and . . ." Her arms fell open, palms up. "I just don't know how to handle it. You see, I'm pregnant and intellectually I'm thrilled, but I can't seem to figure out how to . . . how to *feel* happy about it."

The surge through the mindline reminded Jahir of the time

his swordmaster had surprised him with a riposte that had caught him full in the sternum: stunned and a little dizzied by something that he hadn't been expecting. */What do we do with this?/* Vasiht'h asked.

/The same we do with all our clients. We listen, and we let them rest?/

"I really want this baby," Brenna hastened to assure them. "That must have sounded awful. My husband and I have been planning this for a while. We're both very happy! Or at least, I think I'm happy. But I'm not. What I am is . . ." She looked away, frowned, ears flattening. "I'm . . . angry? Or I feel strange, like I'm not in my body at all. On bad days, I even think that someone's shoved me out of it. Literally, like the baby is now the one in charge of my body and I'm the one who's getting told to find a hotel room somewhere. I don't recognize the inside of my own head most days." Her shoulders slumped. "It's ridiculous. I look at baby clothes and nursery furniture and I don't *feel* anything. This was supposed to be one of the most exciting times of my life and I'm not here for it. Not me, the real me." She managed a little smile. "Help?"

"It's what we're here for," Vasiht'h said. "You know we work mostly through dreams?"

She nodded. "My father told me. A nap sounds nice . . . I'm tired a lot. I guess that's normal."

"Definitely," Vasiht'h said. "Your body is working hard right now. So just plump up whatever pillows look good to you—they all have fresh covers—and pick out the blankets and we'll leave you alone for a bit, all right?"

"Would you like a tea?" Jahir added.

"No, I'm fine. Thank you."

/What do you think?/ Vasiht'h asked outside.

/I don't know,/ Jahir admitted. */I suppose we will see./*

Inside, Jahir joined himself to Vasiht'h and reached for Brenna, and found himself distracted by an unexpected and beautiful complexity. Their sense of her was much the same as any client, but it was not alone.

/He dreams!/ Jahir said, charmed.

Vasiht'h's smile felt satisfied and protective. /They do, yes./

/So young, though . . . !/

/The few times I've chatting with one of my pregnant relatives . . . yes. They're their own thing immediately, with plans and business of their own! If that makes sense. They're busy making themselves from the moment they have all the building blocks, so . . ./ Vasiht'h smiled, a memory tinging his speech golden. /One of my cousins told me she knew the day she conceived. Some women do, I guess. Maybe this is part of why./

/I had no idea,/ Jahir said, examining the bright spark without touching it. /Do you know what they dream?/

/I've never tried to find out. I mean, once they're old enough to kick and push you can't avoid hearing what they're feeling, but by then they're like small versions of us anyway. Not verbal, of course, but they get hungry and curious and sleepy and irritated, just like babies who are outside their mothers do. But this young? I'm a little scared to touch them, you know?/

/Yes,/ Jahir breathed. /He seems so delicate./

/And yet it's a hardy process. My sister will tell you . . . once it gets going, it takes a lot to stop it. That's what makes the Pelted problems with it so tragic. Having parents, growing up, having kids, being part of a family . . . that's really basic to everyone who lives. Being engineered . . . it interrupted that process for a lot of people./

Jahir watched the spark shimmer and dim, then glow brighter . . . busy with its own developing life. He'd never considered the intersection of their talents and children, particularly prenatal. It was magical.

/Me too,/ Vasiht'h said softly. /It never gets old./

/No,/ Jahir answered. /I cannot imagine it does. But we have a duty./

/Let's see what's going on./

Brenna's dreams, when they entered them, were nothing like any other dreams they'd encountered. They reminded Jahir more of the wet hallucinations from the victims on Selnor, though he couldn't decide why. Their content was normal enough: random day to day images of Brenna's life, occasional montages involving babies, or a hazy silhouette they decided must be her deceased mother. But the dreams resisted manipulation; they felt murky and dense, the colors dark except where they were too bright, like a storm-clotted day. Her mind resisted their departure as well, dragging at them like mud.

/What was that?/ Vasiht'h rubbed his arms. /Ugh!/

/I don't know,/ Jahir said slowly.

His partner glanced at him, eyes narrowed. /You don't know but you have an idea./

/I was thinking . . . that they reminded me in kind, somehow, of the patients on Selnor./

A cold shudder, like the call of an unidentifiable animal in a night forest, came through the mindline. /She's not . . ./

/No,/ Jahir said. /But this might have more to do with the changes in her body than what we usually handle./

Vasiht'h was silent for some time, considering the sleeping Seersa. /What we do eventually affects the body, though./

/Yes. But is that a good idea, given that her body is doing things we don't understand?/ Jahir smiled a little. /Unless you understand the biology of pregnancy more intimately than I do . . ./

/Not likely! Despite seeing enough of it in my extended family./ Vasiht'h sighed. /So what should we do?/

/There are several medical therapists at the hospital. I would suggest referring her to one of them./

Vasiht'h nodded. /That makes sense. I hope it goes over well./

Jahir reached for his tablet. /I will see if one of them is willing to see her. Perhaps you might have something ready for her to eat when she wakes? Her dreams did not seem to suggest any experience with nausea./

/Right./

By the time Brenna woke, Vasiht'h had set out a tea tray and Jahir had a follow-up appointment prepared. The Seersa woke groggy and grateful for the drink, nibbling on one of the cookies. "So how does it look?" she asked. "Am I totally broken?"

/Maybe you should handle this one. You're better with words

than I am./

/I would dispute that,/ Jahir said, but he accepted the charge. "We do not believe you to be broken at all. But our suspicion, after witnessing your dreams, is that your paradoxical reaction to an event you have been looking forward to all your life might be partially, or perhaps entirely, the result of the biological changes created by your pregnancy."

Brenna's hand sagged, cookie forgotten. "You think it's physical?"

"The evidence is suggestive."

"That's so *weird*," she said, eyes wide. "Why would my body sabotage itself that way?"

"Your body is not intentionally sabotaging your wellbeing," Jahir said. "Think of it as an unfortunate side effect of its efforts. Your body is new to this particular process; it may be that subsequent pregnancies will not have this effect—"

"Or it might make it worse!" She shivered. "What do I do now? Can you fix it?"

"This is not our expertise," Jahir said. "With your permission, we'd like to refer you to Healer Tenebra at Veta General. She has specific experience with women in all stages of this process, and is a mother herself."

Brenna's ears perked. "That sounds helpful."

"We think it will be," Vasiht'h said. "She's in a better position to help you than we are."

"Here," Jahir said, offering a folded slip of paper. "The appointment time and direction. If you need to reschedule, her contact information is at the bottom."

"You wrote it on paper," Brenna said, sounding charmed. She looked at the paper. "Thank you. Goodness, you have nice handwriting. You should go into calligraphy."

Jahir ignored Vasiht'h's amused look. "Thank you."

"I really appreciate this," she said on her way out. "Knowing that it might be more complicated than just my own feelings. Or at least, that my feelings are wrapped up in something bigger than I am. Does that make sense?" She smiled at them both. "I feel a little better already."

"We wish you the best of luck," Vasiht'h said. "Take care of yourself, alet." Once she'd gone, he surveyed their office and started tidying. "Well, that went better than it could have."

"She will do well with Healer Tenebra."

Vasiht'h nodded. "There's a cookie left. You should eat it."

Jahir eyed him.

"It's that or salmon mousse with your scones."

With a sigh, Jahir took the cookie. But he smiled while eating it.

———❦———

Vasiht'h decided once every two weeks as a reasonable periodicity for his visits to Tiber, to balance his need to talk with his budget. That first visit had refocused him on his priorities, and while he didn't feel he was in serious need of therapy, he valued the way Tiber reset his perspective when it was in danger of going awry. "You'll probably only feel these visits necessary while you're uncertain of your financial status," Tiber said. "Once you settle that, a lot of this will resolve."

"But not all of it?" Vasiht'h asked.

Tiber smiled a little. "Most of us have one or two trigger issues that we never stop grappling with. This might be one of yours."

On reflection, Vasiht'h thought he was right.

A week after they referred Brenna, Vasiht'h followed Trusty into Tiber's office and sank into his customary place on the carpet. The dog waited until he was done and then rested his muzzle on Vasiht'h's paw. As usual, he rambled to Tiber, about growing up, about wishing he knew one way or the other about Veta, about how much he disliked uncertainty—that becoming a philosophical discussion between them over different belief systems that helped people handle those uncertainties, one they punctuated with experiences with clients that had demonstrated them best. Vasiht'h hadn't had as many, of course, and the university system had skewed heavily Seersan in population, but he felt he gave back to the discussion well despite that, and Tiber's experiences were fascinating. Necessarily nebulous, given the constraints of their ability to discuss any personal details, but listening to him, Vasiht'h had a sense of his breadth and compassion, revealed in accidental ways.

It no longer irritated him, finding things to like about Tiber. He didn't even think it regrettable. Most of them time, it didn't occur to him that they had fought at all . . . which suited Vasiht'h, since he didn't have the energy for grudges.

But as their session wound up and Vasiht'h administered one last ear-rub to the enthusiastic dog, Tiber said, "I hear you referred someone to the hospital therapy team."

Because of the time he'd spent unweighing himself to Tiber, Vasiht'h didn't think anything of saying, "We thought she needed someone with expertise in her situation. We didn't have it." Straightening, he said, "She's a Pelted client, so I can ask . . . did she go? We didn't follow up with Healer Tenebra."

"She went," Tiber said, eyes unreadable.

"Good," Vasiht'h said. "I hope it helped."

"That's it?" Tiber's words were reluctant, as if he knew as well as Vasiht'h did that this conversation was . . . inappropriate was a strong word. What would Jahir have said? Ill-advised? Poorly timed? Vasiht'h smiled a little, trying to imagine.

"That's it," he said. "Did you expect us to hang on to someone we didn't feel we could treat?" Tiber looked away and Vasiht'h sighed, resigned. "Allen. Don't you know at least me better by now? And you met Jahir . . . in a towel and a swimsuit, even, which isn't the least vulnerable of times to confront someone. Do you think he's capable of the kind of pride you're accusing us of?"

"I don't think it's pride," Tiber muttered.

"You think it's lack of experience, and a dangerous confidence in our own methods," Vasiht'h said. "I'll grant the lack of experience. And we *are* confident. Really confident, which means when we run into something we can't handle, we can admit it to each other and do the right thing."

"I shouldn't have brought it up," Tiber said with a grimace. "I'm sorry. It wasn't professional."

"It wasn't, no," Vasiht'h said. "But we're all people here, making mistakes, and forgiving each other for them. And, I hope, helping each other through them."

Tiber made an acquiescent gesture, but he remained visibly flustered. Vasiht'h took pity on him and left before either of them could fumble their way into an actual argument.

"So," Sehvi said, listening to this story sometime later. "You decided to start seeing the therapist you hated for your problems, and you're at the point now where you don't want to bludgeon him even when he gives you amazing openings? Seriously, ariihir?"

"I know," Vasiht'h said. "I'm sure it doesn't make sense to anyone else. But it was either keep him as an enemy forever, or make a neighbor out of him. It's hard to hate people you know well. Since he wasn't going to reach out to us, I figured I'd take the first step?"

"Brave of you," she said, her face cushioned on both hands as she watched him set up for dinner through the wallscreen. "But you know sometimes getting to know someone makes you hate them more, right?"

He eyed her over his shoulder.

"Even the humans knew that. 'Familiarity breeds contempt.'"

Vasiht'h wrinkled his nose. "I'm pretty sure that's not what that saying is supposed to mean."

"It's what it means now." She grinned. "Seriously. There's such a thing as knowing people too well. You can learn things about them you don't like, or that confirm your worst feelings about them . . ."

"Like their taste in terrible novels?"

Sehvi sniffed. "I don't know who you could be referring to. The only people I know have *excellent* taste in novels. Particularly me."

Vasiht'h thought about it while breaking the lettuce for salad. Did he fear learning something about people that would make him hate them? In all his life, his experience had been the opposite: learning more about people made him feel more compassion for them. He guessed there had to be people out there with beliefs so awful he couldn't forgive them for holding them, but . . . he hadn't run into anyone like that. The Alliance was full of different people and cultures, but even the most alien ones made sense for those people. As long as a Harat-Shar didn't want him to live like a Harat-Shar, he didn't really care how the Harat-Shar lived. "I think it's fine, Sehvi. I'm not afraid of people's deep, dark secrets."

"Maybe you haven't run into enough bad ones yet."

He chuckled. "Maybe. But I graduated with a psychology degree, ariishir! I've read things that would make your fur fall out. I know bad things exist. But they're rare. And all the other stuff is just . . . those are irritations, really."

"If you say so," she said.

"I do." He smiled lopsidedly. "We're all works in progress. If we don't love each other for that, what have we got?"

She studied him for a long moment, then smiled. "Guess that's why you're the therapist and I'm the one that works with dividing cells that don't talk."

"You talk with prospective mothers and fathers!"

"Who make me wish they couldn't talk."

Vasiht'h laughed. "You're awful, Sehvi."

"You see? I told you people are full of things you don't want to know!"

"I still love you though," Vasiht'h said, serenely. "So I win."

Her smile softened. "We both do."

Vasiht'h brought down the bowl to give them both time to savor that before finishing, "You could never let me have the last word, could you."

"Of course not," she said, eyes sparkling. "I wouldn't want you to get used to winning when we all know the universe is unfair. Think of it as a life lesson."

He sighed and chuckled. "Isn't everything."

CHAPTER 19

T HE LONGER LENNEA REMAINED acting principal, the less she slept for them. Most of the time she didn't even try; she would have tea and a cookie and talk about the week's tribulations. But trying she would often fail, and they would return fifteen minutes into the appointment to find her under the covers with only the top of her face peeping out, eyes wide open.

"It's no use," she told them one day with a sigh. "Every time I try to lie down, I start twitching. All the things I've left undone. All the things I don't know how to resolve. All the things coming next week that I know are coming and are just awful and that I don't want to deal with. They're all *right there* and I'm afraid to close my eyes. Even with the two of you guarding my sleep." She looked at them mournfully. "I'm so tired."

"We could brew you a specific?" Jahir said gently. "It might help you pass the threshold."

"Let's try that next time," she said. "For now, could I just . . . stay here? Under the covers? Can we talk from here?"

"Of course we can," Vasiht'h said. /Maybe we should buy a few stuffed toys./

/Those are not considered juvenile?/

/Depends on the person,/ Vasiht'h said. /And she sure looks like *she could use one./*

/She does at that,/ Jahir said, a little sadly. */This work is not suited to her, in any way. I fail to understand how this school board does not perceive it . . . that they have engaged a gentle spirit better suited to teaching children for a position that needs a crusading warrior./*

/Like Ametia,/ Vasiht'h agreed. */Ametia would love this job./*

Jahir froze as he reached for his cup of tea, a hesitation he hoped Lennea wouldn't notice.

/No,/ Vasiht'h murmured with a frown. */That can't possibly be the right thing to do again. That would be asking too much. We fixed Pieter's problem entirely by sending him to a new job. We can't fix Lennea's too by getting her out of her current one./*

/The situations are not directly analogous,/ Jahir said.

/They're similar enough!/

/Muyhup,/ Jahir said. And added, */But negative stress can be created by our external situations. If the external situation can be ameliorated . . . ?/*

/We're not career counselors!/

That made Jahir smile and he hid it by ducking his head and attending to his tea. */We are a fresh perspective on the lives of our clients. When we see things that they might not, is it not our obligation to speak?/*

Vasiht'h eyed him.

"Are there any cookies, maybe?" Lennea said into their internal monologue, oblivious. "Or, I would get crumbs on your sofa. I guess I should sit up?"

"We clean the couch every day," Vasiht'h said. "But you should definitely sit up."

They concentrated on her for the remainder of her visit, but after it Vasiht'h folded his arms and glowered at him.

"You are only wroth because you suspect I may be right," Jahir said.

That diffused the storm gathering in the mindline, as he suspected it might. Vasiht'h started laughing. "Goddess, that makes me sound like something out of a dramatic novel. No, I'm not . . .

'wroth' . . . ! But sometimes this job . . ." He sighed and chuckled. "Sometimes it asks us to be things we don't expect, I guess."

"As the best things in life do," Jahir agreed, pleased.

"I guess they do, at that."

———⦿———

While Vasiht'h still nursed ambivalent feelings about HEALED BY HER IMMORTAL HEART, by the seventy percent point he wanted to see how it ended, if only to have something to talk about with his sisters next time they saw one another. It also kept him occupied when he wasn't making his attempts at Ilea's garden, or wandering the Garden District, or burning too much incense in the siv't, or wishing he could talk to Sehvi more often. He had just opened the novel when his message alert chimed, and to his delight he found a note from Professor Palland. 'Thought I'd see how one of my favorite students was doing,' was all it said, with Palland's typical terseness; he had never been a fan of electronic communication—some of the notes Vasiht'h had gotten from him in school had been almost unintelligibly short—so receiving one was a high compliment. One of his favorite students! Vasiht'h sat back, wide-eyed. Palland had been a professor for over fifteen years? Twenty? How many students had he had, and yet Vasiht'h had been one of his favorites?

He spread a reply and started typing, describing the starbase, and the satisfaction of working with clients at last, and how dream therapy was differing in practice than it had in the hothouse environment of the hospital or school clinics. As he wrote, the old vocabulary came back to him, and he found himself discussing it in the same scholarly way he'd had to write his research conclusions after the experiments. That he remembered how to talk that way surprised him, and he was a little proud of it. Maybe he'd been listening too much to the voices outside—and inside—his head about how what he was doing was some kind of unscientific quackery. Palland would have been the first to tell him that something's inexplicability made it more of a candidate for inquiry, not less, and that science grew by its questions, not their answers.

Re-reading his message, he saw his own enthusiasm for what they were doing. He really did believe in the work. For all its challenges and uncertainties, this was where he belonged. Maybe not here in particular, on Veta, but doing this, with Jahir. It coursed through him like the breath of the Goddess so powerfully he looked toward the window, expecting a breeze. The window, being closed, provided none, and he grinned and shook his head. And then opened it. A moment later, the breeze capered through.

"And if that's not a symbol," he told his data tablet as he sent the message to Palland, "I don't know what is."

"Should I ask?" Jahir said at the door.

Vasiht'h looked up. "Just thinking. That it's all very well to expect divine messages, but you have to make them possible before they can happen."

Setting his shopping bags on the table, Jahir canted his head. "One would expect the Divine could arrange alternate circumstances, did one make the first impossible."

"Which is the worst possible way to go about it," Vasiht'h said. "If the Goddess feels she has to come after you a second time, she usually does it with a hammer." He dug into the bags and fetched out the salad greens and a long loaf of bread with an unusual smell. He inhaled the steam rising off it and said, "Something floral? Nutty?"

"The flour is ground from the fleshy petals of a flower grown on the world where the Naysha were supposed to have been planted."

"Flower flour!" Vasiht'h inhaled again. "What a delicate smell."

"And a very fine crumb, you will find."

"Which is why you brought home salad." Vasiht'h nodded. "Well, let's see what we can put together."

It wasn't until after dinner that he finally returned to the novel. He plodded through another chapter of mutual adoration and was nearly falling asleep over the narrative when What's-Her-Name shocked him by miscarrying the miracle child. He skimmed the previous chapters, looking for any clues that the happy romance was about to veer into tragedy, but the author had left her readers utterly unprepared. Unless he was simply too unfamiliar with romances to see the signs? He turned on the commentary sidebar and was instantly inflicted with his sisters' raucous opinions.

MANDARA: Sehvi, you have totally redeemed yourself. This book is now awesome.

TAVYI: How can you say that?? This is awful! How can they have a happy ending now?? This is going to haunt them for the rest of their lives!!!!

NINEH: I am more confused at this book's sudden decision to become one with science. Why'd she do that, after building us up to the grand finale of halfling child in the perfect nursery with all the ducks?

KAVILA: It was swans.

NINEH: Birds. Whatever. My point is, why the miscarriage?

SARDA: Maybe she wanted to do a comforting-hurt sort of storyline? I'll be really disappointed if she doesn't go there. We need lots of cuddles and crying together, and growing together through this traumatic experience . . . right?

TAVYI: This was not supposed to be a realistic book. I resent realistic stuff happening in it. Can I rewrite the ending?

SARDA: Only if you share!

MANDARA: I like the horror ending! This is far more interesting than the direction it was going.

KOVRAH: Meh. They should have portrayed her crying against his chest on the cover if they wanted to go where it's going now. Does it get better?

SEHVI: It gets worse, actually. In the best of ways.

KAVILA: This is cruel and unusual punishment, Sehvi. I thought you liked us!

SEHVI: Family should have shared experiences. Awful, melodramatic, and irritating ones as well as good ones.

TAVYI: She's got a point. You've got friends to have good times with. When you need someone to share the trauma of a badly written book with you, that's when you go to family.

Vasiht'h set the tablet down and looked over at his friend's bed, where Jahir was also reading. Sensing his attention, Jahir glanced at him and though his expression was too shadowed to read clearly, his inquisitive glance felt in the mindline like a gentle touch on the hand.

"We're family, aren't we?" Vasiht'h asked.

To his relief, Jahir did not answer immediately. At last, he replied, "What else, with love?"

He did not have to reassure Vasiht'h of that love. Everything they'd been together had demonstrated it beyond any doubt. Smiling, the Glaseah put his tablet on the night table and fluffed up his pillows. As he made himself comfortable amid them, Jahir asked, "Was there a reason why you asked?"

"I just wanted to hear the answer." Pulling the blanket over himself, Vasiht'h said, "Sometimes, I think that's all we need."

He thought that would end the discussion, so he was surprised when Jahir said, "Like the window."

"The window?"

"If we would hear messages from other people, we should make it possible for them to be shared. Yes?"

Vasiht'h grinned against his pillow. "You never stop thinking, do you."

"I fear not." A trickle of humor through the mindline. "I hope it never stops interesting you."

"It won't," Vasiht'h said. "Good night, arii."

"Rest well, my friend."

⸺◦⸾◦⸺

/Now is the time,/ Jahir said to Vasiht'h.

/Are you sure?/

Watching Ametia pace, Jahir knew. How he knew, he couldn't have said . . . only that something in her agitation, in the well-worn rut of her diatribe, in the viciousness of her disappointment and frustration, spoke to him, clearly as the bell from the spire of Ontine Cathedral. /Now is the time./

/It's all yours, then./

". . . and then I ended up right back where I started," Ametia finished. "As usual." She stopped prowling, folding her arms and striking a martial pose Jahir was sure was subconscious. The thwarted warrior, overlooking the grounds of the battle and seeing no way to win. "People are idiots."

"You don't actually believe that," Vasiht'h said.

"Oh don't I?" She dropped onto the sofa. She sighed, flattening her ears. "No, you're right. But it's too easy to be cynical about the entire process."

"When you see its end," Jahir said.

"Its inevitable end," she agreed. "Because people will always coalesce into tribes and turn on other tribes."

"This you do not believe, either," Jahir said. "Or you would have ceased your efforts."

"What if I just can't give up? I'm stubborn."

"But tremendously intelligent, educated, and incisive," Jahir said. "So not likely to waste your time."

She snorted. "Very flattering. Is there a point to this particular line of discussion?"

"That you should consider applying your considerable energy to the beginning of the process, rather than wasting it on its end. Where you yourself have observed people to be too set in their ways to easily change."

"Ah?" She cocked a brow. "This sounds interesting. Go on."

"The city's primary school is seeking a principal," Jahir said. "A position of significant responsibility, charged with shaping the direction of the school and its donors. You would acquit yourself magnificently in such a role, and it would give you the opportunity to target the problem closer to its source. Yes? Surely such children are young enough to respond to your call for clemency toward other species?"

/*Goddess, I think you finally shocked her speechless./*

Apparently he had, for Ametia was staring at him, her ears sagging and eyes wide.

"Perhaps I spoke out of turn?" Jahir said, cautious.

"You want me. To herd littles around. I am *not* a parental type."

"Principals don't teach," Vasiht'h said. "They administrate."

Ametia was tapping her fingers on her leg now, as she did when she was thinking at her fastest. "Still. Children."

"They're just people who haven't grown up yet," Vasiht'h said.

"But they're so unfinished—"

"Is it not that finished quality what dismays you about your current students?" Jahir said.

She eyed them. "You are double-teaming me."

"We're just talking you out of talking yourself out of it." Vasiht'h grinned. "It's just an idea, but you have to give it a chance before you shoot it down."

"Ah!" She showed teeth, eyes lighting. "Yes. Let's *debate*."

The remainder of the hour was the most lively one they'd logged as therapists thus far. Ametia's notion of debate was strenuous, and she enjoyed every word of it. Vasiht'h did his best, but partway through it he said, /*You are so much better at me than this. How can she keep going??/*

/*This is her entertainment, arii./*

/*It's not mine!/*

/*I shall carry the flag for Lennea, then./*

/*You really think she'd work out for it? She says she finds children impossible!/*

/*Do you think she's right?/*

Vasiht'h was silent through the next few exchanges, which involved whether the school board would be as insufferable in its own way as the university board of trustees. /*No. I think she has two separate needs tangled up together. She needs to feel intellectually*

engaged with people. And she needs to feel like she's doing something important. Teaching was a way to give her both those things at once./
    /Perhaps you should say so./
    /Me??/
Jahir hid his smile, shook his head a little. */Do not make the mistake of thinking yourself less intelligent because you dislike conflict, arii. You have your own wisdom./*

∽∞∽

Vasiht'h's ears sagged. */You mean that?/*
    His partner looked at him then, the honeyed eyes gentle. */Can I lie to you thus?/*
    The warmth that drifted through the mindline, like the first rays of a sunrise on a soft spring morning . . . Vasiht'h flushed, and couldn't look away.
    "So," Ametia drawled. "Are the two of you having a moment? Should I take a bathroom break?"
    Vasiht'h cleared his throat. "It was about you, actually."
    The Harat-Shar chuckled. "Oh really. Go ahead, then. Though we're not done with this discussion, Long Tall One."
    "I remain at your service," Jahir said. "But I believe Vasiht'h's observation is pertinent."
    "I like pertinent. Go ahead, then. Awe me."
    "Do you do this to all your students?" Vasiht'h asked, rueful.
    She laughed. "Yes. They're more honest when I fluster them first."
    Vasiht'h shook his head and sighed, but it was a fond sigh. He liked Ametia . . . as a client. As a professor she would have intimidated him straight back out of the classroom. "You need conversation like this, don't you."
    "I don't like being bored, no."
    "And the university gives you that."
    "Sometimes," she said, dry. "When it's not cloaking rank stupidity in pretentious dialectics."
    "You also want to feel like you're accomplishing something worthwhile."

"Doesn't everyone?" she asked, studying him with that distant amusement.

"Why did you decide to go into teaching?"

"Because I have learned a great deal, and disseminating that knowledge is important."

"So why not do that through a primary school, and get your intellectual conversation somewhere else? Where you don't have to deal with the politics and the . . . ah . . . pretentious dialectics?" Vasiht'h asked. "If there's one thing kits are good at it, it's being earnest. They're the opposite of fake."

"And where exactly would I find this intellectual conversation outside my job?" Ametia asked, arch.

"Maybe you could talk to any coworkers you have now that you like?" Vasiht'h said. "There's no reason you can't stay friends with them."

"Or you might start a salon," Jahir said.

/You did it to her again,/ Vasiht'h said, grinning.

The shock didn't last as long this time, because she broke into a peal of laughter. "A *what?* Like something out of a . . . a human historical novel!"

"Is that where it hails from?" Jahir asked, with that ingenuous tone Vasiht'h knew was hiding so much. Amusement. A sweet interest. And memories that he could sense only as a fog, or a taste. Cream on the tongue. The sound of harps.

"I admit, the idea is compelling, despite the absurdity. Or maybe because of it." Ametia tapped her nose, still struggling with her laughter. "Ametia, grand dame of the salon. Come for intellectual amusements! Debates on epistemology! The newest compositions for harp and terspichoric lyre! Wine and imported cheese, explicated at length by visiting sommeliers!"

"You came up with all that off the top of your head?" Vasiht'h asked, bemused.

"She would make a grand mistress of a salon," Jahir agreed.

Ametia lost herself to another full-on bout of laughter.

"I have to imagine the kind of people you'd meet at a salon would make great donors to a primary school," Vasiht'h added.

"They'd be rich and interested in education."

"And dedicated to the preservation of their legacies?" Jahir said.

"You two are fantastic!" Ametia wiped her eyes, still chortling. "Battleangel. What a thought."

"But a compelling one?" Vasiht'h reminded her.

"Despite its absurdity," Jahir agreed.

She snickered. "Stop! Or I'll pull a gut muscle." She exhaled, oozing back on the couch. "Ah, that was good. I needed that. It's almost as if you all think there's some way for all this to happen."

"We do, remember? We mentioned the school is looking for a principal at the beginning of this conversation," Vasiht'h said. "It's what made us think of you."

Ametia sat up abruptly. "Lennea. This is why Lennea's been so scarce lately, isn't it? It's her school that needs help?"

"They've made her acting principal," Vasiht'h said.

"What!" Ametia jumped to her feet. "That's a horrible fit for her! She hates administration work! Why did they do that?"

"They haven't found any better candidate?" Jahir said.

Ametia fisted her hands. "What!" And then planted those fists on her hips. "Why didn't you tell me that in the first place?"

"Maybe we didn't want you to feel obliged to rescue your friend until you decided you wouldn't mind the job without the extenuating circumstance?" Vasiht'h said.

Ametia pointed at them. "That . . . is actually a very good point. So thank you. But I need to speak with Lennea immediately!"

"Just don't do anything rash?" Vasiht'h said.

"Rash!" She snorted. "Of course not. Why else have we been discussing this so vigorously for an hour? So I could knock the stuffing out of it, see where it's vulnerable. That's the purpose of debate. It clarifies one's thinking."

"As long as it clarified yours?"

"You did well enough, for therapists." Ametia grinned, flashing her fangs. "Especially you, Tall Pale. I could get used to bouncing things off you."

"As I said, we are here to serve."

"Next week, then," Ametia said, and marched out of the office.

She left a vacuum behind her when she deprived the room of her enormous presence; feeling it, Vasiht'h said, "She's wasted as a professor. She needs to be a mover and shaker somewhere."

"Perhaps this will be the moment where she decides to make that transition."

Vasiht'h hmmed. "Do you think we convinced her?"

"I don't know," Jahir admitted, and if the mindline was right that possibility tickled him.

Vasiht'h laughed. "You liked that! I didn't think you'd enjoy fighting like that."

"That was not a fight." Jahir rose to pluck up the pillow and begin changing the sheets. "It was an exercise. She was not wedded to either side of the argument—what engaged her was the process of examination."

"And you like that too."

"It was a discussion that harmed no one," Jahir said. "And there is an exhilaration inherent in the exploration of ideas. Isn't there?"

Vasiht'h smiled. "I never really thought of it. I hate debate . . . I always feel like I lose."

"Your intelligence works differently." The Eldritch unfolded the fresh set and handed the sheet down to him. "You are patient and deep and intuitive."

Flushing, Vasiht'h said, "And practical, I hope."

"And practical." The mindline softened. "I meant what I said. I mean what I say now. You are a good partner, arii."

Vasiht'h's ears splayed. "I don't feel old enough to be wise."

"Neither of us is," Jahir said. "That doesn't mean we are not endowed, occasionally, with flashes of insight. A gift, if you prefer."

"I could believe that." Vasiht'h looked toward the door and shook his head. "Poor Lennea. Ametia's going to descend on her like a storm."

"A well-meaning one," Jahir said. "But yes. They are an

interesting pair, to have become friends."

"I can see it," Vasiht'h said. "Sometimes the stormy people need someone to calm them down."

"Then they are admirably suited . . . and I hope whatever comes of this works out for the best."

"Amen," Vasiht'h murmured.

CHAPTER 20

THE DAYS SLIPPED AWAY. Vasiht'h tried to hold them the way he sensed his friend did, as precious and ephemeral things to be enjoyed, hour by hour. Some days he managed. On the days he didn't, he comforted himself that the fact that he could enjoy each day as it came some days meant he wasn't entirely consumed by his worries. In one of their sessions, Tiber recommended he research other worlds as a way to deprive the future of its louring anxiety, so he tried that and actually had fun looking at different planets and settlements and imagining himself living on them. He still wanted to stay on Veta, but considering a different future made him realize how expansive that future was, and how satisfying it would be to introduce Jahir to new parts of the Alliance, or to experience them for the first time himself.

Tiber was a lot more helpful than he'd thought possible, which made the afternoon the receptionist called to cancel his appointment disappointing. "Can we reschedule you next week?" she asked.

"Sure," Vasiht'h answered. "Is Allen all right?"

The Seersa paused, ears flicking outward. "Allen's fine. But Trusty died, so he took this week off."

"Oh no!" Vasiht'h exclaimed, shocked. "What happened? He

seemed fine last time I was there?"

"I don't know," she admitted. "It was very sudden. But Trusty was old for a dog. It was only a matter of time."

The thought of Tiber without his dog was . . . well, it was inconceivable. Vasiht'h kept trying to imagine Allen without Trusty lying at his feet or trotting alongside him and failing. He wasn't an animal person himself, but he felt stricken on Tiber's behalf.

It was their day off from the office; ordinarily Vasiht'h would have spent it puttering while Jahir wandered the starbase, and then going to find them something to cook for dinner. But he lost track of time, and when the Eldritch came back it was to a dim kitchen and a cold table.

"Arii?" Jahir said at the door. "Did you not want to eat?"

"Oh!" Vasiht'h rubbed his face, grimaced as he looked at the room. "I completely forgot."

The mindline's caress felt a little like a probe. "You were not reading . . . something is troubling you?"

Vasiht'h went to the cupboard to see if he could figure something out without resorting to the genie. "This is going to sound ridiculous but . . . Tiber's dog died."

The dismay in the mindline reassured him a little that he wasn't crazy; Jahir found the news just as upsetting. "He must be in great distress."

"He loved that dog," Vasiht'h agreed. Nothing in the refrigerator suggested anything to him. Maybe they should go out for a late supper. As he studied the selection available, the mindline developed an odd flavor, a sideways tilt that kept building until at last Vasiht'h looked over at his friend. "What?"

"You are . . . concerned . . . about Doctor Tiber."

Realizing how unlikely that was, Vasiht'h flushed. "Well, yes. I . . . ah . . . might actually be seeing him now and then. For therapy."

This pause made Vasiht'h very nervous. Unfairly, because nothing he could sense through the mindline was suggestive of judgment or disapproval. Jahir said finally, "Really?"

"I figured you knew?" Vasiht'h said sheepishly. "I mean, I'm drawing from our account for it, and the transaction's labeled. Don't you look at our account?"

Jahir's pause was accompanied by a tender heat in the mind-line, like blushing skin.

"You don't," Vasiht'h said, amazed. "Do you."

"I . . . have little cause. We are not large spenders."

"You're not a large spender!" Vasiht'h exclaimed, still astonished. "But you don't know the first thing about my spending habits. For all you know, I could be buying everything in sight!"

Jahir was standing close enough to the wall to rest his back on it, and there was something sheepish about the set of his shoulders. "And putting it where?"

"Fine, I could be spending it on something intangible that you can't see," Vasiht'h said.

"But . . . that is not in your character?"

Vasiht'h eyed him. "Arii . . ."

Jahir said, weakly, "Perhaps we should eat dinner at the café with the scones? I will even eat the mousse."

The Glaseah choked down an unwilling laugh. "Look, can we just . . . can you just answer this once, and then we don't have to talk about it again?"

Jahir hesitated, then said, "Ask . . . ?"

"Are you rich?"

This pause made both of them nervous. Vasiht'h didn't know what Jahir was thinking, but for his part he found he was scared of the answer either way. So naturally, he got an Eldritch answer.

"Is it enough to say that I feel no need to worry?"

"Only if you know enough about how much it costs to live in the Alliance to say that," Vasiht'h said. "You said yourself it was different on your world. What do you honestly know about the cost of living here? Do you know?"

Jahir looked away. "I know that I need not worry." He drew in a breath, deep enough to be seen across the table, and that meant he was very unsettled. "You need not either."

What could he do? The whole exchange had been so . . . so

Eldritch somehow that he couldn't help but find it endearing. He had loved Jahir from the start, mysteries and all, and Vasiht'h had backed him into a corner and still he could only be, consummately, who he was. Which also entailed a 'what he was.' If Vasiht'h hadn't been willing to grapple with the what along with the who, he would never have accepted the Goddess's gift. And the mindline truly was a gift.

Vasiht'h counted his in-breaths, let them out. "So, you really are rich." When the Eldritch didn't contradict him, he closed his eyes and nodded. "All right. That helps, actually."

Incredulity seeping through the mindline, tinted with hope. "It does?"

Sehvi's quiet good sense; Tiber's gentle corrections to his perspective. He saw their situation through those lenses and it let him understand that his own problem—needing to feel like an adult at last, able to support himself—was entirely separate from the complications of Jahir's money. Vasiht'h would have felt the need to prove himself no matter his situation . . . Jahir's addition to it was a distraction from the real issue he had to resolve. "It does help. I won't pretend I'm comfortable with it, because I'm not. But knowing for certain . . . I can set it aside and deal with the important stuff."

". . . which . . . is?" Jahir asked, tentative.

"That I need to be enough for myself," Vasiht'h said. "And that has more to do with how I grew up and the people I feel I have to prove myself to." He folded his arms. "You're not off the hook, though. I want to be a partner here, not just a kept friend."

"A kept . . . friend?"

Of course he didn't know the original phrase. "A kept man, or woman, is someone a richer person supports financially because they want their company."

Jahir considered that at length, then said, "Then you could never be a kept . . . friend. I am not buying your company, Vasiht'h. I could not, any more than you could buy mine. Do you doubt that?"

It embarrassed Vasiht'h that he hadn't even considered that

angle. "I guess when you put it that way. . . ." He smiled wryly. "I'd say I'm making a mess of things, but we're communicating so it can't be that bad."

"Relationships do require communication." Jahir hesitated. "Are we well now?"

"Yes," Vasiht'h said. "We're good. I mean, I'm not miraculously over my need to be successful in my own eyes, by my standards, but I don't think the fact that I haven't met those standards is your fault."

"Good," Jahir said.

"But we're still going to the café with the scones," Vasiht'h said.

Jahir hid his wince so well Vasiht'h might have missed it had he not felt it through the mindline.

"Don't worry," Vasiht'h said, amused. "If there's cream or mousse or double servings of kerinne, I'll handle them for you."

Jahir opened the door and stood out of the way. As Vasiht'h passed through it, the Eldritch said, quiet, "Truly? We're well?"

There was such wistfulness in it that Vasiht'h had to stop and reach for him. He knew touch should be a rare thing, but this moment needed it. Setting his hand on his friend's arm, he looked up and put every ounce of his conviction into the words, into the mindline. "Arii. I mean it." Smiling, he said, "Honestly, this is small stuff. You know?"

"Money separates many relationships," Jahir said, soft.

"It won't separate ours." Vasiht'h snorted. "And if I let it, I deserve my misery. Sehvi would pound me into the dirt, too. 'You left him because he had too much money? Any other stupid reasons you want to turn people away at the door? Too nice? Too smart? Too funny?'"

Jahir dipped his head to hide the smile Vasiht'h could feel like sunshine through their link. "We do laugh."

"We do," Vasiht'h said. Thinking of Tiber, he said, "We're very lucky."

"Yes." Jahir shook his hair back and said, resolute, "The scones."

"If you eat them all, I'll buy you ice cream."

———— ⚬✖⚬ ————

That conversation stayed with Vasiht'h long after it happened, like incense clinging to his fur. Something about the mingling of Tiber's bad news with the chance to tell Jahir that he'd been seeing a therapist, and the final resolution, such as it was, of the uncertainty of their monetary state . . .

"So you're good with this?" Sehvi asked, incredulous.

"Yes," Vasiht'h said. "No. I'm good with it being something I can't control."

"You are?" she said, eyes widening further.

He started laughing. "All right, maybe it's going to take me a while to work through it. But I see what the problem is at least. Knowing that gives you some tools to keep it from overrunning your life."

"Uh huh."

"You don't have to sound so dubious, you know!"

"You have Jahir to be supportive. Or that guy you're seeing. You need me for some good, solid, practical skepticism." She grinned, before sobering. "It's just too easy."

"It is the *least* easy thing in the world," Vasiht'h said with emphasis. "Just knowing the problem and that it's inside me doesn't do the work of fixing it. A lot of days I'm fine, but there are days where I'm convinced this is all crazy and I'm crazy and I can't believe I'm muddling through it. I'm still waiting to grow up, ariishir."

"Maybe that's why people have kits," Sehvi said. "You have to be a grown-up if you're raising people who actually are children."

Vasiht'h snorted. "There are plenty of parents who haven't grown up."

"Yeah, but we wouldn't be one of them."

Hard to argue that, so he didn't. "Well, I'm not ready for a family. I don't even have a permanent practice yet!"

"Isn't your time almost up?"

"A few weeks now," Vasiht'h said, feeling it like a pressure on his back.

"I bet once that passes and you know, one way or the other, you'll feel better about everything else," Sehvi said.

"I bet you're right."

✥

Tiber said the same thing in their session. "Problems magnify one another's effects. That's why we snap at people about small things so often: we're grappling with the emotional weight of other issues, and it uses up our self-control."

Vasiht'h grimaced. He had his head on the table, in his folded arms, and was using the rake to push one of the rocks through the sand garden. "I know. We only have so much self-control a day. But there must be a way to increase that capacity, you know? Otherwise some people wouldn't have so much more of it."

"Maybe they're just born that way," Tiber said, smiling a little.

Vasiht'h covered his face. "Don't tell me that."

"All right. Maybe they're using up all their power and when they finally snap it'll be nuclear."

That startled a laugh out of Vasiht'h. "Goddess, I hope not." He sighed. "Is it ridiculous to say I wish this would be over, one way or the other, to someone who doesn't want me to be here doing what I'm doing?"

It was Tiber's turn to look away then. "I don't want them to send you away from the starbase, alet."

Vasiht'h looked up. "You don't? But if we don't practice, they'll tell us we're not adding anything useful to the community, and we'll have to go."

"I know. I can find your work problematic and still hope you'll be able to stay here, when it means so much to you."

Which was a lot more nuanced compassion than Vasiht'h had been expecting on the topic. He studied Tiber in the time remaining to them and saw the hollows under his eyes, and felt his heart crimp for the other man. At the close of the hour, Vasiht'h asked, hesitant, "Do you want to talk about it?"

Tiber didn't need that explained. He glanced at the rug, and maybe he saw the ghost there. Vasiht'h did. "No."

Vasiht'h nodded and said, quieter, "I'm sorry for your loss. Is there anything we can do . . . ?"

Tiber glanced at him, let that look lengthen. His head-shake was curt. "No." And a little gentler. "Thanks for asking."

CHAPTER 21

"TELL ME ABOUT SELNOR."

Jahir looked up from his soup and found Helga studying him, spoon loose in her fingers. Beside her, Vasiht'h paused on his way to the bread in the middle of the table.

/Almost six months she's been coming to dinner and she finally asks now?/ Vasiht'h said.

/Yes,/ Jahir answered, because it could only have been this way. /Exactly./

"I assume it was eventful!" the Hinichi continued, spooning up a potato chunk and slurping the cream out from around it, rather like a gleeful child. Jahir was not at all deceived by her demeanor. Beneath the glib façade he could sense the authority the decades had mantled on her shoulders: she was young, as Eldritch counted time, but responsibility had made her the equal of any elder in his society. And like an Eldritch matriarch, she had decided it was now time to evaluate her successors, and for that she wanted this last piece of information, a piece she'd divined was crucial to her understanding of them as people.

She was right, of course. Selnor had changed everything for them both.

"It is a story we both should tell," Jahir said, looking at

Vasiht'h.

"I think of it as more about you than me," Vasiht'h confessed.

"But there would be no story at all without you."

Vasiht'h's ears sagged, but his blush through the mindline tasted of gratitude. */You love me./*

/Of course I do. Do you doubt?/

/No./ Vasiht'h smiled. */You're the truest constant in my universe now, along with Her./*

Jahir closed his eyes to let that settle into him, like the benison it was. Then he pushed his bowl away.

"Oh, no," Vasiht'h said. "Don't tell me you're going to skip dinner because of this."

"I can tell the story," Jahir said. "Or I can eat. And I think I need to tell the story." He met Helga's eyes.

The Hinichi answered, "You need to tell the story."

/One missed meal won't harm me, arii./

/So long as it doesn't turn into a pattern . . ./

/If it does, I ask you to correct me./

Vasiht'h mmmed quietly. "I'll help. But I'm going to eat."

Jahir smiled over at him and said to Helga, "Initially I was uncertain that I would be capable of lingering here in the Alliance. Loving . . ." He paused, gathering his thoughts. "Loving is challenging."

"Especially if you think everyone's going to die on you?" Helga guessed.

"We live a long time," Jahir said quietly. "It makes us uncomfortable with risk."

"And yet here you are."

"Yes." Jahir settled himself with a long breath. */I begin./*

/I'm with you./

/I know./

Telling Helga about Heliocentrus was difficult, but not for the reasons Jahir expected. Divulging personal information . . . he had been conditioned to find that uncomfortable. Gauche, when it wasn't forbidden entirely by the Veil. He avoided it reflexively, and overriding that impulse required effort. But sharing this episode, this very painful, personal episode of his life, with a woman he still thought of as an acquaintance was easy. What hurt was having to live through it again, even at a remove. The punishing fatigue. The grief. The knowledge that he had limits, and he could smash into them so badly he couldn't put himself back together without help. All the reasons, he thought, that made him feel new compassion toward those he strove to aid in his practice . . . in many ways, the root of those reasons grew out of his own experience, failing when he needed so badly to succeed.

As promised, Vasiht'h helped with the narrative, sometimes of his own volition, sometimes at Helga's prompting. Jahir could appreciate the deftness of her approach, for she knew just how to elicit information without coercion. She had a light touch, their guest. As a therapist she must have been marvelously comforting. An avid listener, with sympathy in her discerning eyes, always ready with a quip when the mood needed lightening or a gentle prompt when they faltered.

/It's still with you,/ Vasiht'h observed as they drew near the close of it. /I had no idea how much./

/It will always be with me,/ Jahir replied. /Because it has changed me, in every particular./

/For the better, I hope./

/I would do nothing differently, arii./

"Well," Helga said at last over her second cup of coffee, this one with a dollop of rum. "That was a crucible, and no mistake."

"We learned a lot about ourselves," Vasiht'h said. "As people alone, and as a couple."

"No regrets, it sounds like?"

"None," Jahir said. "Save that I wish I could have done more."

Vasiht'h snorted. "You did enough. Too much more and your heart would have given out. Literally."

Jahir smiled a little. "Sooth. Then . . . I will say I wish I had been capable of more."

"Do you blame yourself for that?" Helga asked.

"No." Jahir thought about it, then said, "At least, I hope I don't. We are all works in progress."

Vasiht'h chuckled a little, rueful. */Aren't we./*

"You could earn a lot of credibility, telling everyone this story." Helga swirled her coffee. "Helping law enforcement shut down a drug ring would validate your modality. Strongly."

"And make us look like heroes?" Vasiht'h wrinkled his nose. "No thank you. We're not miracle-workers, alet. We're just . . . us."

"You're just you because you haven't told everyone you're heroes," Helga said. "I would think you'd want to use every tool in your arsenal to make your case before the housing authorities. That's what you're fighting for now, isn't it?"

"It is not always appropriate to use every tool in one's arsenal," Jahir said. "And this one . . . it feels forced. And we cannot work with people who adulate us. Particularly inappropriately. What we did on Heliocentrus . . ." He shook his head minutely, trying to still the quiver in his shoulders. "That was not heroism. That was . . . tragedy. And lost opportunities. And people trying to make the best of a terrible situation. We helped, but we were a small piece of a large story. To lose sight of that would be to disrespect those who suffered more than we did."

Helga glanced at Vasiht'h and said, affectionately, "And you've yoked yourself to this for your life?"

"I know," Vasiht'h said, grinning. "Aren't I lucky?"

The Hinichi laughed. "I think you are, actually!" She stood, stretching. "Well, ariisen, that was a lovely dinner, and a very interesting conversation. Thank you for trusting me with it."

"We like having you by," Vasiht'h said.

"I'll definitely miss your cooking when I go."

"Go!" Vasiht'h said. "You're leaving?"

Helga nodded. "In two weeks I'm off on my retirement adventures." She cuffed Vasiht'h on the shoulder with a chuckle. "And I'm going with Hector. So yes, you can be smug about your success."

"I'm not smug! I'm just pleased to see two people I like enjoying one another's company!" Vasiht'h said.

/You are smug, though,/ Jahir observed, amused.

/But saying so seems impolite!/

"When will you be back?" Jahir asked as they walked her to the door.

"Oh, I don't know. We don't have plans one way or the other," Helga said. "Part of the pleasures of retirement. No need to be anywhere in particular. But we'll be gone at least two or three months, I imagine. Hector wants to take a colony food cruise, taste the wonders of the borders. And we both have extended family to visit. We're looking forward to stretching our ancient legs." She grinned, ears perked. "But I'll be by before then, so don't start missing me yet."

"We await your next visit with pleasure," Jahir assured her.

"Dinner," she agreed. "Next week." And jogged off into the perfumed evening with its glowing lanterns and soft purple sky.

Jahir leaned against the doorframe and folded his arms, watching her recede. He felt Vasiht'h draw abreast of him. "That was . . . odd."

"That, unless I am mistaken," Jahir said, "was her decision to recommend us as her replacements."

Vasiht'h's ears sagged. "You really think so?"

"I do, yes." Shutting the door, Jahir turned to the plates, and his untouched meal. His stomach was knotted but he was hungry, and he was not surprised when Vasiht'h handed him up the heel of the bread. "Thank you," he said, chagrined.

"Sit and chew on that," Vasiht'h said. "You can't go to bed with your stomach tensed up. You'll sleep badly."

Obediently Jahir lit on one of the chairs and applied himself to the bread. His partner, thinking busily but not sharing, cleared the table, put away the plates, and started a pot of tea. By the time he brought the cups to the table, Jahir was done with the bread and his friend was ready to speak.

"Do you think we're in then?"

"That will depend entirely on whether the authorities privilege Helga's assessment of us over Tiber's."

Vasiht'h sank back on his haunches, dismayed. "Oh . . . that's . . . not going to be an easy decision for them."

"No," Jahir said. "We are not in the clear yet. But she is a powerful ally."

"And good company," Vasiht'h said. "I'll miss her when she's traveling."

"So will I," Jahir said.

The following morning Ametia arrived to her appointment . . . with Lennea. They entered and came to a halt, the taller Harat-Shar behind the shorter Karaka'An, and Ametia rested her hands on her friend's shoulders and raised her chin high like a feudal lady, proud of her charge. Lennea set one of her hands on Ametia's and beamed at them. She was wearing jeweled clips on both of her sandals again, Jahir saw. A dragonfly on the right, and a bumblebee on the left.

"She saved me!" Lennea exclaimed.

Ametia chuffed a laugh. "Like a knight in shining armor, I swooped down the hill and rescued the princess." She described a gliding motion with one arm. "And shocked and awed every person who knew me, by quitting my prestigious job as a tenured professor to take up with drooling kittens."

Lennea laughed. "They're not all kittens. And they're old enough to have stopped drooling!"

"And technically I didn't quit," Ametia agreed. "I am on extended sabbatical. They can't fire me, so." She grinned and kissed the top of Lennea's head before striding to the sofa and curling up on its end.

"You took the job!" Vasiht'h said, surprised.

"I did!" Ametia said. "I actually took it the day after our appointment."

"She really means it, too," Lennea agreed, wide-eyed. Settling on the middle of the sofa, she finished, "She showed up and demanded they hire her."

"It wasn't that dramatic," Ametia said.

"It was absolutely that dramatic!" Lennea confided to them, eyes shining.

"Well, maybe it was somewhat dramatic," Ametia allowed, slouching against the arm of the sofa with a lazy smile. "But it did involve some extended administrivia, like checking my references and considering my qualifications."

"Trivialities," Lennea said, affecting Ametia's demeanor with a lifted chin and a dismissive flick of her hand.

/I've never seen them together this long,/ Vasiht'h said, stunned. /I never would have guessed they'd be this comfortable! That impersonation . . . !/

/She is good at it!/

/And Ametia thinks it's funny!/

Jahir watched the two of them, amused. /Why should she not? It was, and meant with fondness./

"So do you like the job?" Vasiht'h asked.

Ametia grinned. "They have no idea what they got themselves in for."

"She's loving it," Lennea said, laughing. "Absolutely loving it. She gets to tell people what to do and they have to do it!"

"That is a significant benefit. For them, seeing as I know best."

Lennea smothered another giggle. "You see what I mean?"

"We do," Jahir said gravely. To Ametia, "So you have found your bearings?"

"I'm getting there." Ametia smiled, sobering. "It's not a simple job. I was surprised . . . I thought I'd be bored within a week. But there's a lot involved, and a lot of it is frankly fascinating. I had no idea how much went into administration. If I had I might have been nicer to the university board." She paused, snickered. "All right, probably not. They deserve all their headaches. Insipid old cowards." Tapping a finger on the couch arm, she continued, "The primary school is a lot more nimble, if you'll believe it."

"It's smaller," Lennea said.

"Not by much," Ametia said. "It's that the system isn't interested in retention the way the university is. Universities . . . you can attend forever, if you have the money and interest. And the school wouldn't mind keeping you coming back for yet another degree, if you can afford it. But these primary schools . . . the kits keep moving, so there's less fighting over their money. Once they're here, you only get so much out of them and then they're gone. The focus has to be on the education, not the student." Ametia paused. "I'm not sure I'm articulating this well. I'm still wrapping my arms around it. But it's fascinating. And Lennea is kindly helping me understand the day to day operations."

"She's being nice," Lennea said, smiling fondly at Ametia. "She's already got it down. I don't think we've ever had a principal this smart."

Ametia snorted. "You were definitely overdue, then. This is important work."

/*Important work!*/ Vasiht'h repeated.

Jahir smiled at Lennea. "And you, then, alet? Are you content?"

"Oh, I'm *so* much better," Lennea exclaimed. "*So,* so much. I'm teaching again! My kits missed me. And I get to go to work with one of my best friends!" She touched her cheeks and laughed. "This has been the best two weeks of my year! My face actually hurts from smiling so much."

"Would that we all had such problems," Jahir murmured.

/*Goddess, they're so adorable it hurts my cheeks.*/

/*They make an engaging pair.*/

/*Who would have thought it??*/

/*Who would have thought of us, arii?*/

Vasiht'h chuckled. /*Good point.*/ "Well, we have an hour," he said aloud. "Why don't you tell us all about how it happened?"

"Yes!" Lennea said. "But . . . with cookies?"

"No tea this time, though," Ametia said. "Get me coffee. I don't want to sleep."

That was their only appointment of the day, so they let it stretch on past the hour. The interaction between the diffident Karaka'An and her ferocious friend provided an immense source of entertainment and satisfaction; they ate cookies and had coffee and indeed no one slept. Leaving their office for the day, Vasiht'h said, "Goddess, these are the days it's good to be alive."

Jahir looked down at him. "You really believe it?"

"I do!" Vasiht'h loosened his back, a ripple of muscle and limb that started at his head and moved the length of his spine to his tail. Starting down the walkway, he said, "I do, and I'm ready for lunch to celebrate. Let's try the place with the fancy noodles."

"Fancy noodles it is," Jahir said, as his data tablet chirped. He had it damped for their session, so it surprised him to receive an alert important enough to bypass the command.

Vasiht'h stopped. "Arii?"

Jahir spread the message, skimmed it. Became aware of his heart racing and pressed a hand to it before he could quell himself. The memories of Selnor were close.

"Not something bad?" Vasiht'h slunk closer, tail low.

"No," Jahir said. "Not precisely. But we now have an errand to do before lunch."

"Will you tell me what it is?"

"Yes," Jahir said. "This way, please. We will need a Pad station."

"A Pad station!" Vasiht'h exclaimed. "Where are we going?"

"To the port."

"To do . . . what?"

Jahir smiled a little. "You recall I was researching dogs?"

Vasiht'h's ears flagged. "Yes."

"There is a dog at the port in need of rescue."

"But . . . you don't want a dog!" Vasiht'h stumbled, halted. / *You want it for Tiber./*

Jahir stopped as well to look back at him. "I put out a query, indicated I was interested in one if one were to arrive on Veta. I thought we might give it to Helga as a parting gift, since she had indicated an interest."

"But then Allen's died."

Jahir hesitated. "Another reason I left the request public. Yes. It made sense at the time."

"But what if he doesn't want another dog?" Vasiht'h said, joining Jahir to look up at him. "We can't just give him one to replace Trusty."

"We're not replacing Trusty," Jahir said. "And we are not

giving him a dog. We are rescuing an abandoned animal, and hoping that the person who understands dogs best would be willing to rehome him."

"There are a lot of ifs implied in that scenario," Vasiht'h muttered.

"But?" Jahir asked, hearing it in the mindline.

"But it might work. Let's go look."

The moment Vasiht'h saw the dog, his heart crumpled. 'Abandoned at the port' sounded so clinical. The reality was heart-wrenching, because the animal was only a puppy, all big paws and piteous eyes and sad whimpering sounds. "What happened?" he asked the woman standing guard over the box, a Tam-illee in coveralls marked with the port authority's badge.

"We wish we knew," she answered. "One of my techs found the box shoved into a corner of a maintenance tunnel. We have a visual record of someone leaving it there, but they kept their heads down. Our best guess is that it came off one of the big cruise liners; we had a couple put in this week and they've got a ton of crew coming on and off ship. The clothing was consistent with something one of their maintenance personnel would wear."

"And you can't . . . find them? Somehow?"

"And do what?" the woman asked, tired. "We could fine them for littering, I guess, but there's no rule against leaving things lying around. Even if we did, what good would it do? We can't give the animal back to someone who left it behind. What would their next step be? Spacing it out an airlock?" She shook her head, glanced at Jahir. "I saw your note on the feeds. I hoped maybe you could solve this problem for me."

"I may not be able to," Jahir said. "But I may know someone who can."

"Then you'll take the dog?"

"We'll handle it," Vasiht'h said.

"Great," the Tam-illee said, smiling at them both. "I won't

forget it." And covered Vasiht'h's palm before leaving them with the puppy.

"I guess we can take the box?" Vasiht'h said, uncertain. "I don't know how to hold a dog."

"I will carry the box," Jahir said. "If you call Doctor Tiber."

"Because I'm the one who knows him," Vasiht'h said, feeling the absurdity of it.

"He is your therapist," Jahir agreed with just a glimmer of humor, shadowed by the whimpering of the dog.

"The Goddess works in really, really mysterious ways," Vasiht'h said.

Tiber answered Vasiht'h's message as they were heading from the port to the commons. Spreading it, Vasiht'h said, "We should come by now."

"Did you tell him why?"

"I said it was an emergency and that I needed his help."

Jahir looked down into the box. The dog had stopped crying, and had her long nose over the plastic rim, looking out at the world. "That would be an accurate summation. Was there any reason you did not reveal the nature of the emergency?"

"I think if I tell him we're bringing a dog he'll say no," Vasiht'h said. "But if he *sees* the dog. . . ."

Jahir consider that. "Manipulation?"

Vasiht'h wrinkled his nose. "No. But he's got a picture in his head of 'Tiber with a dog' and that dog is Trusty. This dog is smaller, and bright gold and it's got very long fur . . . it doesn't look anything like Trusty. If we want this dog to have a chance, we can't have him fixated on that picture."

They continued walking. "And if he says no?" Jahir asked at last.

"Then . . . we offer it to Helga, like you planned," Vasiht'h said. "And if she doesn't want it, then we keep it until we can find it a permanent owner. It shouldn't be too hard to find someone on the station who wants a dog. There are a lot of people here. Good people."

Glancing at the streams of people exiting the port with them,

Jahir said, "There really are."

Something in the mindline made Vasiht'h look over at him; and he could read that face. It took practice, and a lot of attention, but there, in the tension around Jahir's eyes and the slight tilt of his brows . . . "You're sad?"

"I am wishing it was not so difficult, to gain permission to stay. Because I like it here, arii."

"I know," Vasiht'h murmured. "So do I." He sighed. "This way. At least Tiber's office isn't far from this side of town."

The walk felt like a reprise of their arrival to the starbase. Vasiht'h remembered jogging off the shuttle, scanning the crowds for his much taller friend. That excitement he'd felt, the anticipation of a wonderful future . . . he'd been so eager for it. Even when Jahir had explained there were challenges better explained over a cup of kerinne and a scone, finding a place here had felt do-able. Like the first of many adventures they'd have together. And in a way . . . it had been. Maybe they'd have to leave, and Vasiht'h would regret it. But the six months they'd spent here, making friends, helping people, learning how to live together . . . nothing would take that away. And whatever they did next would be just as special, if in a different way.

Jahir looked at him past the box and lifted his brows.

"It's all good," Vasiht'h told him.

"I would do nothing differently," Jahir said.

Vasiht'h smiled. "You know . . . I wouldn't either. And I didn't know it until this moment now."

The Eldritch looked up at the false sky as they exited the port into the commons. "It has been marvelous."

Vasiht'h laughed. Marvelous! What a word, but so appropriate. Full of marvels. "Yes. Yes, it has."

Tiber's assistant was behind the desk when they arrived, along with one of his clients waiting on the couch. At the sight of them, she rose and then her greeting died in her throat as the puppy peeked over the top of the box. "Speaker-Singer," she exhaled in a breath. "Oh look at those adorable ears. Do they . . . they flop . . . !" Glancing up, she added, "But are you sure this is a good idea, alet?"

"Is he sure what's a good idea?"

Vasiht'h steeled himself. /This is it./

/Your show this time, arii./

Vasiht'h eyed him. /This is revenge for all the times I make you speak for us, isn't it./

Jahir's silent laugh was in his eyes. /Today you are the best person for the work./

/I guess I am, at that./ Vasiht'h faced Tiber as the man joined them and froze at the sight of the dog. "So, our emergency."

"You're so young," Tiber interrupted, reaching past Vasiht'h to dig into the box and bring out the puppy. "Little girl . . . where's your mother?"

"That's the problem," Vasiht'h said. "Someone left her in this box at the docks."

"What!"

"They called Jahir because he's been looking into dogs, and when we got there . . . well. We thought of you."

Tiber was cradling the golden dog to his chest, ignoring her happy licking. "You wanted a dog?"

"No," Jahir said firmly. "I was only interested in how they were acquired when there was no vendor on station. I left a note asking about it, and the port authority contacted me in regards to this dog, hoping I would want her, or know someone who did."

"Poor darling," Tiber said, stroking her back. "Who would do that to a defenseless animal?"

"They don't know," Vasiht'h said. "And even if they did, they don't want to return her."

"Of course not. Who knows what they'd do next!" Tiber lifted her and looked her in the face. "That awful man didn't deserve you." The puppy strained toward him and he tucked her back into his arms. "You really don't want her?"

"We're not ready for pets," Vasiht'h said. "We don't even know if we'll have a place to stay in a week."

Tiber hesitated.

"We thought of you," Jahir added.

Vasiht'h nodded. "You were good to Trusty. This dog needs someone to be good to her."

Tiber looked away, still stroking her head. Squaring his shoulders, he said, "There's no guarantees I'll keep her. We might not get along. But if we don't, I promise I'll find her someone who'll love her the way she deserves."

"That's all we can ask," Vasiht'h said. "Thank you."

Tiber nodded. "See you next week."

"If I'm here," Vasiht'h said.

Again that hesitation. Then Tiber nodded again and swept back into his office. As the door shut, they could just hear the first of his cooing sounds.

/He is not giving that dog to someone else,/ Vasiht'h said, satisfied.

/Absolutely not,/ Jahir agreed.

"I . . . I didn't think that would work," the receptionist said, wide-eyed.

"Neither did we," Vasiht'h said. "But we had to try. For both their sakes."

That made her smile and her ears straighten. Even the client, sitting on the couch, said, "It'll be nice to have a dog at the sessions again. Allen without one is just . . . weird."

They waited until they were outside to laugh.

"Now we can finally get to our lunch!"

"I had hoped you'd forgotten," Jahir said.

"The noodle place? Not a chance. And I want dessert too. If we're only going to be here a little longer, I'm buying all the fancy scones I can get before I have to start mail-ordering them."

Lifting his head, Jahir said softly, "It truly has been grand."

"It has," Vasiht'h said. "And we helped some people." Thinking of Tiber, he chuckled. "Even the ones who didn't like us at first."

"Worse things could be said of people, than that they helped a few of their fellows as they passed through."

"Yes," Vasiht'h said, and thought he was okay with it. He smiled. "Life is good."

CHAPTER 22

THEIR SIX MONTH ANNIVERSARY came and went, and they received no notification about their status despite Vasiht'h checking his mail for one several times a day. He gave up after a week and concentrated instead on their workload. Ametia hadn't made a new appointment, but she'd referred them several new people; Lennea was still coming, and so was Rook. He and Jahir discussed the ethics of taking on new clients when they might have to leave, and decided to handle it by informing their new patients of the situation. All three of them chose to keep their appointments.

It was good to be busy.

His next appointment with Tiber was at the end of that week, and the new puppy had been installed in state in his office. Unlike Trusty, who'd been an old and confident dog, Sarah was shy. She preferred to watch things from the cozy hutch Allen had built for her and filled with soft pillows, chew toys, and a striped pink blanket that set off her long golden fur. She looked much happier—so did Tiber. Leaving the office, Vasiht'h thought they'd done very well there.

In the middle of the second week after their deadline, Vasiht'h finished HEALED BY HER IMMORTAL HEART. Jahir had gone for his swim, so there hadn't been anything better to occupy himself with, and he felt a vague curiosity over how the author was going to rescue her sweetly sappy romance after torching it so completely with the tragic miscarriage. The answer to that puzzle was 'badly,' by his sister's standards, because the two "found strength in their love" and became, again, sweetly sappy, as if nothing had happened. They even agreed to adopt instead, which Vasiht'h's sisters came down on like the fists of angry goddesses.

> **SARDA:** Are you kidding? Did she really just hand-wave adoption as a way to fix everything? How disrespectful is that, when she didn't consider it in the first place? It's like adopting is a poor second best option!
>
> **NINEH:** It is a weird intrusion of practicality into a narrative that's had absolutely no tether to anything concrete or real. Why can't they have another magical halfbreed baby if they conceived one the first time? Adopting seems disappointingly mundane when you've introduced hybrid Eldritch-fox children as an option.
>
> **KOVRAH:** I can't see most readers being satisfied with it as a happy ending.
>
> **KAVILA:** I'm more confused that they seem to have completely shrugged off the trauma of their failed attempt. Why isn't there a 'Book 2: Thaddeus slowly heals his Eldritch partner of her grief?'
>
> **MANDARA:** Because this is HEALED BY HER IMMORTAL HEART. Obviously. She's the one doing the healing, not him.
>
> **KAVILA:** Right, so a Book 2 where he does the healing would have a nice symmetry. Plus it would sell more books. People like things that come in sets, right? You could buy HEALED BY

HER IMMORTAL HEART and follow it up immediately with HEALED BY HIS MORTAL HEART

MANDARA: His mortal something, anyway. . . .

TAVYI: Yuck, Mandara, SO MUCH YUCK.

SARDA: This book has FAILED. Sehvi, we're going
to have words next time I see you.

SEHVI: As long as those words are accompanied
by pillow fights and cookie dough.

SARDA: . . .

SARDA: And we do a point-by-point take-down of
how awful this was and how we didn't deserve
it?

SEHVI: Sure! But seriously, they're a cute couple.

TAVYI: It's hard to argue that. Though I really wanted
the half-Eldritch Tam-illee kid. Without the bilateral
asymmetry. All one thing or the other, but tragic.
Oooh, hey! That would be perfect! This author should
write the story of the sad ghost halfbreed! She can
fall in love with a medium!

MANDARA: Someone should write that book. I'd read it.

KAVILA: Someone's probably already written it.

MANDARA: MY TURN TO RECOMMEND OUR NEXT
BOOK

Vasiht'h found himself grinning and turned the page to study
the happy portrait of the author, a stylized cartoon of a beaming
female Pelted of indeterminate age and species. Oddly, unlike
his sisters, he found the ending heartwarming. Not because
he thought the portrayal of trauma was accurate—it was completely ridiculous—but because Rexina Regina was right about
one thing: love got you through things. Even the kind of love
that he had, which had nothing to do with romance and everything to do with finding the very best of friends, closer than any
brother or lover, and sticking with him through anything. And if
that best of friends was an Eldritch, well . . . somehow that was
even better. For Vasiht'h anyway, because he wouldn't want it

any other way.

"Not to say," he told his tablet, "That love doesn't also create problems, because it does. Or that love solves them, because it doesn't. But it makes things bearable. And you can do a lot when you feel like things are bearable."

Rexina Regina twinkled back at him and he touched her nose. Strange to think he could have enjoyed her novel, but somehow, he had. The ending had made it all worthwhile.

A dialogue box opened under his finger. Startled, he lifted his hand and saw the message header, and his entire body froze.

Just open it, just open it, don't hesitate or you'll never find the courage . . . Vasiht'h tapped it and spread the text.

. . . like to welcome you to Starbase Veta. . . . Thank you for choosing us as your place of residence . . . information on utilities, voting, amenities listed below . . .

Vasiht'h jumped to his feet and spun in place, beating his paws on the floor. And laughed, grabbing his cheek ruffs. They'd done it? They'd done it! He re-read the message just to be sure and let his tablet drop, then his haunches. And Jahir was out! And wasn't typically available while swimming. Sending an emergency alert to him felt extreme, especially when he could wait and do the thing properly. Vasiht'h grabbed his bag and ran for the door.

Jahir entered the cottage to a suspicious tension in the mindline and no sight of his partner. He set his bag on the kitchen table and paused there, one hand lighting on the back of a chair. The windows were open on a bright day, letting in the spiced perfume of Ilea's sun-warmed plants. No clutter in the kitchen, either, nor any other sign of activity. He touched the fullness hanging between himself and Vasiht'h and extended a gentle probe.

/Up the ramp./

On the roof, Vasiht'h was sitting, squinting up at the sky. "You know, I never noticed the one weird thing about Veta's sky."

"What's that?" Jahir asked, taking the chair alongside him.

"There's no sun. I mean, there's an apparent point source, but it's not a sun. I looked it up once it occurred to me, and I don't understand a word of how they make it feel like daytime without an actual burning star. But the takeaway is that you can look directly at that point source, and it won't hurt you. Isn't that strange?"

"Only as strange as a manufactured environment having a summer," Jahir said. "Have you noticed?"

"That it's warmer now?" Vasiht'h nodded. "But not uncomfortable. I guess if you can decide how hot it gets, why let it get scorching. Did you have a nice swim?"

"A good one, yes," Jahir said. He would miss the pool, but there would be water wherever they went. Everything important, he would take with him. "I appreciate the waxing season in that regard."

"I'm sure you do." Vasiht'h chuckled and slid an envelope over to him. "Here, a present. I bought it with our money."

"Our money," Jahir repeated, bemused.

"I'm trying to be less uptight about it." The Glaseah grinned at him. "Not to say I'm about to become a spendthrift, but a few luxuries now and then seem all right. Right?"

"Depending on what they are," Jahir agreed, surprised and charmed. He took up the envelope, and the moment his fingers brushed it, something echoed back to a similar one on Seersana. His hesitation made Vasiht'h look up at him, eyes sparkling, and the mindline effervesced with his joy.

Opening the envelope on two passes to the cultural center's musical season, Jahir said, soft, "We're staying."

"We're staying," Vasiht'h confirmed.

Touch remained so hard, and yet so important, and this moment deserved it; did not just deserve it, required it. Jahir held out his hand for Vasiht'h's and received those alien fingers in his, softly furred, short and strong. And then he let his head sag until it was resting against his dearest companion's. The light on his back was warm, the scent of the garden strong all around them, and it felt right: this fleeting, heartbeat now.

"We could have managed anywhere," Jahir murmured, unwilling to lift his head.

Vasiht'h snorted, his smile like true sunlight in the mindline. "We could have *thrived* anywhere. But this place was meant to be our home."

"And now it is." Jahir sat up and squeezed Vasiht'h's hand once before letting it go. "This calls, unquestionably, for a celebration."

"Ice cream," Vasiht'h guessed, laughter turning up the edges of the words.

"I will consent to a proper meal first. But ice cream after."

Rising onto all four paws, Vasiht'h said, "I wonder what Karina will recommend today?" He laughed suddenly. "I wonder if the menu changes over the course of the year!"

"We," Jahir said, "will find out."

CHAPTER 23

"SO THIS IS WHERE YOU'VE BEEN making do," Helga said, peering into the door of their office.

Vasiht'h said, "Are you our walk-in appointment?"

"I am now!" The Hinichi bent to lift the corner of their brightly colored afghan. "Look at that. Not only Ametia's handi-work, but Hector's as well." She sniffed. "Smells nice in here too."

"A suggestion from a client," Jahir said.

"Good on you for running with it," Helga said. She turned in place. "Still, it's a bit tiny, isn't it?"

"As you said," Jahir replied, fascinated by her air of mischief, "We are making do."

/She's up to something,/ Vasiht'h said.

/She has been since she took up with us, arii./

Vasiht'h chuckled. /She has at that./ Aloud, he said, "You know our news, I'm guessing."

She grinned. "Of course I do. I know everything around here."

"Dare we ask if you had a hand in the outcome?" Jahir said.

"Oh, I put my foot in it, of course." She waved a hand toward the door. "This is my community. I have strong opinions. Particu-larly about people in my own profession."

"Then we thank you for your help," Jahir said.

"I did say I would, back when I found you furrowing your brow over a data tablet and an empty table," Helga said. "I said my starbase needed you two, and I'm sure the long run will prove me right." She smiled. "But you should also go thank Allen. He put in a good word for you, and after trumpeting from on high that you were dangerous, that was big."

"He did what?" Vasiht'h asked, his incredulity bursting between them like fireworks.

"I said 'big.'" Helga tapped her chin. "I should say pivotal, really."

"Allen Tiber? Spoke for us?" Vasiht'h repeated.

"You made a good impression," Helga said. "I don't think he'll ever quite believe in your methodology, mind you, but he can admit when he's wrong."

"A rare trait," Jahir murmured.

"Very," Helga said. "He's a good man. Don't hesitate to lean on him if you need him. Minette's a bit of a specialist in college kids. Allen's your man for broader issues, if you need to refer people. Just don't do it too often . . . he needs to slow down. Which is why I'm so glad you all are here, because now I can saddle you with my existing client list and go haring off on my adventures without a care in the world."

Her existing client list! "You're going to do what?" Vasiht'h said, ears sagging.

"Go haring off on adventures?" she repeated. Her eyes were dancing. "You should be the least surprised about that, given the matchmaking."

Vasiht'h put his hands on his hips. "I wasn't talking about the adventures part!"

She started laughing. "I know!" She clapped her hands. "So, my dears. Ready to move into your new office?"

/If I say 'our what' she's going to laugh at me again, isn't she./

Jahir bridled his mirth. /You should know better, arii. This was coming. Yes?/

/I guess it was./ Vasiht'h said, "Do we have time to pack?"

---❧---

The Healer's Knot was empty of everything but the memory of the kindnesses done in its rooms, and the potential unfolding before them. Jahir followed Helga through its front door into the broad central room and halted as she pointed. "This used to be the waiting room."

"It has a kitchen!" Vasiht'h exclaimed.

"Oh, sure, we used to serve healthy meals," Helga said. "Food is medicine, too." She padded inside. "So that door there, right next to the front door, leads to the two offices we used to use for therapy. And then down this hall . . ." She led them further into the room, "This was where we did physical therapy, and down there's the bathroom. It's got an installation large enough for all the species of the Alliance, though an Akubi would probably find it uncomfortable."

/There is no part of this that isn't perfect,/ Vasiht'h commented, standing in the bathroom and scanning it from sink to shower.

/We could easily live here./

Vasiht'h looked up sharply.

/The physical therapy room would fit us both for a bedroom. And the waiting room would serve as great room./

Vasiht'h's ears perked. /We could put a table in it by the counter, for meals. And a sofa and pillows and a wallscreen in the center . . ./ He canted his head. /Our patients would be able to see our house, though. Is that all right with you?/

/Should it not be?/

Vasiht'h padded out of the bathroom. /You're the private one . . . ? I don't want you to be uncomfortable./

/I would prefer not to share the sight of my bedroom with strangers. A well kept great room . . ./ Jahir trailed off, thinking of the sitting rooms in his mother's house. /Should be inviting./

"Busy talking it out, I see," Helga said, grinning. "Should I leave you to it?"

"You really wish us to use this property," Jahir said. Thinking of Vasiht'h's many uncertainties, he said, "We have not even seen the rent."

"You can afford it," Helga said. "I'm giving it to you."

This time, both of them paused, and the Hinichi let them have their silence before leaning toward them, her demeanor sobering. "You understand what I'm doing here?"

"You are leaving us your community to caretake," Jahir said.

"Yes. And I'm confident you'll do right by them, or I wouldn't be doing this. The property belongs to the therapists who are carrying on my work. It's a . . . a piece of continuity. For me, for the city, for the clients who used to come here." Helga looked from one of them to the other. "You can choose not to say yes to it, if you want to do something different. But I'd like you to have it. I'd feel like it would remind you of what I'd want for Veta."

Vasiht'h blew out a breath. "It certainly would do that! But, are you certain?"

"Completely," Helga said. She grinned. "Let an old woman be extravagant. I've already given my kits and grandkits enough presents. They're tired of me showering them with things."

"But this is no small thing," Jahir said. "This is a legacy, and a mantle."

Smiling fondly at him, she said, "And that's exactly why I'm comfortable handing it on. You understand. So what do you say?"

"Yes!" Vasiht'h exclaimed, so fast Jahir stared at him. The Glaseah said, sheepish, "I can learn."

Jahir laughed. "I did not say you couldn't!"

"This is a very good thing in our lives," Vasiht'h said. "I'm not going to be stupid and say no to it. So . . . yes, please, Helga-alet. We would love to inherit your property, and any of the clients from your list that want to come back, and we're going to do our best for them."

"I never doubted," Helga said, patting the Glaseah on the shoulder. "So let's go do some paperwork, shall we?"

Vasiht'h recalled the furnishing of their first apartment on Seersana with rue in the following days, because his objections to spending his partner's money had utterly evaporated when confronted with their first, actual home as adults. He wanted to *live* in it, properly, not like a student forced to buy a single piece of furniture at a time. Jahir didn't comment on it, save to share what felt like a mental hug when Vasiht'h noticed the absurdity of it. Which might have bothered him more, except their new place was so perfect. The kitchen had been designed to serve commercially, if to a small audience, and all its appliances were top of the line, its pantries and cupboards capacious, and its surfaces elegantly designed. He could use it comfortably despite his centauroid body. The waiting room made an admirable great room and Jahir let him decorate it exactly as he'd envisioned when he saw the space: not too cluttered, but casual and welcoming, a place they could relax at night and either watch the wallscreen, read or work, or look out the false window he had sketched onto the wall on the opposite side.

The bedroom was well and again large enough for them both to sleep, and Vasiht'h's satisfaction when he arranged his pillow nest alongside Jahir's bed the first night they stayed . . .

/I feel it too,/ Jahir said.

Vasiht'h's heart felt like it would brim over, and he pressed a hand to it. /Home./

/For a long time, I feel./

/I hope so./

The patient offices were perfect too, with an outer chamber and an inner one that gave their clients privacy while they drowsed off and insulated them from the world far better than an office that opened directly into a building's foyer. The ability to gradually walk them out of their therapeutic headspace, from one room into a less private room where they could prepare themselves to enter the normal world again . . .

"It's perfect," he said to Sehvi.

She was craning her head, trying to see out of the wallscreen. "What I can see of it is gorgeous. I have the walkthrough you sent me, but it's not the same as looking yourself. Are you done decorating?"

"Of course not. That'll take years. Furniture's easy. Knick-knacks take time."

She laughed. "Right." She shook her head. "I can't believe it!"

"Oh Goddess, neither can I," Vasiht'h admitted. "Some days I wake up and think 'is this real'? And then I walk out into this amazing kitchen . . ." He gestured toward it with proprietary satisfaction.

"And you make the thickest kerinne in the known universe and drink it while laughing?" Sehvi said.

"Not out loud. That would be messy."

She snickered. "You are feeling better, you're making bad jokes again."

"I do feel better," Vasiht'h said. "I mean, I know this is just the beginning, and I still have a lot of things to work out. We both do. But . . . it's the *beginning,* Sehvi. You know?"

"I do," she said, her voice gentler. "I'm really happy for you, ariihir."

"I'm happy for you too, little sister. We're both on our way."

"Who knows where we'll end up, too?" Sehvi said. "I can't wait to find out."

"Me neither."

They shared a look of perfect accord.

A week later, Jahir set the package of scones on the kitchen counter alongside the tray Vasiht'h had set out. He breathed in the aroma of fresh coffee and said, "Today it was chocolate chip pumpkin."

"Scones?" Vasiht'h said, incredulous.

"They are . . . dense."

"I bet they are!" Vasiht'h shook his head and opened the bag so he could start arranging them on the plate. "I have no idea how they come up with these flavors, but they never seem to run out of ideas."

"We shall have to see," Jahir said. "I was told they have a flavor for every day of the year . . ."

"And we'll be here to see them," Vasiht'h said, his satisfaction warm in the mindline, like afternoon sunshine.

"Speaking of us being here to see things," Jahir said, "My mentor would like to stop by on the way to a conference. He mentioned it when we first came."

"Healer KindlesFlame? Of course he should come! I hope he stays several days. Did he say?"

"He didn't," Jahir said, pleased. "But I will tell him he's welcome."

"That couch is comfy enough for a bed," Vasiht'h said, finishing the tower of scones and setting it on the edge of the counter beside the coffee pot. "He can stay with us if he wants to. How's that look?"

"Delicious, if one is minded to eat heavy food."

Vasiht'h chuckled. "Well, some of our clients will be."

"Lennea is due in ten minutes," Jahir said. "Our first appointment in our new home."

Vasiht'h glanced up at him. "Ready for it?"

"More than," Jahir said, and offered his hand. He savored the feel of his friend's as it settled in his. "Things did work out, did they not?"

"They did," Vasiht'h said. "I'm so glad we came here, arii."

"As am I."

The door chimed, pushed open. Lennea peeked past it. "Am I early?"

"You're just in time," Vasiht'h said.

"And always welcome," Jahir finished. "Shall we get started?"

CASE STUDIES

T HESE VIGNETTES WERE originally serialized online and then
briefly made available as a standalone collection with an
anchoring short story, "The Case of the Poisoned House." That
collection is reproduced in its entirety here as a pastiche of the
work done in the first years of Jahir and Vasiht'h's new practice
after the events of *Dreamhearth*.

Avid fans may recall several more case studies; those represent the later years of their practice, and will make their appearance at the end of Book 4, *Dreamstorm*.

NEST

THE PHOENIX ENTERED THEIR room, swept it with a single cursory glance, and said, "There is no place to sleep," and turned to go.

The mindline between his auditors spiked with their combined anxiety, for as therapists who worked primarily with dreams they couldn't work if their patients refused to sleep. "Wait, please!" Jahir said. "We'll have something tomorrow. Come at the same time."

The alien eyed them both with his uncanny gaze . . . and then left. In that silence, they deflated, the agitated colors in the mindline growing pale and finally collapsing into neutral gray. Vasiht'h reached for the data tablet on the table and said, "So now we have a day to . . . ah . . . let's see. Build a nest."

"What kind of nests do Phoenixae sleep in?" Jahir asked.

"Looks like an adherent nest," Vasiht'h said, scrolling through the samples. Jahir didn't have to look over his shoulder; through their link he saw a hazy image. "Like a cup with a long back-rest. It's made of found objects . . . every nest has to be unique."

"So . . . to the park," Jahir said. As he opened the door for his shorter partner, he added, "Of all the things I expected we'd be doing as therapists, I admit this is one of the last."

"Tell me about it!"

Several hours later they were in their office again with a cart of supplies and bric-a-brac.

"How big do you think we should make it?" Jahir asked, lifting a branch with a faint frown.

"You're only a little shorter than a Phoenix," Vasiht'h said. "We'll just make it to your measure with a little extra."

"Right."

They fell asleep on the floor next to their attempt and spent all of the morning completing it, until at last Vasiht'h said wearily, "Well, give it a try."

Jahir glanced uncertainly at it, then stepped into the low pouch. The image Vasiht'h reflected back to him, of his face peeking out of it like a powder-pale baby bird, elicited a quiet chuckle. He twisted around. "Are you certain it's wide enough? Do they have broader shoulders or narrower?"

"Narrower, on average, if the data's right," Vasiht'h said. "Do you need a hand getting out?"

"No, I'm fine," Jahir said, clambering out of it. Together they surveyed their handiwork: a roughly woven thing of branches from the park, held together with twine and what seemed like a day's worth of sweat, mounted on a wooden tablet so it could be rolled away and stored when they were seeing patients who were fine with napping on a couch.

When the Phoenix returned, they watched with seeming nonchalance as he inspected their offering, but the mindline between them shimmered with worry like heat waves rising off crete. Their patient lifted his head, about to speak, when he halted. Frowned. Tilted his head and looked sideways at the nest with that bird-like quality that so many found unsettling.

"What is this?" he said, pointing at something with a golden talon.

They peered into the nest. "Oh," Jahir said, "Pardon me. That appears to be some of my hair—"

"Ah! Very unsual!" The Phoenix hopped into the nest, all its feathers rustling. "I sleep in a nest full of Eldritch hair. Very unusual!" And closed his eyes.

Jahir and Vasiht'h exchanged looks, and in silence, the former endured a great deal of laughter.

LANGUAGE

THROUGH THE MINDLINE came concern, faint as rain pattering. Vasiht'h twisted his upper body around and looked over his back to find Jahir approaching with a mug and a pitcher. His partner sat beside him amid the pillows and glanced at the vista: the balcony, the perfect blue sky through which the base's distant Spindle could be seen as a paler blue lattice.

"Refill?" Jahir asked. "It's kerinne."

"Please," Vasiht'h said, offering his cup for more of the thick cinnamon drink. They drank in companionable silence, the mindline hanging fallow between them.

At last, Jahir asked, "What are you thinking?"

"About language."

"It was rather astonishing," Jahir said.

The dreaming mind of the Seersa who'd been their last patient lingered, clear enough to Vasiht'h's recollection that he could almost think the way she had. He grappled with expression—something she would rarely have done, if his sense of her mind was true. "I was thinking about my people's language. How it became vestigial."

"We didn't discuss languages in depth in any of the classes I took," Jahir said. "Other than to note that the Glaseah abandoned it in favor of direct communion."

Vasiht'h smiled, because the words were almost baroque in their formality, but the mindline between them was suffused with the soft peach color of his partner's desire to be gentle. "It was never much more than a construct anyway. The Pelted gengineers who made us wanted to give us a language of our own, so they created one for us. We never took to it. Mostly we spoke Universal until the discovery that so many of us were born espers there wasn't any need to maintain our own language. So we discarded it."

"And yet," Jahir murmured.

"And yet," Vasiht'h said, "that Seersan woman . . . she wasn't even a linguist and she knew at least half a dozen languages—"

"More, I think," Jahir said.

"More!" Vasiht'h shook her head. "And her thoughts . . . it was as if when she ran into a mental block, she just switched languages and found a way around it."

"Do you think in a language?"

"I don't know," Vasiht'h said. "Universal, I guess. But I wonder . . . is that what we gave up when we abandoned Glaseahn? The few words we retained . . . they do give a . . . a flavor to things. Would we have been different people if we'd kept it?"

"Possibly," Jahir said. Then rousing himself with a distinct, iron-tang taste to the mindline, "Probably. Probably."

Vasiht'h glanced at him. "Do you think in Universal too?"

A twinge came over the mindline, sour like a stomachache. "Sometimes," Jahir said. "More often than not, now." The taint cleared from their link as he continued, "Universal has a much broader vocabulary, more technical terms. It's easier to be precise in it, particularly about technology and multicultural issues."

"And your own tongue?" Vasiht'h asked, careful. He knew Jahir better now, enough to more fully respect the Eldritch's reticence. When they'd first met in college, his curiosity had often been a trifle blunt. He'd meant no harm, but had little notion of the depth of the waters he'd been treading. "What does the Eldritch language teach?"

"To be careful. Very, very careful."

Vasiht'h let that stand. He sipped his now tepid kerinne. "Maybe we should learn more languages. To understand our patients better."

"God and Lady," Jahir said. "We have enough trouble merely dipping into their minds while they sleep. If we spend more time in alien heads, we might never find our way back."

Vasiht'h glanced at him, then looked pointedly at the open-air balcony with the multiple species moving about on it, drinking, laughing, their conversation a textured white noise tapestry. He tweaked the mindline with a bright lemon amusement.

Jahir sighed and smiled.

THE CAPTAIN

THERE'S A BATTLECRUISER laying over," Vasiht'h said as he entered the room.

"There usually is," Jahir said, without looking up from his data tablet, one long hand still on the mug of steaming coffee.

"I sent them a note advertising our services," Vasiht'h continued.

"What?" Jahir put down the tablet. "To what purpose? Fleet ships carry their own medical personnel. They would have no need to contract out for therapy."

"They don't need to, but they might want to," Vasiht'h said, padding into their kitchen to fix his own breakfast. "You never know. And we could always use more business."

"We'd be better off relying on our advertising in the commons," Jahir said, returning to the news.

"You never know," Vasiht'h said again, unperturbed.

/Don't be smug,/ Jahir said through the mindline as their guest stepped into their office and came to a halt at something that looked like parade rest.

/I'm not smug,/ Vasiht'h said, but his sending was threaded

through with ticklish little sparkles.

Jahir blew a mental sigh his way and said, "Alet? What can we do for you?"

"My C-med tells me I need to see someone," the man said, looking harried. "I heard you two work on people while they sleep."

"That's right," Vasiht'h said.

"Lead me to your bed, then—don't bother with a sedative, I won't need one. It'll be such a relief not to be easy to find for a change."

Bemused, they took him in, watched him arrange himself on the couch and . . . within minutes, he had passed out.

"What do you make of it?" Jahir said at the door.

"Human. Probably in his mid-forties?" Vasiht'h guessed. "I can't read these tabs on his uniform."

"Let us look them up, then," Jahir said. He smiled ruefully. "We have at least twenty minutes, since he didn't need any time to settle like everyone else!"

"He didn't even give us his name," Vasiht'h said, bemused.

"At least it's on his breast tab," Jahir said, looking at it. "Amadeo, Paul."

"Right," Vasiht'h said, checking the data tablet. "Looks like he's the captain of that battlecruiser."

"Well," Jahir said, looking at the man's careworn face, now slack; he had rarely seen such a deep sleep in one of their patients. "I suppose we should find out what's ailing him."

"Worried?" Vasiht'h said, padding closer.

"A little," Jahir said. "I have no experience with the military mind."

"I suspect the military mind is a lot like any other. Just with different worries," Vasiht'h said.

"And worries are what we're about," Jahir observed. But he held out his hand, and his partner took it, and together they slipped down the mindline, out and into the sleeping mind of their patient.

---❈---

When the captain awoke, he did abruptly, as if in response to some unheard alarm. He rubbed his temple. "Uhn. Are we done?"

The two therapists looked at one another. "For now," Jahir said. "We'd like you to come back—ah, how long are you staying?"

"Two weeks," he said. "Minor refits."

"Then we'd like to see you all two weeks, if possible."

"My chief medical officer is going to be thrilled. She says I'm a cracked mess and if someone doesn't fix me, I'll explode." The captain grinned, weary. "I get the feeling she was hoping she wouldn't have to do it."

"We'll take care of it, alet," Vasiht'h said seriously. "See you tomorrow."

"Right," he said, and left at a good clip, like a ship under steam.

They stared at the door. Then at one another.

Jahir started to smile. Vasiht'h laughed and tapped the mindline until it sang.

---❈---

Every day, then, exactly on time to the minute, Captain Amadeo arrived for his therapy. Each time, he put his head down on their pillow and fell immediately to sleep. After that first session, however, neither of them did anything more invasive than watch over him and keep the temperature comfortable.

The man who woke on that final day was bright-eyed and focused, with good carriage and straight shoulders. He stretched, rolling his wrists, and then put his hands on his knees. "So, doctors. This is our last session. Tell me, am I cured?"

"You were never sick, Captain," Jahir said. "But I believe your chief medical officer will have no complaints of you."

Rising, Amadeo said, "I'll have the ship's purser square things with you, if that's all right."

"Perfectly," Jahir said.

The captain shook Vasiht'h's hand and politely refrained

from offering to Jahir. "Thank you, gentlemen. I feel like a new man." He paused at the door. "You never did say . . . and if it's all right to ask? What exactly was it that was bothering me?"

The two therapists traded glances and frissons of silver laughter through the mindline.

Jahir said, "Lack of sleep."

"Lack of—" Amadeo stopped. And then laughed, round and rolling. "Good one, gentlemen. Next time I'm in the area, I'll be back. For a nap!"

"We'll keep the pillow plumped for you," Vasiht'h said.

In Dreams

Some of their patients were able to remember their presence in the dreams Jahir and Vasiht'h used to help them. And in that, the two therapists found many moments of amusement.

The Harat-Shar who dressed them both up as one of their intraracial angels, in spotted cloaks that became part of their skins, and masks with fangs and terrible slim swords:

/Do you at least know what to do with one of these?/ a leopard-spotted Vasiht'h asked him, brandishing the sword.

/I've had some small training, but certainly not enough to justify this rather martial loincloth I'm in./

/At least yours is in the right place,/ Vasiht'h said, looking down at his, placed where the base of his torso merged into his centauroid chest.

———

The human who'd come after too much badgering from wife and son saw them as humans; Vasiht'h appeared as a heavyset man with brown skin and wiry white and black hair and Jahir as a pole-thin man so pale his veins seemed to glow.

/You're bald!/ Vasiht'h said.

/So I am,/ Jahir said. /I also appear to be . . ./

Vasiht'h looked at their uniforms. /*A parole officer?*/

/*Our client seems to be repressing feelings of resentment over his having been forced here,*/ Jahir said.

/*This doesn't seem very repressed to me!*/

The enormous centauroid Ciracaana who stretched Vasiht'h up to match his own race's height:

/*Aksivaht'h's breath!*/ Vasiht'h said, looking down some nine feet. /*How do they manage all their paws from this distance? I can barely see my own toes!*/

/*You look . . ./*

/*Go ahead, say it,*/ Vasiht'h said with a sigh.

/*Emaciated,*/ Jahir said finally, amused. /*I think I prefer you short and solid.*/

Vasiht'h snorted. /*At least one good thing about this shape . . . for once, I'm the one looking down at you!*/

Another Harat-Shar this time, who put Jahir in homeworld native clothes. A woman's native clothes.

/*I never thought I'd see you in silk,*/ Vasiht'h said. /*Much less see-through silk.*/

Jahir looked down at the filmy scarves that passed for a bra and the jingly belt and extra scarf that did nothing to cover his nethers. /*This is the only time you will see me in see-through silk, I pledge you.*/

/*I don't . . . uh . . . recall you being quite so . . . endowed.*/

/*That, arii, is a Harat-Shariin addition. Thank God and Lady. I don't know that I would be able to walk otherwise.*/

There was a Hinichi who gave them fur and put them alongside the ancient wolves of the religion that gave rise to their sentience ("We made a handsome set," Jahir observed of their black and white shapes racing alongside one another). And the Asanii who envisioned Jahir as a priest of the Sun and Vasiht'h as a priest of the Moon. The Seersa male who saw them as floating symbols in his race's alphabet, the Seersan Universal Phonetic Alphabet—they'd had to look those up later to find out it had been their names. The Tam-illee engineer had abstracted them into diagrams with diaper pins: he'd been having issues with his children. A Fleet officer passing through had sensed them as vague ships in orbit around an unknowable star, and had woken up complaining of ghost readings on his sensor panels.

And then there was the Glaseahn woman with the spotted back, who after a single session had conceptualized Jahir as Aksivaht'h, the goddess herself, and never once deviated from it in all the sessions since.

"Why you?" Vasiht'h complained outside the chamber while they waited for her to wake. "I'm the Glaseah!"

"Maybe she thought I was more feminine than you," Jahir said, amused.

Vasiht'h snorted. "We don't notice things like that. We don't have the hormone issues the rest of you folk do."

"Is that so?" Jahir said, the mindline dusted with daffodil-yellow amusement.

Vasiht'h's retort was interrupted by the arrival of their patient, who smiled tentatively at them both.

"You're free to go, alet," Jahir said.

"Thank you," she said. And smiled at Vasiht'h. "Ah . . . maybe you can walk me out?"

Vasiht'h blinked at her owlishly, his feathered ears slicking back. "Of course."

Her smile was shy as he fell in alongside. He had the uncomfortable feeling he was about to uncover the source of the issues that had brought her to their door.

Politely, Jahir left them alone and went to strip the sheets from the client couch. He noted the spike of surprise through the mindline without comment and tossed the dirty linens into the hamper, running a decontaminator over the pillow and beginning on the mattress.

When Vasiht'h returned, he said innocently, "Asked you out, did she?"

Vasiht'h grumbled and stomped through the door to the kitchen.

Jahir called, "She was sweet!"

"You go out with her, then!"

Jahir hid a smile and started making the bed for the next client.

THE SAILOR

"I THINK THIS IS LESS PSYCHIATRY and more meddling," Vasiht'h muttered. "Again."

"You may be right," Jahir said, standing at the entrance. "Shall we leave?"

"Nooooo," Vasiht'h said slowly. And sighed.

So they walked under the broad arch with its decoration of shed stars trailing from a solar skiff, into a hemispherical room englobed with curved floor-to-ceiling windows. Amid the chatter of passengers awaiting their boarding calls, they spoke quietly to a steward and were escorted into an office where a surprised Asanii looked up from his tablet. He was middle-aged, more humanoid than feline, lean and focused in a dark blue uniform embroidered with the trailing stars from the arch.

"You're here to apply for the opening?" he asked, looking from one to the other.

"No," Jahir admitted. "We're here to ask a question of an experienced sailing master."

Vasiht'h said, "Jahir and Vasiht'h, xenotherapists. We work—"

"—down past the commons, I've heard of you," the man answered, mystified. "Go on, then. How can I help you?"

"Would you hire a man who'd had a sailing accident?" Vasiht'h asked.

The Asanii leaned back, crossing his arms over his chest, and lifted a brow. "What's this about, then? You have a candidate for me?"

"We . . . might know of one, yes," Jahir said, exchanging a look with Vasiht'h. "He ran small vessels for twenty-two years between Seersana and Karaka'Ana. A bad accident put him on shore. He's come out to the starbase for a change of venue."

"He's healed up," Vasiht'h said. "But he hasn't applied for new work. His wife sent him to us, but we haven't had any luck getting him to open up about what's holding him back."

"We're a bit adrift," Jahir finished. "We came for advice."

"Neither of you've had any trouble in space, eh?" the Asanii said, flicking his ears back. At their expressions, he said, "Then neither of you've been scared enough in your lives to imagine what it's like. Particularly if you're the captain. And if the ship's small . . . well, so much the worse. They come apart quick when they fail, small ships." His eyes lost their focus. "I've had some bad ones, I have."

/You think . . ./ Vasiht'h began, the mindline tinged with the astringence of uncertainty.

/I do,/ Jahir said firmly, making tea of that astringency. */Think of it as a referral to a more experienced practitioner./*

/If you say so,/ Vasiht'h said, but a touch of humor reached him, like honey.

"I don't suppose you'd be willing to do a fellow sailor a favor," Jahir said. "And go out with him for a drink."

The Asanii's eyes grew sharp again. He looked at them. "Eh? I thought you were going to ask me to give him a job."

"We wouldn't do that," Vasiht'h said. "You don't know him."

"But you do know ships, and you do know accidents, and frankly not all the reassurance from two ground-bound souls will convince a man who's spent twenty-two years piloting small craft that we know what we're talking about," Jahir said. "He needs to hear the stories from someone who's been there."

"It is good, trading stories," the Asanii said. "Well, sunspit, no reason not. Haven't talked to someone new about the trade in ages. I'll forward you my card, ah? You tell him to look me up. We'll have a beer."

"Thank you," Jahir said as Vasiht'h offered his hand palm-up.

The Asanii covered it with his, and nodded to the Eldritch. "No trouble," he said.

At the conclusion of yet another unproductive session, they mentioned the offer from the owner of the solar skiff enterprise on the rim. "A colleague," Jahir said. "He thought you'd want to talk shop."

With a grunt, their patient took his leave.

The man missed his next appointment with only a cursory note of explanation.

"We failed this one," Vasiht'h said with a sigh. His voice was embroidered with little rain-clouds in the mindline, which Jahir brushed off vaguely until the sending between them was only a little damp with pessimism.

"Patience," he said over his cup of coffee, reading his data tablet.

"Do you really think we need to have experienced things to help people through them?" Vasiht'h wondered.

Jahir set his data tablet down and looked at him over his small breakfast. "No. Obviously, or we wouldn't be in this line of work. We've helped Harat-Shar with labyrinthine amorous troubles, parents with children, workers with job problems so esoteric they had to explain them at length to us. And they've walked out of our office with lighter shoulders."

"Then why is this one different?" Vasiht'h asked. "Why did we have to give it up?"

"Because, arii," Jahir said, "he needed absolution, not healing. And we are not priests in the religion to which he adheres."

Vasiht'h glanced at him sharply, but the Eldritch had already returned to his reading.

∽∾∽

Three weeks later, they finally heard from their grounded captain.

"Tickets?" Jahir said, bemused.

"Two," Vasiht'h agreed, spreading the message for the details. "On a tourist's skiff. A shot through the spindle for a spacer's view of the inside of the base, and then a skim off the top to catch a trail of passing debris. A 'jewelfall cruise.' And our man's in charge. I guess we got him a job . . . !"

"He arranged that job himself, more like," Jahir said, laughing. "Well, then, arii? Shall we?"

"I'll go schedule it now!"

ℋELPLESSNESS

. . . the devout Hinichi whose medical tests had proven him incapable of fathering children, torn between his desperate desire for a family and the religion that barred him from extraordinary measures, a religion that had given him strength and purpose all his life . . . he could no more turn from that faith than he could from his life, but he could not relinquish his dreams of a family, of children and grandchildren. He came to them because they could meet his eyes without flinching, could bear the anguish there, so gravely mastered so that he could remain functional. But they knew, and their patient did also, that he was dissolving out from under that mastery, and that there was nothing any of them could do about it if he could give up neither of these things that made him who he was.

. . . the woman who'd remembered loving music for as long as she had memory, who had wanted nothing more than to be a musician, and whom had proved utterly untalented despite her devoted studies, her constant attempts to improve . . . she came to them, and wept, and asked them for silence. They tucked a blanket around her thin shoulders and crept from the room, leaving only the ambient noises of their office to distract her

from the symphonies that played in her head, and that she would
never play in any other way.

. . . the Harat-Shar who loved two others; a cripple no longer
able to respond to him physically and too afraid to share him,
and a human who loved him and couldn't bear to admit that love
for another man, and another species . . . on arrival he begged
them to take his dreams from him; in vain they explained that to
do so would be to disable him, to disorder his mind. He refused
to listen. When they entered his dreams that first session, they
understood why, for they were filled with loneliness and the
inexorable sensation of being ripped apart. His soul, asleep, was
nothing but a long, unfinished scream. They guided his dreams in
other directions, vigilant, grieving.

. . . the woman who worked on the starbase, who loved a
Fleet officer from whom she was parted for years at a time . . .
she said to them, exhausted, "We can give up the work that ful-
fills us . . . or give up the love that completes us. Either way we are
condemned. But . . . I miss her so much." She found peace in their
company, speaking of her work or the news of the day, but the
pain central to her life, around which all other weaknesses and
stresses revolved, none of them could resolve and she refused to
broach.

. . . the widower who made his first appointment with them
eighteen years after the death of his wife, who had raised all
three children and seen them into adulthood and never healed
from his loss . . . he never spoke during their sessions, only went
quietly to their couch and stretched himself upon it, and closed
his eyes, and slept.

Week after week, they came, and slept or talked or did not
talk. Week after week, Jahir and Vasiht'h received them, and
stood vigil to their dreams, faced their depressions without judgment, ministered to the pains that shaped them, and could or

would not be removed. And when it wore them down, Vasiht'h found Jahir in the bedroom and sat beside him and silently wrapped his dark-furred arms around his taller friend; and Jahir bent until he could rest his brow against the other's forelock, and set a hand, flat and open, on his back. And there, they took comfort in that they could comfort one another, if they could comfort no one else.

THE HARAT-SHAR

S O, KESHYA-ALET, IS IT?"
"That's right," the Harat-Shariin woman said, leaning on the couch and smiling at him. It was a very Harat-Shariin smile, hinting at happy, lascivious thoughts.

/I get the strange the feeling she is not here for therapy,/ Vasiht'h murmured through the mindline.

Jahir ignored him. "Keshya-alet, then." He glanced at the copy of the intake form she'd filled out on his data tablet and tried not to notice her watching him. "Why are you here?"

She continued to stare, lost in her own private reverie.

"Alet?" Jahir said again.

"Oh!" she exclaimed. "Sorry. Ah, I am here for a therapy session. I filled out the form . . . ?"

Jahir tried not to exchange glances with Vasiht'h; technically he didn't need to, since he could sense his partner's bemusement through the mindline. It tasted like that peanut butter liqueur they'd had once. Confusing.

"We've reviewed the form carefully," Jahir said. "According to your responses, alet . . . there's nothing wrong."

"Oh but there is!" she exclaimed. "I have a thing for unavailable men!"

There was a long silence in the room. Vasiht'h and Jahir looked at their patient. Their patient stared . . . at Jahir. Happily. Almost indulgently. After a moment, she even purred a little.

There was a coughing noise so distinct Jahir almost thought it was real, and not an artifact of the mindline. "Forgive me, alet, but I appear to be misinterpreting you—"

"—you're here to look at Jahir," Vasiht'h said.

She sighed. "You found me out." She grinned. "I've seen the two of you in the commons, and . . . well . . . a real Eldritch. I've never seen one. As far as I know, there's not another one on the entire Starbase. Or in the entire sector. I couldn't resist. I don't want to touch you, I know that's not something one does. And I don't want you for myself. But I thought it would be nice just to look. And maybe fall asleep with the pretty pictures in mind. I'll be good, I promise."

"So you really did pay our consultation fee just to spend an hour staring at my partner," Vasiht'h said.

She sighed, resting her cheek in her hand and continuing to gaze at Jahir. "Yessss. Now, no doubt, you'll send me away. But it will have been worth it."

Vasiht'h cleared his throat. "Ah . . . will you excuse us a moment, alet? I'd like to talk with my partner."

"Of course," she purred.

They walked together out of the office. Once the door slid closed, Vasiht'h's haunches dropped and he grasped his stomach, laughing silently into a cupped palm. Jahir watched his paroxysms with arms folded.

"Done?" he said, resigned, once the Glaseah began to wipe his eyes.

"What do you want to do about this, arii?" Vasiht'h said.

Jahir sighed. "We should send her away. We're not models, we're therapists."

"But?" Vasiht'h asked.

"But her interest is harmless," Jahir said. "I could finish some work while she fell asleep on our couch. She'll leave happy."

Vasiht'h peered up at him. "Are you sure? I thought you'd find it . . . more upsetting. Especially after that incident on Selnor."

Jahir shook his head. "She's not human, arii. The Harat-Shar . . . when they tell you they just want to look, they're not lying. If they wanted more, they'd have absolutely no trouble asking."

"If you're sure," Vasiht'h said, struggling with his amusement. "I can send her away for you if you want."

"You were the one who told me on Seersana that I'd be dealing with this sort of thing," Jahir said. "This is just the first time it's been quite so . . ."

"Obvious?" Vasiht'h said.

"Simple to resolve," Jahir said, with weary amusement.

So they went back into the room together. Their patient was standing already, waiting by the door.

"You can lie back down if you wish," Jahir said. "You don't mind if my partner stays in the room?"

"Oh, not at all," she said, eagerly resuming her perch on the couch. "Your very own chaperone, yes?"

"Something of that nature," Jahir said. He pointed at a data tablet. "I'll make notes on your case while you rest."

She beamed. "Yes, please do."

"And one more thing, alet," Jahir said. "I permit this because you already paid the hour. But there will be no parade of Harat-Shar through this office after you leave. Vasiht'h and I are professional therapists; we have patients to schedule who have real issues, and I would be displeased to have their time displaced by those who don't have their needs."

"You mean . . . I'll be the only one who gets this close look," she said, threading her fingers together. "Oh yes! Absolutely!" She leaned forward, brows lifting. "As far as anyone else is concerned, I *am* here to talk." She leaned back with a sigh. "I really wasn't jesting, the part about unavailable men. When you have the number of lovers I do, it starts to sound soothing, to be able to look and appreciate without having to navigate all the attendant . . . complexities."

"That does sound like an actual problem," Vasiht'h said,

sober. Mostly. The mindline was sparkling, sunlight on water. "Maybe you should cut down on the number of your lovers."

"Oh!" she said. "No, no. For all their irritations, they're worth it." She sighed, fond. "Very much. But yes. I shall enjoy my little respite . . . mmm. Yes. It will be very . . . *healing*." She grinned at them both so winningly that even Jahir had to laugh.

So Jahir sat, took up the tablet and went to work. Their patient put her cheek in her hand again and watched him with deep satisfaction, and eventually slid to sleep with a very happy grin.

"What do you think?" Vasiht'h said later after she'd taken her leave, and a more pleased and relaxed client they'd rarely had the privilege to see off.

"I think that's possibly the easiest we've made someone happy . . . perhaps ever," Jahir said.

Swiping the mindline once, Vasiht'h felt an unnamed weight. ". . . and?"

"I feel a little confused," Jahir confessed.

"Peanut butter liqueur."

He chuckled. "Yes." He shook his head. "Harat-Shar!"

"Yes," Vasiht'h said. And added, "But not together."

Jahir eyed him severely and left him snickering by the door.

THE WITNESS

"INEED YOUR HELP," THE SLIM man in Fleet uniform said. There was a caduceus on his breast tab and a focused look on his face. "We need to get this man debriefed, and to do that he has to calm down. But I can't even start . . . he can't talk without hysterics. He's either like this or catatonic. I was hoping since you work while people are asleep—"

"That we can begin the healing where he's more malleable?" Jahir said.

"Yes," the Fleet physician said.

They all looked through the window at the man pacing . . . pacing. Constantly moving. His face was locked in a rictus of shock.

"What happened to him?" Vasiht'h asked, low.

"He was on his way down-planet when a pirate came through," the physician said. "Destroyed the settlement and the ship he was serving on."

"The ship too?" Jahir asked, startled. "A Fleet vessel?"

"A small one, but yes. So you can see why we need him to talk. He's one of the only survivors."

Jahir looked at the haunted figure, shoulders rounded, head bent, tremors in the arms and knees. "He'll need to sleep."

"I'll give him a soporific."

———⊶⊷———

/*God and Lady,*/ Jahir whispered down the mindline as they looked at their patient, now slack on the facility's bed.

/*He's been through hell,*/ Vasiht'h agreed, compassion threading the words with pained sparks like an irritated nerve. The Glaseah looked up at his much taller partner. /*This is not going to be one of our easier times . . ./*

Thinking of what the man had witnessed, Jahir answered, /*No./* And held out his hand.

Vasiht'h took it, and together they bent toward their patient's tortured dreams.

———⊶⊷———

From within, the maelstrom was unnavigable. Guilt. Pain. Horror. Flashes of images neither of them wanted to see.

/*What do we do?/* Vasiht'h asked, crowding close to him in the eye of the storm.

/*We make an anchor,*/ Jahir said. /*All your gentlest memories, arii. And all of mine. We need to help him feel safe somewhere./*

/*Nothing seems gentle enough!/*

/*No single thing will be,*/ Jahir answered, and began with the sound of a lullaby. Vasiht'h did not understand the words, but they were liquid-long and carried with them the smell of jasmine and the feel of summer sunlight. He saw the Eldritch on campus at Seersana University where they'd met, surrounded by the bustle of the student body, so many species and races. He felt the warm working of muscle against the insides of his legs as his partner rode a galloping horse over a long field. /*Thus,*/ Jahir whispered.

He wove his own in, then. The rough-and-tumble play of his cousins and siblings, wings and paws and too many legs and laughter. The taste of kerinne after a long night's work, the satisfaction of having helped someone and the exhaustion of it. The first time he'd seen a Phoenix flying: flash of light off metallic feathers as the male soared through the low-g gymnasium. And on and on. Choosing memories like bright strands, weaving them into banners hung into that storm.

They rose from their patient's mind dripping with sweat and weary beyond measure. The man was still sleeping.

"Will it be enough?" Vasiht'h wondered.

Jahir shook his head.

It wasn't. They returned the following day. And the one after. And again. And again. Digging deep and finding good and giving it away. The first time Jahir had used a shower—there were no such things on his world—the marvel of feeling the hot spray on skin and wondering how it was issued; Vasiht'h replayed the message from his family, sent on his graduation . . . one so interminable that Jahir had started laughing as one after another, this cousin or that nephew or this uncle or that relative took the place of the next in a never-ending stream of congratulatory Glaseah. They gave the memory of languages buzzing on the promenade next to their favorite coffeehouse. The sight of the spindle seen from the base's interior, shrouded by the shell of atmosphere so that it looked like a pale white arch in the cloudless sky.

They often woke from their work on the floor with their heads on the edge of the bed. Their exhaustion permeated their sendings, and the distant worried hush of the medical staff and the man's commanding officers as they spoke over the therapists' heads. But they kept their vigil . . . until the night they woke to find their patient staring at them from his pillow.

Stunned, neither of them spoke. He studied them, first one face, than the other.

"That makes sense of the dreams about having four feet," he said finally, his voice hoarse but steady.

"You're awake," was all Vasiht'h could think to say.

"I'm ready to talk," he said, pushing himself upright. "Send someone in."

———❦———

They withdrew. The Fleet physician hastily sent for the intelligence officer and then drew them aside. "What did you do? Will it last?"

"We don't know," Jahir said after exchanging a look with Vasiht'h. "But I think you'll be able to use more conventional techniques from this point forward."

Vasiht'h said, "We'd appreciate if you'd keep us apprised of his recovery, if you have the chance."

"Of course," the physician said. "And thank you both. You came recommended, and I see it was well-deserved."

———❦———

They retired then, and canceled their appointments for the next week, and spent several days doing nothing in particular. They were aware of one another's state through the mindline: the fatigue and the grief of having existed amid the man's memories of what he'd seen . . . and knew better than to try to talk. Some things were best left to heal unaided, unmolested.

———❦———

Several weeks later, the physician sent them a note. Their patient had returned to duty and was still in weekly therapy sessions, and was doing well.

'He cites your aid as critical,' the note concluded, 'because it reminded him there were still things that needed protection.'

Looking over Vasiht'h's shoulder, Jahir shook his head. The rue in the mindline felt distantly bitter, like the memory of medicine. "And I thought creating a point of safety was the key."

"And we were wrong," Vasiht'h murmured. And smiled a little. "This is the part where you're supposed to say something poetic."

A surge of amusement washed the mindline, glittering with foam. "And what exactly would you suggest?"

"Like, I don't know," Vasiht'h said. "Health can blossom out of the soil of safety . . . but it's useless to plant it without a sun to grow toward?"

Jahir smiled at him. "You hardly need me at all."

"Hmph," Vasiht'h said. "Only if you know what I'd say, hearing it."

Jahir cocked his head, white hair hissing over one shoulder. His smile grew lopsided. "That needing a sun is common sense. It's knowing what makes the sun shine for someone that comprises the art of the thing."

"Now I know we spend too much time together," Vasiht'h said a sigh, and laughed, and knew they too had healed well.

"Moving on," Jahir said.

"Yes," Vasiht'h said, and brought up their next patient's file.

THE CASE OF THE POISONED HOUSE

S o, why don't you tell us about your family?"
/*Nicely done,*/ Vasiht'h sent on a curl of orange amusement. /*I doubt she even noticed your double-take when she walked in.*/

Jahir didn't even look at his partner as he replied in silent kind, /*And what a double-take it is. No wonder they have had problems.*/

Their client, currently seated cross-legged in one of their chairs, was a woman in her late twenties. That she was Harat-Shariin, one of the the many offshoots of humanity's genetic experiments hundreds of years ago, was not particularly unusual in the primarily Pelted Alliance . . . no, what had surprised both Jahir and Vasiht'h was that the woman's brother had referred her for therapy. Her Hinichi brother. People who looked like wolves did not naturally produce siblings who looked like ocelots.

/*How many problems they're having depends on how old she was when they took her in,*/ Vasiht'h said, continuing their silent dialogue as the woman settled into the chair and began picking at the end of her spotted tail. /*We might get lucky.*/

/*I won't gamble on those odds,*/ Jahir said.

"I'm not sure this is a good idea," the woman began. "I don't think you can understand what I'm going through."

"Why is that?" Jahir asked.

"Well, I've heard that Glaseah have no hormones and Eldritch have sex once every six hundred years and only to procreate, so how can either of you possibly understand me?"

/Nice opening,/ Vasiht'h muttered.

/At least we won't be bored./ Aloud, Jahir said, "Do you think these things are relevant to your feelings about your mother?"

"Of course they are," the woman said. "I'm Harat-Shariin."

"Your brother's very worried about you," Vasiht'h said, speaking for the first time.

Her ears flattened and she looked away. "I know. I came as a favor to him. He says you two have a good record, whatever that means."

"We want to help," Vasiht'h said. "Won't you let us try?"

More picking at her tail-tip. Then a sigh. "If I don't, Barron will only worry more. I guess we can talk." Another pause. "You asked about my family. I love my family!"

"When did you come to live with them?" Jahir asked.

"I was about five, I guess," she said.

/Enough time to imprint on Harat-Shariin customs?/ Vasiht'h wondered.

/Not sure,/ Jahir said. "It sounds like quite a story. We don't get many Harat-Shariin daughters of Hinichi parents, you know."

She flashed her pointed teeth in her first grin of the session. "Yes, well, I am special. My birth parents gave me up for adoption, and Mom and Dad sent all the way to Harat-Sharii for me."

/Homeworld-bred!/ Jahir thought. /This may be more trouble than we thought./

/Do you think a five-year-old would have enough time to become a Harat-Shar culturally?/

/I hope not./ "And you have . . . let's see. Three brothers and two sisters!" Jahir said. "That must have been an adventure."

"A wonderful one," she said. "I love my family a lot. They're always good to me. I never feel alone." She looked into her lap, petting her tail-tip for a moment. Abruptly, she ceased and her voice lost its character. "I miss Mom. I know Barron doesn't think

I do, but I do. Just because I'm not crying about her doesn't mean I didn't care about her. I did. I cared a lot."

/*And there's the block,*/ Vasiht'h said.

/*Obvious,*/ Jahir replied, touching the sending with just a little gray worry despite the words. /*Just how we prefer them.*/

"Are you aware of how we operate, Sarja?" Vasiht'h asked.

"Barron says you work on me while I sleep," she replied, once again worrying at her tail-tip and sounding skeptical. One of her rare grins passed over her face. "I guess that's why the hours."

"It tends to help if we see people before their rest periods, yes," Jahir said with a smile.

"I'm not sure if you're familiar with lucid dreaming," Vasiht'h continued, "but what we do is a little like inspiring you to have a lucid dream. You'll be aware of us and we'll be directing your dream so that you can uncover some of the issues you may not know you're facing."

"Sounds like magic," the woman said.

"It feels like magic," Vasiht'h said. "We have a tea we ask our patients to drink. It'll help you fall asleep."

"When you're done—"

"The dreaming sessions usually take an hour once you fall asleep," Vasiht'h said. "We'll wake you up when we're done."

The woman shrugged. "Fine. Bring me the tea. Let's get this done so I can go home."

/*You think she'll go under quickly?*/ Jahir asked.

/*I have no idea. I guess we'll find out.*/

In the kitchen, waiting for the room monitor next door to sound, Jahir leaned back against the counter and looked the long distance down to his centauroid partner. "So, do you think the problem stems from the cultural mismatch?"

"I don't know," Vasiht'h said, "but it's hard to imagine her not being affected by it. The Hinichi are so stoic when it comes to showing familial affection."

"And Harat-Shar have what amounts to socially-mandated

incest," Jahir said. "Do you think we'll be able to do justice to this?"

"What, me the hormone-stripped and you the cypher?" Vasiht'h asked with a laugh. He stood and stretched, spreading dark wings and wiggling white and black toes. "Haven't we been through this before? We've dealt with plenty of Harat-Shar."

"But not Harat-Shar having problems because their mothers didn't have intimate contact with them," Jahir said. "I'm not certain I know how to help someone who feels deprived because of its lack. Maybe we should refer her to a Harat-Shariin therapist."

"But she's not just a Harat-Shar," Vasiht'h said. "She's a Harat-Shar raised by Hinichi with Hinichi brothers and sisters who are worried about her." He sighed. "Her brother didn't seem all that remote when he came to us, did he?"

"No, but he might not act that way around her," Jahir said. He filled a mug with steaming kerinne and passed it down. "Ah. We're jumping to conclusions, though. We haven't even started the case history. Maybe we'll find out from her dreams that she's afraid of death."

Vasiht'h's paws twitched. "Maybe. But you know, arii, I begin to wonder if the mindline doesn't make us more sensitive to other people. Our intuitive leaps are usually correct."

"Usually," Jahir said. "Not always."

⚬⚬⚬

The monitor sounded, a muted chime.

"To work," Jahir said, putting his mug aside.

Vasiht'h followed him into the room next door, where their client had curled herself into a furry ball, both arms wrapped around a pillow. She wore a stubborn expression, even in her sleep.

/Poor thing,/ Vasiht'h said, /She doesn't even give up her troubles in bed./ He held out a hand.

Working against social taboos centuries strong, Jahir slid his own fingers into the black, furred ones, and the already-strong mindline broadened into a deep, powerful channel, the link that made their special brand of therapy possible. They turned their attention as one and reached for the sleeper, falling through the layers of her consciousness and into the tangle that preoccupied her as she slumbered.

Their client was cleaning, it seemed. The corners of a wooden home. The walls. The ceilings, though how she reached them neither she nor her two observers understood. She spent a long time doing this, until an older man passed through, a stern but absent Hinichi elder.

The man asked her what she was doing. She was, of course, cleaning. There was poison somewhere, and she had to get rid of it all. The elder thought she should keep at it, then.

/Is she the poison?/ Jahir wondered.

/Or her unmet desires, which she's trying to keep away from her family,/ Vasiht'h said. /Do you want to affect?/

They watched a while longer as their client went from room to room, sweeping invisible dirt from walls, searching and becoming frustrated when her search turned up no poison.

/Let's,/ Jahir said. /I'll go first./

/Right./

Jahir took on the seeming of a younger Hinichi, suggesting with a breath, *I'm family*. He made and sat in a chair in one of the rooms, and when the client entered, he said, "What are you looking for?"

The woman, exasperated, thought it was obvious. She was looking for poison.

"There are many kinds of poisons," Jahir said. "What will this kind do?"

This kind would kill her!

/Her?/ Vasiht'h wondered.

Jahir asked, "Kill you? What about us, your family?"

He was ridiculous. Her family couldn't be hurt by poison. They didn't even realize it existed, so how could it hurt them? Now could she return to her search? It was very important.

"Go ahead," Jahir said. /Interesting. Your turn./

Vasiht'h chose to show himself as another family member,

but he did not address her. She cleaned her way around him until she frowned and looked around. She didn't understand.

"What don't you understand?" Vasiht'h asked.

She knew the poison had to be in the house somewhere, but she'd searched it from top to bottom, in every nook and cranny. How had it escaped her? This was very important . . . if she didn't find it, she would die.

"Maybe there's no poison in the house," Vasiht'h said.

This was obviously ridiculous. Of course there was. She knew this with a personal certainty, no matter what her brothers and sisters said.

"We've told you again and again there's no poison," Vasiht'h said. "Why don't you believe us?"

She loved her brothers and sisters very much, but if there was no poison, why was she sick?

"Perhaps because you think you should be."

Nonsense, that was definitely nonsense. All she wanted was love and acceptance, and this poison was in the way. She would just have to go back to cleaning until she found it. Now would her brother kindly move out of the way?

/What do you think?/ Vasiht'h asked.

/I think what you're thinking,/ Jahir said. /She is becoming agitated. We should slip out before she finishes waking./

———— ✿ ————

"So," said the woman ten minutes later. "What did you find out?"

"You tell us," Jahir said. "What did you feel on waking?"

"Irritated," the woman said, tail twitching. "I had this weird dream—did you plant it?"

"No," Jahir said. "We were just watching. What do you remember about the dream?"

She looked at her tail. "I remember being upset because something was killing me and no one was helping me to get rid of it."

/Interesting!/ Vasiht'h said.

"Do you remember what the thing was?" Jahir asked.

"I'm not sure. Some sort of gas," she said. "I kept looking for something, you know, liquid. Like a stain. But there was no stain. I was supposed to be looking for a gas, and I was getting weaker and weaker because I didn't realize I couldn't see what was killing me." She picked at her tail-tip. "I'd rather not dream that again."

"I don't blame you," Vasiht'h said.

"So what's wrong with me?" she asked. "Barron said you usually know within a single session."

/Which of us should deliver, given how she has described us?/

Vasiht'h's snort echoed down the mindline. /Better let me. She'll find it harder to be angry with me./

/No arguments there./

"Well, Sarja," Vasiht'h said. "You were older than many cross-race babies are when they're adopted. Five years is plenty of time to develop expectations of how your parents are going to show their love."

"So this is about me being Harat-Shariin after all," the woman said. "You think I haven't cried about my mother dying because she didn't pet me the way my Harat-Shariin mother did."

"That's what we think," Vasiht'h said.

She picked at her tail tip. There was already a bare spot on it. "I don't remember my birth-mother all that well."

"You don't have to remember her consciously to have developed a feeling about how parents are supposed to act," Vasiht'h said.

She stopped plucking her tail, stared at them, and said, "I think you're wrong." And then she left, back stiff and ears flat against her head. The door slid on their startled silence.

"Did I not state it gently enough?" Vasiht'h wondered, his words echoing up the mindline with a touch of limp remorse.

"We either hit the mark exactly right," Jahir started.

"—or?"

"Or we missed it entirely," Jahir said. "I have no idea which."

"Let's just hope she comes back," Vasiht'h said.

⋙

"What did you do to my sister?"

/This doesn't look good,/ Vasiht'h said.

"We evaluated her as you requested," Jahir said. "But her case is complex. We'd like her to return so we can continue working with her."

"She says you told her that Mother didn't love her!" the man exclaimed.

"We told her that we thought it likely that she didn't interpret your mother's behavior as loving because it didn't match the behavior displayed by her Harat-Shariin mother," Jahir said. "She was old enough to become accustomed to how Harat-Shar families operate . . . not how Hinichi families do."

The Hinichi wrinkled his nose. "We loved her far more than her Harat-Shariin family ever did."

"I don't doubt that," Jahir said. "This is working on a more subtle, subconscious level, alet."

"She doesn't want to come back," the Hinichi said. "I just came to pay for her session."

/Not good at all,/ Vasiht'h said.

/No,/ Jahir said. /But we can't exactly coerce her./ "We appreciate that," the Eldritch continued out loud. "Though we wish we could finish what we've begun. We can often diagnose a problem within a session, but we can't solve it."

"If all she's going to take away from this is that Mother didn't love her enough, it's not worth it," the man said. "She's upset enough as it is without thinking thoughts like that about the woman we just put to the ground."

"Of course," Jahir said as the man counted out a stack of coins. The Alliance rarely used literal money, but on occasion people did prefer to pay them in fin.

The Hinichi began to hand the stack over when he stopped. "Oh, I can't give this to you, can I?"

"You can pass it to my partner," Jahir said.

The man turned to the shorter Glaseah and handed him the money. "It must make things difficult for you, not to be able to touch anyone."

"It's the way we're raised," Jahir said. "It's hard to escape the conditioning we had as children."

"And that's Sarja's problem, is it?" the Hinichi said. He snorted. "Love is what Harat-Shar say love is."

"Exactly," Vasiht'h said.

The man laughed. "Right. So Eldritch love is never touching, and Harat-Shariin love is abandonment. I think I'll stay with what I learned as an adult." He bowed. "Thank you for your attempts, aletsen."

/Arii!/

/I heard it too. Do you suppose—/

/It makes a lot more sense, don't you think?/ Vasiht'h said, urgency compacting the words, black and spiked. /We got too tangled in what we thought the problem was to actually see the problem./

"Alet," Jahir called after the man's retreating back, standing. "A moment, if you would . . . ?"

The Hinichi paused at their door. "Yes?"

"We'll refund you the fee in full if you give us just one more chance to talk with Sarja," Jahir said. "Just talk. No dreams. One more session . . . if she doesn't want to come back after what we have to say, that's fine. We won't charge her again."

He hesitated. "You think you can help? More than you did before?"

Jahir exchanged a look with Vasiht'h. The latter said, "We're sure of it."

⸺∞⸺

"Mother loved me," Sarja said at their door, scowling.

"We know," Vasiht'h said.

Jahir continued, "It was your birth-mother who didn't love you."

The woman's eyes widened in shock . . . and then she let out a long wail.

As Vasiht'h helped her back to the couch, Jahir said, /No wonder the poison couldn't kill her real family. They knew she'd been *abandoned, but they still love her. She's the only one who could die if she found it and looked at it./*

/I wonder how long she's been trying to clean that house?/ Vasiht'h said.

/Probably all her life,/ Jahir said, drawing his chair closer and passing the client a handkerchief through Vasiht'h's hands. / *Hopefully in a few weeks she'll put away her bucket and towels and be done with the whole business./*

/Hopefully,/ Vasiht'h said. /Let's get to work./

APPENDICES

CONTAINING A RECIPE, *information about the species of the Alliance, a sidebar about Rexina Regina, author sketches, acknowledgments, a rundown on other Pelted stories, and the author's (actual, rather than fictional) biographical data.*

Brief Glossary

Alet (ah LEHT): "friend," but formal, as one would address a stranger. Plural is *aletsen*.

Arii (ah REE): "friend," personal. An endearment. Used only for actual friends. Plural is *ariisen*. Additional forms include *ariihir* ("dear brother") and *ariishir* ("dear sister").

Dami (DAH mee): "mom," in Tam-leyan. Often used among other Pelted species.

Fin (FEEN): a unit of Alliance currency. Singular is deprecated *finca*, rarely used.

Hea (HEY ah): abbreviation for Healer-assist.

Kara (kah RAH): "child". Plural is *karasen*.

Tapa (TAH pah): "dad," in Tam-leyan. Often used among other Pelted species.

(Very Basic) Scones

HEAVEN HELP ME, BUT I would pick scones for this book when scones are both finicky and hard to test if you can't eat flour. Or have milk. But there really is nothing like a scone, so I flung myself into the kitchen with a bunch of recipes and hammered them together and came up with these. This recipe makes six largish scones (good if you have a modest family), and tastes mostly of butter (so make sure you buy really good butter). And I am happy to report they are not disappointing, which is the adjective one finds most often on the tip of one's tongue when eating wheatless baked goods. They're a little chewier than most scones, but they're still tasty.

If, unlike me, you can have both wheat and milk, removing the xantham gum and doing a one-to-one substitution should work. Just don't use skim!

Finally, be warned that I live at sea-level. If you live at high altitude, adjust accordingly.

Scones for Eating While Reading

- 1 cup gluten-free flour
- ¾ tsp xanthan gum*
- ½ tbsp baking powder
- ¼ tsp kosher salt
- 1 tbsp sugar
- ½ cup frozen berries
- 2 ½ tbsp unsalted butter, chilled
- ½ cup almond milk

Set oven to 400° F and line a pan with parchment paper. Set aside.

Scone-making is a lot like pie-crust making, which means if you don't have a pastry cutter you will weep bitter tears. I highly recommend one. Also, keep your tools cold. Your bowl, your hands, your cutting board. I usually put a cold-pack under mine.

Combine the flour, gum, powder, salt, and sugar in one bowl, really well. (Double-check your gluten-free flour mix; some of them already contain xantham gum, at which point you can omit it.) Put the frozen berries in another smaller bowl and toss them with a couple teaspoons of this mix to coat them.

Now, praying to the higher powers, dice the butter into the large bowl (keeping it chilled), and then cut it into the flour until it gets chunky and the chunks are all flour-covered and about the size of peas. (If you've never done this, there is almost certainly a Youtube video somewhere that demonstrates cutting butter into flour.) If you don't have a pastry cutter, you can use a knife and fork but it will take you six times as long. I recommend buying your scones from a bakery and saving yourself the grief.

After you have the butter cut in, add the milk and mix it just enough to integrate (it should be an ugly dough, kind of lumpy). Fold in the frozen berries and then drop big dollops of the dough on your pan. Mine were about half the size of my palm, which gave me six. Sprinkle the tops with crystallized sugar, if you like extra sweetness.

Bake for fifteen to twenty minutes, until the edges are slightly brown. I like to eat these after they've cooled a bit. And then I put more butter on them. Because butter.

THE SPECIES OF
THE ALLIANCE

THE ALLIANCE IS MOSTLY composed of the Pelted, a group of races that segregated and colonized worlds based (more or less) on their visual characteristics. Having been engineered from a mélange of uplifted animals, it's not technically correct to refer to any of them as "cats" or "wolves," since any one individual might have as many as six or seven genetic contributors: thus the monikers like "foxine" and "tigraine" rather than "vulpine" or "tiger." However, even the Pelted think of themselves in groupings of general animal characteristics, so for the ease of imagining them, I've separated them that way.

THE PELTED

The Quasi-Felids: The Karaka'An, Asanii, and Harat-Shar comprise the most cat-like of the Pelted, with the Karaka'An being the shortest and digitigrade, the Asanii being taller and plantigrade, and the Harat-Shar including either sort but being based on the great cats rather than the domesticated variants.

The Quasi-Canids: The Seersa, Tam-illee, and Hinichi are the most doggish of the Pelted, with the Seersa being short and digitigrade and foxish, the Tam-illee taller, plantigrade and also foxish, and the Hinichi being wolflike.

Others: Less easily categorized are the Aera, with long, hare-like ears, winged feet and foxish faces, the felid Malarai with their feathered wings, and the Phoenix, tall bipedal avians.

The Centauroids: Of the Pelted, two species are centauroid in configuration, the short Glaseah, furred and with lower bodies like lions but coloration like skunks and leathery wings on their lower backs, and the tall Ciracaana, who have foxish faces but long-legged cat-like bodies.

Aquatics: One Pelted race was engineered for aquatic environments: the Naysha, who look like mermaids would if mermaids had sleek, hairless, slightly rodent-like faces and the lower bodies of dolphins.

Other Species

Humanoids: Humanity fills this niche, along with their estranged cousins, the esper-race Eldritch.

True Aliens: Of the true aliens, six are known: the shapeshifting Chatcaava, whose natural form is draconic (though they are mammals); the gentle heavyworlder Faulfenza, who are furred and generally regarded to be attractive; the Akubi, large dinosaur-like fliers with three sexes; the aquatic Platies, who look like colorful flatworms and can communicate reliably only with the Naysha, and the enigmatic Flitzbe, who are quasi-vegetative and resemble softly furred volleyballs that change color depending on their mood. New to the Alliance (and not pictured in the lineup) is the last race, the "Octopi" of *Either Side of the Strand*.

For a more detailed look into the species of the Alliance, a Peltedverse Guidebook is available through me; you can get it by signing up for my mailing list (from my website), by jumping on my Patreon, or by emailing me directly (haikujaguar at gmail).

THE SPECIES AND RACES OF THE PARADOX PELTED UNIVERSE

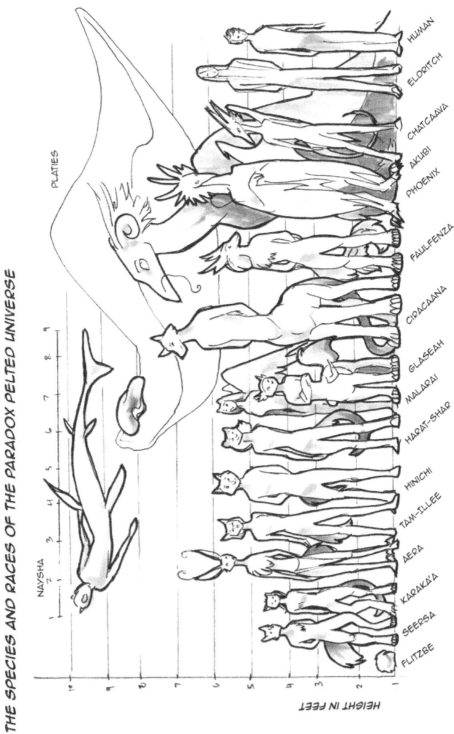

PLATIES

NAYSHA

HUMAN
ELDRITCH
CHATCAAVA
AKUBI
PHOENIX
FAULFENZA
CIRACAANA
GLASEAH
MALARAI
HARAT-SHAR
HINICHI
TAM-ILLEE
AERA
KARAKA'A
SEERSA
FLITZBE

HEIGHT IN FEET

About Rexina Regina

I WOULD LOVE TO SAY THAT Young Me's story of Thaddeus and Alana the Eldritch exists as a finished piece I could share with you, but at fifteen I was very good at starting stories and not very good at finishing them. Since the Peltedverse was in its infancy, I didn't have a handle on anything in the setting, anyway, so it would have been astonishingly non-canonical in places. And their story in particular went through several versions, including a swiftly-abandoned attempt at a B&W comic (back in the era where there was no internet for me to post to—thank goodness).

But I think their story is important, which is what inspired me to include it (sort of) in *Dreamhearth* . . . because it represents my initial attempts to find "the" Eldritch story. I knew instinctively it had to be about an Eldritch and one of the alien species in the universe, but I couldn't decide what that pairing looked like. Thaddeus and Alana (who had several different names in their various drafts) were my first attempt. Then there was a Tam-illee girl and an Eldritch girl who were Best Friends Forever—these two evolved, eventually, into Fasianyl and Sellelvi, the Eldritch and Harat-Shar that Reese learns about in *Earthrise*. The ultimate end of my journey was Reese and Hirianthial, of course . . . but I wouldn't have gotten there without my initial flailing as a teenager.

It's for this reason I feel affection for my first efforts. Even as an angst-obsessed teen, I could sense the bones of a good story, and I was tenacious enough to stick with it until I found the goods. You go, young self.

Some amusing trivia: first, Vasiht'h's comments about the weirdly detailed medical stuff in HEALED BY HER IMMORTAL HEART are true of the originals. The comic's first few pages took place in a doctor's office where Thaddeus is getting lectured about his declining sperm count. (Seriously. I wrote this. As a fifteen-year-old.) While there's not much left of the actual writing of these stories—this is my mournful look at this ancient Syquest cartridge I can no longer read—I did compose the excerpts in *Dreamhearth* by stealing lines from other stories written at the same time, which is where Vasiht'h gets his complaints about comparing someone to fruits and precious stones in the same paragraph. And the author's pen name was actually the one I selected for myself as a teen: Regina Queen. I thought I'd just alliterate it a bit, for the sake of cute, and I chose another name I really liked as a teen. I was big into Latin-sounding names.

While I'll spare you the poor attempt at the comic version, I did find some sketches of the Tam-illee and Eldritch who inspired HEALED BY HER IMMORTAL HEART, drawn by Teen Me. I hope you'll enjoy this evidence of their long lineage. I know Teen Me would be tickled to have any part of what she's done show up in a Real Book at last. I intend it as an homage, and with utmost affection, and I know she knows it.

Here's to our earliest attempts at Story. Even before we have the tools, we know the way. To all the Rexinas of the world: rock on.

mcahogarth.org

mcahogarth.org

Author Sketches

It's typical for me to do sketches while writing, a sort of mental doodling as I work out events and character arcs. These sketches are not intended to be the final word on what the characters look like! In fact, I usually have trouble pinning down people's looks. I just keep at it anyway.

Jahir and Vasiht'h are among some of my oldest characters in this setting. My original drawings of them . . . I think they date back to the early '90s! Needless to say there's a lot of *bad* art of them, by my standards, because there's a lot of art of them in general. Here are some of my favorites that pertain to *Dreamhearth*, or Jahir and Vasiht'h's years on Veta.

1. **Vasiht'h on Starbase Veta:** One of my favorite sketches of Vasiht'h, trotting past a bakery on the commons. I am amused that I took the trouble to tuck a doll into the arms of the sketchy child in the very back.
2. **The Tree:** Jahir and Vasiht'h in winter, on the couch. This piece actually goes with a later case study, which readers who continue onto Book 4 will find in the back of the book.
3. **Sehvi:** A quick, toony sketch of Vasiht'h's favorite sister.

4. **The Veta Apartment:** Here's a floor plan of the Healer's Knot after the two have converted it to their living space. This apartment remains their home for almost a decade.
5. **Dreamhearth Teaser:** Finally, in case you missed the teaser graphic for the book, here's the pair in the commons again, this time in color!

Sehvi

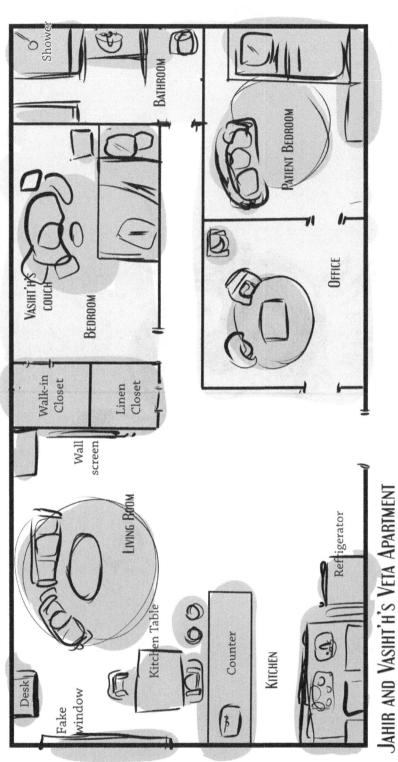

JAHIR AND VASIHT'H'S VETA APARTMENT
mcahogarth.org

Shower

BATHROOM

PATIENT BEDROOM

OFFICE

VASIHT'H'S
COUCH

BEDROOM

Walk-in
Closet

Linen
Closet

Wall
screen

LIVING ROOM

Kitchen Table

Counter

KITCHEN

Refrigerator

Desk

Fake
window

"We're family, aren't we?" Vasiht'h asked.

To his relief, Jahir did not answer immediately. At last, he replied, "What else, with love?"

ACKNOWLEDGMENTS

As usual, books don't happen without a great deal of help. Here are my thank-yous this time around:

◆ My copy-editors/first reader team: Maigen, Cap, Bertha, Therapist Jenn, Kythryne, and Artist Jen. Special thanks to Therapist Jenn who helped me correlate all the research I did on therapy with actual experience. All the hearts.

◆ My Pelted Kickstarter backers, particularly those who bought cameos in this book. I hope you all enjoyed seeing your Pelted alter-egos as much as I did writing them!

◆ My friends in the Furry Writers' Guild, who let me hang out with them even though I write about space elves, aliens, and humans along with my furries. Y'all are the most fun.

◆ Writerfriend L.Rowyn for listening to me whinge through every. Single. Manuscript I write. The patience of saints, you all. (Also, read her books. They are awesome.) And writerfriend Ursula Vernon, for not being sure why she likes Vasiht'h and Jahir so much, but recommending them to people ceaselessly with adorable expressions of puzzlement. Her books are also awesome, so you should read them too.

◆ My Patreon chat subscribers, who listened to me agonize over the recipe and peered at my lumpy scone photos and reassured me that it wasn't all in vain.

◆ And all my readers, who keep my family fed and kept asking me for more Dreamhealers. I listen! Honest! One more after this!

RETURN TO THE ALLIANCE
MORE FICTION SET IN THE PARADOX UNIVERSE

Dear Readers,

THERE ARE SEVERAL SERIES AND interlocking storylines set in the universe of the Pelted. Most of these involve the long lead-up to the conflict with the Chatcaava, barely mentioned in the Dreamhealer's Saga, and by their nature are less pastoral than the story of how Jahir and Vasiht'h met. Of the various offerings, *Earthrise*, Book 1 of the Her Instruments trilogy, is a more traditional space operatic adventure with a strong romance subplot, and involves the irascible human captain of the perpetually underfunded merchant Vessel, the TMS *Earthrise*, and what happens to her when she ends up rescuing an Eldritch prince. I highly recommend moving on to this series next, if you haven't read it yet! Or take a side-tour and pick up my collection of Pelted short fiction, *Claws and Starships*.

For those of you who want darker fare, *Even the Wingless* goes straight into the Chatcaavan Empire itself to show us the iniquity that the Alliance will be facing, and pits an Eldritch ambassador against an entire court of torturers and sociopaths. It is a tense, bloody, and violent book, and sets up the events that will affect the course of intergalactic history. It is, however, full of triggers, and while Jahir and Vasiht'h show up later in Book 2 of Lisinthir's series, it remains a difficult set of books. Readers, beware! Even our gentle healers are subject to their own internal pressures and problems. They survive and come out stronger in the end, but some of you may want to skip the journey. If you would prefer not to engage with more difficult work, or prefer to go into it prepared by spoilers, a Reader's Guide is available via Patreon, the author's mailing list, or if you ask!

Our intrepid mindhealers will return again in one more more Dreamhealers story (*Dreamstorm*), in addition to "Family" which is already available. I also hope to write the story of other Eldritch immigrants like Sediryl. Those will be coming soon! Or if you'd like to detour somewhere more gentle, I recommend trying my romance novel, *Thief of Songs*, or visiting Kherishdar with *The Aphorisms of Kherishdar*.

Stay tuned! Or if you prefer, sign up for my newsletter to be alerted when new books arrive!

—M

About the Author

DAUGHTER OF TWO CUBAN political exiles, M.C.A. Hogarth was born a foreigner in the American melting pot and has had a fascination for the gaps in cultures and the bridges that span them ever since. She has been many things—web database architect, product manager, technical writer and massage therapist—but is currently a full-time parent, artist, writer and anthropologist to aliens, both human and otherwise. She is the author of over fifty titles in the genres of science fiction, fantasy, humor and romance.

The *Dreamhealers* series is only one of the many stories set in the Pelted universe; more information is available on the author's website. You can also sign up for the author's quarterly newsletter to be notified of new releases.

If you enjoyed this book, please consider leaving a review . . . or telling a friend! (Or both!)

mcahogarth.org
mcahogarth@patreon
mcahogarth@twitter